ACTION...
PAGEANTRY...
INTRIGUE...

In this magnificent and stirring novel, Louis de Wohl
turns his famed narrative
skill to the story of the soldier and merchant's son
who might have been right-
hand man to a king . . .
and who became instead
the most beloved of all
saints.

"COLORFUL"
—Ft. Worth Star-Telegram

"HIGH
    ADVENTURE"
—Atlanta Journal and Constitution

Originally published at $3.95
by J. B. Lippincott Company

ABOUT THE AUTHOR

LOUIS DE WOHL was twenty-one when his first book was published and he has been writing ever since. THE QUIET LIGHT, his novel based on the life of St. Thomas Aquinas, was chosen by the Gallery of Living Catholic Authors as the best Catholic book of fiction of 1950 and began the distinguished series about great saints to which FRANCIS OF ASSISI belongs.

Francis of Assisi

original title:
The Joyful Beggar

Louis de Wohl

POPULAR LIBRARY • NEW YORK

POPULAR LIBRARY EDITION
Published in December, 1960

Copyright © 1958 by Louis de Wohl
Library of Congress Catalog Card Number: 58-12276

Published by arrangement with J. B. Lippincott Company
J. B. Lippincott Company edition published in October, 1958
First printing: August, 1958
Second printing: March, 1959

Original title: THE JOYFUL BEGGAR

This novel has been published in Germany, Great Britain and Switzerland

PRINTED IN THE UNITED STATES OF AMERICA   C

CHAPTER ONE
A.D. 1202

"I need money," said the pale young man, elegantly crossing his long legs.

Bernard of Quintavalle nodded noncommittally and started smoothing the folds of his dark green coat, a habitual movement of his when appraising a customer.

The customer could scarcely be more than twenty years of age. His dress was not exactly luxurious: second-grade wool dyed blue, with little and rather artless embroidery, a leather belt with a simple silver clasp. The shoes—always look at a man's shoes—were well made but also well worn and had no buckles. Still, it was the dress of a young knight, and young knights were known to be on the lighthearted side. This could be the son of some minor noble, who had lost his money and accouterments gambling or jousting with opponents too good for his lance, and who was too far away from his father's little castle to get more.

Yet it was difficult to believe that this young man was lighthearted, despite his somewhat direct approach to the reason for his visit. He had a very serious young face, lean, with brilliant gray eyes and a proud nose; he had a firm mouth, with thin lips.

He looked foreign, and Bernard, as a much-traveled merchant, was just a trifle irritated by not being able to decide where he came from. He certainly was not from the North of Italy. His Italian had an accent that was neither German nor French, though it was closer to French than to German.

"Forgive me, Sir Knight," Bernard said, "but I didn't catch your name when my servant announced you. Also my poor Filippo is not too good at pronouncing foreign names. . . ."

"I am Roger de Vandria," the young man said. He seemed to expect that no further explanation was necessary.

"I am much honored," Bernard said courteously. "May I ask why you come to me rather than a banking house?"

Roger de Vandria's smile destroyed some of the good impression he had made; it was bitter and mocking, the veil before the face of defeat.

"My father used to say that banking houses are like women, Messer Bernard. They welcome only those who have already shown themselves to be successful; not those who only expect to be."

"There is something in that," Bernard of Quintavalle admitted cautiously. "But . . ."

"They are always willing to lend money to those who don't need it, and never to those who do," the young man went on. His bitter smile deepened. "I have seen the Frescardi in Bologna and the Pisani in Perugia. I've had my fill of banking houses. And I don't want to go to common usurers. When I came here to Assisi I made inquiries. You were pointed out to me as a man of wealth not averse to business affairs. So here I am."

"Good Christians," Bernard said gravely, "are not supposed to lend money on interest. . . ."

"Oh, I know, I know," the young noble said ironically. "Neither are they supposed to kill or to commit adultery. But they do sometimes, I'm told."

Bernard shook his head. "I have made a number of business arrangements since I retired from selling imported goods," he said, "but always on the basis of a sale."

"I've heard that, too." Roger de Vandria gave a shrug. "You buy; later on the seller can buy his property back. For a higher price, naturally. That way you do not take interest, you break no commandment of the Church, you are an exemplary Christian—and yet you increase your wealth. An admirable custom, Messer Bernard."

Quintavalle frowned. "It is a generally accepted practice. . . ."

"Of course. And it happens to suit me, too. I offer you my castle for sale—on the condition that I may buy it back within, let's say, two years."

"*Your* castle?" Bernard gave the young man a startled look.

Roger drew himself up a little. "I couldn't very well sell you what does not belong to me, could I?"

"And where is it?" Bernard asked somewhat dubiously.

"In Sicily. Two days ride from Monreale. I have all the documents with me."

"In Sicily!" Bernard of Quintavalle began to laugh. "My dear young . . . my dear Sir Knight, Sicily!"

Roger's eyes narrowed. "What, if I may ask, causes you such hilarity at the mention of the most beautiful island on earth?"

Bernard dabbed at his eyes. "Sicily," he repeated, "and on the island itself, moreover. . . . My dear Sir Knight, you told me that banking houses are like women. Well, so are countries. The more beautiful and rich they are, the more suitors will try

6

to win them. You're right, Sir Knight, Sicily is a very beautiful island. No wonder she has so many—suitors."

"Sicily belongs to Sicily," the young noble said fiercely.

"No doubt, no doubt. But it'll be hard to convince the Emperor that this is so—the emperors, I should have said, now that Philip of Swabia and Otto of Brunswick both claim that title. Besides, there are some very powerful German nobles down there whose allegiance to either of the two emperors does not seem to be quite clearly defined. There is a King of Sicily, too, unless I'm mistaken, little Frederick, aged six or seven. . . ."

"Eight."

"Eight, then. There are tribes of Saracens, all of them armed to the teeth and ready to claim anything and everything. And there is the Holy Father in Rome who will have his say too. Sicily! I wager there is no one in the whole world who could say who is going to rule Sicily six months from now."

"True," the young man admitted coldly, "but that makes no difference. My castle is my castle. I inherited it from my father when he died, a year ago, in Mainz."

"Mainz? That's in Germany, surely."

"It is."

Suddenly Bernard understood. "Who is holding the—your castle at the present time, Sir Knight?" he asked softly.

Roger bit his lip. "I wish I knew," he said. "But whoever it is, I shall get him out."

Bernard nodded. "You were living in exile—you and your late father? I thought as much. And what you are looking for is someone who will finance your fight to get the castle back, isn't that it? My dear Sir Knight, I am not rich enough for that kind of thing. And I scarcely blame the Frescardi and the Pisani for not giving you their support."

Again the bitter smile. "I am not such a fool, Messer Bernard, I know that no one would lend me a sum sufficient for an armed expedition. My hopes are far more modest. All I want is to get to Vandria myself. But traveling costs money and I spent my last Florentine guilder yesterday afternoon."

"But then you must be hungry!" Bernard threw up his hands. "Of course you are. Where have my eyes been? Ah well, there at least I can render some assistance. Filippo! Filippo!"

The servant appeared in the door.

"Bring some food at once, Filippo, bread, meat, cheese, anything that's ready. And some wine. Don't you hear me? What's the matter with you?"

There was no need for Filippo to answer. Behind him loomed a large, bulky man, bearded, beetle-browed, paunchy.

"Messer Cuomo," Bernard exclaimed as he rose to his feet. "What gives me the honor of your visit? Filippo, a chair for Messer Cuomo. And then go and get food as I told you. Sir Knight, Messer Cuomo is the newly elected chief constable of our town. . . ."

"And here in his official capacity," Cuomo interposed, with a little bow. "Forgive me, therefore, Messer Bernard, if I do not sit down. May I ask how well you are acquainted with this . . . noble visitor of yours?"

"I was about to make the introduction," Bernard replied with a hint of reproach. "This is Count Roger of Vandria. He hails from Sicily."

"Perhaps," Cuomo said, coldly offensive.

Roger's hand flew to his sword-hilt.

"Please, do not excite yourself," the chief constable told him. "Four of my men are waiting outside. Messer Bernard, I must repeat my question: How well are you acquainted with this man?"

"Well, I only met him today," Bernard of Quintavalle admitted reluctantly. "He came to see me on a business matter. But I have no doubt—"

"I am inconsolable, Messer Bernard," Cuomo interposed, "but I must interrupt whatever business you may have in mind. Sir Knight, you will follow me if you please."

"What is the meaning of this?" Roger asked tersely.

Cuomo bowed again. "A precautionary measure, Sir Knight," he said, with an oily smile. "No more than that. After all, Assisi happens to be at war. Surely you know that, Sir Knight?"

"Now that you mention it, I believe I did hear some mention of it," Roger of Vandria drawled. "You're at war with Perugia, aren't you? I wish you the best of luck, Messer—Messer Chief Constable. But your war has nothing to do with me."

"The war!" Bernard exclaimed incredulously. "But my dear Messer Cuomo, the war has been going on for I don't know how long and nothing ever happens, except that we did lay siege to a couple of castles near by; and *that* didn't get anywhere either. Not that I'm complaining—on the contrary. But why this sudden belligerence?"

"It is impossible to avoid belligerence in war," Cuomo stated with dignity.

"Oh no, it isn't," Bernard protested. "In the war between Cremona and Padua neither one ever attacked, because each

8

town felt that the other was the stronger; and in the war between Siena and Lucca a few years ago everything went perfectly peacefully because Florence lay between them and neither of the belligerents wanted to violate the neutrality of Florence. If you ask me, Messer Cuomo, war should be permissible only between towns without a common frontier. The result is far more humane and—"

"Forgive me, Messer Bernard," Cuomo interrupted stiffly, "but this is not the moment for a lecture on military history. I am acting under orders from Their Excellencies, the Consuls themselves. This man, who you say comes from Sicily, was seen in Perugia a few days ago."

"And why not? He told me so and—"

"Besides, he is a nobleman. You know perfectly well that few of them are on the side of Assisi. You are keeping strange company. If I did not know you for a good Assisan, Messer Bernard, I would . . ."

". . . think that I'm plotting against Assisi myself, together with a Sicilian noble," Bernard interrupted. "And I one of the five best taxpayers of the town. Really, Messer Cuomo!"

The chief constable spread out his enormous hands. "I am not arresting you, Messer Bernard, am I? I *am* arresting your guest. And now we must go. My respects, Messer Bernard, and my excuses for the little inconvenience I caused you. Follow me, please, Sir Knight."

As Cuomo turned to go, he collided with Filippo just entering with a tray and cursed roundly to the accompaniment of much jangling of plates and goblets.

"Good-bye, Messer Bernard," Roger said courteously. "I am sorry I am unable to enjoy your hospitality. This day will remain in my memory as the one on which I found out that a castle in Sicily is not worth even a supper, if fate decides otherwise." He bowed and followed Cuomo.

Bernard waived Filippo out of the room and sat down again. For some reason he felt unhappy. It was silly, for why should he feel sorry for this young fellow with his bitter smile and his ridiculous pride, based on being a nobleman, a Count of Vandria —who ever heard of Vandria? Perhaps the whole story was a lie, to get money. Certainly, he was a nobleman, accent or no accent, those gestures, that way of looking at people. And that fellow Cuomo did look like an ox, standing beside him. But noblemen had no standing these days in Assisi. In Perugia they still counted the quarters on a knight's shield. Most of Assisi's nobility had fled there, when the war started. Perhaps by now they were as impoverished as this Vandria fellow.

Serve them right, many people thought. Bernard was not so sure. Some of them were what they all ought to be, true noblemen, the Galeanos, for instance, and the Scifis—some of the Scifis.

But the spirit of the times was against them; at least in Assisi. There was a new spirit in Assisi, ever since that glorious night when the German tyrant, Count Luetzelinhart, fled to the Pope to plead his cause, and all the citizens rose, stormed his castle and tore down the walls, and then used the stones to build walls around the town! A merchant, especially a successful merchant, liked peace and quiet; but there had been something about that time that made it unforgettable. All the Assisans had been like so many brothers, laughing and working together with a will, and the new freedom had made young men of them all, even of men like wealthy Pietro Bernardone so that he and his precious little son, too, had carried stones for hours on end, young Francis clothed in velvet. And so had Bernard of Quintavalle.

There had been something about that time. They had all felt it; it made them distrustful of those who might become new tyrants, suspicious of all nobles.

Assisi was a republic. It was rather childish to elect consuls, perhaps, as if this were the Rome of the Gracchi and of Cincinnatus. Nevertheless, it was part and parcel of the new spirit.

Why bother, then, about a penniless nobleman with a castle in Sicily? Perhaps he really was a spy from Perugia. Trying to get money out of a man for his journey south! A hundred to one he had never earned a copper-piece in his life. Riding, jousting, hunting, showing off fine armor and fine clothes, that was all they could do. No idea of the value of money. No thought for the labor, the effort, the concentrated work it took to make a success in commerce and trade. Merchants were nothing in their eyes—so long as they didn't need 'em. And even when they did, they despised them. Their very courtesy was no more than the armor of their contempt. Castles in Sicily! Castles on the Moon!

Serve him right, the young good-for-nothing, to spend a few days in jail! How he sneered when he mentioned business practices!

But then, he was young. He didn't know any better. There was not only contempt behind his courtesy; there was unhappiness and even . . . hopelessness.

Bernard of Quintavalle sighed. If he had married and had a son, that son might be of the same age now as this youngster.

Somehow he had never had time to marry, at least that was how he put it to himself, although most of his friends laughed when he said it, Pietro Cattaneo first and foremost, the young canon of the Cathedral—young for a canon, anyway.

"I can't marry," Cattaneo said, "because Holy Church forbids it. You can't, because you are married to your moneybags."

That wasn't true, of course, a man could have respect for money without being married to it; a merchant had to have respect for money or he'd soon be a beggar, and next to eternal damnation that was the saddest lot of all.

However, a merchant did have to travel a great deal, and thus had little time for courtship. And later, when he retired, there was always the wretched thought that he might succumb to the lures of some enterprising young woman who thought of him only as the provider of finery, luxuries. Women loved such things and never more so than now. Why, many of them were going about with more jewelry than the daughters of the nobles used to wear! Was a man to sacrifice his peace and quiet for the sake of such a hussy? And what if she turned out to be shrewish, as so many did? All smiles and kindness until the good priest had said his Amen in the church, and then nothing but foul language, ranting and scolding.

No, a man should give up the sort of life he was accustomed to only when he found something better, something he could be certain *was* better. Certainty. Security.

Most young people did not know the meaning of security, like that young knight who wanted money to finance a mad adventure. Suppose someone had given him the money, a few hours earlier—now he was in jail and the money would have been taken from him. One might as well throw money out of the window.

There was a great deal to be said for the new spirit of Assisi. No more kowtowing to a tyrannical German commander, no more bowing and scraping before arrogant nobles and their even more arrogant ladies. Instead, civic pride, and work and flourishing commerce.

Cuomo was right: many nobles had fled to Perugia and probably were doing their best to rouse everybody there against their home town. Fortunately, Perugians were usually as peaceable as anyone else. Only a chief constable or a military commander could take the war seriously. It was a nuisance all the same, one had to divert business to Foligno or Cortona, and even so only last month poor old Massimo Bordi was severely reprimanded by the consuls for trading with the enemy—the enemy being his brother, living in Perugia.

Who was making that infernal noise outside? There was no election, surely, so why send the town crier through the streets? With drums too, which the authorities only did when they wanted to be quite sure that everyone took notice.

In the narrow little street outside, the drums sounded like heavy thunder, reverberating from the walls too quickly to form a clear echo. The whole world seemed to be filled with the booming, threatening noise. Then it broke off suddenly and the nasal voice of the town crier could be heard; the voice, but not his words. Bernard of Quintavalle's house was very solidly built and the windows were closed. It did not matter. Filippo was sure to be out there, to listen and report. The message was short, it seemed. After a few moments the drums began to thunder again, not quite as loud as before.

"Filippo! Filippo!"

The servant came in, white-faced and trembling.

"What is the matter, Filippo?"

"The c-civic guard," Filippo quavered. "The civic g-guard must assemble tomorrow m-morning, at d-dawn at the Old Gate."

"Is that all? Colonel da Fabriano wants you to do some more drilling, I suppose. It'll do you good."

"N-no, Messer Bernard. We're marching on P-Perugia, and I'm sure I'll get killed."

"Nonsense," Bernard said gruffly. "Nobody gets killed in war these days."

The drums, now fairly far away, sounded like mocking, deep-throated laughter.

CHAPTER TWO

"So this is your spy," said His Excellency the Chief Consul. His Excellency was a man scarcely less obese than his chief constable, and he looked even more forbidding, with his heavy beardless chin, his firm mouth and his small, darting black eyes. Before he was elected consul, he had been the head of a very successful business, dealing with half a dozen countries and, as he liked to say, a man who could do anything.

"Spy," he repeated, as if relishing the word. "Spy, eh? And what makes you think he is one, my Cuomo?"

The chief constable spread out his fingers. "One," he said: "the man says he comes from Sicily. But I *know* he comes from Perugia. He spent last night there, *and* the night before. Two: he is a knight and therefore likely to be on Perugia's side. Three: why should such a one as he come to Assisi at a time like this, if not to find out something useful to the Perugians?"

His Excellency gave a bland nod and Cuomo, encouraged, went on:

"I decided to arrest him and bring him before Your Excellency. I also examined his belongings, of course. They consist of a horse, a rug and a set of documents in Latin. My Latin . . ."

". . . is no better than your horse sense," the consul said. "What about money?"

"None, Your Excellency," Cuomo said contemptuously. "Not a maravedi; not a bezant; not a guilder; not a copper-piece."

The consul scanned the documents. His face was without expression. After a minute or two he said: "Well, Sir Knight, what do you have to say to this accusation?"

"May I ask who you are?" Roger's voice sounded bored.

Cuomo stepped forward. "Curb your insolence, Sir Knight," he snapped. "You stand before the highest magistrate of Assisi —and you a penniless adventurer."

"I have been penniless in bigger towns than Assisi," the young man told him, with a shrug. "Does one renounce one's own name here when one becomes a magistrate?"

Cuomo almost danced with rage. "You'll be sorry for this! You'll be sorry. . . ."

"I am Mario Revini, Chief Consul of Assisi," His Excellency said with some dignity. "And now that we have met, will you be good enough to answer my question?"

"That fellow," Roger said, nodding toward Cuomo, "is a fool."

"If Your Excellency permits," the chief constable said in a thick voice, "I'll take this prisoner down to the guardroom and—"

"No, no, no, my good Cuomo. We leave such methods to the nobility. We are simple burghers. Sir Knight, it so happens that we are at war with Perugia. Is it true that you were there a very short while ago?"

"Certainly," Roger said.

"To visit friends, perhaps?"

"On the contrary. To visit bankers."

A flicker of amusement went over the consul's heavy face and vanished. "Your visit was not very successful, I gather?"

"No."

"In that case," the consul said, "your feelings toward that town are not particularly warm, I suppose."

"They are exactly the same as those I have toward Assisi," Roger replied dryly. "Here they wouldn't lend me money either."

The consul passed a fleshy hand over his mouth. Perhaps he was hiding a smile. "What did you want the money for?" he inquired.

"To travel home, to Sicily. To my castle. There I won't be asked questions of this kind."

The consul grinned outright. "I wouldn't be so sure about that," he said. "Things aren't easy in the South."

There was a pause. From afar came the noise of the drums.

The consul raised his head as if an idea had struck him suddenly. "What about earning money, instead of borrowing it?" he asked, and Cuomo gasped.

Roger grinned back at the consul. "I'm not very good at trading . . ."

"I didn't suggest trading," the consul said. "You're a knight, despite your youth. You must have gone through the usual ritual, fencing, hawking, hunting, riding, jousting. . . ."

"Oh yes," Roger drawled. "I passed before the judges at the court of Mainz.'"

"So I see from this." The consul tapped on one of the documents in front of him. "And the Germans, I'm told, don't make it too easy to win one's spurs. Well then, what about joining our forces? We're marching on Perugia tomorrow morning. They don't expect us, I believe. What do you think they'll do, when they find out? Let us lay siege to the town?"

"Of course not," Roger replied at once. "They can't afford to. It'll be a matter of honor to fight it out before the walls, not behind them."

The consul nodded. "Mustn't be said that nobility didn't dare to meet commoners in the field. They'll make a sortie, we'll beat them and enter the town with the fugitives. Will you enroll in our army?"

That was too much for Cuomo. "Your Excellency can't be serious. Why, the fellow would—"

"He was right about you, my Cuomo," the consul interrupted. "You really are a fool. Have you ever heard of a spy without money? A spy may be a knight who poses as a beggar, but he

14

can't afford to *be* a beggar. After all, he must be able to bribe people for information. Besides, this knight is a Sicilian. I should know the accent. My grandfather learned the silk trade in Palermo—you couldn't learn it anywhere but in Sicily at that time. The Norman kings established the trade there and my grandfather waxed rich on it. We of the house of Revini owe a great deal to Sicily. I shall be happy to repay a small part of it by helping this excellent young knight. My dear Count, here is your chance of winning all the money you need and more in the form of legitimate booty. What do you say?"

"We shall probably be beaten," Roger said calmly. "But I have no choice. What about armor?"

The consul laughed. "You'll be provided with all you need. Have you taken quarters anywhere? No, of course you haven't. Very well, I shall ask one of my friends to give you food and shelter. I would ask you to my own house, but there'll be a council of war there in one hour's time." He wrote a few lines on a sheet of paper which he folded and sealed. "I'll send a man with you—but it won't be the chief constable. Roberto!"

A thin-faced individual came in. "Your Excellency?"

"Here, take this letter and accompany the young knight to the house of Ser Pietro Bernardone. Good-bye and good luck, Count."

When the door had closed behind the two, the consul turned to Cuomo. "The secret of success, my Cuomo, is to make the best of a given situation, not the worst. You would have put that man in jail, where you would have had to watch him. Result: two strong men immobilized. Instead of that he will fight for us and, as you are so suspicious of him, I'll let you join the expedition too. You can watch him in the field as much as you please; but you, too, will be able to strike a blow for Assisi."

"But, Your Excellency," Cuomo stammered, "if the chief constable is not in town to protect—"

"Nonsense, man, your lieutenant will represent you worthily without a doubt. Tomorrow at dawn, my Cuomo, and I feel sure you will cover yourself with glory."

The house of Pietro Bernardone had three doors; the entrance to the house proper; the entrance to the shop; and the door of death, used only to carry out the body of a member of the family who had passed away. The door of death was walled up, as if in an attempt to prevent the entry of the only guest who would use it: Death himself. Most houses in Assisi had these three doors. The custom went back beyond early Christianity to pagan times when it was regarded as unlucky to cross a threshold over which a dead body had been carried.

Thin-faced Roberto crossed himself when they passed the door of death. "Many will die tomorrow and yet the doors of their houses will remain walled up," he said. "May I be permitted to ask whether you, too, will fight with our forces, Sir Knight?"

"I'm in it, yes," Roger said. "And you, fellow?"

"Not me, Sir Knight. They wouldn't take me for the civic guard. It's my chest." Roberto grinned suddenly. "I used to feel sorry that I wasn't in good health. But now I'm not so sure. . . ."

He pulled the bell at the main entrance with relish.

To Roger's astonishment the door was opened by a servant in a kind of livery. But this was only the beginning of many surprises. The hall was filled with costly furniture and in the next room the windows were of glass instead of oil-paper, and the floor was covered with a beautiful carpet. There was no doubt that this man Bernardone was rich, richer, probably, than Bernard of Quintavalle. The castles of a number of German nobles that Roger had seen contained nothing like the treasures here.

He remembered his father remarking on the growing wealth of the merchants everywhere. "They're as busy as bees collecting and piling up honey. One shouldn't interfere with them until it's enough to make it worth while taking it away from them."

If one could. It had been galling, hearing the old man talk like that, knowing that all power had gone out of him and that he had had to spend the last years of his life in countless and fruitless visits to this noble and that, always trying to get backing for the restitution of his castle and fief and, with an almost uncanny knack, always choosing the wrong man or the wrong party.

My heritage, Roger thought, is not a castle and a title. It is a phantasmagoria, a chimera, a mirage. And it would never be more, unless he went to find it himself; alone, if need be.

Meanwhile, here was Ser Pietro Bernardone, his host, a genial, booming, hearty sort of man, fleshy with good living, with bushy black eyebrows and graying temples. He was dressed sumptuously in cloth from Lyons spun by those French wizards, smiling and bowing. His Excellency was more than kind to send him so welcome a guest, the noble count's horse would be looked after at once, *he* knew how important it was to have one's horse well cared for; and supper would be ready in half an hour, if the noble count agreed.

Roger agreed with a mere nod. At the very mention of food his mouth filled with saliva and his stomach ached sharply.

A tall thin woman came in, and for a moment Roger thought that he was not the only guest of noble rank to be entertained by Ser Pietro Bernardone. Hers was what painters liked to call a "face with good bones," the kind of face that would change little with old age. There was dignity and grace in her movements, but somehow it was difficult to imagine her smiling.

"My wife," Bernardone said, with a wide gesture as if pointing out a famous monument. "Donna Pica hails from southern France, the cradle of so many good and noble things. I have a weakness for France, my lord Count, I won't conceal it. You, of Norman origin, will be the first to understand. My wife is née Boulement." He could not have said it with more emphasis if the good lady had been a princess of the blood.

She was embarrassed, but she did not simper. She had probably never simpered in her life. She did not look happy. The light from the lamps was not very strong, but it seemed that she had been crying recently.

There was a commotion outside and a young man burst into the room, dressed with such magnificence that he would have outshone an assembly of German nobles. His brown hair was carefully cut in the most elegant fashion, his hands were white and well kept and he was brandishing a plumed hat in one of them and a red-cheeked apple in the other.

He rushed straight up to the lady of the house, kissed her on both cheeks, whirled around and embraced Bernardone. "You know, don't you?" he asked breathlessly. "Everybody does, the drums have seen to it. Please don't worry about me, Mother. I shall come out of it with honor. You know that, Father, don't you? This is the beginning, the real beginning. What a wonderful thing that it should come now, when I'm ready for it and not when I was still a child or a boy! The colonel has given me permission to fight with his own lancers. He sends his respects to you, and to you, Mother."

But the lady turned away and vanished without a word into the adjacent room.

"She isn't crying, is she?" the young man asked with sudden compassion. "I must go and comfort her. . . ."

"Wait," Bernardone boomed. "My lord Count, this is my son, Francis. Francis, Count Roger of Vandria is going to war with our army too."

17

"A thousand apologies, my lord Count," Francis said, bowing with courtly grace. "Assisi must be very proud to have you on its side."

Roger grinned, he could not help it. The dressed-up little popinjay had a disarming manner. Silk hose, a velvet doublet, that plume on his hat!

"Francis is the apple of my eye," Bernardone said proudly.

"No doubt," Roger replied, "and if we were seen together in the street, it is he who would be taken for a nobleman. I admire your taste in clothes, Messer Francis."

"How kind you are, my lord Count!" Francis said delightedly. "But then I've always known that kindness is the mark of the true nobleman."

He means that, by God, Roger thought. To have one's irony taken at face value was somewhat disconcerting. The worst of it was that one could not really blame the little fellow for his vanity. In fact, he *could* be taken for a young nobleman, and not only because of his clothes, as gay as the feathers of Emperor Philip's best parrot.

Somewhat to his own surprise, Roger found himself stretching out his hand to Francis Bernardone.

Francis made a move to shake it, found that he was still holding his hat in one hand and the apple in the other, laughed, dropped the hat on the floor, passed the apple from his right hand to his left and shook hands at last. "A girl gave me that apple," he said, smiling. "They're giving fruit and flowers to all who are going to war."

"Except to me," Roger could not forbear saying.

"What a shame," Francis said, "but they probably didn't know you are our ally. If you don't mind accepting it from me, my lord Count . . ."

"On the contrary, I am delighted," Roger said. He took the proffered apple and bit into it at once. It took a great effort not to show the Bernardones that he was half starved. Even so, he had eaten the apple before he said, "Thank you very much"; and by then young Francis, too, had slipped into the adjacent room.

Ser Bernardone said apologetically, "His mother is worried about the boy going to war," and Roger could see that she was not the only one.

CHAPTER THREE

The day was hot and Roger sweated freely under his armor. The arsenal of Assisi had provided him with a set made for a larger man and he had not found it easy to put on. A coat of linked mail, plated gauntlets, a steel breastplate, a helmet with a hood and collar of mail drawn closely around the throat and shoulders and leaving no loophole for Perugian arrows. Only the mail on his legs was flexible. The workmanship was rather poor and he thought at first that they had given him something no one else wanted. Later, when he saw the Assisan army assembled, he realized that he had nothing to' complain of.

The Assisan army had a hard core of about one hundred and fifty mercenaries, the devil knew where they got them from; their leader was a swarthy fellow with one eye, a Spaniard, maybe, or a Portuguese. Roger managed to exchange a few words with the man and discovered that he and his troop had arrived in Assisi only the day before. That, then, accounted for the sudden decision to attack Perugia; the consuls had been waiting for the arrival of professional fighters, and now that they were there, they were to be used at once. Mercenaries were notoriously expensive and thrift was one of the main virtues of merchants.

This, after all, was a war of merchants against merchants.

The mercenaries were foot soldiers. There was a detachment of Assisan cavalry, too—lancers, to which he himself was supposed to belong. The horses were fair; they certainly looked more reliable than their riders, the sons of well-to-do burghers, most of them, more accustomed to parading their vanity on horseback than to serious fighting. And then there was the civic guard, six or seven hundred citizens armed with almost anything, swords, pikes, bow and arrows and even clubs, studded with iron nails, a crude imitation of the terrible German *Morgenstern*.

The entire force amounted to little more than a thousand fighting men.

Roger thought of Perugia, the proud town on the hill, the refuge of many nobles with their iron-clad retinues. He wondered what made Consul Revini feel so sure that Assisi would win. Revini looked and talked like a sensible man. But perhaps he counted on the element of surprise, and there he might well be right. No one in Perugia seemed to bother about the war. No one had even spoken to him about it, except the elder of the three brothers Pisani, and he only mentioned it as an argument for not making loans to anybody for the time being. . . . It would be fun to break into that solemn office and take as legitimate booty what had been refused as a loan! It might happen, too. In war everything was possible, as his father used to say.

They were advancing across the wide Umbrian plain. Somewhere over there, in the haze of the early sun, were the hills of Perugia.

Half of the lancers formed the vanguard. Then came the colonel with his staff, Gentile da Fabriano, a noble. However democratic Assisi was in sentiment, the consuls had had sense enough to appoint a noble as chief of the war expedition. Consuls! They were aping ancient Rome, obviously. Four soldiers were carrying the Assisan colors; the flag-staff had a broad, vertical beam with the initials S.P.Q.A.—*Senatus, Populusque Asisianum*. Shades of Caesar and Pompey! These people were blissfully unaware of how ridiculous they were.

But then, this was an absurd age when every little town thought of itself as an independent realm. Ever since Emperor Barbarossa had been defeated by the Milanese at Legnano, twenty-five or so years ago, all burghers seemed to feel that they were a match for anyone on earth.

Colonel da Fabriano was a sturdy man and he at least could ride, which was more than could be said for most of the so-called lancers.

That little Bernardone fellow, Francis, was not bad, though. Vain as a peacock, of course, and thoroughly spoiled by papa and mamma, but at least he had manners and he managed his horse with a natural elegance. Besides, his optimism was . . . touching. He was quite certain that he was going to win fame and glory.

His parents were less optimistic, especially his mother. Roger sighed a little and grinned unhappily. He had retired soon after supper last night—and what a supper; he had exerted all his will power to keep from eating too much, on the eve of a war expedition. Mother Bernardone had shown him to the guest room. When he bade her good night, she did not answer. Instead she just stood there, looking at him as though she wanted to read his innermost thoughts. She couldn't have been very successful in that, since he didn't have any. All he wanted was to go to bed and sleep.

At last she whispered with great intensity: "My lord

Count . . ." and he arranged his features into an expression of polite interest. "My lord Count, I beg of you . . . keep an eye on our Francis tomorrow. He is so young . . . and he has never been in battle before. . . . I am so worried, so terribly worried. . . ."

He had promised he would, of course, and she thanked him tearfully and, bending down, kissed his hands before he could stop her. Then with a little sob she vanished.

All very natural, of course, but rather irritating. He was not much older, if any, than her precious Francis. What made her think that *he* had had any battle experience?

Perhaps it was because he was, after all, a knight, and therefore trained in the use of arms. Or because he did not seem to care what might happen.

Did he care?

Since his father's death he had been living with a single thought: to get home, home to Sicily, home to Vandria. He remembered it with a painful vividness. The small, gray castle with its twin towers rising from the top of a small hill; the sweet-smelling room where his mother used to sit, pale and regal, attended by her maids; the large dogs roaming everywhere; the silver crest above the tall chair in the banquet room; his father, drinking with friends and all talking very loudly; the armory and old Oswald carefully cleaning swords and lances. The garden with his mother's favorite place, overlooking the glorious plain; oleander bushes and lemon and orange groves, palm trees, and the rocks hot under the sun and swarming with little, green lizards, so difficult to catch. He had been too young to understand why they were forced to leave suddenly, one day, and flee for their lives, with the riders of the tyrant behind them—the terrible, the murderous Emperor Henry VI.

During all the years under the gray skies of the North he had dreamed of Vandria as a monk might dream of heaven. But his was no mere speculation, no ignorant hope. He knew that Vandria was there, and that he must return as soon as he could.

He started out the very day after his father's burial, with less money in his pocket than many a noble would spend in six months on the least of his dogs. For the sake of this return he had suffered a chain of humiliations. He had been taken for a beggar, a swindler and a spy. And now the last Count of Vandria was a member of this pitiful army of burghers and would earn his first battle experience under their ridiculous flag with its S.P.Q.A. His first battle experience—and quite possibly, his death.

The Vandrias never had been lucky. Somehow misfortune always seemed to hover over them, ready to strike. Today he knew that his father had been a political fool. He should never have gone to Germany, but to France, where King Philip Augustus might have listened to him. Even the burgher Bernardone knew that there was kinship between Normans and Frenchmen.

Maybe I'd have been a political fool too, Roger thought grimly. But as it is, I haven't even the chance to make a fool's choice. Just as well, perhaps.

Meanwhile, there would be at least a chance to do some fighting. It was stupid to regard fighting as something worth while for its own sake, as many German knights did. There had to be a purpose to it, some goal to be achieved; and there was, and its name was booty. Even if the Assisans did not manage to capture Perugia, there was still the possibility that he might capture a nice, fat Perugian whom he could hold for ransom.

They were crossing the bridge over the Tescio River.

"No guards." Roger was thinking aloud.

"Why should there be?" the young lancer beside him asked. "They're not expecting us."

"We're marching across the plain and they're on the hills," Roger mused. "Unless they're blind, they're bound to see us at a distance."

"Not yet they can't." The lancer grinned. "And later on there are woods enough around the hills. The colonel knows what he's doing. At least I hope so."

"So do I," Roger agreed dryly.

"Besides," the lancer told him, "they're having a feast today in Perugia, in honor of some local saint of theirs, I forgot who he or she is, so they'll all be in their finery and going to Mass. I think that's why the consuls fixed this day for the attack. That, and the arrival of our mercenaries . . ."

Roger nodded. "It must be very encouraging to have leaders of such foresight."

The young man looked up to him quickly, but met a face devoid of any expression. "I wish they'd let us rest for a while, though," he said. "It's getting infernally hot."

But the colonel pressed on and the long column continued to wind its way along the dusty road, past olive groves tempting them with their shadows, and lonely cyprus trees silently pointing to man's true destination, as priests and pious women would have it.

Roger grinned to himself.

About two hours later, when they reached the woodland, da

Fabriano gave them a short rest under the trees and let them have their midday meal. The horses remained saddled, but were allowed to drink their fill at a near-by brook and to graze a little.

"Cold food only," the colonel warned his men. "No fires! And mix your wine with plenty of water, or you'll get sunstroke."

Bread, cheese and a little cold meat. Wine and water. Good enough.

Roger saw with some relief that da Fabriano was sending out a number of guards in advance and that he chose them from the troop of mercenaries. Neither lancers nor civic guard could boast of much discipline. They had camped all over the place and were chatting at the top of their voices, until the colonel sprang into their midst and told them they were behaving like a bunch of old women in the market place.

The little Bernardone fellow was with the colonel's staff officers, and so was the chief constable. So he was going to do more for his native town than arrest innocent travelers. He looked sullen and ill at ease, though.

After little more than half an hour, da Fabriano ordered his men back into formation. He had to repeat his order several times and shout at them before he was obeyed. Many of the civic guard, unaccustomed to long marches, felt that they needed a longer rest.

They felt even more strongly about this when they left the shadow of the trees and resumed the dusty road, with the sun glaring down at them angrily, while the colonel rode forward and back to cheer them up with the rough of his tongue. "Come on, you conquering heroes! If you keep up that snail's pace, it'll be night before we get there; and a night attack is much more dangerous. By the saints, one would think you didn't *want* to get nearer to the enemy!"

Perhaps they didn't, Roger thought. Or some of them.

A glistening ribbon split the plain ahead of the column, another river, much bigger than the Tescio.

The Tiber. It was grayish blue here, not yellowish as it was said to be in Rome.

They were marching past a fairly dense forest on their right when they reached another bridge.

"Ponte San Giovanni," the young lancer said, proud of his knowledge. "We've been on Perugian territory for the last half hour."

The Tiber bridge, too, was unguarded.

Colonel da Fabriano raised his hand and the column came to

a ragged halt. He ordered half a dozen riders to cross the bridge and scout for enemy troops. "If you don't see anything, send one man back to tell us so and keep on looking."

The riders clattered across the bridge. Beyond it were a few bare, sloping hillocks and, still farther along, the road wound its way through woodland again. Fabriano kept tugging at his short beard. For the first time he seemed to be a little nervous.

The riders disappeared on the other side of the river. Several minutes passed in silence, broken only by an occasional clanking of armor or the whinny of a horse. Then one of the scouts came in sight, riding toward them. Halfway across the bridge he reined his horse, made a sweeping gesture with his lance and turned back again.

"No sign of the enemy," the colonel said, not without relief. "Forward, the lancers."

One hundred of the lancers clattered across in a double file. The colonel and his staff followed and after him the rest of the cavalry. Behind them, the first contingent of the civic guard got into motion.

Nearing the opposite shore Roger thought he could hear a new noise above the thunder of the horses, a noise like tinkers hammering their pots, faint and distant, and strange.

The colonel's horse reared. Da Fabriano shouted something, but there was too much din to hear what it was.

Roger felt a strong pressure forcing his horse forward, and suddenly there was no longer a double file, there was no file at all. The whole bridge was crammed with horses and men and everybody was shouting.

Idiots, he thought angrily, can't they keep any discipline at all?

They could not. So tightly compressed was the mass of horses and men that it seemed to form one single animal with a multitude of heads and countless legs, a huge dragon with steely scales and a body too broad and unwieldy to move ahead, so that it could only perform mad jolts, making the bridge shake to its foundations.

One more terrible jolt and Roger and those around him found themselves catapulted off the bridge and onto firm land, and at the same time the tinkers' noise grew. They were hammering a hundred pots in an eerie, irregular rhythm.

Out of whirling clouds of dust came a shrill, long-drawn-out shriek, the agonized death-scream of a horse.

Only then did Roger realize in a flash, that this was not just disorder and lack of discipline. It was an attack, a surpise at-

24

tack, and the tinkers were not hammering pots, but helmets and shields and armor. But where were they?

Spurring his horse, he forced it first to rear and then, with a frantic effort, to get clear of the milling mass and up the slope of a hillock.

From his vantage point he saw that the first contingent of the lancers had ridden straight into an ambush of Perugian pikemen. Most of the lancers had been unhorsed and disarmed. The colonel and his staff had been pushed into the ambush as well and the second half of the lancers was just approaching it, as if driven by an inexorable fate, with the first detachment of the civic guard pressing behind them.

Strong forces of Perugian troops were rushing down from the hills, far too many, and the Assisans were screaming with fear and anger. There was no way to retreat for behind them Roger could also see the bluish armor and the green doublets of Perugia blocking the bridge.

One glance at the distant shore of the Tiber revealed what had happened. A double ambush, Roger thought with bitter fury. The first, on the Perugian side of the river, cut off the Assisan cavalry and one detachment of the civic guard from the rest of the army.

The second, on the other side of the Tiber, roared out of that confounded forest to crash into the main force of the civic guard—now without their leader and without cavalry protection —and into the contingent of mercenaries. And there, too, the enemy was vastly superior in force. The Assisans must fight for their lives but . . . would they? The cloud of dust on the Assisi side of the river was fast moving away. The Assisans weren't fighting. They were running.

Of the many things his father had taught him about the art of war one sentence leaped to his mind: "Remember, son, once an army begins to run, it won't stop easily if it consists of seasoned fighters; and if it consists of raw recruits, it won't stop at all."

The Assisans would not stop running. They had broken ranks. They were sweeping the little troop of mercenaries away with them.

It was the end of the expedition. There would be no surprise attack against Perugia. There would be no victory and no booty.

For a moment or two Roger hesitated. He owed nothing to Assisi, except for a few bits of clumsy armor, a supper and a bed.

A battle was one thing—to be butchered senselessly and

stupidly when all was lost, was quite another. The best, the most reasonable, the only thing to do was to gallop away, due south, following the banks of the Tiber.

Both Perugians and Assisans—what was left of them—were busy fighting on this side of the river. With a bit of luck he would not even be pursued. Da Fabriano was going down under the onslaught of three Perugians, most of his staff was down too.

This was the moment to escape.

Roger's hand tightened round the reins and his horse began to move away. The fight would be all over in a minute, only a few youngsters of the colonel's staff were still defending themselves. Dazed and staggering, among them was one in a gaily colored coat.

Roger dragged his horse's head round and drove his spurs into the brute's sides, making it charge the group.

He broke into them like a thunderbolt, the pikemen recoiled and he drew his sword just in time to hit a large soldier over the helmet with it—before the man could run his pike through the back of the little Bernardone fellow.

Almost at once he was surrounded by half a dozen men, the reins were torn from his hand, he heard a thunderous noise and the world caved in and was no more.

CHAPTER FOUR

"Aunt Bona!"

The plump lady on the garden bench was peacefully asleep. She was breathing mightily, the ample upper section of her robe of brown velvet rising and falling in a series of regular and well-controlled earthquakes.

"Aunt Bo-na!"

Round as the moon and button-nosed, the face above the earthquakes managed to express complete serenity, which, however, it lost as soon as the eyes opened, gentle, flustered, beset again by the troubles of life.

"What is it *now?*" Bona Guelfuccio asked plaintively. "Oh, it's you, Clare. Why can't you go and play with Penenda and Agnes?"

The fair-haired little girl, eight or nine years of age, said politely: "I'm sorry, Aunt Bona, but Penenda is having her music esson and Agnes wants to watch her and I have been thinking . . ."

"I was afraid of that," her aunt said, rubbing her eyes. "Your mother *won't* let you wear a hair shirt, if that's it again . . ."

"It isn't."

"She's quite right, of course. You've been reading far too many stories about monks and hermits."

"It's about the prisoners."

"Whatever next?" Aunt Bona said. "What prisoners?"

"The ones in the dun . . . dun . . ."

"The dungeon. Oh, you mean the prisoners of war, do you?"

"Yes. Uncle Monaldo says they ought to be chained and whipped. Why is he so angry with them?"

"Because they made war on us, I suppose." The plump lady slowly regained full consciousness. "Don't you know we're at war with Assisi?"

"Yes, but we're Assisans, Aunt Bona, aren't we?"

Bona Guelfuccio sighed. "And I wish we were back there," she said. "*You* don't remember much about Assisi, do you, little one?"

"Of course I do. We had a big house quite near to our Lord."

"On the Cathedral square, that's right. But they have taken that away from us."

"The prisoners?"

Aunt Bona rubbed her button nose. "Perhaps," she said lamely. "Anyway, those who sent them here."

"But they already *have* our house," Clare said, frowning heavily. "What more do they want?"

"I really don't know, little one."

"Why did they want our house in the first place?" Clare asked. "Didn't they have any of their own?"

"Oh yes, they did, but . . . that's a *very* difficult question to answer. I don't quite understand it myself. It's because we are nobles, partly. They're—they're enemies of ours."

"Then they should love us," the girl said firmly, "whether we're nobles or not. That's a commandment. And we should love them. Very well, I'll love them at once."

"That's very nice of you," Aunt Bona said.

"But they're in the dun-geon."

"Yes, my dear."

"And who's looking after them there?"

"Oh, the guards, I suppose."

27

"Are they nice to them?"

"Look, little one, you run away and play. I'm sure Penenda will have finished her music lesson and Agnes . . ."

"I've been thinking . . ."

"You're always doing that, Clare."

"If I love them, I must do something good to them. *And* it's good to visit those in prison, Father Onofrio says."

"Yes, but . . ."

"So I think I'm going to visit them in their dun-geon."

Bona Guelfuccio clapped her pudgy hands together, her eyebrows mounted up, almost to the wimple on the head. "Clare! This is madness. Your mother will never permit you to go to such a place. You're still a child, a little girl. . . ."

"Yes," Clare admitted, "but you're not, Aunt Bona."

The lady sat up with a start. "I?" she asked. "What do you mean?"

"I've been thinking . . ."

"Ye saints, protect us from the thinking of this child!"

". . . you are such a good person. Even mother says so."

"Does she?" Bona Guelfuccio asked, with a flattered smile.

"Yes, she does. Only the other day Uncle Monaldo said something about you, I couldn't quite hear what it was and mother said: 'Yes, yes, I know, but she's such a good person.' There! Why are you getting all red in the face, Aunt Bona?"

"Never mind. Never mind."

"So I'm sure *you* want to do what the Lord said and love your prisoners and visit your enemies. And I'll come with you. Mother always permits me to go with you."

"But not to the town dungeons," Bona Guelfuccio said, horrified. "No, no, that's out of the question. Besides, they wouldn't let us in, I'm sure they wouldn't, so what good would it do to go there?"

"I've been thinking about that, too, Aunt Bona. We could take some food with us, bread and soup and cheese and wine. Giacomo and Maddalena would give us all we need."

"Absolutely impossible," Bona Guelfuccio declared emphatically. "Even if I consented to this madness, your mother would never let us go."

"Mother and father have gone to visit the Countess San Severino. We can't ask them."

"And your uncle Monaldo would be very angry!"

Clare nodded. "That's possible, Aunt Bona. But I'd rather have Uncle Monaldo angry with me than our Lord. Come on, Aunt Bona, let's *go!*"

"No, no, no," the lady said. "I won't hear any more of this. Absolutely not."

Clare looked at her, smiling. Bending over gracefully, she kissed her aunt on the nose. Then she ran toward the huge, rambling house behind the cyprus trees.

"Where are you going?" her aunt shouted.

"To the kitchen, to get the food," Clare tossed back over her shoulder, and ran on.

Colonel Gentile da Fabriano spent the first few months of his captivity in a hospital at Perugia, but when the learned physicians declared him to be well enough he was made to join the other prisoners of war. According to custom knights, nobles and officers had been given separate quarters, and the colonel found about seventy of his subordinates in their dirty, subterranean quarters. He looked at the gray, slimy walls, the sooty old oil lamps, the ramshackle tables, chairs and cots. The air was dank.

"If this is how Perugia keeps her noble prisoners, I shudder to think how simple soldiers must be faring."

"We didn't ask you to come," the jailer said gruffly and closed and locked the creaky door behind him.

The officers near by came up to the colonel at once and congratulated him on his recovery.

"Thank you," he replied with a rueful smile. "Perhaps it would have been better if I hadn't recovered. I shall never stop blaming myself for not having discovered that ambush—so simple, so primitive! The lancer who gave us the sign all was well—he wasn't one of our men, he was a Perugian, wearing the helmet and coat of one of our lancers. I should have suspected foul play when he didn't ride up to us, but stopped halfway on the bridge . . ."

Loud and joyful strumming on a lute interrupted him and a clear tenor voice began to sing.

> "Love is no woman and no man
> Love has no body and no soul
> Love is unlike us humans then
> And yet it is the human goal."

"Nice voice the young man's got," da Fabriano said, and he smiled for the first time in weeks. "That's young Francis Bernardone, isn't it?"

"Yes, Sir Colonel," Cuomo answered. "May I say how glad we all are to have you back with us after . . ."

"Shush, man, I want to listen."

"Love's name we know, its nature not;
    Behold, without the grace of God
    Its way to us remaineth barred
    Love never enters faithless heart."

They applauded and Francis bowed to them with easy grace.
"You're kind to me, friends," he said, "but I confess I'm not
the poet, only the humble translator and performer. The poet is
the great German Walther von der Vogelweide."

"A German and poetry," an officer said. "I didn't think they
could produce anything but soldiers. And emperors, of course."

"Poetry knows no frontiers and no race," Francis said. "Mind
you, the noble Walther is something of a soldier as well, and
he must be a man of great courage. He has written poems
highly critical of the mighty ones everywhere, including emperors and dukes. Sometimes he goes too far. . . ."

"He can't go too far, there, in my opinion." The officer
laughed. "Except of course, that he may get himself into trouble."

"Ah, but he has attacked the Holy Father, too," Francis
said. "He must be a very impetuous man. When the Pope ascended the throne, Walther didn't give him time to show his
mettle. He wrote at once: 'Alas, alas, the Pope is young—now
woe to Christendom!' Yet from all we know by now the Holy
Father is a great man."

"He certainly has a very strong will," somebody said dryly.

"Let's forget the Pope," a knight with a bandaged shoulder
shouted. "He won't help us and the Emperor won't either. Sing
us something else, my Lord Velvet."

There was some laughter and da Fabriano asked Cuomo:
"Why does he call him that?"

The chief constable grinned. "When they assigned us to this
prison the jailer didn't quite know where to put Bernardone,"
he explained. "So the captain in charge said: 'Knights' quarters
for this one, of course. Why, the fellow is all velvet.' "

Da Fabriano nodded. "He seems to keep them in good
spirits."

"He does, Sir Colonel. Merry all the time. At first they
thought he must be a bit touched in the head, laughing and singing as if this were a palace and he the owner. So they asked him
about it and he said: 'I'm not in the least mad. I'm cheerful be-

cause I foresee the day when all the world will bow in homage to me!'"

Da Fabriano laughed. "All the world, eh? Nothing less? What does he want to be, a great troubadour?"

Cuomo shrugged his shoulders. "As far as I could make out, he is thinking of a military career."

The colonel shook his head. "It doesn't look very likely at the moment, does it? Ah well, perhaps he is just a little mad. However, his madness seems to be of a helpful sort." He walked up to Francis who bowed to him respectfully, his young face beaming.

In a faraway corner of the room Roger of Vandria was leaning against the damp wall, watching the others welcome their leader.

He had recovered from the blow that felled him—almost the last blow dealt in the battle of Ponte San Giovanni. The helmet had saved his life, but he had been laid up for two weeks and it took almost a month to get rid of a headache so severe that it made thinking impossible—except for a dull feeling that he was the most stupid ass in Christendom. When at last he could use his head again, the feeling became a certainty. He had wantonly thrown away his freedom, and for what? To strike a blow for that fop Bernardone.

What on earth made him do it? It was true the fellow's mother had pleaded with him to look after her son and he had promised her he would. Moreover, some Perugian ox *was* trying to run a pike through young Bernardone's back.

Asinine. It had been asinine to join that absurd expedition in the first place. He should have known better. He could have asked the consul to show his gratitude toward Sicily in some other way.

And now he was locked in this large cell with seventy-odd other jailbirds. He hated them, all of them. They were dirty and they were failures, stupid failures, and they would pay for their stupidity by sitting here for years, perhaps. And that applied to him too. They were like seventy shadows of himself and he hated them for it.

When they tried to talk to him he stared at them icily and gave no answer. So they left him in peace—all except that little Bernardone fellow who never gave up, it seemed. He just went on being nice and courteous, damn him. If it hadn't been for him, he, Roger, would be free and on the way to Vandria.

Young Bernardone didn't know that, of course. There was no one who could tell him, except the man who had saved his life.

31

Which meant that he would never know. That was the only satisfaction left. But to have given up one's freedom for years, perhaps forever, so that this spoiled brat of an Assisan cloth merchant, this gay little butterfly, could go on living was the extreme of all futilities.

"And here," came Cuomo's hated voice, "is our non-Assisan volunteer, Sir Colonel. The great Knight of Vandria. I don't think he's done any fighting. The last I saw of him, he was keeping himself at a safe distance on some hillock."

Da Fabriano frowned.

Roger said nothing.

"In my opinion," Cuomo went on, "the man has never been anything but a Perugian spy."

Roger said icily: "If that scarecrow were a noble, he would pay heavily for his insult. As it is, I can only advise him to shut his dirty mouth."

But Cuomo, too, had a grudge. If it had not been for this good-for-nothing Sicilian he would now be sitting in his comfortable office in Assisi, safe and free, with three good, warm meals a day and all the wine he wanted. Besides, he knew that no one had any liking for the bitter young knight who seemed to regard himself as too good for the rest of them.

Arms akimbo, Cuomo jeered: "How useful to be a noble! One can always avoid fighting by hiding behind a quartered shield."

Roger hit him straight in the face, seized an oil lamp and would have thrown it at the staggering man, if da Fabriano had not stepped between them. "Peace, Sir Knight," he said. "This can do no good to anyone." He turned to Cuomo. "I don't like your remarks about nobles," he said. "And I don't like stupid accusations. If this knight were a Perugian spy, he wouldn't be here with us today."

"He hit me," Cuomo stammered, "he hit me . . ."

"And I shall hit you again, if necessary," Roger retorted. He had reached the limit of endurance. "It's bad enough to be in hell without you adding your flavor to it."

Cuomo looked back at the prisoners crowding behind him.

"Are we going to tolerate this?" he roared. "Come on, let's teach him a lesson."

The former chief constable was not exactly popular, but Roger was even less so. There were shouts and curses.

Da Fabriano tried in vain to make himself heard.

A dozen men and more began to move toward Roger who was still gripping the oil lamp.

Suddenly the attackers froze in their tracks. They had heard the creaking of the door behind them.

The warders, da Fabriano thought with some relief. Just in time, too.

Everybody turned toward the door. And then there was silence, utter and complete.

A little girl was standing at the entrance of the dungeon, a child of the rare beauty born of spirit and purity that allows no other reaction than pure, joyful admiration. A shaft of sunlight broke through the narrow window high up in the wall, as if the sun would not let her enter the dungeon unescorted. So unearthly was the apparition that some of the prisoners crossed themselves.

From one corner of the huge room came the triumphant strains of a lute. Young Francis Bernardone had his own way of showing his pleasure.

CHAPTER FIVE

Count Monaldo Scifi was not only angry, he was furious; and when he was furious, he saw to it that the entire house took notice. His rasping voice could be heard in every room and he had a habit of punctuating his sentences with sharp raps on the nearest table.

"I'm ashamed of you, Bona. How could you do such a thing! How did you dare!"

"I . . . I really don't know myself," Bona Guelfuccio stammered.

"You really don't know, don't you?" Monaldo mimicked his cousin's tearful voice. "By the horns of Satan, don't you know *anything*? Don't you understand that you have exposed your name and ours to gossip and ridicule? It may not matter so much about the name of Guelfuccio. Your late lamented husband's family was not of ancient lineage. But you happen to have been born a Scifi like myself, and the girl you . . . abducted into that den of iniquity is a Scifi as well. We are one of the oldest families of all Italy, with a lineage going back to the most heroic times of ancient Rome and to the great Publius Cornelius Scipio Africanus himself. Haven't I told you that, and more than once?"

"M-much more than once, Monaldo dear," Bona agreed unhappily. "But . . ."

"And then you degrade us all by taking Clare to that infernal place and going there yourself! I never heard of such a thing. I'm *most* upset and so are my brother and my sister-in-law. Aren't you, Favorino? Aren't you, Ortolana?"

Count Favorino, five years younger than his brother, tried to give his weak, amiable face an expression of grim earnestness. "Most upset," he agreed. "Oh yes. Very much so."

Countess Ortolana managed to hide a smile. "Don't be too hard on poor Bona, Monaldo," she said.

"Too hard?" Count Monaldo gave the table another thump. "As the head of the family it is my duty to see that the honor of the house is not put in jeopardy by this . . . this apology for a noblewoman and by your precious daughter."

Countess Ortolana frowned. "My dear Monaldo, aren't you exaggerating a little? I agree that a visit to a prison—"

"*A* visit? Six visits, in six consecutive weeks and all behind my . . . behind *our* backs. Why, it's little less than a conspiracy! And if I hadn't checked our stocks of food, as is my duty, and found them diminished by more than half, we still wouldn't know! Only when I called that churl Giacomo a thief, was he good enough to explain."

"I'll stop that nonsense," Ortolana said calmly. "There's no need for any more excitement."

There was a knock at the door.

"Didn't I say we were not to be disturbed?" bellowed Count Monaldo. "My orders don't seem to count for anything in this house. Who is it?"

The door opened and Clare made her entrance. "I'm sorry, Uncle Monaldo," she said. "I'm sorry, Mother. I'm sorry, Father. I'm sorry, Aunt Bona." Each time she made a graceful little curtsy. Then she straightened up. "But you mustn't scold Aunt Bona, Uncle Monaldo. It isn't her fault. I seduced her."

Again Countess Ortolana hid a smile. "I thought you did," she said. "And I'm glad to see that you are repentant."

"But I'm not, Mother," Clare said quickly. "I mean, I'm sorry I caused you trouble and I'm sorry I caused Aunt Bona trouble, but I can't be sorry about the visits. The prisoners were all so happy about it, and they were hungry, too. They could have eaten much more, only we couldn't carry more, could we, Aunt Bona?"

"Not repentant, aren't you?" Count Monaldo glared at his niece.

Clare gave him another curtsy. "I couldn't possibly be, Uncle Monaldo. Father Onofrio says it's a work of charity to visit people in the dun-geon. He says our Lord said so Himself. How can I be repentant for having done what our Lord told us to do?"

"I shall certainly speak to Father Onofrio about this," Count Monaldo said grimly. "Did he tell you to go and see those men in jail?"

"N-no, Uncle Monaldo. That was my own idea, and Aunt Bona didn't like it a bit, at least in the beginning. But I made her like it. If you had seen how pleased they were, you would've liked it too—perhaps you would have," she added a little hesitantly.

Count Favorino had a fit of coughing and the countess turned her head away.

"It would make it much easier, if you'd come with us," Clare said hopefully. "It's awful heavy—all that food. You see, there are so many of them."

"Are you trying to drag *me* into this absurd scheme of yours, you little idiot?" Count Monaldo thundered. "There'll be an end to it now, do you hear?"

"What is a scheme, Uncle Monaldo?" Clare asked politely.

The count drew forth a silk handkerchief and wiped his brow. "Never mind," he said. "But let's have this settled here and now. There will be no further visits to the dungeon. I forbid it. So do your parents. Don't you, Favorino? Ortolana? You see, Clare? No more visits. And let me tell you one more thing. You had no right to take that food. It wasn't yours."

"But Giacomo gave it to me," Clare said, crestfallen.

"He had no right to do it. It didn't belong to him either. It belonged to your parents and to me. I wonder what Father Onofrio has to say about stealing!"

Clare blanched.

"I'll pay for the food," Bona Guelfuccio said unexpectedly, and both Favorino and Ortolana gaped at her. "I haven't any money, but there's jewelry enough in my jewel box and—"

"You keep out of this, Bona," Monaldo said.

"But I'm in it," the plump lady insisted. "I carried most of the food myself. I'll pay for it. And now there'll be no more talk about stealing, I trust."

"Good God, Bona, what's got into you?" Monaldo said angrily. "Who cares about the confounded food and about your jewelry! All I'm trying to do is to teach this little girl a lesson she badly needs."

"She didn't steal," Bona Guelfuccio declared hotly. "And I think it's cruel and wrong to tell her she did."

Count Monaldo blinked. He had never heard his kinswoman

35

raise her voice before. It was like being suddenly attacked by a chicken.

"Bona is right, Monaldo," Countess Ortolana said softly.

The count drew himself up. "Very well," he said. "If that's how you feel I will not insist on that point. But we are agreed that these visits must stop. Aside from being indecorous, to say the very least, they're putting us all into an impossible position. In every way. Those Assisan commoners will think we want to win their approval, which is infuriating. And the Perugian authorities will doubt our loyalty. After all, we are at war with Assisi."

"Are we always going to be at war with Assisi, Mother?" Clare asked sadly.

"No, my darling, I hope not."

"Then why can't we stop now and send the prisoners home so they can eat their own food?"

There was a pause.

Count Favorino cleared his throat. "We're not in power here, Clare," he explained. "We're only exiles . . . guests. It's for the Perugian government to decide about that."

"But surely they'd listen to Uncle Monaldo," Clare said. "Everybody does."

This time it was Count Monaldo who cleared his throat. "Now we have your daughter going into high politics," he said irritably. "Saints above, whatever next!"

"I've said that many a time," Aunt Bona murmured.

"I'm much honored, Bona," the count said ironically. "Very well, Clare, you've had your say. Now go. And keep away from the prison."

"Y-yes, Uncle Monaldo." She did not cry. She made her curtsies to everyone and slowly walked to the door. There she turned. "I do so wish you'd send them home, Uncle Monaldo," she said sadly, turned again and left.

"Eight years old and mixing in politics," Count Favorino said apologetically. "Ridiculous little thing."

Then he saw to his surprise that Monaldo was deep in thought.

On a hot day, life in the dungeon was sheer torture. The men sat around in listless groups and quarrels were frequent and bitter.

Cuomo wiped his forehead with the back of his hand. "It's a bad sign," he said to no one in particular, and those nearest him looked up sullenly.

"What is?" one man asked mechanically.

"That they've taken away the colonel, of course," Cuomo told him. "They didn't tell him where he was being taken, did they, Tardi?"

"Think they'll kill him . . . execute him?"

"They might," Cuomo said darkly. "Perhaps there's been another attack. Or they want to attack Assisi, and take him with them and force him to explain the fortifications."

"He wouldn't talk," Tardi declared with conviction.

"There are ways and means to make a man talk," Cuomo hinted.

"You know all about that, don't you?" Lancer Officer Bianchi cut in. "You police people are all the same."

Cuomo glared at him. "A man who doesn't like the police has his reasons for it."

"It *is* a bad sign that the colonel's gone, he's right about that," Tardi said quickly, before tempers could rise higher.

"And that's not the only bad omen," a third man spoke up. "I saw a big spider this morning. And our little Lord Velvet is ill."

"That's nothing new, he's been ill for some time," Tardi said.

"I don't believe in spiders and broken mirrors and that kind of thing," Bianchi said, "but it's a shame about little Lord Velvet. They ought to put him in hospital."

"He should have stayed at home with his mother," Cuomo said.

"I wish *you* had," Bianchi flared up. "If you have a mother, that is. It's difficult to imagine. Poor Lord Velvet. And poor us. That lute of his made all the difference. I liked that song about Roland and his horn and the other one about Tristan and Ysolt the Fair."

"It's not only the lute," Tardi said. "It's him himself. The only one who could make us laugh. Always cheerful. Am I right, Bianchi?"

"Right. And this is the fifth Thursday, too."

From a distant corner of the room Roger of Vandria looked up. He said nothing.

"What do you mean, the fifth Thursday?" Tardi asked.

"It's the fifth Thursday that *she* hasn't come. She always came on Thursdays, don't you remember?"

"Bless my soul, so she did. Holy Mother of God, that first time, when she stood in the door! There was some quarrel, and they were going to kill somebody, but when they saw her . . ."

Roger rose and stalked away to the corner of the room where

37

Francis Bernardone lay on his cot. "Feeling better?" he asked in a low voice.

Francis smiled up at him. "Some of these good fellows think I'll die of this fever. Even the doctor thinks so, I believe, though he won't actually say it. How wrong they are. I shall be well again soon and all will be well again soon and I shall be a prince, a great and puissant prince. . . ."

Roger looked at him sharply. A waxen face, an emaciated body, but clear eyes. No fever. At least not at this moment. So he was not delirious. "I know there are people whose dreams come true," he said dryly. "Maybe you're one of them. As for me, I have given up dreaming."

"That doesn't matter," Francis said. "The best dreams are not those we fashion ourselves."

"Meaning?"

"They come to us unbidden—at least by us."

"Lots of things come to me unbidden," Roger said bitterly. "Vermin, for instance. Some with six legs and some with two. Pain. Worry. Sorrow. Injustice . . . above all, injustice."

Francis turned his head toward him with an effort. "I told you weeks ago, Sir Knight, things become what we think them. Therefore it's very important to look at the right things. Remember what Abélard said: 'Rest a while, nightingale—rise up, song of my heart.' The world is full of sweetness. Why think only of vinegar?"

"All I've ever received has been vinegar," Roger said. "Or has changed into vinegar when I put it to my lips. But never mind. I sometimes wonder what makes me come and talk to you as if we were equals—friends, I mean," he corrected himself quickly. "I think I know now what it is. You are the opposite of what I am. To you all is good and beautiful . . ."

"Except myself," Francis said.

"You don't usually give the impression of much dissatisfaction with yourself," Roger said with a half smile.

"That's because I don't think of myself most of the time," Francis answered cheerfully. "There is so much else; there are so many others. . . ."

Roger looked at him sharply, but there was no indication that the words were meant to be a rebuke.

"The little lady who came to visit us, for instance," Francis went on.

Roger's face became rigid. "She has given us up, too," he said stiffly.

38

"She is a great little lady," Francis said, "and she comes from a great family."

"What? You know her? You never told me."

"It all came back to me," Francis said. "I've seen her once before, in Assisi. She was a tiny little girl of three, all dressed in gold cloth, in the arms of the round lady who came with her to bring us food, the Lady Guelfuccio. That was before they fled from Assisi."

"I should never have fought for Assisi," Roger said. "If *she* had to flee from it, the town must be accursed. What is her name?"

"The Lady Clare Scifi," Francis said. "My father said the Scifis have become very influential in Perugia—I have forgotten why." His breathing seemed to be more labored and there were drops of perspiration on the waxen forehead.

He may die in a few days, Roger thought, and to his surprise he felt a spasm of regret. But then, perhaps that was because his death would confirm the idiocy of the biggest ass in Christendom who had turned his horse in the wrong direction. . . .

The heavy prison door began to creak on its hinges and Roger turned with sudden expectancy.

But it was not the little lady.

It was Colonel da Fabriano. So they had let him come back after all. Shouting, more than half a hundred men crowded around their leader.

Slowly Roger walked up to them and as he did, the din began to subside and he could hear what da Fabriano was saying.

". . . most kindly received, both by the Perugian authorities and by some of our own noble exiles, including Count Roberto San Severino and Count Monaldo Scifi, the uncle of the little girl whom he very graciously permitted to visit us here. I have been entrusted to put forward certain suggestions to the consuls of Assisi, which in turn may well lead to direct negotiations of peace—*may,* I said," he cried, raising his hands to quench the loud outburst of enthusiasm.

"We can't be certain yet. But it's a beginning and as far as I can make out, the conditions are such that they will at least be seriously considered by our leaders. Besides, as a gesture of good will, I have obtained the permission to repatriate those who are ill—the six who are still in hospital and those who are laid up here: Davella, Girelli and Bernardone. They will be sent home tomorrow, and I shall go with them, on parole, to report to the consuls. If all goes well, there may be peace within a few months."

CHAPTER SIX
A.D. 1203

"Where is Francis?" Pietro Bernardone asked.

"He has gone for a walk." Donna Pica was busy with her embroidery. She did not look up.

"Has he? Well, I suppose it'll do him good." Bernardone sat down ponderously, folding his arms over his heavy stomach. "He's got his ambition back, anyway," he added contentedly. "Yesterday evening he told me: 'I shall be known in the world, Father, I know I shall be.' "

"If God wills it," Donna Pica said quietly.

"Of course God wills it, woman. That's why the boy was made the way he is. No one takes him for anything but a young nobleman. Even in Perugia he shared the nobles' and officers' quarters, remember?"

"Ten months in a dungeon," Pica said bitterly. "That's what he got for his desire to be a great man of this world. He might have died there. He was so ill, so desperately ill. . . ."

"But you have nursed him back to health," Bernardone interposed hastily. "And now it's all over and done with."

"He is still not well. Far from it. I know him."

"He will be well. At his age one is elastic like those bamboo sticks I bought last year from Mecopuli. In Cathay they build houses from that kind of wood. Can't imagine how, but I sold them well enough. I'm having new clothes made for the boy."

"He is restless," Pica said.

"An excellent sign," Bernardone declared. "Would you rather have him a phlegmatic stick-in-the-mud? His mind and thoughts are flying high, I tell you. He *will* be a great figure in the world, one day, and we shall both be proud of him. It isn't so foolish when he says he'll be a prince. He's got the personality to be one and that's what matters in modern times. Not just birth . . ."

"Goodness matters," Pica said.

"You don't get to the top just by being good," Bernardone told her indulgently. "You've got to be sharp, keen, eager, courageous. You've got to have enterprise, you must keep your eyes open and make the best of your opportunities. I did—and look at me! When I started out I often didn't know where the money would come from to pay for next week's food. Now I'm richer than Cavallieri and Quintavalle—almost as rich as Revini himself. Consuls and senators treat me with respect. Good enough. But the boy will *start* from there. I've laid the foundation. He will build the high towers."

From outside came shouting and shrill laughter.

Bernardone rose, stalked to the window and opened it.

A tall, lean man with disheveled hair and a straggly beard was walking past. A patched-up old mantle covered the rags in which he was dressed. A number of street urchins were dancing around him, laughing, whistling and aping his movements. He did not seem to see them. Looking up to the sky, he sang: *"Pax et bonum! Pax et bonum!"*

Bernardone closed the window with a bang. "It's that fool again," he said irritably. "Peace and the Good! As if he could give anything good to anybody, the beggar. One of the Calabrian madman's disciples, I shouldn't wonder."

"Do you mean Abbot Joachim of Floris?" Pica asked.

"Who else? Preaching about the kingdom to come, the birth of a new age and such nonsense. What's wrong with our age anyway? A man who is industrious and uses his head can get somewhere."

"One town fighting another," Pica said. "Most people thinking only of their own advancement. Almost everybody greedy for luxuries . . ."

"I'm not," Bernardone snapped. "I'm not thinking of myself. I'm thinking of my son."

"I'm still hoping—" Pica broke off.

"You're still hoping what?" Bernardone asked, frowning. "Out with it, woman, tell me."

"That our son will become a true child of God," Pica said quietly.

He laughed. "What do you mean? He was baptized, wasn't he? I was present when he was."

"You weren't present when he was born," Pica said.

Bernardone's frown deepened. He knew all about the strange thing that had happened; the neighbors had told him about it quickly enough when he returned from France. "Superstitious twaddle," he said testily. "Had I been here, I wouldn't have permitted it."

"Then I would have died—and the boy with me."

"Nonsense, woman."

But Pica, usually so soft and gentle, was adamant. "The labor stopped," she said. "I was getting weaker and weaker. Then the

41

blind pilgrim came and when the door was opened to him he did not beg. He just said: 'Tell the mistress of this house that her son must be born in the stable. For such is the wish of our blessed Lord.'"

"You've told me all this before." Bernardone shifted uneasily in his chair.

"So they came and carried me down to the little stable, and the baby was born almost at once. Surely such a child should become—"

"Who knows," Bernardone interrupted with heavy indulgence. "Perhaps one day he'll become a great prelate, a cardinal, a prince of the Church and Bishop Guido will have to bow to him with reverence. Though I must say I don't think he's cut out for it."

From outside again came the shout of the beggar: *"Pax et bonum! Pax et bonum!"*

"The stupidity of it," Bernardone growled. "What good can it do to shout that all day? I bet the fool has never done a good day's work in all his life. But he thinks he's a holy man or some such thing."

"Pax et bonum." This time the cry was farther away.

Francis came in a few minutes later. He was pale and he dragged his feet.

"You are ill again," Pica cried. She jumped up from her chair, her embroidery dropping to the floor.

For a moment Bernardone, too, looked worried.

"It's all right, Mother." Francis smiled ruefully. "It's just . . . I just don't understand, that's all." He sat down. "I don't understand," he repeated.

"What is it, son?" Bernardone asked.

"Just now—" Francis began, then checked himself.

"He's seen the pilgrim," Pica said and no more.

"Yes, I have." Francis shook his head. "He was walking along, shouting of peace and of all that's good. And then he saw me and bowed and . . ."

". . . asked you for alms," Bernardone said sarcastically.

"No, he didn't. He took off his mantle and spread it out before me to walk on. Some people laughed, but he said: 'You can't render too much honor to this young man. Soon he will be honored by all people.'"

Donna Pica remained silent. Bernardone said, with a shrug: "Well, and why not? Even a fool may say a wise thing occasionally. What is it that you don't understand, son?"

"I had had a long walk," Francis said. "I went to San

Damiano and back, and I did so hope things would change back to what they used to be. . . ."

"What are you talking about?" Bernardone asked, startled

"Nature, Father. The sun and the trees and the birds, a thousand things I used to love. I did so long for them all when I was in . . . Perugia. I made myself smell the fresh grass, the tang of the citrus trees, I could see the sweep of the Apennine mountains like a chain of aquamarines and hear the larks, the ouzels and the nightingales. And now here they are, all of them, in reality and it means nothing to me . . . nothing. Have they changed or have I?"

"You are not really well yet, son." Pica smiled. "That's all there is to it."

"Oh, but I am well, Mother, I am. I have taken up my training again, too, with sword and lance, down there in the old shed . . ."

". . . where you were born," Pica said. Her voice was trembling a little.

"That's right. I'm quite well, I assure you. So today I was sure things would be as they used to be. But everything was so quiet, nothing seemed to have any real life—perhaps it was my imagination."

"Of course it was," Bernardone said. "And it doesn't matter at all."

"Perhaps you're right, Father," Francis said meekly. "Perhaps it isn't important."

"That's better." Bernardone nodded jovially.

"I must have been a fool to pay so much attention to such things," Francis went on. "I used to listen to bird calls for hours on end, and there were moments when I quite seriously thought I might learn to understand their language. I *was* a fool."

"I'm glad you've changed," Bernardone said. "My son is not an idle dreamer like that idiot of a pilgrim."

"He may be mad," Francis admitted. "But I wish he weren't, for his prophecy's sake." He rose. "I want to do something, Father, something great and real. But what? What?"

The return of the last prisoners from Perugia coincided with the arrival of a very famous man: Pierre Vidal, King of the Troubadours. For several days all Assisi listened to his songs.

"He is a master of his art," Francis told his father. "His voice filled the Cathedral square as effortlessly as if he were speaking in a small room. I never heard anyone like him."

"I don't care much for the likes of him, as a rule," Bernardone said with a fat little chuckle, "but he's been very useful for my business. I sold half the silk and velvet in the shop. Everybody wants to outshine everybody else in honor of that singing mountebank."

"Oh, but Pierre Vidal is not a mountebank, Father," Francis argued almost indignantly. "He is a great man. The Holy Father himself has sent him to all the towns of Lombardy."

"What on earth for?"

"To call for volunteers in a great cause."

"If it's the crusade we've heard so much about, I refuse to call that a great cause," Bernardone said with a sneer. "Not with the Venetians in it. With them it's business and nothing else. Ah well, it's made them rich and will make them richer still."

"It's not the crusade, Father. It's the reconquest of Sicily."

"Why should we in Assisi bother about Sicily?"

"I'll tell you, Father," Francis said eagerly. "I know all about it now. The late Emperor Henry VI—"

"That brute . . ."

". . . married Queen Constance, heir to the Norman kings of Sicily and they had a son, Frederick Roger. When the Emperor came to die, he made the Pope the guardian of his son. Then Queen Constance died and the terrible old Markwald, one of the Emperor's commanders in the field, suddenly declared that he held the final will and testament of his master and according to that he was *balius regius et regni,* the royal regent of the kingdom. Little Frederick Roger was only four at the time but he had been crowned king six months before . . ."

"Ye saints, give me patience," Bernardone said, raising his pudgy hands. "Do you think I know nothing of what is going on in the world? A good merchant must know all these things, son, if he doesn't wish to lose his goods very quickly. And, by the way, wasn't it Constance who made the Pope Frederick's guardian? This Markwald was a great general. The Pope had his hands full with him, especially as all the Germans in Italy and Sicily were on Markwald's side."

"Even so," Francis said, "he offered the Holy Father an enormous sum of gold if he would acknowledge him as the master of Sicily."

"Twenty thousand ounces of gold down and another twenty thousand after the conquest of Palermo," Bernardone said, with a superior smile. "Isn't that right? And he wrote the Pope that such a deal could in no way be a burden on the Pope's conscience, as he was in possession of documents proving that little Frederick was a foundling, without a drop of royal or imperial blood in his veins. It was a handsome offer, but the Pope refused it."

"And with indignation," Francis added "And that's how the war started."

"It hasn't done the Pope much good. . . ."

"His troops won in Apulia. . . ."

". . . and lost in Sicily proper."

"Yes, but then the Pope appointed the great Count Walter of Brienne to be his general and wherever he fought he was victorious, first at Capua and then at two other places, I've forgotten their names. Then Markwald died, but his henchman, Count Diepold of Acerra went on with the war and is still fighting."

"This troubadour of yours seems to have given you a lesson in modern history." Bernardone chuckled. "I know all that, son, or most of it. But, wait a minute—you said he's calling for volunteers, that Vidal fellow. I suppose he wants them to fight . . ."

"Under Count Walter of Brienne, the greatest commander of our time," Francis said. "We're going to liberate Sicily for the Holy Father as the guardian of little King Frederick."

"*We,*" Bernardone said anxiously and yet proudly. "Does that mean you've volunteered?"

"I haven't yet, but I think I shall, Father. The holy Father has made Walter of Brienne the Duke of Toranto. If I succeed in distinguishing myself in this campaign . . ."

"You have my permission, son," Bernardone said with a grand gesture. "Your new clothes have come from the tailor. And I shall go at once to Ser Olivari, to get you the best armor in town. Come back a knight, son."

Donna Pica wept a great deal that day.

"Be sensible, woman," Bernardone told her. "Our son will rise high. He may become a baron, a count. This is his great opportunity."

"All I want him to be is a child of God," Pica sobbed

Bernardone was exasperated. "By all the devils and foul demons," he stormed, "can't a baron be a child of God too?"

But Donna Pica would not be consoled

The sky was cool and starry over the silent towers of Assisi. It was the last night before the start of the expedition. Francis turned in early. He could not bear to see his mother's tears. His shiny new armor was stacked up at the foot of his bed and he

45

gazed at it for a long time, until sleep came on silent wings and time ceased to be.

Someone called his name and he rose at once and stepped out into a garden full of flowers, the like of which he had never seen before, but then, of course, this was the palace garden, and he walked into the palace itself, all marble and gold and full of glittering crosses, five-crosses-in-one like those on the crusaders' helmets and shields. The entire palace was full of helmets and shields, of lances and swords, never had there been an armory of such size. Who could be the lord of this palace?

In a flash he knew that he himself ruled here, he and his followers, his knights, his cavaliers.

Someone smiled at him, a young woman of pure beauty, but dressed in the simplest gray robe, patched, and ragged at the seams, and he knew that she was his bride. Why was she dressed in such a fashion? But as he looked at her, her robe changed into royal purple, trimmed with ermine, and precious stones shimmered on her fingers and around her throat.

And he woke up.

The first rays of the sun shone into the room and under their spell ruby-red crosses shimmered on his armor and helmet.

They assembled in the Cathedral square, a little troop of thirty-odd volunteers. Tardi was among them and Bianchi and . . .

"You, too, Sir Knight," Francis said, beaming. "Excellent. And this time we cannot fail."

"Full of enthusiasm, I see, as usual," Roger said with his half smile. "I certainly didn't expect to see you again on horseback."

"I told you I have great dreams," Francis reminded him. "Until a few days ago I had no idea how they could come true, but now we're on the way to their fulfilment."

"Perhaps," Roger said. "But I wish the little lady would see us off."

"The Lady Clare Scifi? Here in Assisi?"

"She is either back or soon will be. That's one of the conditions of peace: all the nobles of Assisi must be reinstated and given back their possessions. It would have been a good omen, seeing her again before we leave. Ah well . . . I'll get to Sicily now."

"That's what you always wanted, isn't it? To return to your castle."

"I'd almost given up hope of seeing it again. I think I

46

would have if it hadn't been for the little lady—and for you," he added grudgingly.

Francis laughed. But then he saw that the knight was still wearing, under his clumsy armor, the same clothes he had worn in the dungeon and he frowned.

"I only arrived here a very short while ago," Roger explained with an embarrassed smile. "There was no time to do much about suitable equipment."

"This is not worthy of your rank, Sir Knight," Francis said warmly. "You are a knight—I only hope to become one. We must change clothes . . . and armor, too."

Roger paled. "I never heard you make a rude joke before, Messer Francis."

"But I mean it," Francis cried. He tore off his helmet and with hasty fingers began to unstrap his armor.

"By thunder, I believe you do," Roger said, taken aback. "What madness is this? Your armor and clothes are things of value—"

"How could I dare to offer them to you if they weren't?" Francis interrupted reproachfully, tearing at the straps of his hauberk.

"Stop it, you generous little fool," Roger snapped. "I cannot possibly accept this. Stop it, I say."

"You can try them on, at least," Francis said. "There, that's it. They may not fit you. Let me have your helmet, please. Oh, I forgot, we can't very well do it all here in the open square. Come with me."

"Wait a moment," Roger cried. "I told you I can't . . . Where are you going?"

"Under the arcade, there."

Roger followed him, still remonstrating.

"What are those two up to?" Bianchi asked.

"Changing armor, I think." Tardi grinned. "Maybe they had a bet or something."

"If they had, little Lord Velvet must have been the loser," Bianchi growled. "It's like taking lead for gold."

Under the arcade, Francis dressed a vainly protesting Roger. "The tunic fits you beautifully," he said. "So does the hauberk, and the cuirass, too. We are about the same size, I think."

"I'll wear this today to please you," Roger said, "but we'll change back again tonight, or rather tomorrow. I insist on that."

Francis said cheerfully, "They seem to have been made for you."

"Until tomorrow," Roger repeated. "And . . . thank you."

They reached Spoleto in the evening.

"I hope I shall never have to storm it," Colonel da Fabriano said, grinning. "I wouldn't undertake that task with anything less than ten thousand; I'd need siege machines as well and even then I wouldn't be sure I could do it. Look at those walls, and the citadel on that steep hill."

Not so long ago Conrad of Luetzelinhart had been ruling here, Duke of Spoleto and Count of Assisi, until the Pope, in spite of his appeal deposed him and his former subjects rebelled against him. He was supposed to be in Germany now.

The little troop took quarters in a large inn.

"So tired?" Roger asked as Francis fell rather than lay down on a cot of doubtful cleanliness.

"Yes. Very."

"It wasn't such a long ride."

"No, it wasn't. I don't know what is the matter with me. I'll be better in the morning."

Roger glanced at him sharply. "I hope it isn't a recurrence of that fever of yours," he said.

"I don't think so."

"Shall we go down and eat?"

"I couldn't eat anything, Sir Knight."

Roger nodded. "I'll send you up some wine then."

After a while a buxom girl came in with a pitcher of wine and a tin goblet. Francis thanked her and wondered a little why she was taking such a long time putting them on the table. But at last she left, banging the door behind her.

He closed his eyes, heavy with exhaustion.

No fever, he thought. Just tiredness, surely. He wondered whether he would see the Pope when they reached Rome. But then, perhaps the colonel would choose another way, bypassing the Eternal City. Across the Abruzzi mountains, maybe, and down through Molise.

Sleepless, he tossed on his cot. I haven't prayed yet, he thought. But as he made the sign of the cross someone called his name. That was how the dream had started the other night. Soon now he would see the garden again and the palace.

But all remained dark. However his thoughts concentrated on the strange flowers and the marble gate of the dream, he could see no more than a kind of gray reflection of them which in his heart he knew was due to his own imagination. He found himself thinking, I'm not dreaming at all, and immediately he was called again.

This time he knew he was no longer alone. There was a Presence in the room and he was afraid, so afraid that he did not dare open his eyes.

The Voice was neither loud nor low, neither deep nor high. Nor could he say from where it was coming. But he knew that it was commanding.

The Voice spoke. "Francis . . . who can render you greater favor, the Master or the servant?"

"The Master," he answered, with a childlike joy that he was able to answer the question.

But the Voice said: "Why then do you leave the Master for the servant?"

Francis sat up. He folded his hands and bowed his head, as he had been taught when a child. But for the first time in his life his prayer took the form of a question.

"Lord, what do you want me to do?"

The Voice said: "Return to your city. There you will be told what to do. . . ."

The room was empty, and its emptiness was frightening. It was as if everything had gone out of it, all life and all grace, and he alone, tiny and helpless, was groping in a darkness without end.

Roger returned in the morning. "Wake up," he said. "Here is your armor. You'd better wear it today. Mine's too heavy for you. I thought it would be. There's no use . . ." He broke off.

Francis was lying on his cot, motionless, deadly pale.

"You're ill after all, are you?" Roger asked.

There was no answer. But Roger saw that Francis' eyes were wide open. "The sun is up," he said. "We're leaving in half an hour. Better get up and get ready. Here are your things. You must wear them today."

Still there was no answer.

"Come on, boy," Roger said gruffly. "We can't keep the others waiting."

Francis looked at him. "I can't go," he said almost in a whisper.

"You *are* ill, then?"

"I don't think so. No."

"Then what is the matter?"

"I made a mistake. I didn't understand the meaning of the palace and—everything."

49

Roger made a gesture of impatience. "What palace? What are you talking about?"

"I didn't understand," Francis repeated. "I must go back to Assisi."

Roger stared at him, hard. "But why? What nonsense is this? Back to Assisi! Don't you realize what they're going to say there? They'll say you ran away because you were afraid."

"It doesn't matter," Francis said softly.

Roger's eyes narrowed. "*Are* you afraid?"

"I'm afraid only of disobeying," Francis said.

"Disobeying whom?"

"I can't tell you," Francis said.

Roger gave a short laugh. "I must admit, I had a better opinion of you, Messer Francis Bernardone."

Slowly Francis sat up. "I cannot help that, I'm afraid," he said. "But now at least you can wear the armor. I have no use for it. I don't think I shall ever wear armor again."

Roger said between clenched teeth: "I was beginning to think that you had the makings of a knight. I even thought that perhaps I was right after all, that day, at the Ponte San Giovanni, when I—never mind. I was quite wrong. You are a seller of cloth and a lute-player."

Francis said: "Do take the armor, Sir Knight."

"I will," Roger replied contemptuously. "Not as a present from you, but as my right. You are not fit to wear it. So it shall be mine. I shall tell the colonel about your return. Farewell . . . coward."

"Good luck to you, Sir Knight," Francis said. "I hope you will find your castle. And may God keep you safe."

But the banging of the door made his last words inaudible.

Not long afterward Francis heard the clatter of hooves. The troop was departing.

He rose. There was no weariness in him. He felt as well as if he had never known illness.

An hour later he, too, rode away, northward, to Assisi.

At nightfall he reached the town and his parents' house.

CHAPTER SEVEN
A.D. 1204-1205

"This, my lords and knights, is what I call victory," the Duke of Taranto said, caressing his silky little beard. "At last the Holy

50

Father can sleep quietly. There will be no more trouble from the Germans."

Two hundred-odd voices shouted their assent and cups were raised all along the banquet table.

"You really feel it's as decisive as that, my lord Duke?" Bishop Fornari asked hopefully. "Count Diepold has escaped—and he's a formidable adversary."

"If he weren't, there would be little glory in having beaten him, my lord Bishop." The duke smiled.

"Diepold escaped with only a few hundred men," Commander Crécy told the bishop. "I wish you'd seen the battle! It'll go on record as our great duke's masterpiece."

"History will record it simply as the battle of Salerno," the duke said with becoming modesty. "Though I will admit it was perhaps not unskillfully fought."

"The flank attack was a stroke of genius," Crécy cried. "Julius Caesar himself must have applauded in heaven—that is, if that is where he is."

"The lord Bishop is the only one among us who could tell us about that," the duke said, smiling.

Bishop Fornari gave a little chuckle. "I can't speak with certainty," he said. "But I surmise the treatment he gave to Vercingetorix and other noble commanders of Gaul does not point to an early reception in heaven. As good Frenchmen I am sure you will appreciate my hesitation."

"He's got us there, by heaven, hell and purgatory." The duke laughed. "If a battle were no more than a duel of wits, our dear bishop would be more dangerous than Diepold of Acerra."

"Diepold found his master," Crécy said.

"My good Crécy, when you look at me like that you remind me of a faithful hound I once had."

"I *am* your faithful hound," Crécy said, "and let anyone laugh at me for it, if they dare." He looked about fiercely.

The duke lifted his cup, beautifully wrought of gold and ivory, set with semi-precious stones. "Health and victory to the Holy Father," he said. "And you may tell him, my lord Bishop: after this battle no German will dare attack even an unarmed Frenchman."

There was a roar of enthusiasm.

"What a blow for the Chancellor of Sicily," Crécy said. "It's little more than a year since he refused to obey the Pope's orders to make peace with the Count of Brienne, as he insisted on calling our duke."

"Worse," the bishop said. "He swore he wouldn't obey if the Apostle Peter himself gave that order; not if he went to hell for it. That is the language of the damned. Well, now perhaps he will recant."

"We were in a bad position at that time—" The duke pursed his lips, tasting the new wine poured into his cup: "They have a good cellar in the castle of Salerno— Yes, a year ago things looked different. It didn't take much courage then to utter proud words."

"God is always listening," the bishop said softly.

"One more year," the duke said, "and I shall be able to attack the island of Sicily itself."

"Not until then?" The bishop looked dismayed. "I thought . . . I hoped after such a victory . . ."

"The duke is the greatest commander I ever served," Crécy stated. "But he's not a sorcerer."

"God forbid," the bishop said. "Nevertheless . . ."

"It takes ships to conquer an island," the duke explained patiently. "And both Genoese and Pisans are difficult to deal with, precisely because they know that they're the only people who can provide the ships. I can't attack Palermo with fishing vessels. Don't worry, my lord Bishop—I won't wait longer than I must. Not only I, my commanders also are eager to see that marvelous city. Especially my young friend, Count Vandria. I'm afraid he was badly wounded today . . . Does anyone know how he is?"

"Here I am, safe and well, my lord Duke," Roger said, rising at the lower end of the banquet table.

"Do remain seated, I beg of you," the duke said courteously. "I'm delighted to see you got away unhurt, but how on earth did you manage to do that? You did very well indeed in the attack on the left wing, but I saw you unhorsed, with two Germans hacking away at you."

"Frankly, I don't quite know myself," Roger said, "except that my armor is the best I ever had."

"Take this cup for what you've done today. . . . Give it to him, page! No, no, not like that, put it first on one of those little red cushions on the table there. That's better. Good luck to you, my dear Count, and when we get to the island of your birth, I will see to it that your rights are restored to you."

"Congratulations," murmured Colonel da Fabriano who was sitting opposite Roger, his left arm in a sling.

Roger bowed. He lifted the duke's cup. "Glory and victory to our great commander, Count Walter of Brienne, Duke of

Taranto," he said loudly. Everyone applauded and the duke also bowed most charmingly.

A few months later the Duke of Taranto's camp was attacked without warning, in the middle of a moonless night.

Roger in his tent was wakened by a tumult of confused noises. "Page!" he shouted. But the boy they had given him—since he had no land, he had no squire—did not answer, so he put on his armor himself as best he could in the darkness.

Outside the uproar was mounting to a crescendo. Once or twice he could hear orders shouted in German. He pulled down his visor and walked into a turmoil the like of which he had never seen.

The night was lit by hundreds of torches, none of which remained still for a single moment. The heavens themselves seemed in travail, with red stars fleeing, chased by an unseen power. It occurred to him that this might be the Day of Judgment, but he reminded himself grimly that on that day the orders were not likely to be shouted in German.

He made his way toward the duke's tent. The way for a young knight to rise was to fight under the eyes of his commander in the field. Besides, it looked as though the duke would need all the help he could get.

But as he marched on, cold reasoning told him that once more he was fighting for a lost cause. This was not merely a daring raid. It was an attack not of a few hundred men, but of an army that was following a definite plan. The enemy knew what he was doing, the attacked were fighting for their lives, planless, singly or in little groups. It was slaughter, butchery, and very likely the end. But his place was with the duke and that dark shape, a hundred and fifty yards away, was the duke's tent. What else can I do? he thought fretfully.

A man came running out of the murk, shouting in French: "Flee, all is lost."

"Nothing is lost but your courage," Roger said curtly and hurried on.

Now he could see fighting all around the large tent.

"Torches," a voice roared in German. "Torches, you damned fools. He'll escape us in the darkness."

There was a flicker of light; another, a third, and they began to grow, stars coming to life, blood-red and treacherous.

Roger saw a huge armored man, fleshy and bearded, on a horse of gigantic dimensions. He recognized him at once. It was Diepold of Acerra.

"More light, you stupid louts," Diepold roared. "Set those tents on fire, those over there, not the duke's! If anyone burns that, I'll have him flayed alive. That's where I shall sleep to-night. Get on with it."

Roger felt a wave of red fury rising in him. This brute of a man, with his infernal self-assurance—it would be sweet heaven to run him through the gullet and silence that fat voice forever. He plunged forward. All around him tents were going up in flames. He could see clearly, but knew that he, too, would be seen by the enemy at any moment now. There was just a chance that they might mistake him for a German because he was ar-mored, but by now many of the French knights would be ar-mored too, and, besides, most Germans were much bigger than he.

Small groups of men were running in all directions. He could not seem to get nearer: the brute kept his huge stallion con-stantly in motion; it was an elementary rule for a commander in the field. More than a few moments in the same place and some hidden bowman had time enough to take careful aim.

There was hard fighting going on at the very entrance of the duke's tent, and here was the duke himself, with his retinue, banner and all.

A burly form barred the way.

"You've got a gullet too," Roger murmured, striking with venomous force. The man gave a grunt as he fell and Roger moved on toward the thick of the fighting.

A fresh swarm of Germans were joining it; the banner of Taranto was going down, but only for a moment, for the duke himself picked it up and held it high, shouting. It was a noble gesture, but made him an easy target and, next moment, blood was flowing from his sword arm. Roger found himself in the middle of a number of Germans, pikemen, like that time at the Ponte San Giovanni, except that this time it was night and the men were much bigger.

As he laid about him, he saw a man go down beside the duke with a lance in his chest and recognized da Fabriano.

Mad with rage, Roger clubbed a German over the head, warded off a pike thrust and another and a third and reached the duke just as he fell, with a pike deep in his shoulder.

Roger raised his shield to ward off more pikes aimed at the duke's visor. I'll be dead in a moment, he thought with a strange detachment. It'll be the death of a prize fool who saved a cow-ard's life and came too late to save a hero. He struck out against an enormous knight with a red panther on his shield and

54

saw the man's heavy sword coming down on him. He threw up his own battered shield just a moment too late.

When he came to he was lying on a field bed and a gray-haired man was bending over him. "There we are," the man said with an air of satisfaction. "Now drink this." A cup was raised to his lips and he drank, first in instinctive obedience, then greedily, until the cup was empty.

"That's enough," the gray-head said. "There'll be more soon."

Roger wanted to ask something, but what it was he didn't know. He fell asleep instead and woke up for another cup of liquid. Broth, he thought, good strong broth. But he twitched with pain when he tried to sit up.

The gray-head grinned. "Don't try that yet. It'll be quite different in a week or so. Don't worry. All you are suffering from is bruises, so there's no danger of mortification. You don't know how lucky you are. The Knight of Lanzberg rarely needs more than one stroke to kill a man of his own size, and you're about half that. He thinks it must be magic."

Magic. Kill a man. Lanzberg. Don't know how lucky you are. Kill a man with one stroke. He could not fathom the man's talk, and when he woke up for the third time he had forgotten all about it.

"Where am I?" he asked.

The gray-head raised his brows. "Strange how they all ask that," he mused. "You're not in heaven yet, Sir Knight, though no doubt my broth made you think so. You're in the general's camp."

"Wh-which general?"

"Count Diepold of Acerra, of course."

Roger closed his eyes. "Where is the duke?" he asked.

"Never mind that," the gray-head said. "Best thing you can do is to sleep."

"Where is the Duke of Taranto?" Roger repeated harshly.

"He wasn't as lucky as you," the gray-head said. "I tried my best, but his wounds were too severe."

Roger turned his head away.

The gray-headed physician's diagnosis did not prove to be quite correct. It was more than a month before Roger could leave his bed, and another before he was fit enough to leave the tent. By then he knew that Count Diepold of Acerra had captured over a third of the duke's army, that he was treating all prisoners fairly well and the knights with all the courtesy due to their rank.

"He's not a bad man, for a German," Commander Crécy said, when he met Roger for the first time after that terrible night. "And he's a great general. Julius Caesar himself would have to acknowledge that. I didn't think anyone could get the better of the duke, but there it is, and what's more it's final this time." He seemed to be recovering quite easily from the death of the man he used to admire so much.

"But what is he keeping us here for?" Roger asked.

"I thought at first he wanted ransom," Crécy said.

"He won't get a maravedi for me," Roger sneered. "Everything I possessed in the world was in my tent, including the cup the duke gave me after Salerno—and he's got all of that, of course."

"There have been rumors," Crécy said airily.

"What kind of rumors?"

"Diepold is supposed to be negotiating with the Pope."

"No!"

"Why not? I'm not sure whether it's true, but it may well be. The Holy Father has lost an army just when he needed it most. He may pardon Diepold—and he may even do more."

"Crécy! You don't think, he . . ."

"The Pope is a very clever man," Crécy said. "And Diepold isn't exactly a fool either. That means they'll both do what is best for their own interests. And the best for their interests would be to come to an agreement."

"But Diepold is banned . . . excommunicated!"

"The Pope can always revoke that; and I'm sure Diepold would like to have it revoked. It's not an enjoyable state to be in, even if a man doesn't believe in God or the Devil. In fact it's the Pope's best asset when it comes to bargaining with the German."

"I begin to believe that to be a knight means to be a fool," Roger said. "What have we been fighting for, Crécy?"

"Who knows?" The Frenchman shrugged. "And who cares? A knight can shape his own pattern only in his own castle and fief, a count in his country, a duke in his dukedom. But kings and popes can impose a pattern of their own on them all—if they're strong enough."

"That's what they say about God," Roger said, "that He is forming His own pattern out of man's affairs. Sometimes I find it difficult to believe."

Crécy grinned. "You're not the only one. But someone—I've

forgotten who—said that kings and popes are less than God but more than man."

"What about principles?" Roger said, with his usual half smile.

The Frenchman laughed outright. "If you care for *them,* you'd better enter a monastery."

Three days later a number of captured knights were led into the presence of Count Diepold, in front of the large tent that had once belonged to the Duke of Taranto. Beside the huge German stood a thin, silent figure in ecclesiastical robes. Roger recognized Bishop Fornari.

"My lords and knights," Diepold said in atrocious French, "I want you to hear what the holy bishop has to tell you."

"I have come, as the Holy Father's legate," the bishop said, "to inform you that Count Diepold of Acerra has promised most solemnly that henceforth he will obey the Holy Father in all things; that he will put his sword to the service of the Holy Father and the Church; and that he will not accept any claims on the part of Emperor Philip to the sovereignty of Sicily. Accepting these promises joyfully, the Holy Father has lifted from him the ban of excommunication; and has commanded him to go to the island of Sicily, there to protect the young King Frederick Roger who, as you know, is the Holy Father's ward until he comes of age. I myself shall accompany Count Diepold to Palermo, where the young king is being held in a state unworthy of his rank and incompatible with the Holy Father's guardianship."

He stepped back.

"There is only one thing for me to add," Diepold said. "As you see, I'm going to fulfill what my late adversary, the noble Duke of Taranto set out to do, with your help. Any of you who may wish to accompany me, will be welcome. The cause remains the same—the commander has changed. That is all."

"What did I tell you, Sir Knight?" Crécy whispered. "Come on—let's do it."

"What? Serve under *him?* Under the slayer of the duke?"

"Why not? Didn't you hear? The cause is the same."

Roger stared at the big German, now ringed by a number of knights declaring their assent. Diepold, from his towering height, smiled down at them like a jovial father whose children were bidding him good luck on his birthday.

"Well, I'm going to him," Crécy said and he did.

Roger thrust out his underlip. What business was it of his

whom the Pope chose as his commander? He had fought under the absurd Roman vexillum of the Assisans. He had fought under the banner of Taranto and Brienne. Why not under that of Acerra, wherever the confounded place was?

Both the commanders under whom he had fought had been defeated; and both were dead. Perhaps the bad luck of the Vandrias had infected them? Perhaps this Diepold, too, would succumb to it? Who knows, as Crécy would say. And who cares?

What mattered was that Sicily was within sight again. Sicily and Vandria.

He stepped forward.

CHAPTER EIGHT
A.D. 1205

"I'm hungry," said the king.

The Governor of Palermo, Guglielmo Capparone, looked up from his desk. "I told you before I am not to be disturbed here," he growled. "Where is that teacher of yours?"

"Never mind the old fool," the king said. "I'm hungry."

"Then go to the kitchen and let the cook give you something to eat and, if you please, leave me to do my work. I am working for you, in case you have forgotten."

"That must be why I have nothing to eat," the king said. "And there is no cook. *You* ought to know the kitchen people left because no one paid their salaries."

"It's not my business to pay their salaries," Capparone flared up. "That's up to the royal treasurer."

"And the royal treasurer disappeared when there was no more money in the box," the king said. "You ought to know that, too. Meanwhile I'm hungry."

Capparone threw down his quill. "Is it my fault if there's no money coming in? I didn't start the confounded war."

"True," the king said. "You're not big enough to start a war."

Capparone rose. He was twice the height of the boy and with his thick brows, his large black beard and his great girth he looked like an ogre, ready to devour a very small king.

"Insolence," he said in his rumbling basso voice. "All I ever get for working for you is insolence. You ought to be ashamed of yourself."

"I'm not ashamed at all." The little king shook his long red locks. "I'm hungry. And I want money for my dinner. And it's a shame I have to ask four times."

The curtains were flung back as a thin, elderly man came in. "So here you are," he said plaintively. "I've been looking for you everywhere. A thousand pardons, my lord Governor—he ran away again."

"Money," said the king.

With a deep sigh Capparone produced his purse and took out a silver-piece.

"Put it on the tray," the king said. "Magister Monucci . . . take the tray with the money, if you please, and hand it to me."

Stupefied, the elderly man obeyed and the little king took the silver-piece from the platter in the daintiest fashion. "A papal crown," he said. "In a few years there will be *my* likeness on all coins. That means that all the money will be mine; and no one will eat without my permission."

"Magister Monucci," Capparone said severely, "take the king away with you and another time have more regard for your duties. I have heard you again allowed the king to mix with Saracens. I will not tolerate such an outrage."

"Try and stop me," the king said furiously. "I see whom I like and I like Saracens. They're the only intelligent people on the island."

Monucci looked up to the ceiling. "You see what I have to endure, my lord Governor."

"They're turning the boy's head with their scientific nonsense," Capparone snorted. "In the future he will go out only in your company. . . ."

"He can't run," the king said contemptuously. "He's out of breath at once."

". . . and followed by two guards," Capparone went on. "Really, Magister Monucci, it is most surprising that you should allow a child of ten to impose his will on you."

"I'm eleven," the king protested vehemently. "And at fourteen I shall be of age and then . . ." He broke off.

A palace official came in. "His Excellency the Chancellor," he announced.

Capparone stared at him incredulously. "*Whom* did you say?"

"His Excellency the Chancellor, Bishop Walter Pagliari to see you, my lord," the official said, frightened.

"You mean he is *here* . . . in the palace?"

"Indeed I am, Capparone," the chancellor said, entering. "Ah, I see our little king is with you. Sorry, my child, but I have important business to discuss with the governor."

"I am sorry, too," the king said, wrinkling his nose. "For Sicily, that is."

"Impertinence," the chancellor said, "has never done a child much good."

"Neither have you," the king said. "So it's just as well you aren't allowed to show any."

"Lord in heaven," the chancellor said, aghast. "He gets worse every time I set eyes on him."

"And for that reason," the king said.

The chancellor drew himself erect. "Enough of this. Take the boy away, Magister Monucci, and teach him, if you can, the rudiments of manners."

"You must be courteous to His Excellency," Monucci said reproachfully.

"Why?" the king asked.

"Because he is a very high official."

"No official ranks as high as a king," the king said.

"And because he is a bishop," Monucci added severely.

"He's not an *arch*bishop, though," the king said. "You did want to be Archbishop of Palermo, didn't you, holy Bishop? But the Pope wouldn't permit it. Could you tell me why, holy Bishop?"

The chancellor stamped his foot. "Take that young scorpion away," he said, "and quickly. Capparone, I must talk to you at once."

The governor quickly banished a malicious smile. "Very well," he said. "Guards!"

Two men in helmet and cuirass came in.

"You will accompany the king and Magister Monucci to their rooms."

The king looked at Capparone and laughed. Then he turned and ran out of the room. Monucci followed, gasping admonitions and exhortations. The two guards brought up the rear.

"Insufferable," the chancellor said.

Capparone nodded. "He'll be worse than his father one day," he predicted. "That is . . . if he lives that long."

"He must go on living," the chancellor said. "If he doesn't, it'll be your end—and mine."

"What do you mean?"

"My dear Capparone, we haven't always seen eye to eye . . ."

"That," the governor said, "is putting it extremely mildly. In fact, I couldn't believe my ears when you were announced. I didn't think you'd have the effrontery to come here."

"On second thought, you must have told yourself that I wouldn't do so without grave reasons," the chancellor said dryly. "Well, there are the gravest reasons you can think of. Diepold of Acerra has landed in Sicily."

Capparone's eyes narrowed. "If that is another of your traps . . ."

"Judge for yourself, if you won't believe me," the chancellor said sharply. "Send out your agents, verify it. They won't have far to go. He'll be in Monreale by now."

Capparone sank back into his chair. "Impossible," he gasped. "Out of the question."

"And he'll be here tomorrow night, maybe tomorrow morning," the chancellor added.

"But how? He has no ships! He . . ."

"He ferried over from Reggio to Messina."

"He can't ferry over an army on a few coastal vessels!"

"He didn't. He has only a small retinue with him. Less than a hundred men, I'm told."

Capparone rose again, his eyes blazing. "But this is excellent news," he said. "I thought for a moment you were announcing another German invasion. Less than a hundred men! Surely we can deal with that."

"He'll ferry over more men, Capparone; he'll seize our own ships and use them for that purpose."

"That will take a little time," Capparone sneered. "And one or two things might happen first. But why, I wonder . . ."

"I should think it is clear enough what he wants," the chancellor said with an indefinable expression.

Capparone looked at him. "Well, yes," he said. "He wants what I want—and what you want. The trouble is, each one of us wants it exclusively."

The chancellor nodded. "Now you know why I had the effrontery, as you called it, to come to you. My rights have precedence; strictly speaking mine are the only ones that are legal. I was appointed one of the king's guardians by his royal mother. Hence it is I who should be in charge of my royal ward. You simply appointed yourself . . ."

"As Governor of Palermo . . ." Capparone began.

"But you are at least a Sicilian, and you have Norman blood," the chancellor went on quickly. "This Diepold is a German. And no Sicilian can wish for a renewal of German influence in Sicily."

"The king himself is half German," Capparone said slowly.

"And he shows it," the chancellor said. "But he is also half

61

Norman. Time alone will show which will have the upper hand. But that problem we shall face later. At present there is only one thing we must prevent at all costs."

"Diepold mustn't get him," Capparone said.

"Exactly." The chancellor began to pace up and down, his robes swishing. "To think there was a time when I was jubilant because he defeated the Count of Brienne! And now he is as dangerous as that adventurer ever was and perhaps more so. The Pope can't stop him."

"But I can." Capparone rang the bell. "Four guards to watch the rooms of the king," he told the official who answered. "The king must not leave them for the time being. Explain to him that we are taking this measure because an attempt on his life is planned by . . . by Saracens. And send for Colonel Mallino immediately."

The official withdrew.

"I shall mobilize a thousand men within two hours," Capparone went on. "That should be enough for Diepold. . . . What is the matter?"

The chancellor, standing at the window, turned away with a stifled ejaculation. His face was ashen.

"What is it?" Capparone asked again.

"We're too late," the chancellor said tonelessly. "He's here."

"Who? Diepold? Are you out of your mind?"

The chancellor laughed hysterically. "See for yourself," he shrieked.

Three steps and Capparone stood beside him.

A tight formation of knights was pressing into the courtyard. The sentries and a few officials were protesting, as could be seen from their emphatic gestures. They might as well have protested against the eruption of a volcano. Within the fraction of a minute they had been herded together into a corner, ten of the armored colossi were dominating the courtyard, the others dismounted and made their way ruthlessly into the castle.

The two men in the room gazed at each other.

"He can't kill me," the chancellor said, "it would be sacrilege."

Confused noises came from inside the palace, shouts, orders and the sound of running feet.

The two men remained silent, helpless in the grip of stark terror. The clatter of armor grew loud, the door was jerked open and a huge man stood on the threshold, naked sword in hand, smiling.

"The Governor of Palermo and the Chancellor of Sicily together in one room," he said. "A rare occasion, I should think."

He entered and half a dozen of his knights followed. The whole room was filled with steel and danger.

"My lords," the giant knight went on, "you have probably guessed by now who I am. But in case you haven't: I'm Diepold of Acerra. Who you are, I know . . . who you will be, I shall decide presently. Where is that little king of yours?"

The chancellor, fingering his pectoral cross, spoke out: "Count Diepold, as you know who I am, you know also that I am the king's guardian, selected by his royal mother, Queen Constance of Sicily, the wife of Emperor Henry VI, and confirmed in such office by His Holiness the Pope. It is my duty, therefore, to protect the lawful King of Sicily and I must ask you in the name of the Holy Trinity to respect the rights and the person of King Frederick Roger."

"I'll have no sermon from the Chancellor of Sicily, not even if he is a bishop," Count Diepold said, caressing the hilt of his enormous sword. "When I need a sermon, I can always get it directly from the Holy Father's legate who, you'll be pleased to hear, has come all the way from Apulia with me, despite the fact that we had to travel rather swiftly. Quick, somebody! Let the holy bishop come in here. We may need him."

"A legate of the Pope?" the chancellor asked, paling. "And with you?"

Diepold laughed. "You didn't expect that, did you? I've been around long enough to know how to deal with you people. Come in, my lord Bishop, and tell this . . . colleague of yours on whose orders we're here."

When Bishop Fornari entered, the chancellor, after a formal greeting, began to fire quick questions at him in Latin, to which the legate replied in the same language.

Diepold stood watching them with ill-concealed suspicion, but grinned broadly when Bishop Fornari produced his written credentials.

The effect on the two Sicilians was shattering.

"Now then," Diepold said gruffly. "Hand over the king, and be quick about it."

Capparone mechanically stretched out his hand to the bell.

"That won't help much, my lord Governor." Diepold grinned. "Your servants are all under the eyes of my men. Whom do you want to summon?"

"My secretary . . . Tramino."

Diepold roared: "Get a fellow called Tramino in here," and after a minute the official appeared, trembling like a leaf.

"Give the king my respects and ask him to honor us with his presence," Capparone said with great dignity.

"I'm . . . I'm sorry, my lord," Tramino stammered, "but the king . . . you ordered Magister Monucci to . . . accompany him to his room and—"

"Yes, yes, I know," Capparone interrupted hastily.

". . . but he ran away, my lord."

"What?"

"He ran so quickly, we couldn't catch him . . . catch up with him, I mean. And then these . . . these valiant knights came and . . . prevented any further . . . search."

Capparone looked at Diepold as if he expected to have his ears boxed. His heavy, bearded face a study in woe, he raised his fleshy arms and let them drop again.

The German gaped. An inarticulate noise came from his massive throat. His huge body, armor and all, began to shake convulsively. He threw back his head and howled with laughter. His knights chimed in. Even the dignified papal legate laughed.

Somewhat relieved, Capparone and the chancellor grinned sheepishly.

"The king has run away," Diepold sobbed with laughter. "What marvelous guardians you are, to be sure. Losing a king like a pair of old gloves." He checked himself with an effort. "Very well, we'll look for him. He can't have got very far. Somewhere in this castle, men, or somewhere near by, there is a very small king, aged eleven. He's a redhead, so it shouldn't be too difficult to recognize him. Go and get him. Meanwhile you, my lord Governor and you, my lord Chancellor, will be my much esteemed . . . guests."

"In my own castle," Capparone dared to remonstrate.

"In the king's castle, you mean," Diepold corrected him calmly. "And from now on I'm in charge of it."

That evening Diepold summoned a few of his most trusted commanders for a council. "Sicily is ours," he told them. "It's just as I knew it would be. Boldness does it every time. Bishop Fornari gone to bed? Good. Best thing about priests is that they must say Mass in the morning. Makes 'em go to bed early."

"What about the king?" the Knight of Werth asked.

"We caught him in a food shop." Diepold chuckled. "Quite a little hedgehog, too. Refused to come. Said he was there to give orders, not to receive them. Bero seized him, but the brat drew a dagger and cut off two of Bero's fingers."

The knights roared with laughter.

"Not bad for a boy of eleven, is it? They had to carry him back to the castle, screaming and scratching and using the most astonishing curses. He's back in his old room now. I put a double sentry before it and one of my men is sharing the room with him until we have settled matters here. I've never seen such a state of affairs in all my life, and I've seen a good deal."

"I've never seen a country like this either," the Knight of Lanzberg said. "Why, it's paradise."

There was a general murmur of agreement.

Diepold listened with satisfaction. "It *is* a paradise," he agreed. "And much too good for Sicilians."

They stared at him. He could almost see their minds working.

"However," he went on, "the little brat is the king, we can't get away from that fact. And it's his realm, under the Pope. So what we have to do is to guard him well and see to it that nothing happens to him. Of course, if it weren't for him . . ."

". . . this would be a good moment to start a new dynasty," Lanzberg said slowly. "What with Emperor Philip far away and his hands full with Otto of Brunswick, to say nothing of other troubles . . ."

Diepold's face was a mask. No one dared say anything.

"Who is the knight who will sleep in the king's room?" Lanzberg asked after a long silence.

"The Count of Vandria will alternate with Crécy," Diepold said casually.

"What? A Sicilian and a Frenchman?"

"Exactly," Diepold said.

There was another pause. Then Lanzberg said: "You must feel pretty sure of them."

"Yes."

"How so?"

"I know what they're out for. Crécy wants wealth. The little king can't give it to him. Neither can Capparone or the chancellor. They're both as poor as church mice. I can. And Vandria wants his moth-eaten old castle back. Again there's only one man who can give it to him and that's me. Don't worry, neither of 'em will let the king escape." Diepold yawned. "It's getting late. You'd better start making the round of sentries. For the next three days or so we must go warily. We can't expect reinforcements to arrive before that. Sea transport is slow; and we had the best horses and rode like devils."

"That we did," the Knight of Werth affirmed. "My backside tells me so in no uncertain terms."

They withdrew, laughing. Lanzberg alone lingered on.

"What is it?" Diepold asked quietly.

"I've been thinking . . . if I were to take the place of one of those royal custodians—"

"You wouldn't be any better off," Diepold interrupted. "And you might be worse."

"What do you mean?"

"If anything should happen to the little king," Diepold said in a low voice, "and, mark you, I say *if* . . . you'd be responsible, wouldn't you?"

"I would be responsible to you, yes."

"And what would His Holiness say?" Diepold asked.

"Why should you care?" Lanzberg said, with a shrug.

"But I do care, Lanzberg, I do . . . at least until I have my army here *and* hold all the ports of the island."

"I see. For a moment I almost thought you were taking that oath of allegiance to the Pope seriously."

"I do," Diepold said. "Of course, that allegiance is valid only as long as King Frederick Roger is alive. That's obvious, isn't it?"

"Exactly," Lanzberg cried. "Therefore, if—"

"Not so loud, you fool," Diepold whispered fiercely.

"Therefore if anything happened to the king . . ."

"I could do as I please. But, first, I would have to punish the criminal. Or some people—and especially the Holy Father— might get the idea that the fellow had acted on my orders."

Lanzberg scratched his head. "That's not so good."

"None of my men would do such a thing," Diepold said emphatically. "But I can't be so sure about a man of the late Duke of Taranto's army. Especially if he happens to be a Sicilian, a Sicilian noble who has been gravely wronged by the little king's father."

"Oh, oh," Lanzberg said. "I begin to understand . . ."

"None too soon, either. You are better at fighting than at planning, Lanzberg. Go to bed—and I hope you have a bad memory."

"Why? Oh, I see." Lanzberg grinned. "I have no memory at all."

Diepold nodded. "Sometimes that is the best way to reach old age."

CHAPTER NINE

Roger had the first watch in the king's room. Entering, he bent his knee before the boy who was sitting in a corner, with his legs crossed under him in the Arab fashion.

"Roger, Count of Vandria," he said. "I have come to keep the king company."

"There is no king here and no count," the boy said in a strangled voice. "Only a prisoner and his jailer."

Roger rose. "Have I the king's permission to sit down?" he asked.

"Why are you so courteous?" the boy jeered. "I can render you no favor." Then, as an afterthought: "Sit down, if you wish. Perhaps you can explain to me why you should make common cause with those brutes. If you are a Vandria, you must be a Sicilian."

"I am. And you are my sovereign."

Frederick stared at him from large, greenish eyes, hawk's eyes. He looked altogether like a young hawk, with his sharp, inquisitive nose dominating the thin mouth.

Not a handsome boy, Roger thought: but a face one could not forget easily.

"So I'm your sovereign," the boy said. "That means that you're under my orders, doesn't it?"

"Most certainly," Roger said.

"And if I told you to go and leave me alone, you would obey, would you?" the boy asked.

"Yes," Roger replied, "but I hope you will not command me to do that. Count Diepold would soon know; I'd be arrested, and the king would get another companion and most likely one who is not one of his subjects."

The boy said: "Never mind. I command you to go."

Roger rose, bowed, turned and walked toward the door.

"Stop," the boy said. "I've changed my mind. You may stay." He was staring at Roger. It was not easy to bear, because his eyes, like a bird's, never blinked.

They'll fear him one day, Roger thought. If he lives long enough to become a man, they'll fear him.

Yet at the same time he felt strangely drawn toward him. A boy of eleven—and a mass of suspicion and wounded pride and bitterness. He must have had a terrible life, worse perhaps than . . .

"Vandria," Frederick said suddenly. "The name of the Count of Vandria was on my father's proscription list."

"It was, no doubt," Roger said, amazed.

The king grinned. "I always read what they try to conceal from me. I studied those lists. You were implicated in the Norman conspiracy against my father's life, the conspiracy of Count San Giovanni and of . . . relatives of King Tancred."

"My father was," Roger said. "I was less than your age, at the time."

The boy nodded. "Of course. Stupid of me. So you . . . your father fled. Where to?"

"To Germany."

"Stupid of *him*," the boy said. "He jumped from the frying pan into the fire. Is he still alive?"

"He died, four years ago, in Mainz."

"And your mother?"

"She died during our flight. The hardships of the journey were too much for her. She was . . . very frail."

The boy nodded. "So was my mother. She . . . never mind. Was your father guilty?"

Roger said softly. "I don't know."

Frederick leaned forward. "Can you give me a good reason why I should trust one, who must hate the memory of my father?"

"If my father was disloyal to your father, it was because he was loyal to your mother," Roger said.

Again the boy nodded. "It is a good answer . . . perhaps," he said. "There were some who said that she was in the conspiracy herself."

"I know."

"She probably was, too," Frederick said. "Or why should he —my father—have forced her to stay with him in the room where the rebels were killed? She was made to look on when they heated a crown until it was red hot and then nailed it on San Giovanni's head. My father must have *thought* she was guilty."

"How is it you know about that terrible thing?" Roger asked, horrified.

The boy giggled. "Didn't I tell you I always read what they try to hide from me? I read the entire report of that trial. There was no love between my parents. For years my mother refused herself to my father. . . ."

"Don't," Roger said quickly. "You mustn't talk about such things."

"I talk about anything I want. They made me in the end, anyway. My mother gave birth to me at Jesi under the open sky and in the presence of the people, so that no one would say that I was not her son. That damned swine, Markwald, said it anyway, and now he is in hell, I hope. If there is a hell, that is. Do you believe there is?"

"The priests—" Roger began.

"They *have* to talk of hell," the boy interrupted. "Where would they be, if people stopped believing in heaven and hell? I never trust a priest and least of all the Pope. He's my guardian —because my father when he came to die, became all soft and mushy and appointed him. Mother, of course, confirmed it, and then she died, too. Do you know the Pope?"

"I never met him," Roger said.

"He's a small man," Frederick said, "but they say he's very intelligent. Small men are often much more intelligent than large ones. That Diepold is probably very stupid. Why did you join him?"

Roger told him.

The boy listened with intense concentration. "What you really want is what your father wanted," he said. "You want Vandria back. Perhaps I shall let you have it back, when I'm of age. That is, if they don't kill me first, but I don't think they will, not if Al Mansor is right and he usually is. He cast my horoscope, you know. I'm born with the Sun in Capricorn and well protected, so I should live deeply into what they call the second half of life. Al Mansor tells lies often, but only to stupid people. He's never lied to me yet. Has Diepold told you to kill me?"

It was like receiving an arrow in the chest.

"Yes," Roger said. "But I won't do it."

"I know," the boy said. "You are not as stupid as he is. You could see the trap."

"The trap?"

"Of course," the boy said impatiently. "Or else, why should he choose you, a Sicilian, and once wronged by my father?"

"Because he thinks I'd do anything to get Vandria back."

"That's only half of it. The other half is more important to him. He'd say you did it out of vengeance and have you drawn and quartered."

"That is probably quite right," Roger said, biting his lip.

"Why did you accept?" Frederick asked with an air of indifference.

Roger smiled. "Because if I hadn't, he would have chosen somebody who would do what he wants."

"Then you shouldn't have gone when I told you to leave me," the boy said reproachfully.

"I didn't intend to, really," Roger said. "I thought you'd call me back."

"And if I hadn't?"

"I would have come back a little later."

Frederick threw back his head, laughing. "I think I like you," he said. "I shall take you into my service. I have no power and no money. All I have is a lot of enemies who cannot afford to kill me. I'm a very bad bargain. Will you serve me?"

"I also have no power and no money," Roger said, "and anybody can afford to kill me. I will serve you gladly."

They grinned at each other. The boy stretched out his hand and Roger kissed it. "Now I am the king's man," he said. "And my first duty will be to get you out of here as quickly as possible."

The boy stared at him from unblinking eyes. "How strong is Diepold?" he asked.

"Eighty-seven knights. No retinues. About two hundred more men are expected to join him in three days' time. Then I am supposed to carry out his order—not before."

Frederick nodded. "That gives us time. Have you thought of a plan?"

"I might manage to get you out at night. I know when the rounds are made. I would have to deal with the two sentries first, of course."

"Not good enough," the boy said. "I'd have to flee and I have no place to flee to. The first thing is to let Capparone know. That's the Governor of Palermo. He's stupid, but this is simple enough, even he can deal with it. And he's one of those enemies of mine who can't afford to have me killed."

"I could try to get in touch with him. . . ."

"No. You're being watched, that's certain, and it would arouse suspicion at once. I shall have to confess my sins, I'm afraid."

"Confess your sins?"

"Yes." Frederick gave a mocking smile. "They wouldn't let me have a priest from outside. But I could ask the Pope's legate to hear my confession. Even Diepold can't refuse that. And the legate can go and tell Capparone everything."

"I thought you didn't trust priests?"

"I don't," Frederick said. "But I didn't say a priest wouldn't keep an eye on his own advantage. The Pope is another one of my enemies who can't afford my death. He has a claim on Sicily only as long as I exist. So it's to his advantage if the plot fails. Tell the good bishop I want to confess my sins to him. He'll come. The rest is easy."

"I'll do that," Roger said. "And may I say I never saw anyone so obviously born to be a king as you are."

"That's not surprising," Frederick said. "There aren't any. Al Mansor says I am quite exceptional and he has seen thousands of horoscopes. Get me the bishop. And by my royal word: when I come of age, I shall give you back Vandria; and you shall be among the first at my court."

The Knight of Lanzberg came clattering into Diepold's room —which had been Capparone's study—in a state of some agitation. "What is going on?" he asked. "While I was in command of the watch, a small army of carts arrived and your staff men let it go through—on your personal orders, they said. But when I'm in charge, I'm responsible and when I'm responsible I want to know what's going on."

"Vegetables," Diepold said cheerfully. "Meat. Game. Poultry. Spices. Bread, cheese, fruit and forty casks of wine. Satisfied?"

"Oh, oh," Lanzberg said, "you're laying in provisions for a siege."

"Not a bit of it. We're having a banquet. There'll be fiddlers, jugglers, tumblers, everything."

"What about women?" Lanzberg asked hopefully.

"Sorry, no women. This is a state occasion and there'll be bishops and prelates galore."

"I'd rather have women," Lanzberg said. "I've seen some beauties in this city. Almond eyes and . . ."

"Don't be a fool." Diepold laughed. "Tonight it won't just be revelry. It's the Feast of Unity, the banquet of general agreement, the *Te Deum laudamus* or whatever you want to call it. I've done it, man, I've done it."

Lanzberg scratched his head. "I know you've been negotiating with those Sicilian bigheads. Do you mean to say . . ."

"I mean to say that they accepted *all* my conditions," Diepold said. "And believe me, there were quite a few. I never thought they'd do it before our reinforcements arrived and we could make a show of force, but they did. Do you know what it means? I am the guardian of the king for life. I can make and abolish laws. My men will garrison and supervise all the ports. They hedged a bit about a few points, but when I insisted, they just caved in."

71

"No spine," Lanzberg said. "Never had any. It's a wonder they can walk upright."

"Complete unity," Diepold said, rubbing his hands. "I got their signatures—both the governor's and the chancellor's. Frightened stiff, they were. Everything for dear peace's sake. So now we must show that we're benevolent masters. We'll do them proud. I even went so far as to pay for the food and wine. There's nothing you can't get in this city if you pay for it."

"What about the king?" Lanzberg asked. "Are you going to let him take part in the banquet?"

Diepold shook his head. "Too risky. Impudent little rascal. Nervous, too. He might fly off the handle and make 'em think he's a poor victim, or something. He'll stay in his room, well guarded by the noble Count of Vandria, unless he cuts *him* to ribbons, too, as he did poor Bero for laying hands on him."

"Not Vandria," Lanzberg said. "That young man has a charmed life—or charmed armor, I don't know which. I struck him over the head when we stormed the Duke of Taranto's camp. No one's ever survived that, not when the blow came true, and it did, you know. I . . . I don't like that fellow. Speaking of risks—how many Sicilians have you invited?"

Diepold grinned. "There'll be fifty of them—and fifty of us. That'll leave thirty-seven of us to keep watch. They'll have their own banquet tomorrow, so there won't be any ill feelings. No one's allowed to bear arms."

"How do you know they're not going to have arms hidden on them? Those long cloaks they wear . . ."

"No one will enter the castle before he has been searched. That's another reason why I don't want women to be present. There'd be an outcry if we started searching them. Set your mind at rest, Lanzberg. Drink as much as you like, but watch your tongue. I know what you think of these Sicilians. . . ."

"Same as you." Lanzberg grinned.

"Maybe. But this is not the moment to tell them. We shall be the most amiable, benevolent, generous hosts."

"That won't be much fun," Lanzberg said. "And . . . what about the king? When. . . ."

"Tomorrow our reinforcements will arrive," Diepold said in a hard voice.

Diepold was as good as his word. He received his guests at the entrance of the large banquet hall, unarmed, dressed in a wine-red tunic trimmed with fur, with a heavy golden collar circling his massive neck, his large face wreathed in smiles.

He greeted Capparone with special courtesy and even went so far as to apologize for playing the host in the governor's own palace.

"No apology is necessary," Capparone replied with equal politeness. "After all, you are here as the representative of the king."

"I can see that it will be a pleasure to work with you," Diepold said and turned away to welcome the chancellor.

"I have seated you opposite the papal legate," he said. "You are on one side of the middle table and he on the other. That way you'll keep us wild laymen in order, as befits Holy Church."

The chancellor smiled thinly. "I don't think it will be a very difficult task," he said and swept on.

The musicians, high up in a gallery, were playing.

Lanzberg came up, his bulky frame puffing out a tunic of green velvet, trimmed with white fox fur. "Message just came from the papal legate," he said. "The king has sent for him again. We are to start without him. He'll join us later."

Diepold frowned. "What a tender conscience the brat has, to be sure."

"And what a sense of duty on the part of the holy bishop," Lanzberg said. "Shall I go and fetch him?"

"No. It doesn't matter. There'll be no third meeting between the two, though—I shall see to that." Diepold gave a sign to the musicians. They stopped their fiddling and a fanfare of six trumpets announced the beginning of the banquet.

Light dishes formed the start, *frutta di mare,* olives, spiced titbits of a dozen kinds.

"Why do you Southern people always begin your meal with such trifles?" Lanzberg complained, refusing the dish offered to him. "Surely, at the beginning of a meal a man is at his hungriest for some substantial food."

The Sicilians around him exchanged glances.

"These little things serve to whet your appetite, Sir Knight," one of them said affably enough.

"My appetite needs no whetting," Lanzberg growled. "I could eat a horse tonight."

"Do you mean to say that you eat horses in Germany?" the Sicilian asked in mock horror. "How terrible for you. I am sure you won't have to partake here of anything so unworthy of your tongue. Try those prawns, Sir Knight, they're delicious. You will observe that most of these dishes are salty—which stimulates thirst and makes your palate ready for more wine."

"My palate is always ready for more wine," Lanzberg said. "It needs neither prawns as allies—nor Sicilians."

Diepold darted a warning glance at him, but the Sicilians showed no sign of being offended. They were all smiles.

Lanzberg was drinking deep.

Capparone leaned forward. "A prawn is a kind of knight—all armored," he said. "I'm sure you'd relish eating knights in armor."

"I have dealt with many knights," Lanzberg replied, wiping his mouth with the back of his hand. "And I'll take on any German, any three Frenchmen and any six Sicilians, whether they be of Italian, French or Moorish origin or any mixture, though, by my faith, I believe there isn't any one of you who is not a mixture of half a dozen races." He emptied his cup and had it refilled.

"You must forgive the noble knight, Your Excellency," Diepold said. "He is a little rough. Besides, he always feels naked when he isn't wearing his armor, so he protects himself with the rough side of his tongue." But he gave Lanzberg another warning look.

"Oh, but he's quite witty," Capparone said, with a somewhat strained smile. "Even though his wit may be rather heavy. But then we know, we Sicilians, that manners differ among the nations."

The servants had commenced offering game and poultry.

"That's a little better," Lanzberg said, taking a whole roast hare from the platter and tearing off the head that had been replaced, fur and all, so that guests far gone in their cups could still know what they were eating.

"Palermo will do better by you than that, Sir Knight," Capparone said. "I have permitted myself to add a special dish to this banquet, a dish for such noble company, and here it comes, I think."

A number of stewards were carrying in two enormous carcasses on spits.

"By the beard of St. Boniface, two whole roast oxen," Diepold said. "I tried my best, but you've outdone me."

"At least we're trying," Capparone said. "I mean, we're trying to contribute a little to the splendor of the meal."

"Now that's what I call food," Lanzberg said, with his mouth full of roast hare, "and I don't mind telling you that it's the first thing I've seen of you people that really impresses me."

"Shut up, Lanzberg," Diepold snapped, but his words were inaudible because the musicians had started a particularly noisy piece. Trumpets and drums drowned out not only flutes and fiddles, but also all conversation except that between immediate neighbors.

"What's the matter with the fools?" Diepold murmured and then saw some Sicilians nodding and laughing at the band, as if to encourage them to still greater efforts. Well, if they liked the din, let them have it. They were drunk, of course. These little islanders couldn't take much. A few of them were under the table already and some had begun to dance.

No use making the speech he had prepared for the occasion. He should have made it right at the beginning, but had not wanted to do so until . . . until what? That's right, not until the papal legate was present.

He looked at the end of the table. The legate's chair was still vacant.

Diepold's eyes narrowed a little. He had drunk a good deal himself, but he could still make himself think. Could anything be wrong?

Capparone, beside him, rose. "Now, my lord Count," he almost shouted into his ear. "I will, with your kind permission, carve up the best meat in Sicily and the first portion will be for you and the second for your noble and witty friend, the Knight of Lanzberg."

"Wait a moment," Diepold said, but the infernal music swallowed up his voice and Capparone had already started. Some other Sicilians seemed to have had the same idea as the governor, quite a number were approaching the two huge carcasses on spits.

"Carve them up!" Capparone shrieked. "Carve them up for the glory of Sicily!"

"Swords," a German voice roared. "The damned oxen are filled with swords!"

Diepold jumped to his feet—and found himself seized by two of the stewards. He shook them off as a bear shakes off a couple of hounds. In a flash he was dead sober again. He saw that all his knights were grappling with stewards and varlets; he saw the Church dignitaries flee into a remote corner of the hall; he saw the Sicilians around the two oxen throw swords and daggers dextrously to those who were standing farther off.

Half a dozen hands seized him again and he had to lay about him. He managed to fell two of the stewards, but knew instinctively that he was not dealing with ordinary varlets. They were sturdy and they could fight. Soldiers, he thought—they smuggled in soldiers disguised as varlets.

From the corner of his eye he saw that they had pushed over Lanzberg's chair and there he lay, covered by a heap of Sicilians.

His knights were being driven into a corner of the hall at sword point. There was little resistance.

And still the musicians were blaring away—that was not music any longer. It was signaling, and had been for some time. So the musicians were in it as well.

Capparone and six men came up, sword in hand.

"I surrender to you, my lord Governor," Diepold shouted at the top of his lungs, pushing a steward out of the way. "But I warn you, your victory won't last long. My men . . ."

Capparone gave a sign to the musicians. The trumpets stopped at once. "If you mean the thirty-seven knights you posted as guards," he said, smiling, "they have been taken care of. Listen . . ."

From outside came a noise as of low thunder.

"Twelve hundred soldiers are too many for thirty-seven, however large and valiant," Capparone said. "And if you refer to the two hundred knights who were to arrive tomorrow: they're being ambushed tonight near Monreale."

"This is open rebellion against the Pope as well as the king," Diepold barked.

Capparone laughed outright.

The curtains of the main entrance of the hall were drawn back and a large number of Sicilian knights rushed in, armored and armed to the teeth. Some of their swords were red. So the guards had not gone down without fighting. . . .

A great shout of enthusiasm welcomed them. They responded with a salute of their swords and then formed a double line to the right and left of the entrance.

The shouting became a roar as the little king entered the hall, flanked on one side by the papal legate, on the other by a knight in full armor.

"Long live the King," Capparone shouted. Then he turned to Diepold. "And we shall see to it that no one shortens his life."

"What are you suggesting?" Diepold flared up.

"Quiet, murderer," Capparone retorted. "Do you still think that we do not know all about your plan?"

Diepold stared at the knight at the king's side, his face contorted with fury.

Lanzberg was being pushed over to the corner where the other German knights were standing, bewildered and dejected. "There's the dog of a traitor," he roared. "What did I tell you, Diepold?" With a wild effort he shook off his captors, tore a dagger from the belt of one of them and threw it with all his strength.

Roger flung up his shield to cover the king. The dagger whistled past the boy and stuck, trembling, in Roger's breastplate.

Half a dozen swords plunged into Lanzberg's body and he fell. But his eyes were fixed on Roger who drew out the dagger and threw it down. There was no blood on it.

"Damned magician," Lanzberg said tonelessly. Then he sank back and died.

The little king walked on impassively till he reached the main table. He sat down on Diepold's chair of state. "My lord Capparone," he said in his clear boy's voice. "Have those foreigners taken away to a safe place, and have them chained."

Surrounded by sword points Diepold went to join his knights. The armored Sicilians began to herd them out, one by one.

"This is a banquet for Sicilians alone," the king said, "with the exception of my holy friend, the papal legate. Take the place at my right side, my lord Bishop, if you please. Count Roger of Vandria?"

"My lord King?"

"You will sit on my left." The little king's voice was calm. His green eyes, hawk's eyes, shone preternaturally bright. He looked on, unblinkingly, as they carried the dead Lanzberg out of the hall.

"My lord Capparone," the king said, "why don't the musicians play?"

The governor turned toward the balcony and gave the sign.

Involuntarily, Roger shuddered a little. Eleven years old, he thought. What will he be one day—a genius? A madman? A demon? Or something of all of them? He knew he had found a master; and perhaps the kind of master Sicily—and the world —needed.

Suddenly the king smiled charmingly. "Won't somebody give me something to eat?" he asked. "I'm hungry."

CHAPTER TEN
A.D. 1205-1206

"By my honor," cried Ricardo Parelli, "by the swanlike neck of my *adorata*; by all the money I hope to inherit from all my uncles, I tell you, I won't tolerate it any longer."

The other young men in the back room of the tavern looked at each other.

"He has sworn by the three things most holy to him, starting with the least," Paolo Spadone said. "One might think he really means it. Where is that cursed innkeeper? He said he was going to send us—"

"Never mind the innkeeper," Nino Manetti cut his friend short. "What is it you won't tolerate any longer, Ricardo *mio?*"

"I tell you I won't," Ricardo insisted. "And don't think for one moment that I'm drunk. That'll come later. My trouble is that I'm as sober as an archbishop before High Mass. And I listened to you maligning the greatest leader we ever had, the best and the most generous and your host on top of it all. Who paid for our last three, no, four sessions, at the Blue Knight, the Saracen Tower, the New Haven and now at the Golden Tree? Francis Bernardone. You're about as grateful as a bunch of sparrows, picking up . . . picking up . . ."

"Never mind what the sparrows pick up." Nino laughed. "No one said our Francis isn't generous. So would you be, I'm sure, if all your uncles had died."

"But they haven't," Ricardo said, "and you won't sidestep me that easily. You've been whispering about him—I mean against him all evening."

"I only said he's no longer the fellow he used to be," Mario Luca defended himself. "He used to . . ."

"He is magnificent," Ricardo declared. "Who else has ideas to compare with his? You always do exactly what you do do— I mean you never do the unexpected. You're ordinary, all of you, and all of me too. I could predict at any moment what you and I will do and what we won't do. . . ."

"Do, do, do, do," sang Mario Luca lustily.

". . . and your voice isn't as good as Francis' either," Ricardo told him. "Look, this is what I mean. When that passionate idiot of a troubadour came to town, preaching war against Sicily, you did exactly what was expected of you: you grinned sheepishly and stayed at home. What did Francis do? He joined up, helmet, armor and all, and we all thought, poor fellow, he has gone wrong in the head. But off he goes and all the old dodderers make solemn speeches: there is still martial fire in the youth of Assisi, take young Bernardone as an example, now there's a brave young man; and Papa Bernardone struts about like an overgrown peacock. And what happens? Our Francis comes back next day, he's been thinking it over and he won't

78

do it after all. What a joke! What a hoax! I'm certain he never meant it for a single moment and why should he? Going to war to conquer Sicily! What's Sicily to him? Going to fight for King What's-his-name in Palermo. Ridiculous. But I shall never forget the faces of the old dodderers, and especially my own dear papa, who had been preaching sermons at me about young Francis' valor and general magnificence and now screamed that this was cowardice in the face of the enemy and I said to him: 'Papa *mio*, the nearest enemy was in Apulia. If you're right, Francis is the only man in Italy who ever fled from an enemy five hundred miles away. If he's a coward, you must at least admit that he's the king of cowards.' It was wonderful."

"It was very clever," Paolo Spadone admitted. "But it's an old story, Ricardo, we laughed about it a couple of years ago. In fact that escapade of his was one of the main reasons why we chose him to be our leader."

"And that he still is," Ricardo cried. "What do you want him to do, go to war again for twenty-four hours?"

"A good Assisan never makes the same joke twice. But tell me, frankly, haven't you noticed that he has changed?"

"No. How, changed? I've noticed nothing."

"By the flaming sword of the Archangel Tobias," Paolo began.

"Never heard of him," Mario interposed.

"I mean the Archangel Samson, of course," Paolo said. "That's the one who slew a thousand Turks with the jawbone of an ass, isn't it?"

"Philippians," Mario corrected. "Not Turks. Philippians, and the Apostle Paul wrote them a long letter to console them. You're right about the jawbone of an ass, though. But then that's something you would know about."

"I don't quite know what you mean by that," Paolo said with a certain amount of suspicion. "But I do know what I mean and that is that this Ricardo here doesn't notice anything. He won't be aware of the Day of Judgment even when it's in full swing, as it will be soon enough, if you listen to the sermons at the Cathedral."

"Don't wake up my conscience," Ricardo pleaded. "It's so peacefully asleep, the poor little thing. But I still don't know what you want of our Francis. In what way is he supposed to have changed? But guard your tongue when you talk about him—it's still wet from Francis' wine. Where is he, by the way?"

"With the others in the main room, of course," Nino said.

"All right, I'll tell you. Mind you, it isn't easy. My *adorata* . . ."

"Is it still the little—"

"Never mention a lady's name in public. My *adorata*, never mind who she is, told me that every woman will know when her husband is beginning to be interested in another woman."

"What's that to do with Francis? He's not a woman, neither are you and you aren't married to each other."

Nino threw up his arms. "Ricardo! What's happened to your brain? All I mean to say is: whereas a woman feels a change, a man observes it. Francis used to be the most fastidious of us all in matters of dress and refinement. He never wore the same tunic twice to our sessions and he would not tolerate a stain, not even a tiny speck of dirt. His hands were immaculate. Today he's wearing that blue tunic for the third time running, and his fingernails are no longer what they used to be. I tell you, he's slipping."

"Bah, little things like that . . ."

"It always starts with little things," Mario said gravely. "But there's more than that. He is no longer with us, really. His mind is elsewhere. I think I know what happened. He went to Rome not so long ago and somebody must have got hold of him there, so he's becoming religious and if he's not very, very careful, he'll become a priest."

This time they all laughed.

"Whatever next," Ricardo said, wiping his eyes. "Francis a priest! I can see him, mounting the pulpit with his lute under his arm and giving us a sermon in rhymes. Now if you'd said he wanted to become a troubadour . . ."

"You didn't hear the whole story," Mario told him. "I heard he was seen in Rome at the door of St. Peter's, changing clothes with a beggar!"

There was a storm of laughter. "If you believe that, you'll believe anything, my Mario," Ricardo said. "Ye gods, what nonsense!"

"I'm not so sure," Paolo remarked. "He's quite capable of changing clothes with a beggar today and putting on the Pope's robes tomorrow. He loves dressing up."

"He no longer does, apparently," Mario said sadly. "Think of the blue tunic."

"Oh, forget that blue tunic," Nino said. "But listen, Ricardo, he often disappears and no one knows where to. He comes back late at night, furtively, and slips into his house when everyone is asleep."

"Does he, by St. Amor," Ricardo shouted. "Why didn't you say so at once? Now it's all clear to me. He's in love!"

They stared at him.

"Holy Samson," Paolo burst out, "he's right! Now why didn't I think of that in the first place. He's got all the symptoms."

"Ricardo," Mario said, "I owe you an apology. It all fits in. Maybe that story of changing clothes with a beggar is true as well. Maybe he needed them for a disguise, to meet his *adorata*. But in that case she would have to be a Roman girl and . . ."

"Let's find out," Nino suggested. "Come on, we'll join him and the others."

In the main room of the Golden Tree another dozen young men were sitting, some dicing, others telling each other the latest gossip.

"There you are," Paolo said. "Francis is sitting all by himself. Look at him . . . it's just as I said, he isn't with us at all. He's far away. Hey, Francis!"

Francis sat up with a start. "Yes, of course," he said. "More wine. I'll get it for you at once."

"He was fast asleep." Paolo laughed.

"He was dreaming with his eyes open," Mario said. "Is she fair or dark, Francis?"

"Is she a Roman girl?"

"What's her name, Francis?"

"What are you all talking about?" Francis asked. His fingers were playing with the staff of leadership they had given him, a pretty thing of ebony with a silver knob.

They were all crowding around him now, even the dice players.

"Come on, drop the old stick and take your lute," someone said.

"Yes, do," Ricardo pleaded. "Play us a song in praise of your lady love. No good hedging, Francis, we know you're in love."

Francis smiled strangely.

"He is," Ricardo exclaimed triumphantly. "I told you so. He is."

"Well, yes, I am," Francis said slowly.

"He's admitted it," Ricardo shouted. "Well, it's not too early. You're twenty-two or twenty-three, aren't you? You could almost be a grandfather. Who is she? She is beautiful, that goes without saying. But is she rich, too? She'd better be, your father is good for another twenty years—for ten at least. Like my uncles, more's the pity."

"It's far more important that she come from a good family,"

Paolo said. "If you are going to marry her, that is. Are you?"

"Set your minds at rest," Francis said. "I shall marry her. And I shall have a wife more noble and beautiful and richer than any of you have ever seen."

"Listen to him," Mario crowed. "The girl must at least be a duchess. Who can she be?"

"That I cannot tell you," Francis said.

"Of course not," Nino agreed. "Never mention a lady's name in public, I always say."

"I am going to see her now," Francis said and he rose.

"Heavens above and flames below," Paolo cried. "It's past midnight!"

"I can see her at any hour," Francis said. "Please forgive me for leaving you. I . . . I'm not much good to you as I am. The Golden Tree will be at your service as long as you wish, of course."

"We understand, Francis."

"Love always comes first," Nino quoted solemnly.

Francis smiled at him, took his mantle and left.

"He's forgotten his staff of leadership," Ricardo said. "Hey, Francis!"

But there was no answer.

"I'll keep it for him," Paolo said. "Or you do, Nino. I'm a little tired. I think I'll go to bed."

"Maybe I will, too," Ricardo said casually. "Good night, friends."

Out in the street Paolo said: "You're not drunk after all, are you? You're going in the wrong direction."

"I'm going in the same direction you are," Ricardo said, grinning. "And we both have the same idea."

"You mean . . ."

"You know exactly what I mean. I'm just as curious as you are to find out where he's going at this hour. There he is, crossing the square."

"We must keep more in the shadow, though. Just as well there's no moon tonight."

They followed their quarry as silently as they could.

"That's where the Borroleones live, surely. Do you think it could be Maddalena Borroleone?"

"She's no duchess. And her mother . . ."

"No, he's passing the house. Perhaps it's the Contessa Ruffaldi!"

"Don't be a fool, she's ten years older than Francis."

"What if she is? He never said she was young, only . . ."

"Shhh . . . he'll hear us if you go on gabbing like this."

"He's passed her house, too. But whom can he mean? He's approaching the city gate."

"There are no houses beyond the gate. He's fooled us."

"Either that—or he's having a secret rendezvous with her outside the walls. That's it, I'm sure."

"Very well, we'll find out. It can't be far. He wouldn't let a lady go a long way outside the walls."

"But it's awfully dark."

"No darker than for him and his girl. Come on. And don't make so much noise, you idiot."

"It's not my fault. I stumbled. One's got to be a cat to see in the dark. Where is he?"

"I can only just see him. He's passing that clump of trees. Come along."

But when they reached the trees, Francis had vanished.

The tomb was not very deep. A few steps down and through a narrow passage into the dark hollow, where once, who knows how long ago, an old man was laid to sleep, an Etruscan they said he was, who had lived when ancient Rome was young or did not yet exist. There was nothing left of him in the tomb, not even a single bone, though the dust under one's feet might have been his. Neither the joy nor the terror of the tomb had any meaning for the Etruscan. His time was over and had been for a very long time.

Since then the world had been redeemed at the most costly price of all and everything had been made new, though most men seemed to have forgotten it and to have fallen back into the old ways, grown men who chose to live like children.

The joy and terror of the tomb came from another source.

"Everything I ever saw and loved I can forget," Francis prayed in the dark, "but not the Voice nor the dreams Thou hast sent me. When shall I dream again, Lord, when shall I hear Thy voice again?"

He knew that if this was to happen, he must be alone. He knew, dimly, that he had to be born anew in some fashion and for that reason he withdrew into the womb of his mother, the earth.

This new birth, like all birth, would no doubt entail much pain. Many a time his mother had told him of the pain she felt when he was born but this time it was he himself who would feel it.

He was ready for it, he thought. He hoped he was.

83

Or did he still join his friends because he dreaded the pain and felt safe in their company, shielded from Dream and Voice alike by the fumes of wine and the sound of laughter?

And by that did he himself delay the event he came here to pray for?

Most likely that was it. For there was no joy left for him in those nights of carousing, ending up, usually, in some mad and noisy procession through the dark streets. Strange that he had ever liked those glittering shadows, those spectral joys, that were nothing when one looked at them sharply.

I *am* afraid, Francis thought. They were right, he knew, who chided him for being a coward, the Knight of Vandria first and his father and Consul Revini and many others—except that what they had taken for cowardice had been courage; of his true cowardice they knew nothing.

It was one thing to be generous, especially to the poor and most of all to beggars, but quite another to undergo the ordeal he felt was drawing closer and closer.

The Voice had not spoken again. But there was inside him a tugging force, a bitter longing, a mounting desire. There was no coercion and he knew that there would never be. It was much more like a temptation, a good temptation, a stirring-up of the heart.

He knew that it was for him to give his assent, that nothing could happen to him without such assent. He did not know—not for sure—what was expected of him, though he did know this, that it would mean a change more complete than his mind could grasp.

The true beginning of all this was not the dream in which he saw the garden and the castle and the stacked arms, helmets, armor, shields and swords—things born of his own sleeping mind—and ignored the crosses that adorned each and every one of them, the crosses that were the real message.

The beginning was much further back, in his early childhood. There was mother, teaching him that the Lord said: "As long as you did it to one of these my least brethren, you did it to me." And father whose supreme expression of contempt was the word "beggar."

He had learned soon enough to combine the two thoughts. Beggars then were the least of the Lord's brethren.

Then one day, much later, he was selling silk cloth to Donna Revini, the consul's wife. She liked to buy from him and always smiled at him when she did. An old beggar, more daring than others, entered the shop, asking for alms, and Donna Revini

84

picked up her skirts and lifted her nose, because the beggar was dirty.

It was a most embarrassing situation and Donna Revini looked at him in a somewhat pained manner for not dealing with it as in her unmistakable opinion he should.

So he waved the beggar aside, he shooed him off and the old man left dejectedly and Donna Revini, after the customary haggling, made up her mind about the silk cloth—yellow silk it was and she wanted it for a dress for her eldest daughter.

And all the time he was thinking, he could not help thinking, of what he had done to the Lord in one of the least of His brethren; his fingers wrapping the silk and taking the money were moist and trembling. As soon as the lady had left, he fairly leaped from the shop, he did not even think of closing the door behind him, and ran up the street in the direction the beggar had taken.

Nothing, nothing in the world was as important as to find the man. He raced across the Cathedral square, looking about him wildly; he chased up and down the streets, sobbing with excitement and strain. He prayed that he would be allowed to find his beggar; he asked half a dozen people and was shrugged off. One man told him: "You must be the fool of all fools, young man, to run after one of those who are only too willing to run after you and me." And another, "Has the wretch stolen something from you?" But he ran on and on and there the beggar was at last, stretching out his tattered hat to someone, and he caught him. He wanted to apologize to him, but found that he had no breath left. His arms and hands still obeyed him, though, and he poured into the beggar's hat every coin in his pocket and then fled before the astonished man could stammer his thanks.

Back in the shop he swore a solemn oath that he would never again refuse help to any of his Lord's least brethren.

Then there was the moment in Rome when he suddenly realized that it was not enough to share his money with the poor cripple at the door of St. Peter's; that it was meet and just to share the man's humiliation as well. Putting on his dirty rags had not been pleasant. Even less pleasant was it to be kicked out of the way by that young officer, entering the church with his lady. But then—as he still smarted from the pain of the kick —there was one single, fleeting instant when he knew that he had made his body a shield and warded off an indignity to the Body most sacred, and in the same instant a white column of joy had leaped up in him and he could have sung aloud the praise of God.

And now—impossible to doubt it any longer—he knew that this also had been no more than one small step on the journey and that the great tests, the great perils, the real toil and labor and pain were all ahead of him.

There were so many things he could not do. Some brave men, like the Lazarists, were looking after the lepers. He had never been able to bear the mere sight of one of those unfortunate people who were decomposing while still alive. And leprosy was contagious, every child knew that and ran when there was a leper about. Lepers were not allowed in the town, of course, but sometimes roamed the countryside in search of food.

To be like them was an unbearable thought. It was bad enough to be poor, to be dressed in rags and eat what others left. So many poor people became ugly, too. There was one woman in town whose ugliness was monstrous. No one could look at her without a feeling of revulsion. Now if he must be like that . . .

He groaned. Why should the Lord want anybody to be like that? Why should he, Francis, not be satisfied with what the Lord had given him? It was ingratitude, surely, to despise all the good he had received.

He stopped the miserable chain of thought with a fierce effort of his will. Fear was at the base of it, fear dressed up as a leper, as that disgusting old woman.

He began again to pray, and at once the thought came to him of quite another woman, the beautiful, the eternally young woman in the simple gray robe he had seen in his dream. She, not that horrible crone in Assisi, was Poverty. She was his *adorata*, his bride. Of her he had thought when the young men at the Golden Tree teased him about being in love.

Lady Poverty, the great lady who would not be courted with presents of gold and precious stones.

To be worthy of her a knight must perform deeds of great daring, greater by far than riding into battle against odds. Her knight must dare what others did not. . . .

He went on praying, he had no idea for how long. But after a while the tomb was no longer dark but gray. The dawn was coming and he must return to his parents' house before his father awoke.

When he emerged from the tomb the stars had paled and the city walls were whitened by the first light of day.

As he walked toward the gate a lonely figure came up to him very slowly. It was a man, a man in a long robe.

Francis stopped with bated breath. The figure was luminous.

Could it be that his prayers had been answered so quickly and with such overwhelming grace?

But as the man came nearer, Francis had the feeling one sometimes has in a dream, except that this was a hundred times stronger: the sinking, frightening, nauseating sensation when a dream of beauty suddenly changes into nightmare. It was utter disintegration, a plunge from heaven into hell.

The man was a leper. The luminosity was due to the light of the morning playing on the large whitish stains of the horrible disease.

As in a nightmare, Francis wanted to run and could not.

The abominable apparition drew nearer. He could see that the man no longer had a human face. The eyes had almost disappeared under bulging, ulcerous matter. There was a gaping hole instead of a nose, and as his lips, too, were eaten away, his teeth stood out like teeth in a skull. He was so near now that Francis could smell the stench of decay and putrefaction.

Perhaps it was this stench that gave Francis back the power to move, and immediately the thought flashed into his mind that if he turned back and ran, this wreck on his bleeding stumps of feet would never be able to catch up with him. But at the same time he saw the man stretch out his hand, on which there were only two fingers left. The leper was begging.

Francis braced himself. With all the strength at his command he forced his trembling feet to stand firm. His hand flew to his belt and managed to extricate a number of coins. He need only throw them before the leper and he would have kept his oath and could escape.

Instead, he placed the coins into the doughy, stumpy, two-fingered hand, and bending down, pressed on it a light kiss.

Drawing himself up, the dreadful face was so close that he could see a few hairs sticking out between ulcerous patches. The stench of corruption was overwhelming.

The leper stood quite still.

And Francis laid his arm around his shoulder and gave him the kiss of peace on his cheek. He felt the leper's teeth touch his own cheek in response.

Then and then only he stood back a little and bowed and walked on toward the gate of the city.

Incongruously, he wondered why neither the leper nor he had spoken a single word and whether the man might not regard it as a lack of courtesy. So after a few yards he turned around to wave at him.

The leper was gone.

There was no tree in the immediate vicinity, no cave, nothing that could serve as a cover.

Yet he could still feel the touch of the leper's teeth on his cheek.

As he walked on, he heard the call of a lark, answered at once by a second and a third. A chorus of chirping, twittering and warbling came from all sides and the rush of countless wings, all mounting and mounting, until the air was filled with a song of jubilation and triumph such as he had never heard before.

CHAPTER ELEVEN

Fabiello, chief clerk to Pietro Bernardone, lowered his long, thin nose over Francis' shoulder. "The Head desires to speak to you, young master," he announced, glancing at the same time at the figures Francis was entering in a large ledger and giving a little sniff, as always when he saw something he did not find entirely satisfactory.

Francis had heard that little sniff countless times in the past and he bit his lip, although Fabiello had long ceased to have any jurisdiction over him. Fabiello would always see at once that a column of figures was not added up correctly, to say nothing of minor mishaps like a blot or a dogeared page. And he would never become accustomed to Francis' handwriting. How often had he not said: "It may be very well to be generous in one's actions, young master, so long as such generosity is paired with and, indeed, controlled by great prudence. But there can be no such thing as generosity in handwriting. In a commercial ledger or in a business letter words and figures must be such that they can leave no doubt whatsoever of their significance."

"What does my father want of me, Fabiello?"

"The Head no doubt wishes to convey that to you himself, young master."

The correct answer, if given in a rather surly manner.

"Very well, Fabiello."

Did father know anything? It was not likely. But if he didn't know, he would have to be told, either now, or very, very soon.

Francis rose and, passing the two sub-clerks and a row of workers, went into the small office where Pietro Bernardone was sitting alone.

The merchant signed a letter, pushed it aside and raised his massive head, not unlike that of a tremendously large pinkish cat.

"Ah," he said. "My son Francis; my young partner in business. And at what time did you come home the last three nights?"

"I . . . was out, Father. I came home very late."

Bernardone nodded. He began to smile. "That's nothing to worry about," he said. "You were at your desk this morning, weren't you? There! You're a young man, you must have your pleasures. I'm not an old tyrant, am I? By all means, have your fun, as long as you do your work. I was young myself, once. I know." He rose. "You'll be a man of substance one day," he said. "I'm setting aside five thousand Florentine guilders for you—a very tidy sum, you will agree—and I intend to let you use it for independent deals. Mind you, I shall look over your shoulder and see what you're doing with it. But I didn't call you in to tell you about that. I—"

"Father, I must tell you—"

"I called you in because I wanted to say good-bye to you, for a while. I'm going to Arezzo on the matter of the Brothers Corsini. They're the kind of customers one must always visit in person, especially when they owe you money. Which they do. But I'll get it out of them. It'll take a few days, but it'll be all right, so don't look so worried."

"I'm not worrying about that, Frather. . . ."

"You should, you know," Bernardone said. "They owe me—us—fifteen hundred Florentines. *And* no order has come in from them these last four months. I inquired about them, through our agent, Maldivio. One never knows, does one? Well, Maldivio says they're still solvent, so that's all right and I shan't go there for nothing. Fabiello has ordered my old carriage. I have already said good-bye to your mother. Now I must go and see whether my case is in the carriage and the bag with the samples. That's what I'll show Alfredo Corsini first. Some things in there will make his greedy mouth water. He *will* give us an order and only when that's duly booked, shall I remind him of the fifteen hundred. That's the way it's done, son. There isn't a soul who likes paying old debts and why? Among other reasons, because one's supposed to pay for something that gave pleasure in the past. But give them something that promises pleasure in the future and they'll pay like lambs. I must go."

"Father . . . I feel I must tell you something."

Bernardone clapped his son on the shoulder. "I think I know what it is. You're in love. Nothing wrong with that, my boy, and if she's suitable, all will be well. Surprised that your father knows all about it, aren't you? Well, well, young Ricardo Parelli, you know, Consul Revini's nephew, made an allusion the other day, so old Revini became curious and asked me. He swore he didn't know who the lady was. His nephew, apparently, didn't know either. All I said was that I was quite sure you wouldn't marry beneath your station. That's true, isn't it, Francis? Come on, tell me now, *ragazzo mio*. Who is she?" There was more than a trace of anxiety in the merchant's voice.

"There is no one . . . no, Father," Francis stammered. "You're very good to me and that makes it still more difficult to . . . to disappoint you. You see . . . I don't think I shall ever be a merchant."

For one short moment Pietro Bernardone looked startled. Then he grinned hugely. "Don't be a fool, Francis."

"No, Father, I mean it. You see—"

"That'll do, son. Youth often feels uncertain and I suppose you're a little intimidated. I know I'm very good at my business and you feel, very naturally, that you won't be as good as your father. Don't let that worry you too much. There are things you can only learn from experience. To know people for what they are, for instance, to know their faults and weaknesses and play on them in the right way to get the result you want—and many such things. That'll come, Francis, that'll come, believe me."

There was a knock at the door and Fabiello came in. "The carriage is ready, Messer Bernardone."

"Good. I'm coming."

Fabiello withdrew.

"Father, I'm afraid I can't be a merchant. I must explain to you . . ."

Bernardone put both his pudgy hands on his son's shoulders. "Look," he said indulgently, "a few years ago you thought you'd become a great soldier, a knight, a baron. The whole world would be at your feet. And, like a good-natured fool, I fell in with your plans. You were wrong, you now know that yourself. This time you tell me you won't be a merchant. You're wrong again. You *will* be a merchant. Nobody can fool old Pietro Bernardone twice. Good-bye, son."

A minute later the carriage rolled away in the direction of the western gate.

Solitude in the old Etruscan tomb outside the eastern gate was almost like paradise. It was waiting for orders in the Lord's own antechamber. He would call for him, whenever He saw fit.

Fear no longer existed since . . . the leper. He now could go to the Lazarists and help them with their work without the slightest feeling of repulsion.

And then there was, beyond the tomb, less than a quarter of an hour's walk away, the ramshackle little church of San Damiano and on its altar the crucifix he most loved, with its golden ground and topped by a tiny picture of the risen Christ, blessed by the Father's hand and surrounded by serene-looking apostles. The angels, flanking the horizontal beam of the cross looked serene, too, and so did even the figures watching the crucifixion: St. John and St. Joseph of Arimathea, St. Mary Magdalene and St. Mary Cleophas. Only the Blessed Virgin looked a little sad, as if in the middle of heavenly triumph she were thinking of what had taken place twelve hundred years ago.

The Lord on the cross was grave rather than sad, with his arms opened wide and fixed by the nails in the gesture of universal blessing. And it seemed at first glance that the Lord was holding up the cross and not the cross the Lord.

But such triumph could not be won without pain and the pain was there too, if one looked long enough—as the Blessed Virgin did. It was not there for all to see. The Lord hid it, almost as if, in His divine courtesy, He did not want to show to those who came to Him how much He had suffered for them. It was all there, if only one looked long enough and did not shy away from it; it was deep as heaven itself and took to itself all the world's sorrows, all its troubles and fear and hardship and confusion, all bloodshed and vice and horror, all atrocities, all cruelty and cowardice and above all, all injustice.

There was so much of it, he thought that one thing more, even a tiny thing, might shatter the patient Bearer of all Pain. It was terrible beyond endurance to think that one had to add one's own burden of sins to the rest. . . .

But suddenly Francis was made to think of St. Bernard, of a story told about the great saint to whom the Lord spoke many a time. And once the Lord said: "Bernard, give Me something." And Bernard opened his arms wide and said: "What is it I can give You, my Lord. You know that all I am and all I have *is* yours." And the Lord said: "Bernard, give Me something." And Bernard wrung his hands and said disconsolately: "But, Lord, what else can I give You, but what I have given You already?" And the Lord said: "Bernard, give Me your sins."

That was the answer to all fear, that He *wanted* to carry

91

men's sins, knowing that they could not carry them themselves without His help. He claimed all sin and the pains of sin for Himself. The King of Kings, dying for the least of His subjects, Himself present in all human pain.

What was a knight to do for such a king? What could he do?

Be with Him, so close that he, too, would have his share in pain and suffering and humilation. Ascend the Tree of suffering, stretch out one's arms and share the terrible burden.

In a sudden flash, for the first time, Francis understood fully what had made him change clothes with the beggar at the door of St. Peter's; what had made him kiss the leper.

Overwhelmed, he offered himself to the Crucified, soul and body. He was sobbing, but he did not know it.

"Francis," said the Voice, "you see My house is falling into ruin. Go and repair it."

Father Eufemio Livoni, the priest of San Damiano's, was seventy-nine years of age and did not look a year younger, except when he was asleep when his wrinkly face relaxed and lost its habitual waking expression of worry. He was dozing in the morning sun, sitting on some fallen masonry when Francis came storming out of the church.

"Father Livoni! Father Livoni!"

The old man opened his rheumy eyes and promptly his face assumed a woebegone expression. "What is it, my son?"

"Please, Father, take this and buy oil with it—and keep a lamp burning before the crucifix. I shall get you more money soon. I'll be back, Father, I'll be back."

Francis raced away.

Father Livoni's surprised old hands could not hold the little stream of coins. Some of them dropped on his lap and he picked them up mechanically. Surely that was young Bernardone who often came to pray here—the son of a rich man in town he was.

What a heap of money! And silver, most of it, scarcely any copper coins, silver-pieces of all sizes, enough to buy oil for a long time. Such a nice young man. There was no need to buy a lamp, the old one was in good working order, except that there was no oil.

Hadn't young Bernardone said something about still more money? Father Livoni shook his head. What for? He had everything he needed. It was dangerous to have too much money in the house.

He looked very worried.

Francis raced home, pressed a kiss on his mother's cheek. "Tell Lauro to get a horse ready for me, Mother, please." Then he ran into the office, where Chief Clerk Fabiello looked up sourly from the ledger.

"Good morning, Fabiello. Will you let me have some money, please."

The chief clerk's eyebrows seemed to disappear in his hair line.

"Money, young master?"

"Well, yes. I need a thousand Florentines."

"A thousand . . ." Fabiello gave an audible sniff. "I'm afraid that is quite out of the question, young master."

"It can't be, Fabiello. Father told me he wanted to put several times that amount at my disposal."

Another sniff. "In that case, young master, the Head will give you the amount required when he returns from his journey. I am not entitled to make any payments except those explicitly ordered by the Head and this . . . this demand of yours is not among them."

"Oh, very well," Francis said airily. "It doesn't matter."

He walked away.

It doesn't matter, Fabiello thought, outraged. He wants a thousand Florentine guilders and when he can't get them it doesn't matter. Saints above, has that young good-for-nothing no respect for anything? Going off on one of his little excursions with his rich friends again, more likely than not, and borrowing the money from one of them. That's the way it would be. That's why it didn't matter. He gave a last, determined sniff. A thousand Florentines always matter, he thought; and he knew that the Head would fully agree with him.

Francis, in the meantime, had gone down to the store. "Magano," he said, "make me a double pack of this bolt of silk—and that one—and that one, too. Put it on my horse."

"That'll be too heavy for the horse, I think, young master," the storekeeper said, scratching his head.

"Then make up as much as you think it can carry," Francis said, "and don't forget it's got to carry me as well."

"Depends how far you want to go, young master."

"Yes, of course. And the horse mustn't suffer. I . . . I think I'm going to Foligno."

"Quite a little way, then. I'll see what I can do."

From the window of the office Fabiello saw Francis ride off on a horse, heavily laden with goods. He did not sniff, this time.

He whistled through the five teeth he still had in his upper jaw. Then he went down to the store to assess the damage.

Getting to Foligno was easy enough, although the bolts of silk in their hampers on each side of the horse impeded progress more than a little. Nor was it difficult to sell the silk.

Francis knew the people who were dealing with his father's firm, he had even visited them a couple of times, as his father's clerk. The sale was concluded within a few minutes.

However, the price was not as high as he had hoped it would be, not anywhere near the sum of a thousand guilders. Perhaps, if he had haggled with old Moscardo? His father could do that for hours on end and seemed to like it. Perhaps Moscardo would have raised his bid then. But he did say he couldn't and that a single guilder more would make it impossible for him to make even a small profit. The old man almost wept when he said it, so what could one do, despite the feeling that he was perhaps not quite sincere?

To make up for it, Francis sold his horse to a dealer Moscardo recommended to him and returned on foot. More than once he felt a regret about this second deal. The region was by no means safe—no region in Umbria was—and he was carrying, if not a thousand guilders, nevertheless a fairly substantial sum in the little yellow leather bag Moscardo had given him as a parting gift.

It was late in the evening when he reached San Damiano's and he was so tired that he could scarcely hold himself upright.

Father Livoni was again—or still—sitting on his heap of fallen masonry and he had to wake him up again.

"Ah," the old man said, "my benefactor. You disappeared so quickly, I had no time to thank you properly. Will you come into the church with me? The lamp is burning before the crucifix."

"I am glad," Francis said, "but there is more to be done, much more, before the church is fully repaired."

"Fully repaired?" Father Livoni repeated. He looked quite startled. "My good young friend, there is no chance of that, I'm afraid. This is no more than a wayside shrine. It belongs to Assisi, of course, but the good bishop has his hands full with the churches there and no money left for San Damiano's. It's been crumbling away for years and years—just as Holy Church is crumbling away all over Italy and everywhere else, too, I suppose, what with people thieving and robbing each other and behaving in the most shameless way, as if they did not know that our blessed Lord might come back at any moment . . . I told the people that when I last preached. But do you know what my congregation amounted to? Five people, my dear young friend, and two of them children. Holy Church is crumbling just like San Damiano's—just like me, I might say. Only on Sundays can I get an acolyte because little Giorgio, the goatherd, has to go to work early on weekdays and there is no one else to take his place."

"There is from now on," Francis said. "Will you permit me to be your acolyte?"

Father Livoni goggled at him. "You couldn't do that every day, surely."

"I can and I will," Francis said. "And if you will have me, I shall stay with you altogether, until the church is rebuilt."

The old priest began to laugh. "I told you, it never will be. There's no money for it. Besides, the good Lord comes down on my altar every day despite the holes in the roof and the masonry missing from the walls."

"But He would like to see His church repaired," Francis said, and he almost added: "He told me so Himself," but managed to check himself in time. He drew his precious yellow leather bag from his belt and opened it. "Here, Father. This will help to set things right, I hope."

Father Livoni clapped his hands together, horrified. "My dear young friend . . . I cannot possibly . . . this is the most frightening sight. Take it away, I beg of you."

"But . . . I got it for you . . . for San Damiano's. . . ."

The old priest suddenly sat bolt upright. "Who gave it to you?" he asked quite sternly. "Was it your father?"

"No. Not directly."

"Does he know about it?"

"No. But he told me he wanted to give me money of my own and . . ."

"No, no, no," the old priest said, his hands wobbling in the air. "I will have nothing to do with this."

"But . . ."

"Absolutely not."

Francis sighed deeply. "You'll still take me as your acolyte, Father, won't you?"

The old priest smiled. "By all means."

"And I may stay with you? I won't take up much room and I eat very little."

"Stay with me? Here?" The old man shook his head. "Surely you are much better off where you are."

95

"Please, Father, let me stay. I want to be near the . . . I . . . let me stay, Father, I beg of you."

Father Livoni shrugged. "You're a strange one," he said. "You have a good bed in a big house full of servants and you want to stay in my little tumble-down abode. Youth, youth . . . full of strange quirks. Ah well, stay, if you like. You'll soon want to return to the fleshpots of Egypt." He giggled. "I always say Mass in the morning at six o'clock. Not that I have a clock or a sundial or any such thing."

"Then how do you know the time, Father?"

"Saints above, don't you know that the sun rises every day, by the grace of God? Always when it does, it's six o'clock. Now I shall go to bed." The frail little figure hobbled away in the direction of a shedlike structure beside the church. Once it had been a house. Now it was a ruin with a few wooden planks nailed together to form some sort of a room.

Francis was still holding the yellow bag, the useless result of the efforts of the day. He was too tired to think, but he knew that he could not possibly keep it himself. It was a mockery, a silly nothing as long as he held on to it. He wanted to be angry with Father Livoni and found that he could not.

On a sudden impulse he threw the bag through an open window into the church and turned away. There was no defiance in his gesture, only disappointment and frustration. When Father Livoni found it in the morning, let him do with it what he liked. Then he followed the priest into his ramshackle abode.

CHAPTER TWELVE

Five days later Father Livoni saw a little cavalcade approaching his church from the direction of Assisi. It was led by a large, well-dressed man.

A thunderstorm on mule back, he thought with a wry smile. Just as well the young man's mother had sent a warning with that last food parcel of hers. And just as well the young man had taken heed of the warning too. These people did not look as if they could be trifled with.

The cavalcade came to a halt. Two of the riders helped the large man to dismount. It entailed some amount of indignity which did not exactly improve his temper.

"Good morning, Father," he said gruffly. "I am Pietro Bernardone. I have come to fetch my son Francis."

Father Livoni raised his hands with an expression of polite regret. "It is unfortunate that you should have inconvenienced yourself for nothing, Messer Bernardone. The young man has left."

"He's been staying with you," Bernardone snapped. "No use denying it."

"I have no intention of denying it," the old priest said calmly. "But as I said, he has left."

"When do you expect him back?"

"He said nothing about that, Messer Bernardone."

"Will he be back tonight, then?"

"I doubt it very much, Messer Bernardone."

"Where has he gone, then?"

"I don't know at all, Messer Bernardone."

The merchant stamped his foot. "He's a thief. He has stolen money from me," he shouted.

"That is indeed a grave accusation," the priest said, frowning. "And now I must tell you that he has given me some money for my church. If it is yours, I must, of course, give it back to you."

"Every maravedi he has is mine," Bernardone said.

"He gave me thirteen Florentine guilders and four maravedis," Father Livoni explained and the merchant's face fell. "He wanted me to buy oil for the lamp in front of the altar. I spent some of the coins for that purpose, I am sorry to say. Also he . . ."

"Nonsense," Bernardone snarled. "Thirteen guilders! Why, he has robbed me of hundreds of yards of the finest silk and of a good horse to boot and sold the lot in Foligno. I know everything. I have investigated the matter. The horse alone was worth . . ."

"Also he wanted to give me more money," Father Livoni went on, "but I didn't accept it."

Bernardone's eyes narrowed. "You didn't?" he asked sharply. "Then where is it?"

"I am sure I couldn't tell you that, Messer Bernardone. I suppose he still has it with him, though I do not remember having seen the bag it was in for some days—not since he showed it to me when he arrived."

"Perhaps he left it in his bed?" one of the riders remarked deferentially.

Bernardone nodded. "Maybe, Fabiello. If you will permit me to have a look, Father . . ."

"By all means, if you wish," the old priest said quietly, "but there is no need for that. You see, he had no bed to sleep in. He slept on the floor and I had much trouble to make him accept an old coat of mine as a pillow for his head. The pillow is still there, in case you wish to see it. So is the floor. But no bag and no money."

"He may have put it into the church box," Fabiello suggested.

But Pietro Bernardone had had enough. "I want *him* to give it back to me," he said testily. "I have no quarrel with this priest."

Father Livoni took some coins from his pocket. "The guilders he gave me—" he said, "you'd better take them back, Messer Bernardone."

The merchant hesitated for a moment. "I will," he said then. "It is a matter of principle. I'm not a mean man, Ser Priest. I have spent thousands on this wretched son of mine; nothing was too good for him. And then he steals from me."

As he was speaking, Father Livoni was pressing coins into his hand and counting in a low voice. "Twelve," he said. "I told you I spent some of the money. How expensive oil is these days! I can remember when it was cheap, but now the merchants are buying it up wholesale and sell it at their own price. But let me see . . ." He produced a number of copper-pieces.

"Never mind the last guilder," Bernardone said with a generous gesture, taking no notice of the old man's rambling. "But you must promise to deliver the boy to me if he comes back. And I want you to give me your word as a religious that he is not hiding in your house or in the church."

"You may go and see with your own eyes," Father Livoni said, frowning.

"Shall I go and look, Messer Bernardone?" Fabiello inquired obsequiously.

"No," Bernardone roared. "We're going home. But I'll catch him yet and God help him when I do. Good-bye . . . Father." They helped him to mount his mule and the cavalcade clattered away.

Father Livoni shook his head sadly and settled down again on his favorite seat, the heap of fallen masonry. "Money," he said to no one in particular. Then he spat.

When his mother's warning came—a hastily scribbled note attached to the parcel of food she sent to San Damiano's—Francis knew that he would have to leave at once and where he must go. He would be safe in the old Etruscan tomb.

He did not tell Father Livoni, because the priest was sure to be questioned, and the less he knew the better; but he managed to get hold of little Giorgio, the goatherd, and sent him to Madonna Pica with a short message. With her his secret was safe.

On the second day a package of food dropped into his tomb with a thud. So mother had found ways and means to look after his needs. Her love helped a little to assuage his feelings of disappointment and frustration.

At long last the Voice had spoken—and when he set out to obey it, his work had come to nothing and he himself had been driven from the Presence.

The stage of self-pity was soon over. He was not serving a moody human master who blew hot and cold as the fancy took him. His Master was Truth, Justice and Mercy in One, the Way, the Resurrection and the Life in One. Above all He was Love. And His servant Francis was an ignorant pupil, a babbling child who had not yet learned to walk, let alone to think.

The answer to hours of passionate prayer was a thought welling up, the memory of a short passage in Scripture: "Nor your ways my ways, saith the Lord."

That indeed was the answer and all he could do was to accept what had befallen him and wait for new orders. He would not leave the tomb before he knew what was expected of him. He was a vessel ready to be filled, a rational body waiting to be moved by the will of God.

But as days went by he began to ask himself whether his own will was really as subdued as he thought it was. He felt certain of his readiness to serve his Master—and yet there was something else, a feeling of relief that all he had to do was to wait. Why should he feel relieved about that?

Searching his conscience without mercy he found that behind his relief an enemy was lurking—his old enemy, fear.

He was afraid to leave the tomb, afraid to meet his father who would shout and bellow at him, afraid most of all that his father might curse him. A father's curse was a terrible thing, everybody knew that. And would God accept the service of one whom his earthly father had cursed?

Yet the basis of it all was fear and that he could not tolerate. Whether his father was going to curse him or not was uncertain.

Certain it was that a knight in the service of the King of Kings must not act out of fear of man.

It took several more days before this train of thought had thickened to a decision. But the decision was made, and one day —almost a month after his disappearance from San Damiano's

—Francis emerged from the tomb, blinking in the light, and began to walk, on legs weakened by lack of use, toward the city.

Pietro Bernardone was in his office when it happened.

Nothing seemed to have changed here. Fabiello was at his desk as usual, with his long, pointed nose so close to the ledger that he seemed to be writing with it, with the quill serving merely as a standby. The sub-clerks, too, were working as usual. Yet they all knew, of course, and outside the office they all talked. Everybody had at least one person to whom he talked. The whole of Assisi knew by now that Pietro Bernardone's son had stolen money and run away.

Bernardone knew he should not have taken the clerks with him to San Damiano's, only Fabiello would have done, or perhaps better still, Consul Revini. But one could not go to Revini with such a story. Not that *he* did not know about it, he and his wife and his family and everybody else. They all knew. Nothing like it had ever happened to the house before. Nothing like it had ever happened to him.

It was not the money. The amount stolen was ridiculous for a business like his. Again and again Pietro Bernardone told himself that it was not the money. It was Francis.

He had lost a son. If Francis had died in the battle of Ponte San Giovanni, it would have been a great misfortune, a terrible blow. But he would have died gloriously and his name would be mentioned with respect.

If he had died from his illness, after having been released from captivity in Perugia, one might still say that was an honorable death.

But a runaway, a thief with some strange, twisted ideas about money! How was it possible that a son of his could have strange, twisted ideas about money? He had offered it to that old dodderer of a priest, who like a sensible man, refused to accept it because he knew that Pietro Bernardone was not the kind of man who would allow himself to be robbed under any pretext whatever or for any purpose.

Francis' mother, of course, tried to speak up for him. He had cut her short at once. "A child of God doesn't steal." That silenced her. Much of it was her fault, without doubt. She had put wrong ideas into the boy's head, and now that the terrible consequences were there for everyone to see, all she could do was to cry her eyes out.

Meanwhile they all knew. No one spoke to him about it, of course, but what they said behind his back was easy to imagine.

He was a marked man, the father of a thief. Some of the businessmen in town might even go so far as to say that Francis had done clumsily what his father was doing by stealth. Sheer envy, because more than once he had managed to get the better of them in some deal or other. They would have done exactly the same to him, of course, if they had been able to. But now they would be gloating. . . .

It was not surprising that it happened while Pietro Bernardone was immersed in such thoughts. They never left him, however hard he tried to concentrate on his work. Twice he discovered only at the last moment that he had made mistakes in important business letters, clumsy mistakes which might have cost him large sums of money.

From outside came scattered shrieks and a gust of laughter. More shrieks followed and the patter of many little feet. The street urchins were on their way to whatever it was that promised entertainment, a criminal assault, an accident—perhaps a man had fallen from a window; or there might be a fight between two drunkards.

Testily, Pietro Bernardone walked over to the window to close it and thus to exorcise the vulgar noise. There was a group of boys milling around somebody and throwing things at him. Some wretched lunatic, probably, or a drunk. They were pelting him with mud and filth and their victim, instead of defending himself or running away, walked on slowly, with his head down and one arm raised to protect his eyes. It was a disgusting sight. But in the act of closing the window, Bernardone stopped.

The fellow was wearing rags, but they were the rags of what must have been a good coat. A very good coat, with embroidery.

Bernardone realized that he knew that coat. He himself had paid for it, with good money. The fellow had stolen Francis' coat.

He rushed out into the street. The arrival of a large, well-dressed and very angry man made the urchins draw back a little.

And then only Pietro Bernardone saw, horrified, that their victim was Francis, thin, haggard, disheveled and dirty.

For one moment the merchant stood quite still. Then he went into action. He seized his scarecrow of a son by the neck, turned him round and frogmarched him along the street, back to his house and into it. Roaring, he pushed him down the stairs to the cellar and into a storage room. He hit him straight in the face. He hit him over the head. He thrashed him from one end of the room to the other and when he fell, he raised him to his feet again and, holding him up, went on thrashing him.

When he was completely out of breath he released him and the emaciated body crumpled on the floor in an inert heap.

Bernardone stared at it with bloodshot eyes, his breath whistling. He kicked twice, hard. Then he turned away and locked the door behind him. He put the key in his pocket. Slowly he ascended the stairs. A number of people were standing up there, staring at him, he could see them only dimly at first. He was reeling. Every step was a painful effort. Maids and servants. Pica, too.

He reached the ground floor and they drew back from him. His face was purple. He looked about him. "No one," he gasped, "no . . . one . . . is allowed to go . . . to the storage room in . . . the cellar. No one . . . anywhere near it. If anyone does . . . I'll throw him or her out of my house! Never mind who it is!" He stumbled on to his bedroom.

Everybody in the house went on tiptoes and spoke only in a whisper, even when Pietro Bernardone was in his office and could not possibly hear them. The merchant allowed no one to address him, except for the purpose of asking for orders. He dismissed Lauro for having laughed, although the servant protested that he had only been coughing. He forbade his wife to leave the house. "We cannot afford to show our faces in public. That is what this criminal son of yours has done to us."

Donna Pica went to her room and stayed there. She did not come to the evening meal and the merchant dined alone in gloomy silence.

The three servants in the kitchen jumped to their feet in terror when the master of the house suddenly appeared among them. He had never done so before. Without a word to any of them he took a loaf of bread, filled a pitcher with water and stalked out again. The cook and her two helpers looked at each other. They said nothing.

The merchant went down to the cellar. Donna Pica, listening anxiously from a place near the top of the staircase, could hear only her husband's voice. "Shut up," he bellowed, "not a word out of you." Then the door banged and she could hear him locking it. She fled back to her room.

Four days passed and Bernardone did not relent. On the morning of the fifth day he announced that he had to go on a business journey again, this time to Rieti. He would be back in less than a week.

"In regard to Francis Bernardone," he said coldly, "my orders still stand, except that you, Fabiello, will bring him a loaf of bread and a pitcher of water in the morning and a second pitcher before you leave at night. Here is the key. You will give it to no one else. You will not talk to Francis and if he talks to you you will not answer. Is that clear?"

"Yes, Messer Bernardone."

The merchant left.

No one dared stop Donna Pica from approaching the storage room in the cellar. No one even dared to try to hear the long, whispered conversations that went on between mother and son, time after time. But the servant observed a strange thing. The first few times when Donna Pica came back, she was crying. Later she was grave and pensive. Still later she seemed to be quite cheerful, as if she had come back from a gay gathering and was still enjoying the memory of it.

But when they saw her, one evening, opening the little chest where tools were kept, the servants began to worry, and their worrying grew to deadly fear when, on the morning of the third day, Fabiello, going down to the prison as they had come to call the storage room, found the door pried open and the prisoner gone.

Fabiello himself was trembling. After all, he had been shouldered with the responsibility, he alone had the key. He comforted himself with the thought that he could always point out to the Head that the lock had been forced.

Donna Pica assembled the frightened servants and tried to put them at ease. "I shall tell my husband the truth. I alone have freed my son. Don't fear that any blame will be attached to any of you."

But they remembered Lauro who had been dismissed for a coughing fit and they were still afraid.

Two days later Pietro Bernardone returned from Rieti. Fabiello at once reported what had happened and went down to the cellar with him to show him the forced lock.

The merchant only nodded. When they went up again, Donna Pica was waiting for her husband. "You don't have to ask who released Francis," she said. "It was I."

"Fabiello, go back to the office," Bernardone said tonelessly. Then he took his wife's arm and led her to his room. He closed the door. His face was ashen. "So far I thought only my son Francis had forgotten what he owed me. Now I find that you have too. I am no longer master in my own house, it seems. My orders are regarded as so many empty words." Suddenly he roared: "How could you dare do such a thing, woman! How could you!"

"I am his mother," Pica said. "That alone should be enough."

"Enough to go against my orders?" he roared.

"Enough to save the poor boy from your cruelty."

"Madonna! The woman's mad, mad. So I am cruel, am I? I suppose I ought to have received that criminal like the prodigal son! A fatted calf for the wretch who stole from me and then made me—and you—the laughingstock of the town. God, what have I done, to deserve a son like this! I've always done my duty. I worked. I wasted money on him, perhaps that's what I am being punished for. Nothing was good enough for him. And now he treats me—us—like this. And my own wife lets him loose again, my own wife!"

"He wants to live for God alone," Pica said. "Neither your nor anyone else can stop him."

"He certainly made a wonderful start," the merchant jeered. "He stole and he dishonored his parents. Two commandments broken—that is the surest way to please God, I suppose. What a fool you are to be taken in by him! He's a madman, a criminal lunatic, posing as a . . . a saint or hermit, or whatever he pretends to be."

"I know more about that than you do," Pica said. "If you will listen to me . . ."

"I will not listen to you and to the pack of lies he told you to make you set him free. Spoiling a good lock, too. *And* the door. You heard what I said: if anyone, never mind who, goes against my orders, I will turn that person out of my house. You heard me say that, didn't you?"

In a toneless voice Pica said: "I will go then."

"Yes," Bernardone stormed, "now that I am dishonored, now that people point at me—that's the father of a crazy beggar—now you want to leave me. You didn't want to go as long as I was respected by everybody. . . ."

"Now you are being unjust to me as well," Pica said. "I don't want to go. You said you were going to turn me out of the house."

"I said nothing of the kind," the merchant raged. "I said . . . I said . . . oh, never mind. You are as mad as your precious son. Perhaps it would suit you to go, so that people will say: There must be something wrong about Pietro Bernardone; not only his son, but his wife, too, has left him. Oh no, woman. You are going to stay. As for the criminal, you will see what I shall do. You'll see!"

He stalked out of the room, banging the door with such force that the house seemed to shake to its foundations.

Donna Pica began to pray for strength, not to bear the wrath of her husband—she felt sure she could, even if he were to beat her and kick her and lock her in the cellar, but for strength to bear the fulfilment of her prayers. For years and years from the very birth of Francis she had prayed that her son would become a child of God. She knew that she was asking for a great and dangerous thing. Now the fulfilment was upon her. Francis had told her everything. It meant that she had lost him, as a mother must lose a son when he gives himself to God alone. He had said nothing about it, but in her heart she felt certain that she would never see him again.

CHAPTER THIRTEEN
A.D. 1207

"Are you sure that is what you want, Bernardone?" Consul Revini walked up and down his office.

"Quite sure."

"You're an obstinate man, Bernardone, and an irascible one. In a few weeks, in a few days perhaps, you'll regret it."

"I shall never regret it."

Revini stopped in front of the merchant. "I understand your feelings, believe me," he said. "It isn't easy for you. One should be less sensitive about people's gossiping and all the kind of thing we call scandal, but one isn't. I'd feel exactly the same if one of my children had . . . errh . . . behaved badly. But is it wise to press matters?"

Pietro Bernardone glared at him. "That's an easy way to talk. Your children have not, as you call it, behaved badly. They haven't stolen your money. They haven't transformed themselves into lunatics to be jeered at by street urchins. They haven't dishonored the name of Revini. May it never happen to you! But don't blame me for trying to regain at least my self-respect. And there is only one way to do that. I shall cut off all ties between him and my house."

"You can do that," Revini said, "without demanding his arrest."

"What? And let him keep the money he stole from me? Never. I want it back to the last maravedi."

"He may no longer have it."

"He has it. He may have given it to that old priest in San Damiano, but I doubt it."

Revini shook his head. "As an old friend of yours—"

"Forgive me, Your Excellency," Bernardone interrupted coldly, "but I did not come to see you in that capacity. Not today. Had I so wished, I would have visited you at your house. I have come to the town hall, to see the supreme magistrate of Assisi, the Consul Revini. Before him I have placed a formal accusation of theft against Giovanni Francis Bernardone. I have given you all the information you need about the amount of money he stole from me. I have even found out for you where the thief is: in the church of San Damiano."

"Yes, yes, I know, but . . ."

Bernardone rose. "Now I must ask you: Are you going to have the thief arrested and brought to trial or are you not? Are you going to force him to reimburse my money or are you not?"

Consul Revini spread out his hands. "I'll do as you wish," he said. "But remember this: Once I have given the orders to my clerks, there is no way back. Don't come to me afterward, pleading for the boy."

"I swear I won't," Bernardone shouted. "And the heavier the punishment, the better I shall like it. This is what Cato would have done, and Cincinatus and the Gracchi."

"Very well," Revini said, with a shrug. "I shall give the orders now. I shall send for you as soon as the accused is in the town jail."

"Thank you, Your Excellency," Bernardone said fiercely. He gave a formal bow and left.

In the early afternoon he was summoned back to the town hall.

"I am extremely sorry to disappoint you, Messer Bernardone," Revini said.

"He . . . has escaped again?"

"No. My officers spoke to him but he refused to come with them."

"What? And they didn't enforce the arrest?"

"They could not. He informed them that he had left the world."

"What nonsense is this?" Bernardone shouted.

"No nonsense," Revini said gravely. "Your knowledge of the law seems to be extremely limited, Messer Bernardone. Don't you know that a man who dedicates his life to religion alone is no longer subject to the civic authorities?"

"I shall go and break his neck with my own hands," Bernardone snarled.

"You forget that *you* are still subject to the civic authorities, Messer Bernardone," Revini said grimly.

"This is a trick," Bernardone roared, "another dastardly trick of his. He isn't a priest. He isn't a monk. He isn't anything. And now I suppose he is to be responsible only to God in heaven, eh?"

"And to the Church," Revini said.

The merchant stared at him. He thrust out his massive chin. "The Church," he repeated slowly. "That's better. I shall go and see Bishop Guido at once."

The news that Francis Bernardone was going to be tried before the bishop ran through Assisi like wildfire.

The tongues had been busy for some time with the great controversy between father and son and there were factions on either side. The issue was taken up in the *palazzi* of the nobles and in the houses of citizens rich and poor, in the guardroom of the town jail and the chapter-hall of the Cathedral, and on the day of the trial so many people appeared at the gate of the bishop's palace that a servant came, pale and bewildered, to Canon Cattaneo, the bishop's legal adviser, to ask what should be done about it.

The canon raised his brows. "Done about it? Why? Are they creating disorder?"

"Well, not exactly that, but . . ."

"Not even that? To look at you one should think there was a bloodcurdling riot outside. Have the gate opened and let them in."

"But . . . but there are hundreds of them, and many are women," the servant stammered.

"That's quite ridiculous," the canon said. "You know as well as I do that women are not allowed to be present at a trial, not as spectators. Now go and let the people in, the men, I mean. There's room enough in the big hall for over two hundred people at least."

"There are five or six hundred people at the gate, and . . ."

"Then some of them will have to stay outside. What's the matter with you, Gaetano, can't you keep your head in such a small emergency?" The canon walked away and went to see Bishop Guido. "Half the town seems to be outside," he announced cheerfully. "If we had such an attendance at every Mass, Assisi would be an exemplary town, the good Lord might

107

even spare the whole world for its sake. I told Gaetano to let two hundred people in and no more."

"What on earth for?" the bishop asked, baffled.

"Why, to be present at the trial of young Bernardone, my lord. The public . . ."

"But they won't be able to get in! The hall is filled."

"Filled?" the canon repeated, round-eyed. "Now?"

"It has been for almost an hour."

"Excuse me, my lord." Cattaneo rushed out to find Gaetano. He arrived just in time to see two hundred people streaming into a hall where they tried in vain to find seats on the rough benches, already filled to capacity. Some of them settled down on the floor, others on the window sills. The canon raised his arm to draw attention and then dropped it with a shrug. It was hopeless to try to get these people out again. There was a lot of noise, of course, some protestations, some exchanges of doubtful courtesies and a few gusts of laughter.

There was room left only on the dais, where the bishop would be sitting under a panoply with a canon on either side, and in front where a small section of the hall was roped off and jealously guarded by four of the bishop's clerks.

On one side of that exclosure Cattaneo saw Pietro Bernardone, massive and immobile, with a thin, cadaverous-looking individual beside him, his chief clerk, Cattaneo remembered the man's face, Favello or Fabrielli or some such name.

Fairly close, in the first row of the spectators' section, sat an old friend, Bernard of Quintavalle. Whenever there was a dispute about money, all rich men were as interested as if it were their own.

Cattaneo smiled and nodded, but Bernard did not see him. He was looking at the accused who was sitting on the other side of the enclosure. But surely that was not Francis Bernardone? The canon remembered the gay youth who used to be king of the moneyed young revelers of the town. He was still dressed gaily enough, but within his finery he seemed to have shrunk and his face . . . Was it guilt or was it something else? If only he would lift his eyes. But he did not, he kept them lowered and his hands were folded in his lap. Praying?

There was an old priest sitting beside him, and fast asleep. Father Livoni of San Damiano's, of course, or of what there was left of San Damiano's.

And over there: Consul Revini *and* Consul Torreone, and those young revelers as well, noted for nothing but their fathers' money.

Cattaneo turned away and went back to the bishop's room. "There's never been such an audience, my lord," he announced dryly. "Not since the days of the great Pierre Vidal, King of Troubadours."

The bishop frowned a little. Then he laughed. "I'm afraid they're going to be disappointed," he said. "It's a simple enough case, surely. What is your impression of that young man, Canon?"

"I don't quite know, my lord. I couldn't see his eyes. He's dressed nicely for the occasion, though, I will say that for him."

"Wearing a long tunic and thinking himself better than his brethren?" the bishop asked quizzically.

"I'm not sure whether he is like Joseph, son of Jacob, my lord," the canon said, smiling. "But there certainly used to be a good deal of vanity under his long tunic."

"His father, too, is a vain man, though for different reasons," the bishop said. "It is extraordinary about how many different things we can feel vain."

"There goes the bell," Cattaneo said. "And just as well, my lord. With all these people crammed in the hall we would have them fainting right and left, if they had to wait much longer."

When the little procession entered the hall—four priests, two canons, Cattaneo and Broga, and finally Bishop Guido— the assembly rose, by no means an easy matter with so many people sitting on the floor between the benches, to say nothing of those on the window sills.

The noise woke up Father Livoni and he looked about, much worried. Then he, too, struggled to his feet. "Francis," he whispered. "Francis . . ."

"Yes, Father?"

"Have you got that bag?"

"Yes, Father."

"Thank God and San Damiano."

Never in his life had Father Livoni been so frightened as when he discovered the yellow leather bag, lying under the hollow pedestal of the statue of San Damiano. He recognized it at once and ran to fetch his acolyte. "Your bag is in the church! The bag with that money. How did it get there?"

"I threw it in through the window," Francis said, "but that was weeks ago, the day I came back from Foligno. I thought you were keeping it safe."

"I only discovered the thing this minute," the old priest said. "Now you take it. I will not even touch it. And when we go to see the bishop, you'll take it with you. I insist on that." He also insisted on Francis putting on the good tunic his mother had given him when she helped him escape from the cellar. "You're my acolyte," he said. "I won't have you appear before the bishop in rags."

Meanwhile the bishop had taken his seat on the dais and Canon Groga read out the names of the accuser and the accused.

Father and son rose. A hush went across the packed room. It was difficult to believe that these two men were related at all, that they were father and son seemed incredible.

"The old cloth-seller is a real giant," young Ricardo Parelli murmured. "He could crush our Francis with two fingers."

"You forget that little David slew the giant Jonathan," Paolo Spadone whispered.

"Bethsabee, you mean, not Jonathan," Mario Luca corrected. "And David and Bethsabee were not father and son, as far as I remember."

"Sh . . . the bishop is speaking."

"According to the imperial privilege granted to the See of Assisi in the year of our Lord One thousand and eighteen," Bishop Guido proclaimed, "and according to the brief of the Holy Father, Pope Innocent the Third of the year of our Lord One thousand ninety-eight the Bishop of Assisi has sole jurisdiction on all dependants of the Church and no secular court may judge a cleric or an inhabitant of houses or territories belonging to the see. The accused before the court, Giovanni Francis Bernardone, having taken up his abode with Father Eufemio Livoni on the ground and territory of the Church of San Damiano, has become a *dimorante,* a tenant of the episcopal see and therefore comes under our jurisdiction."

The hall was quiet now, so quiet that the clerk's quill could be heard scratching wildly as he attempted to write down the bishop's words. Bishop Guido spoke very fast; most clerks complained that they had difficulty in following, especially as the bishop did not like to have to repeat anything. The bishop knew that and he paused deliberately to give the clerk time to catch up with him.

Pietro Bernardone thought the time had come for him to make his viewpoint clear. "Your Lordship, I wish to state here and now that this man, so far known as Francis Bernardone, has forsaken, by his criminal action, any place in my house and any share in my property. I wish to state . . ."

"Messer Pietro Bernardone," the bishop interrupted, "I must ask you to wait until I have finished and until permission is given you to speak. The court knows the facts of the case as

110

presented by both parties to this most regrettable conflict. The accused has freely admitted to the court that he sold certain wares from the store in his father's house. . . ."

"Two bolts of the finest silk!" Pietro Bernardone could not stop himself.

". . . as well as a horse," the bishop went on calmly, "in the belief that his father, who was absent on a journey, would not grudge him the use of these things, seeing that they were destined for the rebuilding of the Church of San Damiano which is in great need of repair."

"There was no ground whatsoever for such an assumption," Pietro Bernardone shouted angrily.

"Messer Bernardone," the bishop said coldly, "you will, I trust, permit me to present both views of the case without interrupting."

Pietro Bernardone sat down, muttering to himself.

"The young man declares that he never had any intention of enriching himself with this money," the bishop went on, "and that he thought he was entitled to it because his father intended to give him a much bigger sum for business transactions of his own. As he put it, he could think of no better business."

The merchant gave a short, contemptuous snort, but did not dare interrupt again.

"Francis Bernardone," the bishop said, looking sharply at the accused. "You say you wish to serve God?"

"Yes, my lord."

"You must give back the money to your father."

Pietro Bernardone took a deep breath. He found Fabiello smiling at him.

"Yes, my lord," Francis said mechanically.

"The money was not yours to give," the bishop continued, "and as you see your father is much perturbed and scandalized. His anger, I trust, will abate when he gets his money back."

Pietro Bernardone jumped to his feet. "May I be heard now, my lord Bishop?"

Bishop Guido looked at him evenly. "Yes," he said.

The merchant cleared his throat. "This young man has no personal assets," he said. "It is true that I intended to let him have some money, but at some future date, not yet fixed, and subject to my supervision. Up to now he has had no possessions of his own. Every maravedi he spent was mine, every-thing, down to the very tunic and belt and shoes he is now wearing, is the result of my efforts, the fruit of my labor, the

111

outcome of my work. Yet he got hold, behind my back, of what belongs to me and not to him—as you said yourself, my lord—and he refused to give it back to me so that I had to go to court. I have no words for such ingratitude and I will have no further ties, none whatever, with one who has disgraced my good name." He looked about him in righteous indignation. Perhaps they would understand now why the reconciliation the bishop hinted at was out of question. It was impossible that they would not see on whose side was right and decency.

Francis said nothing. He looked wan and forlorn and very small.

"Don't be afraid, young man," the bishop said cheerfully. "He who wishes to serve God must trust God, behave like a man and fear nothing. God Himself will help you and provide you with all you need to repair His church. He would not want you to use this money. For all we know it may have been gained by methods not pleasing to Him. . . ."

Pietro Bernardone's face was a dull crimson. He could see Consul Revini drawing in his head a little and smiling ironically. From somewhere farther back a voice said in a very audible whisper: "The lord bishop is remarkably well informed," and there was suppressed laughter.

The merchant was still trying to formulate a protest when the bishop spoke again, a trifle impatiently: "I told you to pay back the money, Francis Bernardone."

Suddenly the young man came to life. He leaped to his feet. "My lord," he said, "I will gladly give back everything that belongs to my father." Stepping forward, he drew the yellow leather bag from his belt and put it on the dais. He took off the belt, too, and then his tunic.

The spectators began to cheer.

"What the devil is he wearing underneath that tunic?" Ricardo Parelli asked, startled.

"A shirt, of course."

"That isn't an ordinary shirt. There's metal on it—nails! He's wearing a nail-studded shirt!"

"I told you he's mad. I knew it all the time."

"He's as sane as you are—no, I beg his pardon, he is sane. I'm not so sure about you."

Francis did not hear them. He was busy kicking off his shoes and stripping off his hose.

The cheering stopped as they saw the frail, emaciated body and the many little patches of blood on the penitent's shirt.

"Listen, all of you," Francis said in a clear, calm voice. "Until now I have called Pietro Bernardone my father. From now on I will say: Our Father who art in heaven."

In his voice was not the slightest tinge of indignation, hardness or anger. He sounded remote, aloof, and as if he were speaking from a great distance.

Pietro Bernardone tried to make himself heard. His face was distorted with rage.

"Messer Bernardone, don't excite yourself," babbled Fabiello, "Messer Bernardone, there's no need . . . you won the lawsuit. You won it. The money is all yours!" Greatly daring, he tugged at his master's mantle.

"Take your hands off me, you fool," Bernardone snarled. Lowering his massive head he took two steps toward Francis, his fists clenched. Then he stopped.

The bishop stood between father and son. "Take your property, Messer Bernardone," he said mildly, pointing to the bag and the clothes. Turning to Francis he took off his own mantle and with a gesture of great tenderness hung it over the thin shoulders so that its folds would hide the many little wounds caused by the nails.

"There should be a veil before the temple," he whispered. Francis, looking up, saw that he had won a friend for life. And he allowed himself to be led away, into the bishop's room.

Pietro Bernardone stood transfixed. What they were doing to him here was insufferable. It was turning right into wrong. They were treating him as if he were the thief and not that insane spendthrift, that rebel who had disgraced him in public. That was what he got for leaving more silver coins in the church box than any other man in Assisi. But he would not give them the satisfaction of seeing that he felt defeated. "Fabiello," he said, "pick up that bag and the clothes and give them to me."

Fabiello obeyed and the merchant took them as if he were accepting a well-merited reward. And that, in a way, it was.

The crowd began to jeer at him.

"Got everything you want, Messer merchant?"

"Don't you think you better count your coins first? Your son may have hidden a few under that nail-shirt of his. Count them, count them, one never knows!"

"Yes, the nail-shirt! That's yours too, surely, Messer Bernardone. Why don't you go and get it? It might do you a world of good to wear it a couple of years."

They made way for him as he stalked out of the hall, sweating profusely and trembling with rage, but with his jaw stuck out in a last gesture of defiance. But they did not step back as people do out of respect for greater power or higher dignity; they recoiled, as if he and his money were unclean.

Behind him the crowd merged again into a whole and when somebody started shouting for Francis they all applauded and repeated the shout.

The dais was empty now, but after a while Canon Cattaneo appeared. "Go home, good people," he said. "It's all over, you know." His smile was good-natured and the crowd laughed and began to disperse.

Half an hour later Francis left the bishop's palace. He was wearing an old tunic that had been given him; it used to belong to one of the bishop's gardeners, and Francis had chalked a white cross on it. Behind him hobbled Father Livoni who for once did not look worried at all. At the corner of the square Ricardo Parelli, Mario Luca, Paolo Spadone and Nino Manetti were waiting. They had been discussing the case, the bishop, old Bernardone and their enigmatic friend Francis, at great length. As he walked past them, they smiled at him almost timidly, suddenly at a loss for words.

"Thank you for coming to see me on my wedding day," Francis said cheerfully.

They gaped at him.

"Your . . . wedding day?" Ricardo Parelli asked.

"Yes."

"But . . . who is the bride?" Paolo asked.

"My Lady Poverty," Francis said and he walked on, hatless, shoeless and beaming. After a while he began to sing.

He had not gone so far but that they could hear him.

Paolo Spadone shook his head. "I really thought he was going to be a saint; and now he's singing like a troubadour."

"Perhaps he's going to be both," Ricardo said. "That would be a new one." And they all laughed.

CHAPTER FOURTEEN
A.D. 1207-1208

He sang in French. Provençal French, the very language of the troubadours.

Father Livoni could hear him for a while, but not for long; for soon Francis turned to wave at him joyfully, and then walked on in a different direction until he had vanished from

114

the old priest's sight. Instead of going to San Damiano he passed through the eastern gate and went on and on, singing all the time.

A goatherd heard him and two old women whose weather-beaten faces lit up for a moment. Grazing sheep heard him and a lonely donkey lifted its long ears with grave interest and brayed to him. The hens heard him and the crows and the larks and the ouzels. And God heard him, too.

He had to be alone in this new, priceless freedom of his, but his loneliness was not that of the hermit or the penitent, but that of a lover who craves to be alone with his *adorata*. And the Lady Poverty smiled as she saw him walking on, singing, in the discarded tunic of the gardener, and there was no need for her to wish him joy, for he was filled with joy to overbrimming.

This was his honeymoon with her, the glorious time before he would settle down to his new station in life.

It was not entirely uneventful. Crossing the wood on the mountain path to Valfabbrica he was held up by six men. The quality of their dress compared very favorably with his own; nevertheless they were highwaymen.

The idea that anybody should wish to rob the bridegroom of Lady Poverty proved too much for Francis' sense of humor and he burst into uncontrollable laughter.

Accustomed to striking terror into the hearts of lonely wanderers the robbers felt decidedly uneasy at such an unusual reaction and one of them asked: "Who the devil are you?"

He replied cheerfully: "I am the herald of the great King. Is there anything I can do for you?"

After a moment's stupefaction it was the robbers' turn to laugh. One of them, a burly fellow, seized him and searched him thoroughly. His method in doing so was simple: he tore Francis' tunic off him and threw the pieces away. "Not a copper-piece," he reported contemptuously. "Just our luck: not a single soul all day and then a beggar."

"A herald, you mean," another man corrected solemnly.

"All right, herald," the burly man said, "off with you. Take his feet, Tonio."

They swung Francis back and forth a few times, then sent him flying into a snow-filled ravine.

"Give our respects to the great king," one of them shouted and the others guffawed.

And Francis did. When he had finished praying he struggled back to the road and went on, almost naked. He reached a little

115

Benedictine monastery where he was given food. It was not much, but the monks did not have much themselves. They could not or would not supply him with anything to wear. Off he went again, to Gubbio, where the Lazarists allowed him to look after their lepers.

A stranger took pity on him and gave him a hermit's outfit, habit, belt, sandals and staff.

It was then that he realized what God wanted of him: complete dependence on Him. He had been working for the Benedictines in the scullery and now for the Lazarists, yet neither of them gave him clothing. A stranger did, a man for whom he had done nothing. His task then was not to earn his keep, but to do the will of God and if he did that, God would look after him as He looked after the lilies in the field.

That was the end of his honeymoon. Singing, he went back to San Damiano, prayed before the crucifix and then went to wake up old Father Livoni who was sleeping in his usual place.

The good priest was not exactly enthusiastic about his return: "Don't tell me you've got another bag of money."

Francis laughed. "I haven't and, please God, I never shall have again. Father, I've been a fool."

"Ah," said the priest noncommittally.

"I thought one needed money to repair a church."

Father Livoni opened his eyes wide. "Now, whatever could have made you think so?" he asked ironically.

"Wrong upbringing," Francis said, "and as I told you, foolishness. What one needs is stones and mortar and good will. I've got the good will. So all I need is stones and mortar. I'll go and get them. I'll be back. By the way, the lamp before the crucifix is no longer burning. I'll get some oil, too."

He walked straight on, toward Assisi. Father Livoni shook his head, sighed and fell asleep.

In Assisi Francis walked through the streets. "Give me stones, good people," he sang. "Stones to rebuild the Church of San Damiano. He who gives a stone will have a reward. He who gives two stones will have two rewards. He who gives three stones . . ."

They laughed. They gave him stones.

"They gave him oil as well," said Canon Cattaneo.

Bernard of Quintavalle smoothed the folds of his coat. "Who told you that?"

"Young Paolo Spadone, you know, Guilio Spadone's hopeful son. He and his boon companions were having one of their

116

feasts at the Golden Tree and Francis turned up in the middle of it."

"And begged?"

"He was in a very agitated state, apparently. 'Look at me,' he said, 'I'm a coward. I came here to beg from you and felt so ashamed that I didn't dare come in, but sneaked away again. Then I felt ashamed of that, so here I am.' They laughed. They thought it was a good joke—or some of them did. They wanted him to have a drink with them, to sing a song for them. Then they wanted to give him money. He refused point-blank. He did not want money. He wanted oil. They thought it was extremely funny, but they gave him his oil and he blessed them and left. Outside he had a huge sack full of stones, so many he could hardly carry them."

"He is mad, after all," Bernard said.

"If he is, it's a strange kind of madness," Cattaneo said pensively. "It seems to be infectious. Because these young good-for-nothings began to collect stones too. . . ."

"They took it as a joke."

"No doubt they did. But they got a cartload of them and a cart and a horse and took the stones to San Damiano."

"You can't repair a church that way, it's ridiculous," Bernard said. "I know these young people. They did it once and then lost all interest. Am I right?"

"You are," Cattaneo told him, "but in the meantime Francis got other people to help him, a shoemaker, a tailor, a harness-maker—I think they all used to provide him with their goods in the past—and he himself is carrying stones day after day from Assisi to San Damiano."

"Look here," Bernard said, "you know as well as I do that one needs an architect and skilled artisans and craftsmen for such a task . . . why are you laughing?"

"Dear Bernard! The church itself is sound enough. There's no need to build a new one. What it needs is no more than some repairing—a good deal of repairing, I should think. But for that you don't need an architect. The man who built the church originally knew his craft. Our lunatic is quite right . . . the only things necessary are stones and mortar and good, solid work. And from what I've seen, if he goes on for a little longer, he will have done it."

"You have gone there yourself?"

"Well, yes. I . . . wanted to have a look. Besides, the church belongs to the diocese, you know; and the bishop ought to know what's going on."

117

"Well, and what if little Francis succeeds?" Bernard asked, drumming with his finger on the table before him. "It's no great achievement, is it?"

"It is and it isn't," the canon said soberly. "It isn't, because it's a very small church and even when restored won't be a center of the faith. And it is . . . for two reasons."

"Now you have made me curious."

"First, because all Assisi is talking about it," Cattaneo said. "Which means they're concentrating on a matter of religion, of faith and of the love of God instead of the last drinking bout of the revelers or the latest fashion in Perugia or the extension of the silk trade and the profits made by their neighbors."

"And second?"

"Second, it makes one think," Cattaneo said. "We have come to take our spiritual heritage for granted—most of us. We have grown tepid and there's a very terrible warning against that in Scripture."

Bernard shifted in his seat. "That can hardly mean you, can it? You have given your life to the Church. You're a canon, a doctor of laws, a legal expert, serving the bishop to the best of your ability. You—"

"I'm an official," Cattaneo interrupted. "I do my work and I try to do it well. But I'm not all aflame like that astonishing little man, Francis. I'm not running backward and forward with a load of stones. I don't beg for the glory of God; and when I come home from my office I do not go out to look after lepers. . . ."

"Well, if you're so taken with little Francis, why don't you join him?" Bernard asked maliciously. "If he can carry stones, so can you. Why don't you?"

"Exactly," Cattaneo said. "Why don't I?"

Bernard began to laugh. "You should look at yourself, friend . . ."

"That's just it," Cattaneo said, "I don't want to look at myself. I don't think I'd like what I'd see."

"You erudite people are all the same," Bernard said indulgently. "You are too highly educated to have real opinions of your own. Now, I'm a practical man, a businessman, and I'll tell you why you can't do such a thing. Because you have a position. Because you've built up that position over the years with patience and zeal and intelligence. And it would be madness to throw it all away and become a stone carrier and a beggar, even if you did beg, as you put it, for the glory of God."

118

"So that's what you've been telling yourself," Cattaneo said astutely.

"Myself?"

"Of course. That's *your* set of excuses. Every word of it fits your own position."

Bernard pondered that. "You may be right," he admitted.

Cattaneo smiled warmly. "You see, that's what I like about you, Bernard. You're one of the very few merchants I know who have kept their integrity. I don't mean business integrity—"

"That's difficult to keep too. Remember what the bishop said about poor old Pietro Bernardone . . ."

"You're not like that old mule. Besides, a doctor of laws has his temptations too. We do so love to be right, you know, and we do so hate to admit it when we're not. So with a little twisting of facts . . ."

"You don't try to get the better of people as so many merchants do—*and* pat themselves on the back for it."

"Oh, don't we? We try to advance ourselves all the time, spurred by ambition, by obstinacy, by vanity—instead of letting God move us as that little man does. . . ."

"Do you really think so? I mean, do you really think he is 'moved by God,' as you put it?"

"I'm afraid so," Cattaneo said. "Can't you see what he's doing to us—yes, to you and me? He forces us to search our own consciences; and though we're trying to comfort each other, we still see things as they are with us and we don't like what we see."

"Saints above!" Bernard exclaimed. "You really sound as if you might join up with the little man."

"That would worry you, wouldn't it?" There was a tinge of bitterness in Cattaneo's laughter. "My, my, you're waiting for counter-arguments like a dog for his bone. I'll give you your bone. I like my form of life too much for such a wrench. I can't do it, heaven help me! And now I must go. I've got to compose a rather lengthy document for the bishop. There may be a lawsuit, you know, over the estate of old Panelmo. The will isn't clear and . . . never mind." He passed a weary hand over his forehead. "Fancy men like you and me talking about this kind of thing in all seriousness," he said. "It's quite absurd, really." He grinned ruefully. "I tell you what, friend, I'll join the little man when you do. The same day. But not before. So you see, we're both quite safe."

He waved his hand airily and left.

"You are next," Francis said to the tiny chapel. He had known the chapel a long time and he had thought of it more than once while working on San Damiano's and, later, on the chapel of San Pietro's just outside the city walls. St. Damian and St. Peter would forgive his thoughts, because this was a chapel dedicated to the Queen of Saints, though probably the smallest she ever had, except for a man's heart. Anyway, the work on both San Damiano's and San Pietro's was now finished.

Santa Maria degli Angeli was old, very old. They said it had been founded by four pilgrims from the Holy Land who had gone to Rome to visit the tombs of the apostles Peter and Paul and then decided to live somewhere in Italy as hermits. The Pope—almost eight hundred years ago—told them to go to Umbria. Because he knew what was good.

Francis looked at the tiny chapel. The very stones, lying scattered about, seemed to weep and the weeds looked as if they were trying in vain to hold up what remained of the walls.

The four pilgrims, they said, had left again after a while, to go back to the Holy Land, but before they set out, they buried a relic from the tomb of Mary under the altar and commended the chapel to the protection of the angels of the Queen of Heaven. And people said that when a wanderer who was a devout man passed it at dawn, he might hear the angels singing the praise of God.

Perhaps that was why St. Benedict had stopped here for a while, a hundred and fifty years later. He loved the place and it was he who gave it its new name: Sancta Maria Portiuncula. St. Mary of the Little Portion. When he left, he sent some of his monks up from the great monastery of Monte Cassino to look after it, but they, too, had not stayed but went over to Mount Subasio where the good Benedictines still were today.

A little enough portion it was. But if God did not despise little things—and how could He, when He had made so many—then the Mother of God wouldn't either.

Brushing the weeds aside with great care, Francis entered and knelt at the altar.

When he left, three hours later, he knew that neither San Damiano's nor San Pietro's but this tiny chapel was the place to which he was bound as a child is bound to its mother; and he decided to build himself a hut beside it.

Feeling hungry, he walked back to the town and begged for bread.

Assisi was accustomed to his begging now and he had a hundred and more friends to help him with his building too. Some

120

would work with him for days on end, others only occasionally.

Some people still jeered at him—like Fabiello who once saw him pass by with a load of stones and said: "Will you sell us some of that sweat of yours?" To which Francis, grinning broadly, replied: "I'm sorry, but I sold it to the Lord at a much higher price than you could pay for it." Far worse was the fact that Pietro Bernardone would still break into a stream of invective and curse his son whenever he saw him. Fortunately that did not happen often, but each time it did, Francis blanched and turned away until in the end he never went anywhere near a place where he might meet his father without first asking an old beggar, Alberto by name, to keep him company and to bless him each time old Bernardone cursed.

But most people liked him, the lighthearted among them for his infectious cheerfulness and charm, and because he seemed to be quite carefree; others because they felt what the source of his joy was; and all of them because of his unvarying courtesy.

Those who had worked with him on the churches liked him best of all; but their liking was mixed with a feeling of uneasy respect. They had come to know moments when his young face had a strange, almost an unearthly expression and when those moments happened they nudged their neighbors to be silent so as not to miss anything he might say. He would not proclaim nor even raise his voice. There was nothing exceptional but that expression on his face—some said it was as though he were hearing something or listening to somebody—to indicate anything of importance. Once when they were working on San Damiano's he said: "The Poor Ladies are going to live here one day," and there was a great deal of guessing about what he meant, for how could ladies, whether rich or poor, live in a church?

CHAPTER FIFTEEN
A.D. 1209

The Little Portion of the Queen of Heaven was rebuilt and Assisi was richer by three churches. Soon afterward the Assisans saw Francis in a new attire: he had discarded his sandals and his staff; instead of his hermit's robe he wore a habit of sackcloth and instead of his leather belt a simple rope.

The rumor went that he had made the change after the first Mass said at the Portiuncula, when the Gospel spoke of the command Christ gave His apostles to forego all earthly possessions, and to wear no shoes and carry no staff on their wanderings.

It was then that Francis began to preach. Not in a church or chapel, but in the streets or open fields, in barns or shops or vineyards—wherever he happened to be.

"I suppose you'd call it preaching," Canon Groga reported to the bishop, "though heaven knows it's very different from what is usually said in the pulpit."

"How is it different?" the bishop inquired attentively.

"Well, you know how it is, my lord, we must interpret the Gospels. . . ."

"And he doesn't?"

"At least I haven't heard that he has, so far. He quotes frequently from Scripture, but there is no learned interpretation and indeed, how could there be? He's no scholar, he never studied theology. . . ."

"No," the bishop said. He seemed to be a trifle uneasy. "What *does* he say?" he asked. "Is he thundering away against the mismanagement of the authorities, secular or otherwise? Against the weaknesses of the clergy?"

"Not that I know of, my lord."

"Does he tell the people Judgment Day is just around the corner? Most of these lay preachers relish that kind of talk; or they give their hearers the most detailed descriptions of the sins going on in their town or village."

"No, my lord; I mean, it isn't that either."

"Well, what does he say?"

"I've only heard him once myself," Canon Groga said, "but I've been told about half a dozen of his . . . sermons. He talks of heaven, mostly."

"And what does he know about heaven?" the bishop asked a little ironically. "Come on, Groga, out with it. You don't normally hedge as much as all this."

"He speaks as if he had just come from there," Groga said.

The bishop eyed him sharply. Groga was an old man, set in his ways and not easily moved, and yet his voice was unsteady and he blinked as if to subdue tears.

"How so?" the bishop asked, more gently.

"I don't know what it is," Groga said, "I'm sorry if my . . my report seems a little incoherent and hazy, but it is not an easy thing to describe. He talks like a man who has just been

122

sitting at the feet of our Lord. But it sounds all wrong when I say that, pompous and swollen and fulsome. I couldn't repeat it in his own words. . . ."

"Why not?"

"Because . . . because they are so simple."

Bishop Guido laughed and then stopped himself. "God is simple," he said as if to himself.

"Exactly," Canon Groga said quickly. "And you see, my lord, that is the kind of thought he raises in a man's mind and soul all the time. Even my poor way of trying to express it made you say what you just said. You see, he . . . he is so full of joy. 'Can't you see how good the Lord is?' he says. 'Look at Him. He is your true security and your peace, He is patience and humility, He is strength and prudence, hope and gladness, joy and beauty. And He is your ally for the asking! Why don't you ask Him? Don't you want to share all that with Him and a thousand good things more?'" Groga stopped, breathless, "That's the kind of thing," he murmured, "only you see, the way he says it . . ."

"Comforting the poor . . ." the bishop said.

"The poor in spirit," Canon Groga said, smiling. "I saw a good many well-to-do people listening to him as well as the poor. My learned colleague Canon Cattaneo tells me . . ."

"Cattaneo? Does he listen to him, too?"

"He has, several times, I believe."

"Strange . . . he has never said anything about it to me. I'm glad you did," the bishop said. "I was a little worried, for a moment, that he might have another of those wild-eyed lay-preachers here, like that man Waldo, or like those in the South of France, who denounce the Church, the Pope, the priesthood as a whole and from there go on to things still worse. I'm glad he isn't like that."

"I don't think he is like anyone else," Canon Groga said. "Except that he is like . . . that he is trying to be like . . ."

"Canon! What are you suggesting?" the bishop asked severely.

"Well, aren't we all supposed to try to be as much like our Lord as we can?" Canon Groga said boldly. "St. Paul tells us just that: 'Put ye on the Lord Jesus Christ. . . .'"

"I've read St. Paul too," the bishop said crisply. "Now go and fetch me Canon Cattaneo, if you please."

"I will, my lord. He can tell you much more about Francis than I can," Canon Groga said, not without relief.

"Unfortunately," the bishop said, "he will have to tell me

about the legal aspects of a very disagreeable letter I've just received concerning the Panelmo lawsuit."

The canon bowed and walked to the door.

"By the way," the bishop said, "you might get in touch with Father Silvester of San Giorgio's . . ."

"Yes, my lord?"

". . . and tell him he can let young Francis preach in his church, if he wants to."

"Thank you, my lord," Canon Groga said, beaming, and withdrew.

"They say you received your vocation for preaching at the Mass of the Apostle Mark," Bernard of Quintavalle said, after the service in San Giorgio's.

Francis looked at him. "Why do you say that?"

"Because," Bernard said, "in the Gospel of that day it says that the apostles may enter a house they deem worthy and stay there a while. Will you stay with me at my house tonight?"

"I will, gladly," Francis said.

They stayed together that day and talked of many things.

It was a little strange, perhaps, that Bernard had Francis' bed prepared in his own bedchamber, although there were plenty of other rooms.

In the morning he said to his guest: "I have been a cautious man all my life. Before I entered into business with anyone I took great pains to inquire whether or not he was worthy of my confidence. I sent out agents to find out as much as they could about such a man. I did the same with you."

Francis said nothing.

"My agents in your case were my eyes," Bernard said. "You thought they were closed last night, and that I was asleep. But I was not and I have been watching you all the time."

Francis looked away. "I need very little sleep," he murmured.

"Two hours," Bernard said. "Then you rose and prayed and only now do I know what praying is."

"I have much to make up for," Francis said.

"In that part of the Gospel of St. Matthew from which I quoted to you yesterday it says also that when an apostle stays in a house that is worthy, his peace will come down upon it. It did, and thus I know that you come from God. Now I must ask you this: What should a man do, if he has possessed much wealth for many years and now feels that it is no longer a blessing to him?"

"He should return it to the Lord."

"Then that is what I want to do," Bernard of Quintavalle said.

Francis' eyes shone. "We shall meet at San Niccolò's church tomorrow morning, before the first Mass," he said. He drew a sign of the cross over the head of his host and so vivid was the movement of his hand that the cross seemed to remain there for a heartbeat or two. Then he left.

The first Mass at San Niccolò's was at dawn, so it was still quite dark when Bernard entered the church. He was shivering a little in the cold of the early morning. At first he thought that there was no one here, but after a few moments he saw the figure of a man approaching him. But that could not be Francis. It was a much taller man. Then he recognized Canon Cattaneo and they both stopped in incredulous surprise.

"You, too?" Cattaneo whispered. "Is it possible?"

"That's what I was going to say," Bernard whispered back. They grinned. They almost broke into laughter.

"I'll join the little man when you do," Cattaneo gasped. "That's what I said to you a year ago, wasn't it? Or is it two years? And now look at us."

Suddenly Francis stood between them, smiling. "Come with me," he said. "We want to make quite sure of what is wanted of us. Therefore we shall ask the Lord Himself." Seizing their hands he walked with them toward the altar. Before the rail they knelt together.

Francis was the first to rise and he led them up the altar steps to the Epistle side, where the large missal was lying in its place, closed.

The men stood close together. A fragment of the Pater Noster danced and whirled in Bernard's head: "Thy will be done . . . Thy will be done . . ."

Cattaneo thought: That's what St. Augustine did at the decisive moment of his life. He wondered whether Francis knew that, but his will banished the thought and all other thoughts and laid itself at the foot of the crucifix.

The book was open and Francis read out the text: " 'If thou wilt be perfect, go sell what thou hast, and give to the poor . . . and come follow me.' "

Bernard gave a long sigh. Cattaneo smiled.

Francis' thin fingers closed the book and at once opened it again. And he read: " 'If any man will come after me, let him deny himself, and take up his cross, and follow me.' "

Again he closed the book; again he opened it. " 'Take nothing for your journey, neither staff nor scrip, nor bread, nor

125

money; neither have two coats.' " He turned to them and laid his arms on their shoulders. "This is our life and rule, brothers," he said jubilantly. "For ourselves and for all who will join our company. Go and fulfill the word you have heard."

As they descended the altar steps, there was the sound of a bell, and behind a very small acolyte the priest came in to say the first Mass of the day, the sixteenth day of April, One thousand two hundred and nine.

The Bishop of Assisi was worried because Emperor Otto IV was coming down from Germany with an army. The monarch was not coming to make war; on the contrary, the Pope was going to crown him in Rome and there would be great festivities and rejoicing.

But when troops in great numbers passed through a city there was always trouble and the bishop did not think that Emperor Otto's soldiers would prove an exception to the rule. Thus he was not in the best of moods when Father Silvester of San Giorgio's came to see him to ask him for a special favor.

"I'm afraid I want a very great favor, my lord," the elderly priest said.

"Then you must ask God for it and not me," the bishop said curtly.

"I did, my lord. But as a priest of your diocese I must ask you as well. I want to join Brother Francis and his companions."

The bishop pushed back his chair. "What? You?" he asked incredulously.

Father Silvester looked down. "Your very surprise shows how much I am in need of it, my lord."

"What's come over all of you?" the bishop asked testily. "First one of my canons deserts me for this . . . this . . . I don't know what to call it."

Father Silvester smiled under strain. "The Friars Minor . . . the Little Brothers," he said. "That's what Brother Francis calls us."

"Us?" the bishop repeated sharply. "You're not one of them yet. And now I'd like to know what made you think of such a . . . of this thing. I never knew you had any connection with the man at all, except that I gave permission to let him preach at San Giorgio's. He seems to have moved you more than your congregation. As far as I can make out there has been no appreciable rise in the revenues of the church although I know that you are eager to collect as much as possible."

The priest nodded. "You have laid the finger on the wound,

126

my lord. It was that eagerness of mine that made me . . . I don't know how to start, my lord."

"You had better start at the beginning," the bishop said, "and what is more, be brief about it. I have a great deal of work to do."

"It started with the building of San Damiano's," Father Silvester said. "Perhaps you knew, my lord, that Francis went about asking everybody for stones. . . ."

"Yes, yes. So?"

"I gave him some. And I let him preach. Then the day came when Ser Bernard of Quintavalle and Canon Cattaneo distributed their money to the poor. The square was black with people."

"So I'm told. Briefer, Father, if you please."

The priest gulped. "So I . . . went to Francis and reminded him of the stones I had given him. He had promised a reward for them."

The bishop chuckled. "That's more like you, Father. Never miss an opportunity."

Father Silvester hung his head. "What you say is only too true, my lord. Francis looked at me, turned to Ser Bernard, took two fistfulls of coins from the chest in front of him and gave them to me. I put them in my pocket and at once he filled my hands again. 'Now then, are you satisfied, Ser Priest?' he asked quite cheerfully. I was overwhelmed. I just muttered some words of thanks and slunk away."

"I think I begin to understand," the bishop said. "Go on."

"I was troubled about it," Father Silvester said. His lips moved inaudibly before he could continue. "I have always been keen on collecting money. Not for myself, I told myself all the time, certainly not for myself, but for the church, for the poor of my parish, for a new altar cloth, for this and that. But was it really so? I remember the joy I felt at the first moment when all those coins were filling my hands and I remember that I thought: I must count them at once; and that thought, too, was joy. But at that moment I was not thinking of the poor and the joy it would give them. The joy was all mine, my own." Father Silvester clenched and unclenched his hands. "Then I knew more about myself, my lord, more than I ever knew before, even when I was going to confession, may God forgive me. And a certain dream came to me . . . three nights in succession the same dream."

"Of Francis?" the bishop asked quietly.

"Yes, my lord. So I went to see him and we talked; and once

127

more I was full of joy. But what a different joy it was, my lord."
With a sob Father Silvester fell on his knees. "In the name of
our Lord . . . may I join him?"

The bishop blew out his cheeks. "I suppose I must give you
permission," he growled. "If I don't, you wouldn't be much
good, yearning for it all the time."

"Thank you, my lord, thank you." Father Silvester rose,
beaming.

"Not at once, mind you," the bishop said. "First, put your
house in order. I shall send your successor to San Giorgio in a
few months' time . . . three months, shall we say? Then if you
still feel as you do now, you may join the little man. It might
be as well for him to have a priest at his side; though I wish
he'd choose a few simpler men for the kind of life he and his
—what was it?—his little brothers are leading. A wealthy merchant—a canon and doctor of laws; and now a priest!"

"Ah, but there is Giles," Father Silvester said, smiling. "He
used to be a field-worker. And Sabbatino and Giovanni da Ca-
pella—all from Assisi; and Filippo Longo; and Morico who used
to work in the leper hospital of San Salvatore; and Barbero
and Giovanni of San Constantino and another Bernard, too,
Bernard della Vite; yes and Brother Tancredo from Rieti who
used to be a knight. . . ."

"Twelve," the bishop said, his voice high with surprise.
"That's astonishing. And you will be the thirteenth."

"Oh no, my lord," Father Silvester said cheerfully. "As I
must wait till my successor arrives I shall probably be the
fiftieth or so."

The bishop shook his head. "Where are you going to live?"

"At present the brothers are staying near the Portiuncula. We
. . . they are going to build a shed soon, near the chapel."

"I hope so, for your sake," the bishop said wryly. "Very well
. . . you may go now, Father."

Father Silvester knelt to kiss the episcopal ring and for the
first time the bishop could see what the priest must have
looked like as a boy.

When he had gone, the bishop sat for a while in a deep
reverie. The idea was not new, he told himself. In fact, it
seemed to be stirring in the minds of men all over Europe.
Peter Waldo . . . the Humiliati . . . the Poor People of
Lyons; even the Albigenses—they all seemed to long for poverty and simplicity in some form. But there was a difference.
All those others had had a grudge. They thundered and screamed
at those who would not live as they did. They wanted to

force others to comply with their rules. They foamed at the mouth, they put forth new laws and dogmas, more often than not in contradiction to the teaching of the Church. This man Francis seemed to have no grudge against anybody. He compelled no one—except by some kind of infectious cheerfulness, by the contagion of his own joy. And he taught nothing that was wrong.

It *is* a new thing, after all, the bishop thought. And Father Silvester of all people! Never had he looked so young and happy. One could almost envy him. How had Canon Cattaneo put it once: "No longer moving, but being moved by God"—or some such words. The simple life, the kind of life the apostles themselves used to live, free of the burden of possessions and therefore free from lawsuits and other troubles about land, estate and money.

Heaven above, the bishop thought, but I *do* envy him! He'll be living in squalor, he'll beg for a few crusts of bread, he'll work for his fellow men without pay; yet I envy him. This was folly. But then, didn't St. Paul speak of the Folly of the Cross?

For the duration of seven heartbeats Bishop Guido of Assisi quite seriously considered whether Francis, who would take a priest for a companion, might take a bishop as well. Then he looked with regret at his feet, swollen and hot in the evening, although he did not walk much; he thought of his labored breathing whenever he ascended a staircase. It was a little late to change one's life as drastically as all that, at the age of sixty-two.

He grinned ruefully. The Lord would have to use him as he was. Then he began to wonder whom he could send to San Giorgio to replace Father Silvester.

CHAPTER SIXTEEN
A.D. 1209

When Roger of Vandria was called, on a day in October, to see the queen he only just managed to hide an expression of exasperation. Instead, he gave a ceremonial bow to the stiff little Spanish lady-in-waiting, Doña María de Sotomayor, and followed her upstairs, downstairs and up again through the rabbit warren that was the royal palace of Palermo.

It was perfectly obvious to him why the queen had called for him. In fact, he had almost expected that she would, although she really ought to know better.

Frederick was a genius, but a genius not quite fifteen years old—two good reasons why she could not very well expect him to behave the way she wanted him to behave: like the average king, if there was such a thing, and like a mature man. Her own maturity ought to make up for this lack. After all, she was twenty-four, almost ten years older than her husband; and she had been married before.

Doña María de Sotomayor drew back the curtains of the anteroom of the queen's apartments and he entered, and bowed to two ladies-in-waiting who curtsied. He remembered that Frederick had at first been amused by the stiff Spanish ceremonies the queen insisted on. Now the king was accustomed to them, which to him was tantamount to being bored. Roger wondered what the Hungarians thought, when Constance was the late King Emerich's wife.

"The Count of Vandria, Madame."

Queen Constance was sitting in her favorite armchair and for the hundredth time Roger told himself that she was really quite a beautiful woman, even though her large dark eyes and the proud, longish nose gave her an expression of perpetual solemnity. Behind her stood, as always, Doña Pilar de Moralès, sixty, gray and venerable.

"My dear Count," the queen said when he came up from his bow, "I am extremely worried. The king has not left his rooms for a week and will speak to no one. I can understand that the latest news has been somewhat upsetting, even though I have not heard it in detail. But surely something ought to be done to . . . to save him from this self-inflicted loneliness."

"What can a mere servant do, when you yourself did not succeed, Madame?" Roger said.

"There are moments, perhaps, when a wife is less able to help than a loyal friend," the queen said.

"A loyal friend will soon lose whatever value he may have, if he dares to go against the king's explicit command, Madame."

The queen sighed. "Have you any explanation, of the king's behavior?" she asked. "All I know is that there has been news from Rome about the coronation of the new Emperor. I know it is most unfortunate that he should come of that terrible family whose enmity against the House of Hohenstaufen has created so much trouble in Europe. But surely His Holiness the Pope would not have consented to acknowledge him, if he had not given the most solemn pledges for the safety of the king's realm."

She doesn't understand the king at all, Roger thought. And as a woman she can think only in terms of security. He said: "It has been a great disappointment nevertheless, Madame. A year ago, when Emperor Philip was murdered, the king, his nephew, was the only surviving Hohenstaufen. He could not conceive that he would be passed over and the imperial crown given to his most powerful enemy."

"Oh, I know *that*," Queen Constance said. "But that, as you say, was a year ago. We weren't even married at the time, and so much has happened since, hasn't it? He has known all the time that that awful man was going to be crowned in Rome, too—but he was quite cheerful nevertheless."

"Perhaps he hoped the Pope might change his mind," Roger said. "Though that is mere conjecture on my part. The king doesn't often speak to me about these things—or to anyone."

"Very true," the queen said sadly. "Who would have thought that one so young could keep so many secrets in his heart."

"The king," Roger said, "had to learn that at a time when others of his age were playing with toys."

"I wish I could understand this beautiful country of yours a little better, Count. One never seems to know quite what is going on. The chancellor, Bishop Walter of Pagliari, Governor Capparone, Count Pietro of Celano, Count Riccardo of Fondi and other nobles—they all pretend to powers difficult to reconcile with the king's position. It was not so or did not seem to be so when I arrived with my poor brother Alphons, in January this year."

Of course not, Roger thought. Prince Alphons arrived with no less than six hundred Spanish knights and their retinues, a formidable factor that made less powerful ones hold back and lie low. But the plague had broken out, Prince Alphons and many of his knights succumbed to it and a number of others chose to return with great speed to Aragon. The plague had done what neither chancellor nor governor could do: it had reduced the king's power to a mere fraction of what it was when his bride arrived. Of course the king could not reveal that to anyone, so he appeared cheerful and gay and seemed to enjoy life. But he knew all the time that he could not rely on any of the many and powerful factions—the last bit of news was that Count Pietro of Celano, appointed by the Pope to look after the king's interests, was in secret correspondence with the new Emperor.

131

"I am sure the king regrets the untimely death of Prince Alphons almost as much as you do, Madame," he said quite truthfully. "And it is sad, too, that you should be deprived of the company of so many of your compatriots." He did not dare to go further. But she was queen enough to understand.

"I am afraid I cannot ask my father to send an army here to protect our interests," she said. "Aragon must be on her guard too, against the Moors in the South. They are a constant danger. That also is one of the things I cannot understand: that the king deigns to receive Saracen nobles, to entertain them and spend hours conversing with them in their own horrible tongue."

She must have been bored very often, Roger thought. He *will* speak Arabic at the slightest provocation. Blandly he said: "There are learned people among them, Madame, and the king is very eager to learn from them as much as he can. Knowledge is always useful."

"No," the queen said sternly. "There is knowledge no good Christian should try to acquire and what can be expected from the followers of Mohammed but impious and corrupting arts and crafts. I shudder each time I see those fiends here in the palace. We know them well, we Spaniards. They are as false as their smiles and what could be falser? They're as famous for their treachery as for their knowledge of the black arts and I have yet to learn that the Saracens of this island are different, although the king tells me they are. He is so young, Count, so very young. . . ."

"I, too, have learned to speak Arabic, Madame," Roger said. "I had a smattering of it as a boy, acquired before my family went into exile, and I have studied the language with much zeal these last years, so as to be able to participate in the king's discussions with Moslem sages."

"Sages! Say wizards or magicians."

"Not once have I heard them speak of such forbidden things, Madame, only about the science of the stars and about medicine."

"Yes, yes, I know, they're pastmasters at that. The University of Toledo is notorious the world over for the training of such people. And many of those who affiliated themselves with them have come to believe in their own abilities alone, to make light of the power of God and speak with contempt of the Church and of all things holy. . . ."

"And why not, my dear?" asked a harsh, metallic voice.

Despite almost half a century of training Doña Pilar de Moralès could not suppress a little gasp of surprise before she swept into a deep curtsy.

"Federico!" the queen exclaimed, curtsying as well. "Oh how glad I am that at long last . . ." She stopped. She had seen his face.

The king looked like neither a boy nor a man. There was something inhuman about that clear-skinned face with its beak nose and unblinking eyes.

Roger remembered Hassan ben Mubarek, the physician, telling the king that the ancient Egyptians believed in a god with the head of a hawk. "He was not very powerful in his youth, but he became so later," the old Saracen said with a strange smile, as if he were paying the king a compliment instead of telling him another of his many fantastic stories. But—that was what the king looked like.

I shall never get accustomed to his face, Roger thought. And he could not help wondering whether the queen ever would. She had not as yet. He could see that.

"Why not?" the king repeated. He stood quite still and yet he seemed to move. He was trembling. "Why not speak with contempt of what is contemptible? Or don't they teach you at the court of Aragon that treachery is contemptible?"

"I do not understand," the queen said, paling.

"Don't you? Don't you? But I mustn't be impatient. You're always telling me that, my dear Constance, aren't you? Very well. I will be very patient. From the beginning then. When my father died the princes in Germany chose my uncle Philip to be king and to become emperor, because I was only a little child. That was wrong. Child or not, I was the heir to the throne. But the Pope agreed and who could gainsay the Holy Father. He most graciously allowed me to keep the crown of Sicily—under his tutelage, naturally. Then my uncle Philip was murdered, foully murdered by that thrice-accursed man Otto von Wittelsbach. His wife had to flee for her life, with her baby still unborn. The hardships of the flight proved too much for her and mother and child died. I was the last male Hohenstaufen. And what did the Pope do? He gave the imperial crown, the crown of Charlemagne and of my great forefathers to the Guelph, Otto of Brunswick."

"But what else could he do?" the queen asked pleadingly. "He is not all-powerful. You told me yourself that the German princes . . ."

"The German princes would not have dared to go against the Pope if he had come out for me, as was his duty."

"His duty! Is there a law . . ."

"No one interrupts the king," Frederick said, stamping his foot. "The Pope had the power to cast the lightning of his ban against those opposing his will. But did he? He gave in; and he gave in very willingly. He thought it was—how did he put it? —permissible, decorous and useful. Here at long last was the opportunity to get rid of a family which had caused the successors of St. Peter a fair amount of trouble in the past. He was quick to seize it. And Otto was crowned. The wise Pope, they call him; the statesman Pope. And he is both—if it is wisdom to be on the side of the more powerful party and if treachery can be called statesmanship."

The queen said, outraged: "In Spain we do not talk like that of the Holy Father."

Frederick gave a short laugh. "You had better realize that you are no longer in Spain."

"I do," the queen said, "and not without regret. If my husband permits, I will retire."

"On the contrary," Frederick said, "as your Spanish ears are too tender to hear the truth, it is I who will withdraw." He bowed ironically and left, giving Roger a sign to follow him.

Roger's bow to the queen remained unobserved. She had turned her back to him to hide her tears.

The king walked fast, as if he wished to escape the very air of the queen's suite. He climbed the stairs up the western tower with the agility of a cat, so that Roger did not find it at all easy to keep pace with him. At the top he turned and frowned when he saw Roger emerge from the stairway.

"Stay with me," he said, "but don't speak." He looked across the wide, blue bay and once more Roger was forced to think how much he resembled a hawk, a hawk poised to fly from the tower, to pounce on its prey, wings extended, talons ready to tear into soft flesh.

"I have been in Rome," the king said hoarsely. "I saw it all happen, everything. And if a man could die of hatred, I would have died."

For a moment Roger thought that the king had lost his reason.

"A great, big, lumbering ox of a man," Frederick went on. "He came down from the Brenner Pass with his following, tramp, tramp, tramp—they're all as heavy as oxen, big-footed, bull-necked, fleshy. Tramping across the Umbrian plain to

Viterbo. That's where the holy man received him, that's where he and Otto exchanged the kiss of peace, Judas kissing Judas in an unholy union. They say the Pope is a small man and Otto towers a full head over his own knights. It must have been quite a sight. They can't be friends for long, those two. Mark my words, they can't. Their horoscopes mix as little as their tempers and that is only natural, one being the consequence of the other. But their union lasted long enough for the infamy of the coronation. Will you believe that I saw it all with the eyes of my soul? The sacred crown coming down on the Ox's head and the silver trumpets blaring away in honor of the blasphemy. *My* crown! The plague on them both, the traitor and the Guelph." He clutched the hilt of his sword as if it were the Guelph's throat. "Seven feet of avarice," he said. "They hate him. Almost all the princes hate him. He's as coarse as a peasant and he swills like a pig. Oh, I've studied him closely. It isn't true that hatred makes one blind. At least, I am not blinded. I see him as clearly as if I were inside him." He turned away from the glorious, the majestic sight of the bay. He had not seen it at all.

"They'll fall out," he said dreamily. "But that won't help me. Celano is in touch with Otto. Fondi may be, too; I have no proof of it yet, but I shall get it. Celano—do you know what that means? It means the Guelph wants Sicily. Quiet! I don't want to hear you speak. I'm thinking aloud and you are allowed to listen. There are few to whom I would grant that favor. But I think you are loyal to me. In any case *you* would have nothing to gain by changing sides. Otto has too many clumsy Germans whom he must reward with duchies, counties, baronies. I alone can get you Vandria back—in time, I haven't been able to, yet, not with the chancellor's creatures residing there, armed with documents as well as crossbows. You must wait. Diepold has joined Otto, of course. I could have killed that idiot Capparone for letting him escape. I wonder how much Diepold paid him for it. Diepold, that's another of the bull-breed. His army had gone, naturally; crumbled away, dispersed in all directions —what else could happen when men aren't paid for over a year. But that type of man will always find a following. He isn't big enough for Otto, though, not since that coronation. His best dreams are over, but as Otto's general he's dangerous enough for me. And I can't do anything. I am helpless on this island, with everybody thinking of his own little sphere of power, everybody ready to sell himself to the highest bidder. If only I could rely on the Saracens, by God's head, I'd raise the cres-

135

cent on this palace tomorrow and make an alliance with the Dey of Tunis and the Sultan of Egypt." Suddenly he began to laugh. "You think I'm raving, don't you? People have always thought that of those few, those very few who could throw all ordinary ways of thinking to the dogs."

"Have I the king's permission to speak?" Roger asked.

Frederick heaved a great sigh. "Speak," he said. His voice sounded tired.

"I think you're doing the Pope an injustice, my lord King. When you sent that letter of yours to all the reigning kings and princes of Europe, drawing their attention to the injustice of your position, the only one who replied with more than mere honeyed words was Innocent III. He sent you two hundred of his own knights. He negotiated with King Peter of Aragon for you and the Princess of Aragon arrived with six hundred Spanish knights. . . ."

"Stop defending my holy ex-guardian," Frederick sneered. "He is in no position to thank you for it. Yes, he did what you say, but why? Not to save the last descendant of the hated House of Hohenstaufen, but to reaffirm the Church's firm grip on Sicily. He chose my bride accordingly. Anyway, all that is past history. What I want to know is what happened at Viterbo. You can be quite sure Sicily was discussed there. I only wish I knew whether the Pope managed to keep it out of Otto's clutches. And perhaps I shall know that soon . . . there is somebody coming up the road to the gate, somebody on a very tired horse. Can you see him? It's Martino."

"Martino, my lord King?"

"The best man I have in Messina. That means news, and most likely from Rome. Martino wouldn't come himself without grave reason."

Clattering down the spiraling stairs behind the king, Roger wondered how the astonishing boy always managed to have secrets not even the closest of his entourage knew anything about, and that living in a palace where everyone was in somebody's pay and secrets were about as difficult to guard as a bag full of fleas.

The king received Martino in the same small study where he liked to converse with his Arab physicians and astrologers, a cabinet furnished with a desk, a few shelves for books, drawings and only two chairs. When the man had gone Frederick called Roger in.

"I am a good prophet," he said. "They have already fallen out."

Roger's eyes widened. "The Pope and the Emperor?"

Frederick nodded. "The beginning is there. It's not final yet, but I think it will be soon. Didn't I tell you that the Ox is avaricious? That's a fatal vice for one who wants to wear a crown. They didn't get on too well in Viterbo. The Pope insisted that Otto must renounce any claim on Sicily, and apparently the Guelph did, after much struggle. He swore an oath to respect our integrity."

"But this is excellent news," Roger broke in. "I told you you were doing the Pope an injustice. . . ."

"And I told you he will try and save Sicily for himself," Frederick said. "In any case they fought over it, the Pope won and they both set out for Rome, smiling as if all were well with the world. The Ox of Brunswick and the Fox of St. Peter—what a pair! But Otto had his army march with him, and Rome had to let him in with his troops. He wanted to make sure that there would be no last-minute hitch, and he felt sure only in the midst of his army. The Romans didn't like it. They had to think of their wives and daughters—and of their valuables as well. The Pope was Otto's prisoner. . . ."

"What? The Emperor dared . . ."

"Oh, he didn't put St. Peter in chains," Frederick jeered. "There was no need for that. But the people of Rome armed themselves . . ."

"To free the Pope?"

The king threw back his head, laughing. "How little you know them. They wouldn't care a maravedi whether the Pope were free or a prisoner, alive or dead. No, no. They wanted their tribute. A good old custom, Count. They call it the coronation tax. Every emperor to be crowned must pay it. That's how the mob always reacts to generosity. A liberal prince gives them largesse. Another, not to be outdone, follows his example. The third one *must* do it, for now the mob claims it as its birthright. Too bad that third one was the Guelph who turns a penny three times in his hand and then puts it back into his pocket rather than give it to a beggar. He refused point-blank. It cost him the lives of two thousand men. Rome was a battlefield! They had to clear the square of St. Peter's and the area all around it by force so that the coronation could take place at all. Fighting went on all day and all night. The Guelph paid his tax in blood and much of it was German. Now they have left Rome and gone north, though not very far. They'll make their winter quarters in Tuscany and Ancona and they are treating the Papal States as if they were enemy country."

"I didn't think the Emperor would be so foolish," Roger said.

"I'm not so sure he is," Frederick replied. A deep line formed between his brows when he was thinking with much concentration. It made him look double his age. "I can rejoice in the news only because it serves them right, both Ox and Fox. But the danger for me has not decreased—on the contrary, it is probably much greater than before."

Roger shook his head. "I don't understand, my lord King. You just told me that the Emperor has sworn to respect the integrity of Sicily. So . . ."

"So you are a fool," Frederick told him dryly. "Think, man, think. Until now Otto needed Innocent. No Pope, no coronation. Now he is crowned. His bull's head is anointed with holy oil. The imperial sword has been given into his hand. He needs the Pope no longer. He's over the wall. There's nothing to stop him from kicking away the ladder up which he climbed. He has Italy. Why should he stop there? And who is to stop him if he doesn't?"

"You really think . . ."

". . . that he will attack us, yes. Apulia first, of course. Then the island. Italy is a boot. He has slipped pretty far into it, but he won't be able to walk until he's got the boot on properly. I know that's how I would feel. And if he doesn't think of it himself, Diepold of Acerra will. And Diepold knows how weak I am."

There was a pause.

"Of course," the king said lightly, "if I had a knight so loyal to me that he was ready to risk his life for my cause—and if that knight could manage to approach the Guelph and kill him —a slight wound would be quite sufficient if the dagger were dipped in a certain substance I could easily get from one of my Arab friends—then everything would be quite different. The princes in Germany would have to hold a new election. There would be another coronation. And this time they could pass me over no longer. But where could I find such a friend?"

Roger felt the unblinking eyes watching him closely. There was great need to think quickly. "My loyalty to you is second to no other, my lord King," he said in a steady voice. "But the odds are a hundred to one that I wouldn't succeed in this. The Emperor is bound to be well guarded. The loss of my life would not be a great thing. I'm nobody and I doubt whether there is a single person, man or woman, who would shed a tear for me. But I am told that few men remain silent under torture. They'd soon find out who sent me. As it is, we don't

138

know whether the Emperor will dare to attack Sicily. But if it were known that the King of Sicily had tried to have him killed, we would furnish him with an excellent pretext to do so, in the name of revenge."

The ghost of a smile was hovering around Frederick's thin mouth.

"I did you wrong, my dear Count," he said pleasantly enough. "You're not a fool. What a nice piece of reasoning. You are right, I can't get rid of the Guelph so simply."

He didn't mean it, Roger thought. He was testing me—and most likely for intelligence rather than loyalty. Which means that I have stood the test. He reads me like a book.

But Frederick's mind had gone back to the great issue at stake. "The Guelph cannot strike immediately," he said slowly. "But the clouds are gathering fast. And within a year the storm will break."

CHAPTER SEVENTEEN
A.D. 1210

Of all the armies that ever marched on Rome this was the strangest: twelve men in tunics rougher and simpler than those of peasants, ill-kempt, bearded and unarmed, yet as cheerful as though protected by myraids of warriors. Some people thought they were lunatics, others took them for monks of some kind and still others for beggars. But if asked who they were they answered: We are the Little Brothers.

Their leader was not Francis but an older man, slow and conscientious: Bernard of Quintavalle. Francis had insisted before they left the Queen of Heaven's Little Portion that they should choose a leader other than himself for this journey—until they came to Rome.

They sang their way, that November, down the Umbrian valley to Spoleto, across the plateau of Rieti and through the Campagna and then walked in reverent silence through the streets of Rome itself.

After a visit to the tombs of the apostles Peter and Paul they walked to the Lateran Palace and there Francis said: "I shall enter alone. Wait for me here, brothers, till I have spoken to the Holy Father. And pray as hard as you can that he will grant us our Rule and the permission to preach."

Brother Pietro Cattaneo had learned a great deal in the short time he had spent in Francis' company; even so he found it hard not to ask whether Francis really thought he could visit the Vicar of Christ on earth, the Ruler of the Papal States, the Liege-Lord of all Christian kings and princes as if he were a friendly neighbor in Assisi: *"Buon' giorno*, nice weather we're having; now listen, Holy Father, I must ask you something . . ."

He only just managed to say nothing. But Francis looked at him, smiling: "I know someone much higher still who said: 'Ask, and it shall be given you . . . knock, and it shall be opened to you.'"

Brother Pietro Cattaneo grinned ruefully. "I should have known better," and the others wondered what it was all about.

As Francis vanished among the slender columns of the palace entrance, Cattaneo explained, without, however, causing much surprise. Each one of the brothers had had similar experiences. Francis always seemed to know what they were thinking or feeling even when he had his back turned to them. Not long ago when he came back from a lonely journey to Rieti he had told them of a vision he had had about the fate of their brotherhood; it came just at the moment when for some reason they had all felt discouraged—and that, too, he knew and had even foretold. "I am compelled to tell you what I have seen so that you may be encouraged to advance on your way. I would rather be silent, but my love compels me to speak. I have seen a great multitude of men coming to us, desiring to put on the habit of our vocation. Their sound is in my ears. I have seen the roads of all the nations full of men coming into these parts. The French are coming, the Spaniards are hastening, the Germans and the English run and great is the crowd of them who hurry along speaking other tongues." They had not appeared as yet, but they would.

Now Father Francis was going to see the Holy Father and see him he would. Meanwhile they had been ordered to pray hard and they did, a cluster of grayish brown scarecrows in front of the center of the world.

Francis stepped out with a will, in search of the Pope. The habit of the brotherhood, both drab and formless, became almost invisible in the chiaroscuro of the Lateran corridors.

Once a varlet made a move to stop him and ask who he was and where he was going, but the little man strode along so full of purpose that it was quite unthinkable he had no business

140

here; he probably was a messenger to the Grand-Almoner or some other high official and to stop such as he would never do.

The secretary of Cardinal Hugolino of Ostia, in charge of German Affairs, called out severely: "You there! Who are you?" But before the question was out, Francis, never for a moment suspecting that the call had been addressed to him, had vanished round the next corner.

He crossed one court and a second and found himself in a huge hall, empty, with a throne under a canopy on one side, and he marched across the beautiful, cool mosaic floor protesting snobbishly and in vain with low, grinding noises against the touch of a pair of clumsy sandals.

In the corridor behind the throne hall a magnificent officer looked askance, his moustaches and beard competing with the fur trimming his doublet. Francis smiled and waved at the gorgeous creature as he passed and Count Narcisio Vitale stared after him, wondering who the little man was who seemed to know him so well.

It never occurred to Francis to ask anybody where he would find the Holy Father; after all he was somewhere here in the palace and one just had to use one's eyes.

There was a large room full of clerics, debating something quite fiercely, but as they were *all* sitting, the Pope could not be with them and Francis withdrew and walked on.

On a broad terrace a lonely man was walking up and down, rather hurriedly, with his hands folded, not in front of him and hidden in his sleeves as a monk would, but at his back as if he wanted to prevent them from committing an impulsive action. He was a small man and his body seemed to carry the head with difficulty; the poor head kept trying to find repose on the chest; and on that chest was a pectoral cross, sparkling blue fire. He was wearing a red cap, trimmed with ermine.

Francis could not see his face, but he knew that this was the Pope and his heart leaped.

He rushed out on the terrace and up to the formidable and restless little figure and fell on his knees: "Holy Father, eleven brothers and I have come from Assisi to ask for your gracious permission . . ."

From under the red cap a face loomed, dark and powerful and quite obviously the face of a man in a very bad temper. "Who are you?" asked Innocent III in the steely tone that struck fear into crowned heads and cardinals, archimandrites and commanders of armies.

141

"Your most humble servant Francis, Your Holiness. I have written down a Rule for our brotherhood and . . ."

"Guards," said Innocent III. He did not shout and he was by no means perturbed at what might well have been an attempt on his life. But he was annoyed as a man will be when his very disagreeable thoughts about very disagreeable things are interrupted.

"Holy Father, please, hear me. . . ."

The magnificent officer appeared and from the other side of the terrace two guards came at the double.

The Pope told Count Vitale what he thought of him by shaking his head twice, and resumed his walk, hands folded at his back, chin now down on his chest.

Francis felt himself propelled away with a kind of irresistible yet careful energy and, in a very much shorter time than he had spent on his way in, found himself back at the slender columns of the entrance.

"And *stay* away," the officer said grimly. He was very red in the face and breathing hard.

Slowly Francis returned to the little cluster of men, still praying. They stopped as he appeared, but their faces fell when they saw his sad little smile.

"We haven't prayed hard enough," he said and walked on. They followed in silence, and no one dared to ask a question.

Up and down went the solitary little figure on the terrace. The absurd little incident no longer existed, except in the form of a mental note that the matter of guarding the palace needed overhauling. The note was stored away and would come back to awareness tomorrow at seven in the morning, when the Governor of the Sacred Palace would have his daily three-minute audience.

Innocent was back at the main problem, the problem that probably would have to be decided within the next twenty-four hours. The consequences of that decision might well shape the next twenty-four years and perhaps a period ten times longer. It was touch and go.

Better than any other statesman of his age he understood the great art of timing. Deadlocks that seemed unsolvable, impasses that defied the most brilliant intellect, powerful single personalities seemingly invincible—time put an end to all of these.

Yet there were moments when such wisdom was not permissible, when inaction was a sin as grave as the worst action might be. And this was such a moment.

There was something demonic about what the imperial crown did to those who felt it circling their heads. The Caesars of old had been driven to madness by such magic, and now it was the same with its German wearers. A man came to Rome to be anointed and crowned. He swore a solemn oath to uphold the rights of the Church; and then, anointed and crowned, he seemed to feel that the oath had been taken by the man he used to be and not the man he had become—and thus it was no longer valid.

It was only too clear that Otto of Brunswick was no exception. Indeed, he was the most flagrant and fundamental example of the lot. He had not even troubled to wait for a few years, for a single year of mourning for the Otto of Brunswick he used to be, before he acted as the new man he thought he was; he practically ran off, with the feel of the crown still warm on his head, to break every oath he had sworn.

He had sworn to respect the boundaries of the Patrimony, the Papal States. Yet he stationed his army in it, causing untold damage. Complaint after complaint came from every town and village about the robberies and the licentiousness of imperial troops, about the burning of houses and even of whole villages —the entire gamut of crimes committed by hostile occupational forces.

Otto had made his henchman, Azzo of Este, his liege of Ancona, Ascoli, Firmo, Camerino, Osimo, Sinigaglia, Fano, Pesaro and Fossombrone and had given that paragon of faithlessness, Diepold of Acerra, the dukedom of Spoleto—yet these towns and lands were not his to give but belonged to the Papal States.

Otto had sworn most solemnly to respect the inviolability of both the Sicilies—but his army, as soon as winter ended, went south, crossed the Abruzzi mountains and broke into Apulia, aided and abetted by Count Pietro of Celano. . . .

Advice, admonitions, warnings, nothing seemed to make the slightest impression on the huge, bull-headed German. Innocent knew by heart the text of his last letter to Otto. He had written it more than four months ago: "The Church has raised you. Remember Nabuchodonosor who in his pride put all his trust in temporal power and was changed from a man to an ox and ate grass. In our time Frederick the First died before he set eyes on Jerusalem and his sons have perished very quickly. Why can you not be satisfied with that which was enough for so many of your predecessors? If you insist on this course, the

Church will not leave you unpunished. Take care then, lest God destroy you and tear out your roots from the land of the living."

The answer came, after much delay: "I am rightly astonished that Your Apostolic Clemency has taken such pains and length to raise so many unmerited reproaches against me. He who distributes Holy Communion has nothing to do with judgment over life and death. I have no intention of interfering in matters spiritual, but in all other matters the decision is mine everywhere."

Pride and sarcasm. But to cap the arrogance and impudence, the letter had been sent from—Naples which the imperial perjurer had conquered. By now most of continental Sicily was in his hands; only the strong castles of the faithful Count of Aquino were still holding out against tenfold odds —Aquino itself, Rocca Secca and San Giovanni.

Innocent went on with his tiger-in-the-cage walk. It was so easy, so human to hate that crude conqueror for whom he had done so much over so many years and who now repaid him with jeering pride. And there was that far subtler danger: the burning anger against himself for having been Otto's dupe, for having himself forged the sword that now wounded him. How great the temptation to act out of that feeling, to avenge on Otto what he reproached himself for, his credulity, his wrong estimation of the man's nature and value. For years he had given Otto preference over Philip of Swabia, until the German princes had forced his hand. Otto, after all, was not a Hohenstaufen, that terrible family from which nothing but trouble came to the Church and the world. Yet here was the proof that Otto was worse than any Hohenstaufen. . . . The role of dupe was galling to the lowliest of men.

The Pope knew exactly what he *wanted* to do. The tug toward action, immediate and deadly, was almost overwhelming. But as long as his motives were not pure, as long as injured self-esteem or injured pride could poison the root of a decision, he must not make it.

What did God want of him? That alone was the question that decided the issue. But there was no sign, no answer to hours of agonized prayer, not from within and not from without. He was wrestling with God for a decision as Jacob wrestled with the angel for a blessing.

A letter from young King Frederick had arrived, smuggled through the area already occupied by Otto's troops. He had a son now, little Henry whom he recommended to the Pope's prayer and care. But how, Frederick asked, could he rejoice at this event, the cause of pride and joy to the least of his subjects, when a powerful enemy was marching against him, threatening to destroy him, and that enemy the new Emperor, crowned by the Pope's own hands? What would the Pope do to save him from this Behemoth, lumbering down upon him with irresistible strength?

Could there be anything more painful and indeed shameful than to be unable to render help to those for whom one was responsible?

And yet . . . there was, perhaps, still the possibility that Otto would stop now; that he would content himself with continental Sicily. There was still the possibility of a compromise.

Slowly Innocent walked off the terrace and back to his study, where a secretary was waiting for him. "His Eminence Cardinal Hugolino of Ostia begs to be received in audience as soon as possible, Your Holiness."

Wearily, Innocent sat down. He nodded, and the speed with which the secretary withdrew mirrored the cardinal's fretting impatience.

He came in almost at once, a little flushed and his eyes blazing.

"News?" the Pope asked curtly.

"Yes, Holy Father. The gravest news. First: King Frederick has made an offer to the Emperor to cede all Apulia to him as well as his paternal heritage in Germany—the dukedom of Sivabia—if the Emperor will desist from an attack against the island of Sicily."

The compromise. And coming directly from Frederick, so the young king could never complain that he had been forced into it by papal interference.

"The source is reliable?" Innocent asked.

"The Bishop of Capua was present when the letter arrived at imperial headquarters."

"So that's how you know about it," the Pope said. "Not through a letter from King Frederick."

"He may have written to us," the cardinal said, "but if he has, the letter did not get through as his previous one did."

"Is there any news about the Emperor's reaction?"

"Yes, Holy Father. The Emperor read the letter aloud publicly, he laughed, threw it on the ground and spat on it."

"The imperial manners are regrettable," said the Pope coldly. "Has he given an answer in writing?"

"He intends to give no answer at all. But he signed an agreement with Pisa that same day."

"Galleys?" the Pope asked quickly.

The cardinal nodded. "Two hundred Pisan ships are to assemble at the port of Procida next spring."

The Pope rose. "I have asked God for an answer and He has given it to me—" he said. "It is the same answer He gave to Samuel: 'It repenteth me that I have made Saul king'—a ban against Otto the Fourth."

The cardinal shivered. He had known the Pope all his life. They had played together as children. They had risen together in the service of the Church and there was so much similarity in their characters that they used to joke about it, although it was not very surprising, really, as they came from the same family, although from different branches. But Innocent III could no longer be identified with Count Lothario of Segni. No other man in the whole world wielded such power as he. And now the lightning had struck. The cardinal had expected it to happen and he knew that he himself would probably have done the same thing. But the excommunication of an emperor was bound to shake the entire Christian world. With its proclamation Otto the Fourth became a spiritual leper and all his subjects were released from the bonds of loyalty and obedience.

But the Pope was quite calm now. The decision was made and he went into action. He rang the bell. "All the cardinals, archbishops and bishops in Rome will assemble in the main hall of the Lateran tomorrow morning at ten o'clock," he told the secretary. "A proclamation will be made to the people to assemble at noon in the Basilica and on the square to hear the curse on Otto of Brunswick, formerly Emperor, and to receive our blessing. Go, and send in Prelate Cortano."

Cortano, head of the department of correspondence, came in within a moment.

"I shall dictate letters for the rest of the day and the better part of the night," the Pope said. "See to it that there are enough secretaries at hand and have the first one sent in now." As the prelate withdrew, Innocent turned to the cardinal. "I want you to stay with me for the time being. The Bull comes first. Then I must write to the German bishops and to the German princes. You know them well. I may need a word or two of advice from you. Where is that first secretary? Ah, here he is. Get up. Sit down. Write."

The Latin words flowed easily and swiftly, every sentence clear, eloquent, polished and deadly. Otto's deeds were enumerated, one by one and each crime called by its name; perjury, breach of peace, bloodshed in an unjust cause, disobedience, greed, acts unworthy of a Christian ruler. . . . Piece by piece the crown was hammered off the giant's head, its precious stones coming down in a sparkling rain to be trodden underfoot. The ermine fur of the coronation cloak was torn off in strips and under the imperial trappings a huge, clumsy body revealed, covered with shame and the livid spots of putrefaction.

The great anathema was spoken over Otto of Brunswick, he was deposed as unworthy and accursed, and all his subjects, princes, dukes, counts and barons, knights, squires and free men were released of their allegiance to him. No one, on pain of excommunication, was to stand by him, to give him help, assistance, food or shelter. About Otto of Brunswick and around him was death and damnation. Tomorrow it would be proclaimed to the clergy and the people of Rome; and on the back of a hundred horses and in many ships the terrible curse would travel to all Christian countries.

As soon as the Pope had spoken the last word the secretary hurried off to have the document copied and recopied. That work would go on all night.

A new secretary was sitting in front of the Pope to take down the letter to the German bishops and abbots. Within a few weeks they would have to read the Bull from the pulpits of their cathedrals and abbeys, in Cologne and in Munich, in Meissen and Trier, in Aix-la-Chapelle and Mainz, in Magdeburg and Jülich, in every single diocese of the huge realm. Powerful men would whisper behind closed doors in Speyer and Worms, in Basle and Vienna.

There was a moment of hesitation—a fairly long moment—before the Pope dictated the name of the man who was entitled to wear the imperial crown. It was not easy to pronounce the name of a Hohenstaufen. But there was no choice, not now, not any longer.

The letter to the German princes was a masterpiece. Cardinal Hugolino of Ostia who knew most of them personally and had been in constant correspondence with every one of them listened with an admiration akin to awe. Many of these men had always been against the rough, arrogant ruler of Brunswick. Others would accept the new Emperor because he was still half a child and therefore much less likely to interfere seriously in their own spheres of power. But even Otto's closest friends and allies would find it difficult to resist the relentless logic of the letter and particularly the stern warning that a man like Otto,

147

who did not hesitate to break a solemn oath still warm on his lips to make war against a great German prince, the King of Sicily, without the slightest provocation, was not likely to show much respect for *their* rights and privileges once he returned to Germany. . . .

At ten o'clock at night the cardinal asked for permission to retire. He had not eaten so much as a crumb of bread since breakfast. The Pope had not either, but he granted permission and began to dictate a letter to the King of France. Philip Augustus was a shrewd man and an efficient one; he had sent several letters to Rome, warning against Otto, some of them years ago. Not exactly surprising—considering that Otto was a nephew of King John of England, the bitter enemy of France. Nevertheless . . .

". . . I admit freely that you understood him better and earlier than I did. . . ."

The Frenchman was a good ally, although he had only one arm free; the other was raised against King John, as self-willed, brutal and arrogant a ruler as Otto, though weaker of character. But how obstinate a weak man could be! Things in England were still at their very worst; all bishops had had to flee into exile and hundreds of priests were in prison while the royal robber ransacked abbeys and monasteries at will. Any day now the Emperor might give similar orders. . . .

Sighing, Innocent finished dictating the letter to King Philip Augustus and at once began a list of high-ranking prelates who would travel to Germany in support of the Bull and the letter to the German bishops.

The letter to Livonia . . . He was dead tired. His voice was hoarse. But Bishop Albert of Riga needed his consent to the measures he suggested for the conversion of that country. Christ would not leave him without immediate support, therefore His Vicar could not afford to delay it.

He tore the rays of his attention away from other problems and concentrated them on cold, faraway Livonia as if there were no other place in the world.

When he rose at two o'clock in the morning his legs almost gave way and yet he knew that sleep would not come to him for a long time. Only the outer shell was tired. The mind, sharp and clear as ever, would not be appeased.

"I want someone to read to me," he told the varlet who helped him undress. Sitting in bed, propped up with cushions, he waited until a young Benedictine entered, knelt and kissed the ring.

148

"Sit down. Take the Bible. Read . . . read from the First Book of Samuel. The fifteenth chapter."

The young monk opened the book and read. " 'And Samuel said to Saul: The Lord sent me to anoint thee king over his people Israel; now therefore hearken thou unto the voice of the Lord . . .' "

"Go on a bit further. To verses ten and eleven."

" 'And the word of the Lord came to Samuel, saying: It repenteth me that I have made Saul king; for he hath forsaken me, and hath not executed my commandments. And Samuel was grieved, and cried unto the Lord all night. . . .' "

"All night," the Pope repeated, nodding. Ten verses only between a man made king and unmade because he had disobeyed. "Another ten verses or so later. When Samuel speaks again."

" 'And Samuel said: Doth the Lord desire holocausts and victims, and not rather than the voice of the Lord should be obeyed? For obedience is better than sacrifices . . .' "

How difficult it was, for one crowned, to obey, to obey even his own words, his own sacred oath. . . .

" 'Because it is like the sin of witchcraft, to rebel: and like the crime of idolatry, to refuse to obey. Forasmuch therefore as thou hast rejected the word of the Lord, the Lord hath also rejected thee from being king.' "

"Now read what the prophet Ezechiel says to Pharao, in the twenty-ninth chapter."

" 'Thus saith the Lord: Behold I come against thee, Pharao, king of Egypt, thou great dragon that liest in the midst of thy rivers and sayest: The river is mine, and I made myself. But I will put a bridle in thy jaw . . .' "

The pride of kings, through the centuries, the millennia. Would they never learn?

" '. . . and I will cast thee forth into the desert . . .' "

"A little further on," the Pope said.

" 'Therefore thus saith the Lord God: Behold, I will bring the sword upon thee; and cut off man and beast out of thee. And the land of Egypt shall become a desert and a wilderness. . . .' "

"Enough," the Pope said. And the young monk saw with terror and anguish that he was crying bitterly, yet without a sound.

Sleep would not come. Praying was arid and for that very reason not to be abandoned.

The burden of the world was heavy on his soul. Wherever he looked he could see the enemy at work. Eight years ago the

149

Christian army had gone on crusade, but instead of landing in Palestine to free the places most sacred to every follower of Christ, the leaders decided, on their own, to attack Byzantium. For such was the advice of the Doge of Venice, Dandolo, ancient beyond human span, and blind, yet still greedy for booty. By the grace of God some good came of it nevertheless, and once more the East was reunited and the Robe of Christ seamless again. But for how long, men being what they were?

Islam, more powerful than ever, was in full possession of the entire northern coast of Africa, of a great part of Spain and even of parts of Sicily.

England was under interdict, with King John still regarding his fancies as supreme law and keeping his people under the rod of tyranny. That would change, certainly, but meanwhile the people could not receive the sacraments, the Lord's Body was withheld from them, no one could marry validly, no one be buried in hallowed ground.

And as if that were not enough, strange sects were forming, springing up like poisonous fungi in many countries. The worst by far were the Catharoi or Albigenses, who taught the pernicious dualism of Manes in a new form and infected tens of thousands of people. They denied the Incarnation of Christ and the Resurrection and declared the entire visible world to stem from Satan instead of God. "Purity" was all that mattered to them and they regarded marriage not as a sacrament, but as legalized prostitution. For ten years they had disregarded every warning. Then one of these fanatics murdered the papal legate, Pierre de Castelnau, and at long last the King of France decided to act against them. But the methods of his commander, Simon de Montfort, were downright barbarous. He conquered, not for God, not even for his king, but for himself.

Worst of all: within the Church things were not as they should be, and stern measures had to be taken against many prelates and priests whose ways of life made a mockery of their holy station. Had it not been for them, the Albigensian fanatics, mistaking sterility for purity, would never have become so powerful.

All that . . . and now the ban on the Emperor, the very man whose duty it was to protect the Church as its strong right arm.

Essential, inevitable as it was, the ban was certain to have the most frightful consequences. "And the Land of Egypt shall become a desert and a wilderness. . . ."

The Pope groaned. The barque of Peter was in a terrible storm. He had to steer it and no one, not even Hugolino of Ostia, must see him shaken. Yet in his heart he felt utterly powerless and incapable of stemming the flood rising against him. And for the first time in his life he prayed as the apostles did in the storm on Lake Genesareth: "Lord, save us, we perish."

He woke up with a start. And through the haze of familiar things around him he still saw what he had seen in his dream: the huge form of the Lateran Basilica horribly aslant, so much so that its fall was inevitable. Yet it did not, could not fall. There was someone holding it up and slowly pushing it back to safety, a man, a little man, disheveled, in a ragged, grayish brown robe; a beggar.

Suddenly he knew he had seen that man, not in a dream, but in waking life. The little beggar who had suddenly turned up on the terrace, babbling something about a Rule he had made and a permission he wanted.

Innocent III rose from his bed. There was work to be done. Mass first; then the examination of the Bull, of the letters to the German bishops and princes, to the King of France, to Bishop Albert of Riga, the dispatching of the prelates to Germany, the audiences to the chamberlain, to the Master of the Sacred Palace; the address to the clergy assembled in the main hall at ten, to the people assembled on the square at noon. . . .

Horribly, horribly aslant . . . and that little man . . . sometimes God spoke through the medium of a dream. There had been nothing in his own mind that could have suggested his dream of that strange little man holding up the falling Church. He tried to remember whether the man had given his name or the name of the place he came from and the word "Assisi" came back to him. Assisi? Ascoli? No, Assisi.

He rang the bell. "Yesterday, in the morning hours, I was disturbed by a man of small stature, bearded, in very poor clothes, resembling those of a peasant rather than an ecclesiastic. I believe he hails from Assisi. He was expelled by the guards under Count Vitale. Ask the count whether he knows anything about him. I want the man found and brought to me."

"Yes, Holy Father."

But in the afternoon of the same day, after the tiring ceremonies in the Basilica and the address to the people massed on the square, the secretary came to report that no one knew anything about the man and that he could nowhere be found.

151

CHAPTER EIGHTEEN

"You couldn't have chosen a worse moment," said Cardinal Giovanni of San Paolo. "And what's more, you ought to know it. You were present with us at the Lateran and you must have gathered some idea of what is going on there."

Bishop Guido of Assisi nodded. "There is history in the making, and I for one feel like thanking God on my bended knees that it isn't I who has to make it. I feel intensely sorry for the Holy Father. . . ."

"Our entire policy in these last years—" The cardinal broke off. "I mustn't," he said, smiling. "I keep forgetting that I have no longer much share in matters political."

"That must be a strange thing for you," Bishop Guido said, "after all those years under Pope Celestin, when it was really you who formed Church policy."

"The Pope was ninety," the cardinal said. "And yet, you know, his mind was clear as polished silver. . . . *Tempi passati.* Innocent III is a very strong man, a good man, too. Have you read his ascetic writings? You should, you know—"

"I didn't know he had published anything," Bishop Guido confessed. "And my work in Assisi . . ."

"Of course. I understand. He has also written six treatises on the Mass and he is probably the finest expert on canonical law the Church has had for a long time. Hugolino of Ostia told me he dictated the entire Bull against Otto alone and in one day. That kind of thing usually takes weeks and, often enough, months of preparation. But he works too hard and he doesn't delegate details to others. Hugolino of Ostia admits it and he is the Pope's right hand. Another very strong man. This ban, incidentally, is an extremely dangerous thing."

"From what the Pope told us today it was inevitable. The way he spoke and looked! Like destiny incarnate."

"It was inevitable, I agree. But Otto won't give in. And if even a part of his leaders remain faithful to him, he may march on Rome, and massacre us all."

"You really think he is capable of that?"

"Certainly. He has nothing to lose."

"But the man's supposed to be a Christian!"

"Ambition has made a murderer and a pagan out of many a

Christian. You can be quite sure that Innocent has thought of that possibility. He will probably stay where he is, in spite of it. A lesser man might flee to France."

"But there is bloodshed in France as well."

"So there is, though only in the South. In any case, you can imagine what it's like in the Lateran, at present. As I said: You couldn't have chosen a worse moment to ask for this audience."

"But I didn't choose it, Eminence. It . . . it just happened that way."

"You've been here for more than a week, friend."

"But I only came across Francis and his merry men yesterday night. And I had no idea he was in Rome, still less that he would try to see the Pope on his own. It's just like him, though. By the way, I am most grateful to you, Eminence, for giving them shelter here."

"Not at all. But what a foolish thing to do . . . to try to storm the Lateran!"

"Oh, quite," Bishop Guido agreed. "And that's what people always seem to think of Francis—at first. Who but a fool would try to see the Holy Father without an appointment, without an introduction from anyone. But when I told him so yesterday, he said: 'I have read nothing in the Gospel about who introduced the poor lepers to our Lord. They simply went up to Him and shouted for help and He heard them and cured them.' "

The cardinal smiled. "Unanswerable," he said, amused.

"Exactly."

"Even if I could get him in to see the Pope for a minute or two," the cardinal said, "I don't see why this Francis should be allowed to found a new Order of his own—because that's what it is, let's be frank about it, even if he speaks only of a brotherhood. There are good and well-established Orders enough that he and his men could join. In fact it might do some of those Orders a great deal of good to get fresh blood pumped into them and, on the other hand, it would rid your little man of some of his . . . errh . . . exaggerations."

Bishop Guido said innocently: "Why doesn't Your Eminence tell him so? He's waiting in the next room."

The cardinal grinned openly. "In other words you want him to give me the withering answer directly. Very well. I will ask him. But I warn you, dear old friend. I have seen so many of these would-be-reformers come and go. I'm not an easy man to impress with a few pat answers."

"Don't bother about the answers, then, Your Eminence," Bishop Guido said cheerfully. "Just look in the man's heart."

The cardinal glanced at him sharply. "Very well. I'll be back in a minute." And he walked briskly into the next room.

Bishop Guido remained where he was. The cardinal's minute began to stretch out. The bell of San Paolo chimed and chimed again and then a third time. Outside, a carriage arrived for His Eminence. His crest was painted on it, the famous crest of the Colonna.

At long last the cardinal returned. "Come along, friend," he said. "We must leave immediately. I have ordered my carriage."

"The carriage is here, I saw it from the window," Bishop Guido said. "But where are we going?"

"To the Lateran, of course. I must get Brother Francis an audience with the Pope. . . . Why are you laughing?"

"I'm not laughing," the bishop protested. "But it's strange, how he always gets what he wants." They were descending the staircase.

"He didn't with me," the cardinal said grimly.

"Didn't he? Here we are, hurrying to try and get him his audience . . ."

"Oh, that, yes. But I didn't join his brotherhood."

Looking straight ahead and firmly pressing his lips together, Bishop Guido managed to keep a sober face.

"I am fully aware that Your Holiness is pressed harder than ever with business of state," the Cardinal of San Paolo said. "And I crave Your Holiness' pardon and so does the Bishop of Assisi here. If in spite of that, I plead most strongly that you grant an audience, however short, to Brother Francis . . ."

"Brother Francis," Innocent III said quickly. "That's right. That was the name. Where is he?"

"He is waiting in my house," the cardinal said. "I hope Your Holiness will forgive him for his somewhat . . . spontaneous attempt to see you. He has given me the Rule he has written down for his brotherhood. . . ."

"I've had the city combed for him," the Pope said, and it was difficult to decide whether he was jubilant or furious. "Bring him here at three o'clock. In the meantime I will read that Rule of his."

Cardinal and bishop left in a flurry.

Count Narcisio Vitale saluted the cardinal and the bishop, but as he came up from his bow, he saw the small streak of grayish brown between the scarlet and the purple and recognized the hermit or monk or whatever the man was. His eyes popped. Twenty of his agents had been searching for the man in vain and here he was, walking along as unconcernedly as when he entered the Lateran for the first time.

The count rushed up to the group. "Your Eminence . . . my lord Bishop . . ." he spluttered, "His Holiness has given orders that this . . . this person should be brought to him at once. . . ."

"But of course, my dear Count," the cardinal said genially. "We are on our way to His Holiness now."

"I see," Vitale stammered. "Ex-exactly. Yes." And he followed, perspiring profusely.

The Pope received them in one of the smaller audience rooms. To their surprise he had several cardinals with him: Hugolino of Ostia, Cenzio Savelli and the Cardinal Archbishop of Palestrina.

Innocent's face was stern. He had read Francis' Rule and he had shown it to the cardinals; it demanded absolute poverty, without any provision for even the most immediate future. Everything was left to the care of the Lord and to the charity of man. One man might be able to live like that, if he was holy enough. But a whole brotherhood of saints was more than one could hope to find on earth. Even the austere Cistercians could exist only because their order owned large estates. Besides . . . in his dream, one man had held up the falling Church. One man. Not a brotherhood.

"My dear son," Innocent said, "I have read your Rule. But the life you and your brothers lead seems to me too severe."

Dismayed, pained, deeply disappointed, Francis was for a moment at a loss for words.

The Pope saw it. "I do not doubt your zeal and enthusiasm," he went on in a gentler tone. "But one must think of those who will come after you and may not be quite as zealous and enthusiastic."

By now Francis had recovered from the first thrust. "Lord Pope," he said, "I depend entirely upon my Lord Jesus Christ. He has promised me eternal life and happiness. How then could He deny us the simple necessities of life in the present?"

"Quite true, my son," Innocent replied indulgently. "But man's nature is weak and seldom able to maintain the same purpose for long. You had better go and pray that God will reveal to you how far your wishes are in accordance with His will."

For one moment the eyes of Innocent and Francis were in silent conversation. Then Francis knelt, kissed the ring, rose and withdrew from the glittering assembly.

Bishop Guido drew a long, sighing breath.

The Cardinal of San Paolo stood in frowning silence.

But Innocent III asked almost airily: "What do Your Eminences think?"

There was a pause. Then the Cardinal Archbishop of Palestrina said in a rumbling basso profundo: "Impossible."

Gentle old Cardinal Savelli smiled. "It is a beautiful thought, and the man is sincere. I wish it *were* possible to give him what he asks for."

"But is it?" asked the Cardinal of Ostia. "Wouldn't it be a terrible pity if so much zeal and enthusiasm were defeated by the incapability of followers to live up to the Rule? Yet that is what is bound to happen."

"And then he would turn sour," the basso profundo voice chimed in. "And a saint turned sour is as near to heresy as makes no difference. Another Waldo. The egg from which another nest of Albigenses will be hatched."

"Human nature . . ." began Cardinal Savelli.

But Giovanni of San Paolo could contain himself no longer. "Your Holiness," he said, "and Your Eminences . . . let us think what we are about to do. All this man wants is for himself and his followers to be allowed to live after the manner of the Gospels. Therefore if we say that such a way of life is impossible, we declare that the Gospels cannot be followed. And that would be blasphemy against Christ."

There was complete silence.

Bishop Guido of Assisi manfully fought an insane urge to giggle. So it had happened to San Paolo too, that unfathomable, infectious thing that overcame those who came in touch with little Francis. Canon Pietro Cattaneo or Father Silvester, Canon Groga or His Eminence Giovanni Colonna, Cardinal of San Paolo—once little Francis got hold of them they were lost. They carried away with them something of the man's own enthusiasm; they were ready to defend him and his cause against anybody anywhere. And their number included the Bishop of Assisi as well. He, too, had balked at the idea of absolute poverty, it was not realistic, it simply would not work. Even if the individual had no property, the brotherhood as such should have. But Francis replied, "If we have property, we must have arms to defend it; and from property comes strife with neighbors and relatives. . . ." There was no answer to that, not

156

when on one's very desk lay the documents of two most disagreeable lawsuits.

But what would the Pope say to San Paolo's bold words? Everybody looked at Innocent.

The Pope seemed to be quite unmoved. He was the judge, listening without expression to the various testimonies given before him, withholding his own view. But quite suddenly he spoke: "Let Brother Francis be recalled."

There was a flurry of steps and silence again and after a while Francis came back with alacrity, knelt, and at a gesture of the Pope rose.

God forgive me, Bishop Guido thought, but he looks as if he had just dined and wined with all the saints in heaven.

"Lord Pope," Francis said before anybody had time to address him, "I have carried out your command and talked to God, and now there is a story I must tell you and the lord cardinals: Once upon the time there was a woman living in the desert. She was poor, but beautiful, and the king happened to see her and married her and she gave him many sons. . . ."

The Cardinal Archbishop of Palestrina cleared his throat, as if he were going to interrupt, but when he saw the Pope listening intently he decided to reserve his remarks for later. An amazing thing, really. The whole world was in turmoil and here they were, listening to some outrageous fairy story from a young man who insisted he wanted to be a beggar and to collect more beggars around him. A sincere enough man, no doubt, a devout man, certainly. But what was the importance of it all?

". . . but as the king did not call her or her sons to his court, she sent those who were old enough to see him there. The king saw that they all had a likeness to himself and asked them whose sons they were. So they said, 'We are the sons of the poor woman in the desert.' And the king embraced them and acknowledged them as his sons with much joy and said, 'Do not worry, my sons. If I can feed so many strangers at my table, how much more you who are my own sons.' And he sent to the woman and asked for all his sons to be brought to his court as soon as they were fit to travel."

Innocent took it all in: the story, so silly and so wise, so childlike and yet such pure theology; the way the man told it, the eloquent, passionate movements of head and hands and feet. Something of a jester about the man, and something of a dancer. Old Savelli had tears in his eyes. Facile emotions? No. The thing was genuine, from the depths. Old Savelli had a right to his tears.

157

Sharp as a blade, the Pope's mind put it all together. This beggar was a troubadour, a *Minnesänger,* as they called them in Germany, a "singer of love," but for once here was one who was singing in praise of the Love of God.

"I am the poor woman in the desert," Francis explained merrily. "And I trust my Lord, the King. He will look after my sons."

A jester and a dancer; a beggar and a troubadour; a preacher, a monk, a teller of parables and perhaps a saint: there was no end to the man. If Satan could distort the minds of many to preach against the Church in the name of purity, here was one who could preach for the Church in the same name; here was, perhaps, the antidote against the poison in the veins of Europe, the man to give fresh life to a world grown cold. And therefore this man could be, nay, was the one who held up the falling walls of the Church. And that was all Innocent wanted to know.

"My son," he said aloud, "your request is granted. Go and with your brothers preach as God shall inspire you. And when the Lord has increased your numbers, come back to me and I will entrust you with still greater tasks. Will you promise obedience to me?"

"I will," Francis sang the words.

"It is well," Innocent said. " 'Confirm thou thy brethren.' " He made the sign of the cross over the little man. Francis knelt, crossed himself, too, rose, walked away and was gone.

Into the silence came of a sudden the sound of deep, rumbling laughter and all faces turned toward the Cardinal Archbishop of Palestrina. "Did you see that?" he asked, controlling his laughter with an effort. "Did you see the joy on the little man's face? Holy Father, the man's a child, but he is right and he's right because he is the kind of child he is. And I was a fool."

The Cardinal of San Paolo grinned openly at the Bishop of Assisi.

The Bishop of Assisi grinned back.

Old Cardinal Cenzio Savelli shook his head. "It reminds me of something," he said.

Cardinal Hugolino of Ostia said: " 'And all that heard him were astonished at his wisdom and his answers.' "

"The finding of the child in the Temple!" Cardinal Savelli exclaimed. "That's it. Of course."

"I am glad about your decision, Holy Father," Hugolino of

Ostia said. "God forbid that the Church should have no place for men who wish to live as he does."

The Pope woke from his thoughts. In a voice that seemed to come from very far away he said: "I wish this man could be at my side in the hour of my death."

CHAPTER NINETEEN
A.D. 1211

"Have you packed everything?" Frederick asked sharply.

"Yes, my lord King." The majordomo's smile was greasy. The man was a liar—they all were, and why shouldn't they be? Why stick to a ruler who was finished—for years to come and perhaps forever—before he even started?

"The manuscripts?"

"Yes, my lord King."

"The gold plate? The carpets of my study and of the green room? The queen's possessions?"

"Assuredly, my lord King."

"I shall inspect everything this afternoon. We may start at any moment for Catania. You may go."

The man bowed and retired. Frederick was fairly sure he would never see him again; he would not wait for the inspection, but would leave the palace quickly and vanish like so many others. Like Capparone himself, two months ago, in September, and the Count of Fondi last week. Like the second chamberlain, Massimo, only yesterday, and two dozen servants of the royal household with him. Rats.

Astonishing how quickly news traveled across the island; as if reports of disaster were fumes, the smoke from something burning. Yet the fire was across the Strait of Messina—at least it had still been there yesterday. But it wouldn't be for long. Otto was bound to come. He was slow like many large men, like the ox he was. Slow, but sure. Not for him the surprise attack of a Diepold of Acerra, a hundred knights and a papal legate to make it all legitimate. Perhaps that very raid of Diepold's made him feel that this time nothing must be left to chance.

He had almost two hundred ships at Procida, most of them Pisan galleys. Six thousand knights, each with his own retinue and the Emperor's majesty himself with his bodyguards. Everything.

159

Martino's reports these last weeks had gone from bad to worse. Stores put into the ships. A review of troops. Speeches against the "usurper," the "Pope's baby," the "infamous infant" Frederick. The arrival, in full view of the troops, of a deputation from Emir Ibn Abbad of Jato, with a ceremonial purple cloak for *Imberadour* Otto. Well, perhaps one should not be surprised that Saracens could be as disloyal and opportunistic as Christian princes or prelates.

Grist for the mill of the queen, of course.

Martino had arranged for a chain of messengers from Messina to Palermo. As soon as the first ship from Procida was sighted, the first messenger would speed off from Messina, carrying, instead of a letter, a small piece of red silk. At any moment now Frederick expected the little silken dagger. . . .

The varlet Agostino, somber and sullen, announced the Count of Vandria.

"He may come in." One who had not vanished yet. "Well, what is it, Count? In a low voice, please. Agostino has his ear glued to the door."

"I have been down to the port to supervise the loading of the first crates you sent there and to get the feel of things. The captain is all right, I think, an old enemy of the Emir Iban Abbad, some blood feud as nearly as I could make out. The crew has been sailing with him for several years. No new men on board at all."

"How many altogether?"

"Thirty-five, with the captain."

"And our party?"

"Sixty-two, my lord King, apart from the queen and her ladies."

"You made him swear on the Koran?"

"Yes, my lord King."

Frederick nodded gloomily. "It's a pity we had to start loading the ship. No one in his senses will believe that we're going to Catania. It couldn't be helped, though. Anything else?"

"Only one thing—there's a ship approaching the port."

The king jumped up. "A surprise raid after all!"

"No, my lord King. It's a very small ship. If it is full to capacity it couldn't have thirty people on board. I only mentioned it because it's the first ship to enter Palermo harbor for weeks. She may have sprung a leak and come in for repairs or she may want to buy goods for France, perhaps."

"Possibly. Nevertheless double the sentries all around the palace. Tell Beraldo and come back."

When Roger returned, the king was watching the sentries from the window. "That's one of the things I most dislike about our . . . voyage, Count. We still have a few hundred men on whom I think we can rely. But I can take only sixty with me."

"It will be an advantage to have loyal men here when we return," Roger said.

"Oh, certainly," Frederick said dryly. "But a guard of sixty men isn't much in a strange land. I don't know the Dey of Tunis from Adam. But then, I would have to take fifty thousand with me if I wanted to be safe. The queen, of course . . ." He shrugged his shoulders.

"It must be hard for the queen."

"It isn't exactly easy for me either," Frederick flared up. "I can't help her Spanish qualms about going to the land of infidels and all that rubbish. I wish I needn't have told her, but what else could I do when I had to have her things packed and kept in readiness? The tears, the reproaches . . . as if it were my fault that the Guelph cares nothing about the Pope's ban."

"I've wondered about that. . . ."

"Who hasn't? A full year has passed since the proclamation of the ban, and there he still is, keeping his army together, increasing it for all I know, and lying across Italy like the big dragon over his treasure in that new story of Siegfried and the Nibelungen."

"The dragon was killed," Roger said.

Frederick gave a bitter smile. "So he was. But first Siegfried had to get himself a sword. Nowadays you can't get a sword, except for money, and I haven't got any money. But perhaps I can get hold of a blade forged in Damascus. They are good, I'm told. What a joke, if the Pope's elect should win back his land with it! He won't like it much, but then why didn't he give me a Christian sword? Easy for him to speak big words; but they don't seem to count for much outside Italy. What am I saying: outside the Lateran. If there is one thing I've learned, it is that the Pope with all his pomp is no longer a real power. The princes may pay lip service to him to assuage the consciences of their superstitious subjects, but they will do what suits them best. Either they don't want to stand up against Otto or they don't dare to." He began to march up and down the room as he always did when his mind was keyed up. "In a way I shall welcome the news that the Guelph is coming," he said grimly. "Better an end with terror than a terror without an end. Waiting for a catastrophe to happen is the worst agony I know. Let's get it over with." He stopped abruptly. "There is still an-

161

other way out," he jeered. "To go to Messina, wait for the landing there and die fighting. I told the queen that and she said even that would be better than to seek shelter with the infidels. And why not? She's been a widow before and survived. Maybe Otto will spare her and make use of my son to establish a legitimacy for himself he sorely needs."

"The queen didn't think of that, I'm sure, my lord King."

"How can you be sure? We can't be sure even of our own innermost motives. And the brat means more to her than I do. I told her there was nothing noble or courageous about allowing oneself to be slain when one could avoid it. It's only stupid, it's the last and greatest of all stupidities, for there's no way of repairing it. When you're dead, you're dead."

He may be right at that, Roger thought.

"I despise grand gestures when they please the enemy," Frederick went on. "Otto could ask for nothing better."

I should have left that young Assisan to his fate, Roger thought. What in the name of hell was his name? Francis . . . Francis something.

"Thinking of yourself, aren't you?" the king asked. "Until about a year ago I still felt fairly certain that I could get you your Vandria back. Now I doubt it." The unblinking eyes were as enigmatic as ever. "If you wish to leave my service—you are at liberty to do so."

Roger grinned wryly. "I also have no wish to please the enemy, my lord King. Nor am I given to seasickness. Besides, Tunis should be a new experience."

Frederick grinned back at him. "Very well then. The second load of things should go on board. Leave a few picked men there, too, or the captain may see fit to sail without us, Koran or no Koran."

"Yes, my lord King."

The varlet Agostino came in. "A message, my lord King."

Frederick paled. "Where is the man?"

"In the first anteroom, my lord King. Count Beraldo sends his respects; he says it is a German nobleman, with three of his followers, asking for an audience."

"A German nobleman?" Frederick repeated incredulously.

"The ship," Roger murmured, "the small ship I saw coming in . . ."

The king nodded. "Send in Count Beraldo."

The chamberlain was a colorless man in his early fifties, the kind of man who out of sheer lack of imagination cannot contemplate a change. "The noble knight Anselm von Justingen has arrived, my lord King," he said, and Frederick could not help thinking that he would have announced the arrival of a victorious Otto in exactly the same manner. "He has three squires with him and he comes from Nur . . . Nurberg."

"Nuremberg," the king corrected calmly. "Has he told you the reason for his presence?"

"He insists that he can tell only you, my lord King."

"He certainly won't see me alone, if that's what he is driving at," Frederick said. "My uncle Philip had to pay too dearly for that kind of trust. The audience is granted and will take place in half an hour; but I want thirty armed guards in the main hall, three of them on either side of the throne. Count Vandria will command them. And, Beraldo . . . keep an eye on the four Germans all the time. This may be an attempt on my life."

"My lord King, there are crates and bundles stacked up in the main hall. . . . I do not know for what purpose."

Frederick bit his lip. "Have them taken away," he ordered. "Put them where they cannot be seen. Be quick about it."

The chamberlain bowed impassively and left. The king turned to Roger. "It would be such a simple way out for Otto," he said. "I'm the Pope's elect, but the Holy Father's proclamation is null and void if I'm killed. Justingen . . . that's in Swabia, my own dukedom, the man's my subject, but that doesn't mean much these days. I will take no chances."

Frederick sat down on the throne and looked about him. The main hall had been hastily cleared; there was nothing left to give away the secret of immediate departure. Count Beraldo stood at the door opposite the throne, with four varlets on either side of him. The guards in their armor were in position, with Roger of Vandria on the king's right side, sword in hand.

Frederick's own sword was ready on his knees. He nodded, the chamberlain gave a sign and the door was flung open. "Knight Anselm von Justingen and retinue," Count Beraldo announced.

The four Germans marched in. Anselm von Justingen was a tall, fleshy man, dressed in a dark blue, fur-trimmed doublet. Neither he nor his squires were in armor. As he approached the throne Frederick saw a round face, fair-haired, with intelligent brown eyes. The man walked with the measured dignity peculiar to some stout people. At a distance of four yards from the throne Count Beraldo stopped him by stretching out his staff of office. The German knelt on one knee, rose, and one of his squires, a white-bearded man, gave him a document. He un-

163

rolled it, but when he spoke, he did not look at it. He knew it by heart.

" 'Your Majesty! The Congress of Princes of the German realm salute the most noble Lord, King of Sicily and Duke of Swabia. We, King Ottocar of Bohemia, Archbishop Siegfried of Mainz, Archbishop Albrecht of Magdeburg, Landgrave Hermann of Thuringia, Landgrave Dietrich of Meissen and all others undersigned, empowered by ancient custom to elect our King and Overlord and to enthrone him as Roman Emperor, have assembled in Nuremberg to have council about the common welfare of the realm, to depose Otto of Brunswick for his misdeeds and to elect a new ruler. We are looking to you as the man who to us seems most worthy of such honor, a young man in years, but old in wisdom and experience, endowed with all noble gifts, scion of those august emperors who never spared their lives or riches to increase the empire and to bring happiness to their subjects. And we invite you to leave your kingdom and to come to Germany, to assume the crown of the realm and to defend it against the enemy of your House. All this we do of our own will and election, though taking into account the advice of His Holiness the Pope who has banned Otto of Brunswick publicly and released all princes, noblemen and ministerials of their oath of allegiance to him. And we do so in confident trust in the power and the justice of God. Amen.' Signed and attested by all the princes afore mentioned."

Anselm von Justingen stepped forward and, kneeling once more, gave the document into Frederick's hand.

"Thank you, Herr von Justingen," the king said. "The honor offered to us is great indeed. We must have time to consider it in all its implications." He handed the document to Count Beraldo. "Meanwhile we trust you will enjoy the peace and quiet of our hospitality after what must have been a long and arduous voyage." A nod, both distant and friendly, dismissed the deputation.

Anselm von Justingen's intelligent face could not entirely conceal his surprise at such royal brevity, but Roger could see that he was impressed and so, by thunder, he ought to be. Not every day was a royal and imperial crown offered to a young man of seventeen. But when that young man dryly asked for time to think it over, instead of greedily grasping the supreme prize, and at a moment when he had every reason to believe that all was lost. . . . It was difficult not to roar with joy and laughter. He saw Frederick give a sign to the chamberlain over the heads of the retiring Germans.

164

The door was flung open once more and they marched out, followed by Count Beraldo, all courtly grace and elegance.

Frederick looked at his guards, at every one of them in turn and each man felt that he was taken into special, conspiratorial confidence with his king: Do you see, Roberto? Did you hear that, Ernesto? What do you say to that one, Carlo? That's what things are like, you're on the right side, my man, aren't you?

Then the king rose and left, slowly, quietly, without the slightest sign of excitement. Never before had Roger felt such admiration for him. He ordered the guards to return to their stations and then went to the king's study.

Frederick was lying face downward on a couch, his legs in the air. "How do you think the man got through Otto's blockade?" he asked and then went on, without waiting for an answer: "They sent a simple nobleman and three squires. Clever of them. Such a one can travel without fear of being recognized. What's Otto going to do? He's bound to have heard about the Nuremberg meeting by now. He *must* come and finish me off. And we can't sail north, with all those Pisan galleys about. They'd catch me within a couple of days and Otto could take me back to Germany with him in a birdcage and hang me in sight of King Ottocar of Bohemia, the archbishops and the landgraves. So it's likely to be Tunis for us all the same. We could take Justingen with us. From Tunis we may be able to get to Spain or to France. By St. Mohammed and St. Peter, what is Otto waiting for?"

The answer came two hours later when a man galloped into the courtyard of the palace and only just managed to jump off his horse before it fell, frothing at the mouth.

A minute later Agostino announced Martino.

"Stay," the king told Roger. "I may have to give orders instantly." His eyes were preternaturally bright.

Martino came in, a bow-legged little man with a long moustache in a face full of wrinkles. As he tried to bow he fell on his knees and collapsed.

"Wine," the king ordered. "Quickly."

Roger rushed out, passed on the order to Agostino and raced back. The king had managed to get the exhausted man on a couch and was tearing his doublet open. Agostino came with decanter and goblet, Roger poured the wine and the king dipped his fingers in it, sprinkled a few drops on Martino's face and rubbed the man's temples. Then he put the goblet to his lips. Martino groaned and managed to take a few sips. He opened his eyes. They were so bloodshot that no white showed in them, but he smiled and at once the king smiled back at him.

"Gone," Martino gasped. "Gone . . . north."

"What?" the king shouted. "Martino! Martino! Pull yourself together. . . . No, wait, drink your wine first. There. Now! Talk, man."

"He's had news . . . from Germany . . . deposed . . ."

"I know. I am the Emperor-elect and you'll get everything you care to ask for. The army, Martino, what about the army?"

"Going . . . north . . . except for . . . garrison troops."

Frederick drew himself up. "That mistake is worse than getting oneself banned by the Pope," he said. "The Ox is mad. Roger, tell Beraldo I want the Council of Familiars to assemble within an hour."

"The members are not all in Palermo, my lord King. . . ."

"As if I didn't know! Those who are, of course. I must establish a regency for the time of my absence."

"You are leaving despite the news, my lord King?"

"Holy Jerusalem! Holy Mecca! I'm surrounded by fools. I'm leaving because of the news; as soon as I can, that is. Justingen must come with me. Otto is going to Germany, of course; and so am I, to see that he doesn't get the princes round again. I know them. Like women they'll choose the man who is *there*. We must find out what route I can take so that we don't run into Otto's men by sea or by land. That's your next task, Martino—to find out as much as you can about the Guelph's retreat. We shall travel in his wake as soon as it's possible. And I've got a task for you, too, Roger: you'll go to Lombardy and win as many friends for me as you can. We'll work out the arguments. The best of them is money. I haven't got any, of course, but I think I'll get some through Justingen. He comes from a rich family."

"I think I better go to the port first and get those crates out of the Moslem ship, my lord King."

Frederick threw back his head, laughing. "Good-bye to Tunis," he said. "You're right. How pleased the queen will be! And . . . oh, I almost forgot: I'd better tell them now that I have decided to accept the imperial crown."

CHAPTER TWENTY
A.D. 1212

"More," said Clare, "tell me more, Cousin Ruffino."

The young friar beamed. "There's so much to tell, there is no end to it. Father Francis is like . . . like the sea. I tell you of a thousand ripples glistening in the sun and while I do, a thousand new ones are born."

She was busy embroidering an oblong piece of white cloth. Outside on the Cathedral square the flower market was in full swing and the scent of spring blossoms wafted through the open window on the soft March air.

"I need not ask you whether you're happy in the brotherhood," Clare said. "It's written all over you and it hasn't always been like this with you, has it?"

"I don't think I had a happy day in all my life before I joined him," Ruffino said. "I often thought there must be something wrong with me and, of course, there was."

"No more than with everyone else, which is quite enough," Clare said. "But you didn't laugh very often; that's why I was so surprised when I first heard that you had joined him. They're all so merry."

"I'm learning fast," Ruffino said. "But the worst was my shyness. I almost didn't dare speak to him at all because of it."

"And your parents? Are they still angry?"

"I'm afraid so. But it was no different with Father Francis himself. His father never became reconciled. *Your* parents were not exactly delighted about me either."

"Uncle Monaldo," Clare said. She gave a little sigh, but she was smiling.

"Ah, yes, Uncle Monaldo. He doesn't find it easy to think of a nephew who is a beggar."

"No," Clare said quietly, "and that is why I often feel sorry for him."

"Still, I'm allowed to come and see you and your family from time to time," Ruffino said lightly, and Clare knew that he was still not allowed to pay a visit to his parents' home.

"Please, tell me more about Father Francis."

"He is Brother Francis, really," Ruffino said, "but we call him Father; and he is like a mother to us. No, don't laugh, I really mean it. What father observes everything about every one of his sons? For instance there is Brother—well, one of us who is not very good at fasting, and once, in the middle of the night he cried out that he was dying. Father Francis rose at once and saw that the poor brother was starving. So he got all the scraps of food we had for him, but then the brother was ashamed and wouldn't eat. Father Francis said: 'I'll eat with you. We'll share everything alike.' And they did, until the brother had recovered. Then Father told us that each of us must pay heed to his own nature, as some of us needed more food than others. 'Each one,' he said, 'must eat what his body requires and must not try to imitate those who need less, so that all will have bodies strong enough to serve the spirit. Just as we must guard against too much food which is a hindrance to body and soul, we must also, and even more, beware of too much abstinence. The Lord will have mercy rather than sacrifice.'"

Clare nodded attentively. "One can soon find out about oneself," she murmured. "Tell me . . . is it true that he speaks the language of animals? Of the birds?"

Ruffino hesitated.

"It might well be so," she went on calmly. "I think Adam and Eve could, before the Fall in paradise. It is part of perfection, surely. And Father Francis—" She broke off.

"He loves them," Ruffino said after a long pause. "All of them, I think. Brother Giles says he found a hare once which had caught its paw in a trap and he freed it and carried it to him, and Father said: 'Little Brother Hare, why did you let yourself be tricked like that! Come here.' And the hare hopped straight into his lap, to be comforted."

"Brother Hare," Clare repeated, smiling.

"Oh yes, they're all brothers and sisters to him, and not only the animals. There is Brother Sun and Sister Moon and Brother Fire and Sister Water. With anybody else it would sound funny and all too sweet, like mixing honey with sugar, but it's not a bit like that with him, it's—natural. I don't know why. . . ."

"Because he means it," Clare said, eying her needlework critically.

"You're right, you know, *Sister* Clare," Ruffino said, laughing, and to his surprise she blushed deeply. "We had a pheasant staying with us for a while," he went on, "and there was Father's cicada which always chirped when he told her to and—" He broke off abruptly.

"So it *is* true," Clare said. "I heard about some swallows . . ."

"Yes," Brother Ruffino said, and as she looked up she saw that he had lowered his head.

"Oh, I see," she said softly, "you were present, were you?" He nodded.

"Has he forbidden you to talk about it?"

"N-no. Not specifically. He couldn't. There were so many people present, a hundred, perhaps, or more. But . . . it's difficult to talk about it. It's . . . it's so unlikely."

"Nothing is unlikely with him, except evil," Clare said. "Go on, Ruffino."

"Well, we were in Alviano and he was going to preach, not in the church this time, but out in the open. He was standing on a raised piece of ground so that the people could see him and he asked for silence. Everybody fell silent . . . except the swallows. There must have been a number of nests near by and the birds twittered away and sang, the air was full of the sound. Father Francis was quiet for a while—perhaps that made people think that he understood what the swallows were saying. . . ."

"Perhaps," Clare said.

"And then he spoke up: 'Dear swallows, it is time that I speak. You've had your say. Now you listen to the word of the Lord and keep quiet till the sermon is over.' "

"And they did?"

"They did. When he said, 'Amen,' they started again quite loud, as if they wanted to make up for the time of silence. You can imagine what people said."

"They said he was a saint, of course, and so he is," Clare stated. "And you are feeling shy because you are one of his brothers, and people might talk about you in the same vein, when in your heart you know that you are not a saint, or not yet."

"Clare, you mustn't . . ."

"It's true, isn't it? Can't you forget about yourself and just think of the real glory that is neither yours nor even his, but of the One who made you and him and the swallows?"

He looked at her pensively. "What a pity you are a girl," he said. "If you weren't, I'm sure Father Francis would love to have you."

"Such nonsense," she said severely. "It can't be a pity that I'm a girl because that's what God wants me to be. That's obvious. Of course, if I were a boy, a man, I mean . . ."

Bona Guelfuccio pushed her button nose into the room. "Clare —oh, it's you, Ruffino, I didn't know you were here."

"The countess knows," Ruffino said. "Good afternoon, Aunt Bona."

"Good aft . . . Clare, your mother wants you to put on a good dress and come to the hall. We have a visitor."

"Again?"

"Yes, again, though *he's* never been here before, I think. He's a Sicilian and, my, what an elegant young man! A Count Roger of . . . I've forgotten the rest." Bona Guelfuccio waddled in at last, her eyes sparkling. "Such a funny thing happened," she said. "He was talking to us, Uncle Monaldo and your father and mother and me and, all of a sudden, he jumped up from his chair and said: 'Lady Clare!' and we all looked and there was little Beatrice coming in. . . ."

Clare shook her head. "I don't understand. How did he know my name and why did he think . . ."

"That's exactly what is so funny," Aunt Bona declared. "I asked him, of course."

"Of course," Clare said.

"Well, I *did* want to know. But all he said was that he thought it was you, I mean Beatrice was you or rather . . ."

Clare began to laugh. "You must have mixed that up somehow, Aunt Bona."

"I didn't," the ample lady protested. "He did."

"Beatrice is ten years younger than I am!"

"She does look rather like you when you were her age," Brother Ruffino interposed. "But how could this man know that, when he's never been here before?"

"I really don't know," Clare said, putting her needlework away. "I must go and change."

"Indeed you must," Bona Guelfuccio cried. "But don't frown like that. He is a very handsome young man. Come along. You must excuse us, Ruffino dear—Brother Ruffino, I should say, but that's a little funny, too, me being your aunt."

"Most interesting," Count Monaldo said. "So the young man down there in Palermo is not only gifted but brilliant. We've heard that before, naturally, but then there's so much flattery on the part of interested people. . . ."

"He is more than brilliant," Roger said. "He will form a new age. His own age."

"We could do with a new age," Count Monaldo declared. "Look at the state the world is in. Isn't it, Favorino? Ortolana? It could scarcely be worse. Two emperors at once; first Philip and Otto, now Otto and Frederick . . ."

"Otto," Roger said, "is no longer Emperor."

"Maybe not," Monaldo said wryly, stroking his beard. "But he certainly acts as if he were. We had part of his army passing through on the way to Germany, thousands of them. They created havoc in Perugia and Rieti and Spoleto four months ago."

Roger nodded. "The man is desperate."

"I wonder," Monaldo said with a diplomatic smile. "From what little we hear, there are still many German princes who favor him. And King Frederick—or should I say Emperor Frederick? Not yet, to be sure, he's not crowned yet—well, in any case he is still in Palermo."

"The Pope has called him Emperor in his speeches, lately," Roger said. "And as to where he is now, I cannot tell you."

"Oh, oh, you seem to know more than you can tell us, Count."

Roger raised his brows. He said nothing.

"Have you been in your king's service long?" Count Monaldo inquired.

"It can't be so very long," Countess Ortolana said, smiling. "You are still young, my dear Count, though not quite as young as the king . . . the Emperor, I mean."

"He is in his eighteenth year," Roger said, "but his mind is triple that age. I have never encountered anything like it. Is the new Duke of Spoleto still in Italy?"

"Duke Diepold? I think he has gone to Germany with Emperor—with Otto of Brunswick."

"Wise of him," Roger said coldly. "I venture to say there will be changes in the near future."

"Ah, yes," Count Monaldo said, "but what will they be? That is the question."

"A new Duke of Spoleto is a fairly safe prophecy," Roger told him. "Diepold is not in favor with my master. I must pay a visit to the town."

"I hope you will not be in too much of a hurry about that," Count Favorino said graciously. "We shall be delighted to have you here for a little while. Not that Assisi can offer too much for a young man of the great world like you. . . ."

"I had a strange experience here this morning, when I arrived," Roger said. "I don't like carrying large sums of money with me, so I had my bankers give me a number of drafts on various houses in Lombardy. Now I had been informed that Ser Bernard of Quintavalle was the man to approach about such matters and I paid him a visit at his house. But he seems to have vanished. . . ."

Count Monaldo snorted. "He's given up his house—and his

171

good sense as well. Now he is one of those something-or-other brothers, Friars Minor or whatever they're called, and begs for his living."

"Impossible!" Roger exclaimed incredulously. "Why, I was told he was a very wealthy man. How did he come to lose it all?"

"He didn't," Count Favorino said. "He gave it away."

"To his family?"

"He has no family. He distributed it among the poor."

"Madness, of course," Count Monaldo said. "The poor are poor because they are not intelligent or industrious enough to acquire riches. But nowadays, in this age of general insecurity, it is far more difficult to keep riches together than to acquire them. If a man lacks the intelligence and industry to acquire them, how can he be expected to keep them? Right, Favorino? Ortolana? Madness. But that man is not the only one who was bitten by this new bug. Suddenly quite a number of people seem to have discovered that it's a wonderful thing to throw away all they have and join that brotherhood. The fellow who started it all, Francis Bernardone, was the son of one of the richest men in town. Broke his poor father's heart, too."

"Francis . . . Bernardone . . ." Roger repeated, startled.

But at that moment Bona Guelfuccio appeared with three young girls, the countess began to make introductions and Roger found himself bowing and murmuring the compliments permissible to young and unmarried ladies of nobility. Originality would have been insulting. Only traveling troubadours were allowed to step over the mark. It was just as well. Roger could not have thought of anything original at that moment.

"My daughters Clare, Agnes and Beatrice—but then you've met Beatrice."

"Yes," little Beatrice said eagerly, "he has met me, but he thought I was Clare. Why did you think I was, Sir Knight?"

"And where did you learn to ask such questions, my girl?" her mother said severely.

"I'm sorry, Mother," Beatrice said. "It's only because I am curious." The laughter of the grownups came as a distinct surprise to her. Even Uncle Monaldo almost smiled.

"I must admit I share my niece's curiosity," Bona Guelfuccio said with a high giggle. "How *is* it that you could mistake our little Beatrice for Clare, Sir Knight, when you had never seen any of us before?"

"But he has seen you before, Aunt Bona," Clare said quietly. "And he saw me when I was eight, as Beatrice is now."

"What are you talking about, Clare?" Count Favorino exclaimed. "This noble knight is a Sicilian and has just arrived from Palermo."

"And where did I have the great good fortune of meeting you?" Roger asked breathlessly.

"In Perugia," Clare said. "We met in the dungeon."

"Clare," the countess cried, "what are you saying!"

"But it's true, Mother. Aunt Bona and I went to the dungeon with some food to give to the prisoners from Assisi, and the knight was one of them."

"Perfectly true, my lady," Roger said, "and when you came in the first time you probably saved my life, because some of my fellow prisoners were about to kill me."

"I am glad I came, then," Clare said gravely, lowering her eyes.

"You looked like an angel straight from heaven, and at the sight of you everybody fell silent."

Now this was troubadour language and the countess became uneasy. "This is all most surprising," she said. "Sit down, girls, you make me feel quite nervous standing around in a row like a lot of ducks."

"I'm not a duck, Mother," little Beatrice protested. "I'm like an angel straight from heaven."

"What?"

"Yes, I am. The knight said that was what Clare looked like when she was young, and when he saw me he thought I was Clare. So there!"

"Bona," the countess said, "Beatrice must have a lesson in deportment. Please take her with you and instruct her at once."

Surprisingly, Beatrice curtsied before Roger. "If you will kindly excuse me, Sir Knight," she said solemnly, "I must go now." She then curtsied to the others and walked away so quickly that Bona Guelfuccio, waddling after her, could not catch up with her.

"And how is it that a Sicilian nobleman thought fit to join the burghers of Assisi in their onslaught on Perugia?" Count Monaldo inquired, frowning.

Roger grinned. "I was a knight errant in those days, returning from exile in Germany and ready to join any adventure that came my way. Or, if it pleases you better: I was very young and inexperienced."

"You're still very young," Countess Ortolana said gently.

"But no longer inexperienced, noble Countess. One gains experience quickly at the court of my sovereign." And he began again to extol the virtues of King Frederick, his sagacity and wisdom, his generous ways, his great erudition, his courage in the many trials of the past. The words came easily enough—he had used them so many times before, talking to influential people in town after town, preparing the ground, raising hopes, infusing confidence. He knew it all by heart and he could let his eyes rest, from time to time, on the vision of perfect beauty that was Clare at eighteen, from the masses of fair curls, not yet imprisoned in the close fitting headdress of married women, but flowing freely over her shoulders, to the tiny feet just visible under the hem of her blue robe.

He was thirty and indeed no longer inexperienced. But the few amours, furtive and short-lived, with the dark-eyed beauties of Palermo, receded into oblivion. There was no comparison, there could not be. He felt like a street urchin who was meeting a queen, and only the veneer of good manners saved him from being clumsy and awkward. He had had no intention of recalling the past, or admitting that he had met her before, and he had been furious with himself for exclaiming "Lady Clare!" when he first saw little Beatrice. But there had been no escape when the real Clare recognized him with such certainty, and it never occurred to him to deny his identity. In fact, he felt overjoyed, absurdly, overwhelmingly so, that she remembered him, although she had been a mere child then and had met him together with scores of other men.

"Young King Frederick has a good advocate in you," Count Monaldo said. "And what has he done for you, if I may ask?"

"For me?" Roger had to readjust his thoughts quickly. "His last words to me before I left his presence were: 'After my coronation I shall raise Vandria to a dukedom.'" It was true, too, and did not fail to impress the count.

"He seems to be very different from his father," he said. "Or from his grandfather, to say nothing of the Emp . . . of Otto of Brunswick."

"There is no one like him," Roger said. "As I told you, his reign will be the beginning of a new age."

"In any case the German in him is softened by his Sicilian blood . . . ennobled is perhaps the better word," Count Monaldo said pontifically. "We must hope for the best. It is high time that this poor country of ours should come to some semblance of order again; what with towns warring against each other, burghers thinking themselves better than noblemen, and half-made beggars preaching to the people in the market place and the open fields."

"But, Uncle Monaldo, how can things come right, unless we change our hearts," Lady Agnes said unexpectedly. "Clare says the Little Brothers are doing more good than many prelates."

Roger looked at Agnes. She was quite unlike her sister, pale, fragile, dark-haired, with enormous black eyes, the kind of face one could visualize in a picture with a golden background, in the Byzantine style. Her age was difficult to guess, fifteen perhaps or sixteen—she was certainly younger than Clare.

"The young ladies in our family have a tendency to hold strong views of their own," Count Monaldo said with some acerbity.

"Agnes' opinions and views are usually the same as Clare's," the countess said indulgently, "and both seem to have listened too much to their cousin Ruffino who joined that strange brotherhood last year."

"Didn't you say that Francis Bernardone started it, Count?" Roger inquired.

"Yes," Count Monaldo replied irritably, "and what's more, he managed to get some kind of sanction from Rome for his . . . errh . . . way of life. They say he had an audience with the Pope himself, which is nonsense, of course. Innocent III has other fish to fry."

"Brother Francis did see the Holy Father, Uncle Monaldo," Clare said. "Ruffino . . . Brother Ruffino told me all about it."

"Really, Ortolana, it is quite insufferable the way these girls are always interrupting their elders. . . ."

"I am sorry, Uncle Monaldo," Clare said, "I thought you had finished speaking."

"I had not," Count Monaldo said hotly, and then promptly fell silent.

For some moments no one dared to say anything.

Roger decided to break the ice. "The last I knew of young Francis, he wanted to become a great leader in the military field. Now he seems to have quite different ambitions and it may be just as well. I don't think he would have made a good commander."

"Better a good beggar than a bad commander, eh?" Count Monaldo said dryly.

"However, I don't quite see the logic of what you told me about him and Ser Bernard of Quintavalle," Roger went on, with a mocking smile. "If possessions are to be regarded as an evil, why inflict them on the poor?"

The count laughed heartily. Favorino and Ortalana smiled politely. Clare looked down and said nothing, but Roger saw her pressing her sister's hand as if to say "Don't answer, just let him talk." For some reason it made him angry.

"You don't seem to agree with me, Lady Clare," he said. "Do you really hold such a high opinion of that strange brotherhood?"

"The opinion of ignorant young girls can scarcely be of much interest to you, my dear Count," Count Monaldo said quickly.

"Ah, but it is," Roger insisted. "Anything else would be churlish on my part in the case of a great lady to whom for all I know I owe my very life. Quite a responsibility for you too, Lady Clare. The Saracens say that if one saves a man's life, one must care about what he does with the rest of it."

"I am not a Saracen," Clare said bluntly. After a moment she added: "I will pray for you," and Roger, out of sheer embarrassment, laughed a little louder than he intended to. "You haven't told me yet what you think of my theory regarding the poor," he teased.

"Yes, I have," Clare said. "I said I would pray for you."

This time he could not help showing his anger. "I have been poor myself for many years, my lady," he said, "and I could see no particular advantage to my soul in it. It made me envious and doubting, and I could see no justice in the world. Also I don't think a man is better than his fellows for begging from them."

"Exactly," Count Monaldo said. "Listen to the Count of Vandria, girls."

"Nevertheless," Roger said in a gentler tone, "I am most grateful to you, my lady, for wishing me well."

"It is my duty, Sir Count," Clare said flatly.

Just then the majordomo announced that dinner was ready and before Roger could say anything, Countess Ortolana asked her daughters to retire, which they did after a polite curtsy.

During dinner the talk was confined to matters political and very shortly afterward they all retired. The majordomo showed Roger to his room, where his two servants reported to him.

"Are the horses well provided for?"

They were and so were the servants themselves.

"We shall probably stay here a little longer than I thought we would," Roger said airily.

CHAPTER TWENTY-ONE

The hospitality of the noble Scifis was most enjoyable. The large house on the Cathedral square was run smoothly by a large staff of servants, and more than once Roger thought of the royal household in Palermo, at least as it had been before the king married, where things had been done in the most slipshod manner. There was far more formality here, too, than in easygoing Palermo before the queen established her Spanish customs, or even since then.

The Scifis were a proud family. Even if Count Monaldo's claim that he could trace their name back to old Scipio Africanus was nonsense, there was no doubt that they were one of the finest families in Umbria and decidedly powerful. One needed no excuses for prolonging a visit here.

All was well then; and yet it was nothing. It was a most enjoyable time and thoroughly exasperating. Two weeks—and he had seen Clare only three times and never for a moment alone. What made it worse was that she seemed to manage that in some subtle and courteous way. None of the daughters joined their parents for meals—very well, that was customary with the more old-fashioned type of noble family. In the morning the young ladies had lessons in music and needlework, in the afternoon they went out for lengthy walks in the company of that fat, pug-nosed aunt of theirs and it would have been a grave breach of etiquette to join them.

Yet he knew that her parents liked him and, indeed, why shouldn't they? Even that old grouch Monaldo seemed to take a fairly benevolent attitude toward him, the result of many hours of patient listening to his political ramblings and his lamentations about the deterioration of the nobility's privileges and the rise of plebeian customs as well as plebeian power all over Italy and the world. "My dear boy, if your king does not stop it and stop it soon, the whole of Europe will be a hotbed of power-drunk burghers, heretics and holy beggars, with all the noble families reduced to selling their castles and peddling silk and leather goods." After which one had to assure him that King Frederick would change all that.

He had won over almost the entire family, but not the one who mattered to him and she was as elusive as a mirage.

He told her so when at last he managed to meet her, with the inevitable aunt, just as she was leaving for one of those long walks, and she said quite severely: "It is better to keep away than to hear what one is not willing to hear."

"I promise I will say nothing that could possibly offend you. I have spent hours trying to understand in what way I have incurred your displeasure, and whatever it is, surely there must be forgiveness for one so truly repentant?" That seemed to soften her a little and he hastened to add: "Will you not tell me what I can do to gain favor with you? Not even the Queen of Sicily, proud Spaniard that she is, has treated me with such coldness."

"God forbid that I should act out of pride," she said, looking past him. "But you spoke in an unseemly way of a man of great holiness."

"I? I do not recollect at all. . . . It is true that in political talk I may have mentioned His Holiness the Pope in a way that could perhaps be misunderstood. . . ."

"I am not referring to the Holy Father," Clare said, "but to Brother Francis."

"But your uncle, Count Monaldo, seemed to have views even more severe than I about him. . . ."

"Uncle Monaldo is the head of our family, and I have no right to criticize what he says. Nor would I speak to you about it, if you had not asked me."

"I am glad I did, then, Lady Clare, and I would rather be the poorest beggar in the world, than to know that you are displeased with me."

"If you *were*, I wouldn't be," Clare said, "but I doubt whether that would make you join the Brothers Minor."

Was there a spark of laughter in her eyes? He could not make her out at all. But at least, by raising the right subject he had got her talking. "Perhaps I do not understand him well enough, Lady Clare. I cannot see why it is such a great spiritual advantage to throw away one's possessions—or give them to the poor," he added quickly. "If it is, please enlighten me."

"Can you imagine our Lord Jesus Christ living as a wealthy man on earth?" Clare asked. "Can you see Him trying to accumulate gold and silver and yet be who He was?"

"Perhaps not," he admitted, "but with all due respect, the good and holy Francis is not Christ."

"He is the one whose life comes nearest to that of our Lord of all the people I have known in my life," she said.

He had to break that cool, stubborn resistance, to tear it down at any price. "Well, if he means so much to you, I am glad I saved his life, ten years ago."

178

Her eyes widened. "You . . . saved his life?"

He kicked aside the protest of his honor. She was listening now, and eagerly. "Yes—in the battle of Ponte San Giovanni. I knew the battle was lost and I could have escaped quite easily. But I saw a man trying to run little Francis through the back with his pike and I rode back into the fracas and hit him over the helmet. A moment later I was hit myself and woke up in Perugia, a prisoner like Francis himself. It cost me a year of my life, spent in the dungeons of Perugia. He doesn't know about it."

She said in a quavering voice: "I didn't know how deeply I was indebted to you."

"It was ample repayment to see you come into the dungeon," he said and he almost meant it.

Aunt Button-Nose murmured something, Clare gave him a deep curtsy, the two ladies departed and here he was, satisfied with himself for having made some progress at last and yet not happy about his disclosure. The more he thought about it, the less he liked it. She was grateful to him now for saving another man's life. What good was that to him? Gratitude was the palest of all the aids to love, and the shabbiest. And why should she be so impressed with that strange little man? Holy, she said. Why should it be holy to beg? Christlike! That was only too often the ambition of those who did not have the courage to get on in life, or of dreamers; or both. He remembered Francis in the inn at Spoleto, ill and incapable of rising to meet adventure and danger.

Bah, the girl was passing through a religious period, as well-bred young ladies often did. Let some handsome young priest talk to them about a lovely heaven beyond the clouds and off they went with noble enthusiasm and ardor to "do good," or more frequently, to talk about the "good." Fortunately, that kind of thing became rather boring after a while. There was nothing wrong with Lady Clare that marriage would not cure.

"I have asked the Count of Vandria to stay with us over Easter," Count Monaldo said, "and, I am happy to say, he has accepted."

Count Favorino and Countess Ortolana exchanged glances. Aunt Bona sat bolt upright. They all knew the head of the family too well to say anything. In due course he would tell them more. And so he did. "I have made diligent inquiries about his status, rank and position and I must say that I am entirely satisfied. He is what he says he is, he stands high in his young

179

king's favor and I have reason to believe that he is well off, to say the least."

"You know I have the greatest admiration for your perspicacity, Monaldo," Ortolana said, "but I cannot imagine how you could have found out so much in so short a time."

A little to her surprise, the count seemed to be embarrassed rather than flattered. "I had to use somewhat unorthodox methods," he said stiffly, "precisely because there was no time to make inquiries in Palermo—quite apart from the fact that it is still far from easy to learn what is going on there."

"What *do* you mean?" Ortolana asked.

Monaldo cleared his throat. "I . . . well . . . I went into his room and had a rather thorough look at his luggage."

"Holy saints," Bona Guelfuccio said and was given a withering look.

But Favorino and Ortolana, too, looked dismayed.

"What else could I do?" Monaldo asked crossly. "*You*, of course, did nothing at all, as usual. You let things drift, as usual. Somebody had to do something."

"The man's our guest," Favorino said in a tone halfway between reproach and fear.

"So he is," Monaldo affirmed, "and therefore I am prohibited from committing a hostile act. And, indeed, I didn't. In fact, quite the opposite."

"Well, frankly, I cannot see how ransacking his luggage can be called exactly a friendly act," Ortolana exclaimed.

"Of course you don't see," Monaldo said. "You aren't very clever, any of you. Why did I do it, if you please? Because I wanted to find out whether or not the man was worthy to join his name with that of our family. Surely, if I want to accept a man into our family I am acting in his interest at least as much as in our own."

"I am sorry, Monaldo, but what do you mean?" Bona Guelfuccio asked, goggle-eyed.

The count ignored her. "I am glad to state that I found a letter written by King Frederick, officially recommending him in the most courteous terms as his special envoy, and also a number of bankers' drafts amounting to a fairly substantial sum and signed by the name of Justingen, a man quite well known to be financially reliable, as old Mario Revini tells me. So there is no impediment and we may even consider that his marriage to Clare will be of some advantage to us."

"Marriage to Clare?" asked Bona, her voice absurdly high with surprise.

180

Monaldo turned toward her. "I trust you did not imagine the prolongation of his stay in our house was due to his secret ardor for you, Bona."

Bona Guelfuccio gasped for breath, but Ortolana said: "I don't think Clare cares much for the young knight, Monaldo."

"Cares, cares, who cares what she cares about," the count exploded. "You ought to have reared your daughter to do as she is told by her elders and betters."

Count Favorino peered shortsightedly in all directions.

"She can't hear us," Ortolana assured him. "She is in the garden with her cousin . . . with Brother Ruffino."

"And that must stop," Monaldo said. "She's seen much too much of that wretched young man lately and there's no doubt he's putting wrong ideas into her head. I rely on you to tell her so, Ortolana. Religion is a very good thing, especially for a woman, but it mustn't be overdone. And that young beggar ought to know that a monk or whatever he calls himself should avoid the company of young and susceptible girls. I shall tell him so myself. By the saints, one would think you were all blind! Emperor Otto is banned and young King Frederick is to be crowned in his stead. When he is, he'll reward those who were loyal when he was *not* powerful. That means young Vandria will be a duke. Do I have to persuade you on my bended knees to accept a future duke into our family, and the favorite of the next Emperor to boot?"

"What do you want us to do, Monaldo?" Favorino inquired lamely.

"Nothing," his brother snapped. "You'd only spoil things. Just leave it all to me; and it will be all right by Easter, if not before."

He had never seen her look so beautiful. He could not tear his eyes from her, though for the sake of good manners he gazed through lowered eyelids.

The Cathedral was packed for the Pontifical High Mass of Palm Sunday. Bishop Guido was sitting under his canopy and the ancient ritual was taking its course before the high altar.

Roger had chosen to stand. That way he could move about just a little so as not to miss a single expression, a single movement.

She did not see him. She did not look around, not once. Her eyes were fixed on the altar, even during the sermon, given by one of the canons of the Cathedral. What *did* she see? And was

181

it possible that so sensitive a girl did not feel the presence of a man who could think only of her?

She looked radiant, a queen surrounded by her retinue, a queen far more royal and noble than Constance of Sicily. She was dressed like a queen too, all golden and shimmery, from her magnificent, jewel-studded headdress to the tiny golden shoes embroidered with pearls.

Roger had seen her first when the family assembled in the main hall before proceeding to the Cathedral, and he observed that even her parents looked startled when she appeared. Little Beatrice's eyes widened and she whispered to him: "That's her best dress. But today is only Palm Sunday. What is she going to wear for Easter?"

Little Beatrice was right. Such beauty could not be surpassed, the very riches of Cathay could not enhance the glory of her appearance. She was seated between her mother and Agnes, the whole family grouped together as families were all over the church.

The singing swelled to a note of triumph, the Lord was riding into Jerusalem on an ass' colt and all the people shouted Hosanna; from afar threatened the voice of Caiaphas that it was better that one man should die than that the whole nation should perish, but the people's voices rose again, shouting triumphantly.

The sanctuary was filled with palm branches, they were blessed and the people went forward to the altar rails to receive them. Count Monaldo among them, and Count Favorino and the countess and the girls, Agnes and Beatrice, who was not much bigger than the palm she was given. But Clare stayed alone in her seat, immobile, the golden statue of a goddess with a face of ivory, of snow, and her cheeks wet with tears. A girl might cry like that on her wedding day, when she left the home of her parents forever and the happy past seemed to crumble to pieces behind her. But why did Clare cry? Perhaps they had told her about him and that they had given their consent? Old Monaldo Scifi said they would tell her "in due course," whatever that meant, though no engagement could be made official in Lent. Don't cry, my Queen, my beautiful Queen, I will make you happy beyond anything you can conceive and your pale dreams will fade into the mist of that halfway-world between childhood and womanhood, where they belong.

But still she wept.

Then a strange thing happened. The bishop himself rose from his throne, he took a palm branch and came down the altar steps and walked toward her. She looked up, startled, and sank on her knees and he gave her the palm and turned and walked back again. It was a lovely thing to watch and yet Roger felt a shiver go through him, he did not know why. The sight of the mitred old man bending over her with the palm . . . it was as if he were blessing her, as if she were ill, were dying, it was all wrong and he did not like it. Yet she seemed happy now, the tears were forgotten and she even smiled a little.

What was it about her that made him watch out for the tiniest of details, why was every emotion, every movement a thing of importance? Love, they called it, but what was it that made the difference between her and every other woman he had set eyes on? It was not because she resisted him, although that spurred his desire. Nor even because she was so beautiful. There was a mystery about her, a secret, some magic of her own, yet it was the very opposite of what a man thought of at the sound of that word. Could there be such a thing as the opposite of a witch?

But they were forming the procession now and the chanting rose to sweet and powerful majesty: "Fear not, O Daughter of Sion; behold thy King cometh to thee. . . ."

She wore her golden dress all day. And once he managed to speak to her. Rather, Count Monaldo managed it, calling her as she passed through the main hall on the way to her room.

"Lady Clare," Roger said, "I have acquired the permission of your parents to give you a small present. Oh, nothing of great value, no more than a token of my admiration. And here it is." He gave her a small flagon of crystal, filled with a golden brown liquid. "I know you do not care for Saracens and their customs," he said, smiling, "but this may be one thing where your sense of beauty will allow you to make a concession. It is a perfume from the very land of perfumes, and even there they say it is the finest there is. They call it the Perfume of Heaven, and an old Arab sage told me how it was blended. It contains the essence of royal roses and Persian roses, sweet basil from Samarkand, the petals of the zedrat tree of Tabaristan and of the Albanian water lily; the triple essence of Indian aloe; musk from Tibet and ambra of Sichr. And Hassan ben Mubarak swore, by all that is holy to him, that there is nothing like it in the world. My king owned three such flagons, and of his kindness he gave me one. No perfume in the world can be worthy of the glory of your hair. But this one comes as near to it as is possible."

She was caught unawares, the flagon pressed in her hands. Before she could find the words for a polite refusal, Count Monaldo said sternly: "As my niece seems to be at a loss for a suitable expression of her gratitude, allow me to tell you in her name as in that of her entire family that we feel much honored in three ways: that you have found a member of our family worthy of such a present; that the present comes through you from the hands of the king; and that it should be a thing of such rare value." After which there was no way of refusing it.

Clare curtsied deeply and slipped away.

Count Monaldo smiled. "It is all shyness, my dear Count. Set your mind at rest."

But Roger's mind did not find rest and he could not find sleep easily that night.

"Aunt Bona . . ."

"Who is it?"

"Shshsh . . . it is time to go."

After a series of divers noises, sighs, coughings, murmurings and the pushing of chairs Bona Guelfuccio appeared in the door, fully dressed. "Clare, my dear, are you quite sure you—"

"Shshsh . . . follow me, Aunt Bona. On tiptoe."

They made their way down the main stairs. Once the voluminous lady slipped, caught herself and broke into a nervous giggle. Claire pressed her nails into her palms and said nothing.

In the main hall they suddenly stopped. They could hear footsteps outside the house—a servant on night guard.

"We must use the rear door," Clare murmured.

"We can't," Bona Guelfuccio whispered. "It's locked."

Clare shook her head and gave her aunt a sign to follow her. To Bona's surprise she crossed a narrow corridor and went down the stairs into the basement. There was another door here, leading to the back street.

The two women stopped in their tracks. The door was blocked against intruders with a pile of huge stones.

"I knew something like this would happen," Aunt Bona murmured. "We can't get out. Now you be reasonable and . . ."

Clare leaped forward as if she were going into battle. She tore the uppermost stone away and laid it aside. She seized the next stone and put it beside the first.

Bona stared as if she were seeing her niece for the first time. The stones were big. She remembered how Tullio, the gardener, had piled them up, sweating and cursing. Yet Clare was dealing with them as if they were pebbles, her movements so sure and quick and yet so cautious that there was no noise. Twenty . . . twenty-five, and still they came. There was something almost terrifying about the speed with which Clare was working.

At last the door was free. But what if it proved to be locked as well?

Clare took a deep breath. "In the name of God," she said, and pressed down the iron handle. The door opened. The women slipped into the street and started walking in the direction of the gate and the Portiuncula.

The brothers came to meet them with burning torches. As soon as they arrived at the chapel, Clare bade good-bye to her aunt.

"That's all very well," Aunt Bona groaned, as Clare embraced her, "but the family won't let you go like this, I know they won't . . . and they'll tear me to pieces."

"Nothing is going to happen to you, Aunt Bona, dear Aunt Bona," Clare said in a firm voice. "As for me, I am in better hands than I could be anywhere else in the world."

"I still say it's madness," Bona Guelfuccio sobbed. "Don't forget me. And if I had ever had a daughter—" She broke off, turned, waddled away, incredibly fast, and vanished in the dark.

Francis was standing at the entrance of the chapel, with brothers on either side of him. There were more than sixty of them. Smiling, without a word he greeted her and led her into the room that was dearest to his heart. Together they prayed before the picture of the Queen of Angels.

Then she was led to a small hut, one of the brothers left a torch with her and she exchanged her golden dress for the same kind of drab robe that the brothers were wearing; her belt of noble French camlet for a knotted rope; and her pearl-studded shoes for rough sandals. She cast her headdress aside, but did not yet fasten the simple black veil on her head. Instead, she left it hanging over her arm as she returned to the brothers who were singing what she had heard the choir sing in the Cathedral that morning: "Fear not, O Daughter of Sion; behold thy King cometh to thee. . . ."

Once more she stood before Francis, the man she had chosen as her guide into the only life that mattered to her and who had chosen her long ago as one who would be a perfect bride of the Lord. With his own hands he cut off her hair and one of the brothers put the fair tresses into a little casket. Before the crucifix in the chapel she made the three vows and promised perfect obedience to her spiritual guide. Thus she was divorced from the world.

In the first light of the morning the brothers escorted her to the Benedictine Convent of San Paolo, a few miles away, where she was to stay until Francis could provide the three things he now wanted for her: a dwelling-place of her own; a community; and a Rule.

The peace of the Benedictine Sisters of San Paolo was disturbed in the afternoon of the very next day.

The abbess came to see Clare in her cell. "They are here," she said. "And they threaten to break into the enclosure."

"With your permission, Mother Abbess, I will go into the chapel."

The abbess nodded. She looked very worried. "They have come armed," she said.

Clare smiled.

In the chapel she prayed before the altar. The footsteps came before the end of the first Ave.

"There she is." . . . her father.

"Clare! Come to us at once!" . . . Uncle Monaldo.

"Lady Clare!" . . . the Count of Vandria, too.

She turned. There were a dozen men in the chapel. They had brought armed servants with them. "This is the House of God," she said.

But Count Monaldo leaped forward and seized her arm. "You are coming home with us this minute."

She wrenched herself free with a strength that made the count stagger, rushed back and up the steps to the altar. Turning, she tore the veil off her head.

"My God in heaven!" her father exclaimed, and a groan went up among the men behind him.

Clare stretched out her hands till they touched the altar behind her. "I claim sanctuary," she said in a loud voice.

There was no sound except for the labored breath of the men.

Roger stood transfixed. There was no ugliness about her. There was indeed great beauty. But it was the beauty of a strange, unearthly being, a spirit from another world, strong, pure and forbidding, a being before whom a man must stand in awe. He felt—and with a stab of pain—that what he saw was the essence of what he loved most about her, that which made her utterly different from every other woman he had known. But, at the same time, he knew that there was between them a

186

distance a hundred times greater than that between the uttermost ends of the earth. . . .

As Count Monaldo made a move toward her, Roger seized his arm with a grip of iron. "If you touch her, I shall kill you," he said.

Monaldo stared at him, not believing what he heard. But as Roger released his arm, he turned and marched out. Favorino and the servants followed.

Roger stood for one moment more before the living crucifix in front of the altar. He bowed deeply. Then he, too, withdrew.

Two hours later he left the house of the Scifis after a cool, formal farewell.

As he was riding through the city gate, one of his servants said: "The Lady Agnes asked me to give you this, my lord Count."

"The Lady Agnes?"

"Yes, my lord Count."

A flagon of crystal. The Perfume of Heaven. He flung it away and heard it crash to pieces on the stones of the road.

The Perfume of Heaven, he thought grimly. He knew better now. There was nothing sweet and alluring about heaven; it was a stark, lonely place, austere and terrifying. He must go as far away from it as possible. For it cut into a man's heart.

CHAPTER TWENTY-TWO
A.D. 1215

"History is a moody wench," Frederick said. "You never know what kind of face she'll show you next. I act . . . but is it I who am acting, or am I being pushed by some force or power I know nothing about? And if such a thing can be true in my case, how much more in the case of lesser men? My Moslem friends may be right, you know, when they speak of kismet, of the fate that no one can escape. All is written in the Book of Life."

"Your Majesty has chosen a strange place to expound such views," Roger whispered with a half smile.

The thin royal lips broadened. Herr von Justingen laughed outright and then clapped his hand over his mouth.

A steady stream of high Church dignitaries was flowing past the long row of raised enclosures, moving deeper into the huge nave of the Lateran Basilica without taking any notice of the Emperor-elect. No more than a dozen people in the immediate household of the Pope knew that Frederick was in Rome and would be present at the opening of the Fourth Council of the Lateran, the Twelfth General Council of the Church on this eleventh of November.

Frederick was traveling incognito, as Count of Monreale; a small loge had been arranged for him, for the Count of Vandria and for Anselm von Justingen, who carefully abstained from using his new rank and title of Lord Chamberlain of the Empire. They were dressed simply, much more simply than the envoy of the Doge with his group of magnificent Venetian noblemen, on their left, and the glittering deputation from the great city of Milan, on their right. Also they were far removed from the great enclosure where the ambassadors of royalty were sitting, gorgeous in gold and velvet and including the representative of King Henry of Sicily, Frederick's son, now four years of age. Not all the seats were filled as yet. Frederick had insisted on coming early. "Such an excellent opportunity to study the faces of my future friends and enemies," he said. They had seen the list of all the dignitaries who were to be present. Seventy-one archbishops, four hundred and twelve bishops, the patriarchs of Jerusalem and of Antioch, envoys of the patriarchs of Constantinople and Alexandria, almost eight hundred abbots; the ambassadors of the kings of France, England and Hungary, of Aragon and Cyprus, and of course of the Byzantine Emperor. The Roman Emperor-elect, Frederick, too, had his ambassador present—the Chancellor of the Empire, Conrad of Speyer—and he, of course, knew that his emperor was an unofficial observer.

"That's the Abbot of Walkenried," Justingen said suddenly, "Otto's envoy—there, the old man who looks as if he had been drinking vinegar and gall."

"And so he has," Frederick said. "He had an audience with the Holy Father yesterday. It lasted one minute and a half and Walkenried left, looking like his own corpse. It's just like the Ox to send a man like that when he's hard up. A good, loyal ass. If I hadn't known before that the Guelph was finished, I'd know now. That's what I mean about kismet. There! That's Cardinal Hugolino of Ostia. Have a good look at him, Justingen. There's another Innocent for you. Same family, too. Erudite, for a priest, and yet a man of action, a rare and dangerous mixture. I wonder what *his* kismet will be. . . ."

188

"I've never known you to be so intrigued with kismet as here in the Lateran, Your Majesty," Roger said.

Frederick sat back in the shadows as the French ambassador passed by with his retinue. "How can you be surprised," he said in a low voice. "Think, man. A little over three years ago I set out on my journey. On Palm Sunday . . ."

—Palm Sunday. Palm Sunday. The Mass in the Cathedral of Assisi. The unearthly beauty of the girl. She looked like a bride, that day, like *the* Bride—and that's what she was, they would say, the Bride of Christ they would say, together with a hundred thousand other brides, large and small, pretty and plain. And next day her hairless skull—

". . . how angry I was in Rome when that old scrounger of a cardinal, Savelli, wouldn't give me money enough. I can still hear him wailing. The Sicilian account, my lord King, the Sicilian account, I've been watching it for years and it has always been in the red.' By the Kaaba of Mecca, I *had* to have money and who else could give it to me but the Pope? Except Justingen here, and *he* was at the end of his tether. Who ever tried for an emperor's crown with sixty horsemen and a few thousand silver-pieces? . . ."

—The living crucifix before the altar, no longer of this world, dead and yet alive in a cruel, joyless heaven—

". . . certainly glad to see you, when you joined us in Genoa, but not as glad as the Genoese were when we left, merely because they had to pay for our sojourn among them. Everything went so well till Pavia, but when we tried to cross the Lambro . . ." Frederick began to shake with laughter. "I'll never forget the Lambro, with the Milanese swine waiting for us in ambush. . . ."

"Your Majesty—their delegation is sitting next to us. . . ."

"I don't mind. Once we were on the other side of the river we were safe. . . ."

"That's the Cardinal Archbishop of Palestrina."

"I'd like to see *him* trying to cross the Lambro while being shot at by two thousand Milanese archers."

"You did marvelously well, Your Majesty," Justingen said. "I got the fright of my life when you suddenly tore off your saddle and rode across the ford, bareback like a Saracen."

"In the meantime the Milanese and the Pavians were fighting it out." Frederick laughed. "But a thousand miles away, in Germany, in Nordhausen, Otto married poor little Beatrice of Hohenstaufen. Fifteen she was, and frail. She did not survive the

189

embrace of the Guelph and no wonder. Only death could result from the marriage of a Hohenstaufen and a Guelph. How she must have cried, when they forced her into that abominable union! They say his merry ladies gave her poison. I can well believe that. What a cowardly attempt to get *my* followers into his camp. Poor little Beatrice!"

—Beatrice. Beatrice Scifi. There was another Clare growing up, another prey for Brother Francis and his mad beggars who killed the flower of womanhood before it could unfold its petals—

". . . so here's one emperor having his wedding night, and there another, riding through the night for his life. Talk of kismet! And that lunatic ride across the Alps? The Ortles? The Engadine?"

"I thought we'd never get out of those mountains," Justingen said. "I began to feel better only when we got to Chur."

"And from there to St. Gall, bless the town."

"In the name of St. Mohammed?" Roger asked with a grin.

Frederick took no notice. "Then the miracle," he said, "the miracle of Constance, when Otto woke up at last and came tearing down—too late by just an hour. The Bishop of Constance had his speech ready for *him*. I don't think he made a single change in it, when he solemnly read it out to *me* instead. I was in my own country now, though I'd never seen it in my life before. And the Ox, in his hurry, hadn't taken enough men with him to be able to throw me out. . . ."

"He couldn't," Roger said. "The ban of the Church was having its effect."

Frederick nodded. "Old and hopelessly old-fashioned as it is, there's still some strength left in that strange institution, or we wouldn't be sitting here today, watching it hold a review of its army. What would happen, if all the people in this building were killed? Three thousand soldiers could do it easily enough. The Pope, the cardinals, archbishops, bishops and abbots, the learned theologians . . ."

"The Church would still survive," Justingen said gravely. "I'm not much of a Christian and I'm not speaking as a Christian now. But I'm sure the Church would survive."

"You may be right," Frederick said. "The heads of the Hydra grew again as quickly as Hercules cut them off. . . ."

Roger laughed. "The Pope's help doesn't seem to have put him back in your favor, Your Majesty."

"And why should he be, my good fool?" Frederick asked. "He didn't help me for my sake, did he? By the way, where is

190

he? This building is so full now, you couldn't get another bishop in with the help of a battering ram."

"It's just as well we came early," Justingen said. "Judging from the noise, all Christendom must be assembled out there on the square. These Italians have no military sense, no order, no discipline. Everybody's on his own. There'll be hundreds of casualties outside, I wager."

"And none of them has an inkling that he is going to die, instead of seeing a great spectacle," Frederick said. "Kismet, friends. The entire duel between Otto and me was a chain of odd and unforeseeable events. We never set eyes on each other. What would ordinary common sense expect to happen with two emperors fighting each other in the same country? A battle, of course, or at least a duel, man to man . . ."

"*That* would have suited Otto," Justingen said. "All seven feet of him."

"But David killed Goliath," Frederick said somewhat acidly. "However, that's a Bible story. What happened in real life? Otto had to go to the assistance of his uncle England against my great, glorious and extremely shrewd ally, Philip Augustus of France."

"Yes, and we—" Justingen broke off.

"Quite right." Frederick smiled. "We did nothing—although I had collected a good-sized army by that time. We didn't sacrifice a man."

"But if Otto had won . . ."

"He would have had to meet me with what the French left of his army. I wasn't very keen for that battle, Justingen—not before I had more experience in such matters. But dear Philip Augustus did my work for me beautifully and even sent me Otto's banner, as if I were his liege-lord, which I am not—yet. What more can I ask? That battle of Bouvines must have broken the Ox's heart. He did magnificently, of course, riding and killing as if he were in a gigantic tournament. In the meantime the French won the battle and suddenly he found that he had to fly and fly quickly, if he wanted to get away with his life. And that after killing seven or eight French knights single-handed. What a shame! I wish I could have seen his big, stupid face when they stopped him in his butcher's work to tell him that all was lost. And . . ." The rest of his words were lost in a crashing fanfare, long-drawn and triumphant, as the Pope was carried into the Basilica. As he passed by, everybody knelt.

"Is he going to speak right away?" Roger asked, when the trumpets were silent again.

191

"No," Justingen replied, "they'll start with the invocation of the Holy Ghost. They always do."

"Yes, but is he going to oblige?" Frederick asked out of the corner of his mouth. He had met Innocent III three years ago. They had had a number of conferences and discussions. "He couldn't have been more gentle and . . . paternal, but I never had a clear idea of what was going on in the back of his mind. The only thing that gave me comfort was the hope that he didn't know what was going on in mine either. The man is not calculable, friends. Do you have any idea of what he's going to say today? No? Exactly. All the finest brains from a dozen Christian countries are assembled here and I'll bet Sicily against a handful of hair from Otto's beard that none of them knows either."

"*Veni, Creatore Spiritus . . .*"

There was something touching and humble about the hundreds of voices, most of them elderly, many of them cracked, praying for enlightenment and for the gifts the Holy Spirit alone could bestow. Why had He bestowed so many of His gifts on Frederick who did not really believe in Him, Roger wondered.

The light of thousands of candles made the scarlet, purple, gold and lace of the ecclesiastic robes look like one, large, pulsating organ. The heart of the Church? The mind of the Church?

"Yes, my good Roger, look closely," Frederick said. "This is a great show of power and there is nothing like it in the world —as yet. But don't let it overwhelm you. I do wish Innocent would start. This is his supreme hour, the summit of his career. The Albigenses are as good as finished. So is Otto, though he's still alive. He'll sit behind the walls of Brunswick until he dies. I certainly won't try to assail the thick walls of the Ox's stable. I preferred to have my first coronation in Aix-la-Chapelle. But how is Innocent going to take this hour of victory and triumph? What does such a man say at such a moment?" His face was tense.

The king is not interested in causes, except, of course, his own, Roger thought. But he is interested in men, though only as potential servants or potential enemies. Perhaps a man must be like that if he wants to rise to the summit. Perhaps this Innocent was like that, too.

"Now," Frederick whispered fiercely. "What does one say, if one wants to rule the world?"

192

So that was what Frederick wanted. Was it what Innocent also wanted? If so . . .

A hush fell over the great assembly. Then the Pope's voice rang out, clear, strong, without either tremor or inflection.

"With desire I have desired to eat this pasch with you, before I suffer."

A thunderclap could not have had greater effect than the Pope's first sentence. The words of Christ at the Last Supper, announcing His passion! For the better part of a moment the tight mass of scarlet, purple, gold and lace waved in the storm of minds.

Roger stared at Frederick. He looks like a demon, he thought, fascinated. Like a young but very powerful demon.

The Pope went on: "This Council may indeed be called a Pasch. For the word means a passage and such is the command of the hour in a threefold sense. First: the passage to the Holy Land . . ."

"A crusade . . . that's what he's out for. A crusade again."

"Second: a passage from vice to virtue . . ."

"He wants to clean up the stable of Augeas! It'll take more than a man to do that, but then he did once say that the Pope was less than God but more than man, didn't he? Didn't he?"

". . . and third a passage from temporal life to life eternal. Now I call the Almighty God to witness that I have not called you together, the Fathers of the Church, for the sake of temporal ambition . . ."

"Of course not," Frederick jeered between his teeth.

". . . but so that the Church might be reformed and the Holy Land be once more in Christian hands. If God will not grant that I see these desires of mine accomplished, I will not refuse to drink of the chalice of Christ's passion, I will not struggle against death, though I would that I might live in the flesh until the work now to be begun, is consummated. Yet not my will, but God's will be done."

"There's some illness in the man," Frederick said. "He's had a warning. His soul is feverish, even if his body isn't."

Innocent spoke of the Holy Places, whose glory, the very glory of mankind, was destroyed and yet Christians all over the world went on about their petty affairs as if they did not care and as if their own troubles were the only ones that mattered.

"Jerusalem, the city of sorrow, is calling to all who pass by to come and see if there be any sorrow like hers; and shame and disgrace will it be to those who pass by unheeding. But

193

there is one other sorrow, calling out from amidst the Christian peoples: the Church is defiled by the peoples' sins. Listen then to the voice of the prophet Ezechiel . . ." And he quoted the words of the terrible wrath of God, the command to His angels to strike all those who were not marked with the sign Thau.

A little man, kneeling in the crowd, and dressed in an old grayish brown robe, a beggar, looked up and listened breathlessly as the Pope expounded on Thau, the last letter in the Hebrew alphabet. "Thau," he murmured to himself. "Thau."

"It is formed like a cross," the Pope said. "Like the cross before Pilate had our Lord's title affixed to it: a vertical beam with a horizontal beam laid across the top of it."

The last letter of the alphabet—the sign of humility and of suffering, the sign of those who regarded themselves as the last and the smallest of Christ's brethren. This and no other would be the sign of the Friars Minor.

At a distance of a hundred feet from the beggar, Frederick said: "They're going to sell Thaus now, in bronze, silver and gold. How fortunate for Otto. He has two in his name. Innocent has one and I have none at all. But I shan't buy one."

"The Church must strike at heresy and sin, but, like the Lord, she hates sin, but not the sinner. And the command of the Lord to his angel was: 'Start ye at my sanctuary.' Where the priest sins, he makes the people sin, too. How can the pastors who live evilly, reprimand those who live in iniquity? They will reply: the son cannot do but what he sees the father doing; it is sufficient for the disciple to be as his teacher; and thus is the prophecy fulfilled: 'There shall be like priest like people.' And all that is done to one thing only, the lack of love, that makes us leave all responsibility to our Lord, and makes us unwilling to take up our cross and follow Him. . . ."

The little man on his knees wept with joy, for the words of the Pope were his own innermost thoughts and now they were lifted up for all to see and hear.

Justingen whispered to Frederick: "I've just heard an official behind me say that Archbishop Matthew of Amalfi has been crushed to death in the crowd while trying to enter."

Frederick raised his brows. "There are still plenty of them left," he said. "But his chief, too, will soon be crushed. He is trying to do too much. And his listeners are not all Innocents —fortunately. Things won't go as he wants them to go. And a man may die of disappointment. I have seen and heard enough. We're going back to Germany tomorrow . . . or else they may ask me to lead their crusade."

"But . . . you took the cross after the coronation of Aix-la-Chapelle," Roger said. "Quite voluntarily too. You said you wanted to go. . . ."

"So I did," Frederick said, smiling. "But I didn't say when. . . ."

CHAPTER TWENTY-THREE

Francis was walking through the streets of Rome and as usual few people gave him more than a casual glance. He blended with the gray of the houses as well as with the brown of the earth.

The words of the Pope had opened new horizons for him, or made clearer, and even crystal clear, what he had so far seen through a haze, as the sun may illuminate a distant landscape.

Now he knew what he wanted was exactly what the Church wanted. And what the Church wanted was what Christ had ordered him to do in San Damiano: "You see My House is falling into ruin. Go and repair it." He had taken the words quite literally, at the time. He had rebuilt San Damiano with his own hands; and now Sister Clare was living in a convent there, with the first eight of her nuns. The Poor Ladies, people were calling them. But even then it had seemed to him that the Lord must want more of him than merely the restoration of one small wayside shrine, and he had gone on repairing others. All the time he had felt, dimly, that this, too, was only a beginning, and perhaps only a symbol of the real task; and now he knew with certainty that the Lord had meant the Church as a whole. That also he took literally. And how else? What knight or soldier would dare to distort or minimize the command of his king? When the Lord was speaking in parables, He said so. When He said: "Behold, I make all things new," He meant exactly that, and He made people new by His love and that love He gave them for the asking; and those who received it were eager to pass it on to others. He did not give His love to men only, but to the whole of His creation, and in so doing, He ennobled it beyond all bounds.

A baby was sacred, for He had once been a baby.

A woman was sacred, for He had been born of a woman.

A priest was sacred, for he had been made a priest by the laying on of hands by those who, in turn, had been sanctified in previous ordinations, and so back across the centuries to the holy hands of Christ Himself, ordaining the apostles.

A leper, a blind man, a lame man, every kind of ill or infirm man was sacred, for by curing such as they He had proved His divinity.

Brother lamb was to be loved, because Christ had been led like a lamb to slaughter, as Isaiah said; and because Christ asked Peter to feed His lambs.

A lamp in a house was ennobled, for Christ was the Light of the World.

Sister Water had been honored in the most signal way, for through water Christ performed His first miracle; and He ordained that man must be reborn not only from the Holy Spirit, but also from water.

Brother Fire was the vehicle of the Holy Spirit at Pentecost.

Air was hallowed, for the Lord had breathed it.

The earth was hallowed for He had walked on it.

Bread became royal, for He deigned to assume its form in the Holy Eucharist, and wine, because He had changed it into His blood.

Flowers could bloom in innocent pride, for He had made them an example to men.

Trees were sanctified through the one from whose wood the cross was shaped.

Every rock spoke of the one on whom Christ built His Church.

From the stars which were eyewitnesses of His life on earth to the worm to which He compared Himself when He intoned the Twenty-first Psalm of David, on the cross, all creation was hallowed.

What could a man do but dance with joy?

"Forgive me, but I must speak to you."

Francis stopped, the light of overwhelming happiness still in his eyes. Before him stood a man in his mid-forties, bearded, pale, with deep, dark eyes and a dark beard. He was dressed in a fleecy white robe with a black cowl.

"I do not know who you are," the man said, "but I have seen you once before."

"When?" Francis asked.

"Last night."

"Where?"

"In a dream."

Francis said very slowly: "Some dreams are sent by God."

"This one was. I saw you and me together, chosen for certain work. I am Dominic Guzman. Will you do me the kindness to tell me who you are?"

"I am Brother Francis of the Friars Minor."

A light of recognition broke over the stern, Spanish face.

"Brother Francis . . . of Assisi?"

"The Lord's servant, and yours."

"I might have guessed it even in my dream," Dominic said, and there was something very touching about his undisguised joy. He embraced Francis. "You and I are allies," he said. "If we stand together, no enemy shall overcome us. You do not know me, of course. . . ."

"Oh yes, I do," Francis said happily. "You are the leader of those who regain erring minds by force of mind. No wonder you are here on a day when Pasch and Pentecost seem to coincide."

"The Pope spoke as a prophet," the Spaniard said. "There will be much work for you and me and for our sons. Yours, at present, are more numerous than mine. My visit here is for the purpose of obtaining the Holy Father's permission for the foundation of a new Order."

They were walking on now, Dominic carefully watching out, so as not to lose his way, and Francis trotting along beside him, without paying any attention to where they were going.

"Pray that I may get that permission, I beg of you," Dominic went on. "I heard that one of the items on the agenda of the Council is that no new Orders should be allowed."

"God always wins," Francis said, and the Spaniard smiled as a man does when he receives the confirmation of his own thoughts.

"It is not good that spiritual error should be fought by the sword," he said. "Worse still, it is futile if the mind of the erring is uninstructed and unconvinced. That is why I refused to take part in the campaign against the Albigenses. I want to instruct and to convince. And I know that it cannot be done unless I manifest in my own life what I preach to others. I shall wage war on heresy by preaching and by a life of asceticism. That is where we meet, you and I. But I have reached the house where I am going—I hope I have not led you too far out of your own way. . . ."

"It would not be likely, would it?" Francis said, smiling. "As it is, we are both going to the same place." And he pulled the bellrope at the door.

Cardinal Hugolino of Ostia, next to the Pope the busiest man in Rome, had a number of visitors, both ecclesiastic and secular, and each of them had problems which demanded his full concentration. He had to command, to persuade, to warn and to

197

instruct, to help to build up and to avoid causing disappointment, to break down defenses and to give comfort and encouragement. Yet when he saw the two men entering together, dressed as simply as could be, one in white, the other in grayish brown, for one glorious, uplifting moment he felt that the future was walking in.

As soon as possible, without offending his other guests, he drew them aside. It did not take him very long to find out that they had met and that they understood each other. So he could talk to them together. "I have discussed your petition with His Holiness," he told Dominic. "You realize the difficulty: it is as good as certain that the Council will decree against any new Order being established."

Dominic's face seemed to turn to stone, but he bowed his head. "If God wills it, there will be a miracle," he said.

"There may be no need for that," the cardinal said, with a subtle smile. "If for instance you were to draw up the charter for your fraternity according to the Rule of St. Augustine or of St. Benedict—the former might suit your case better, I think—I can see no reason why your petition should be refused."

For what seemed to be a long time, Dominic stared in front of him. Then life came back into his face and he nodded. "Blessed be St. Augustine," he said and the cardinal tried hard not to show how relieved he was. Dealing with personalities of the first magnitude was dealing with wills of steel and iron. One had to know how to temper the one and how to melt the other. "As for you, Brother Francis," he said, "you seem to feel quite happy."

"The great Council was opened on St. Martin's feast," Francis said cheerfully.

"What do you mean by that?"

"Well, lord Cardinal, he gave half of his coat to the poor."

"So he did," Hugolino of Ostia agreed, "and we may take it as a good omen for the lover of Lady Poverty. I shall remind His Holiness to notify the Council of the approbation of your brotherhood three years ago; in your case there is no question of a new Order."

"Thank you, lord Cardinal," Francis said, beaming. "You have given me half your coat. But I am a greedy pauper. I want the other half also, leaving you nothing at all."

Hugolino of Ostia shook his head. "What is it you want this time?"

"The extension of the great privilege of poverty to Sister Clare and her Poor Ladies at San Damiano."

198

"I'll make a note of that, too," the cardinal said. He knew about the tiny community—eight or nine little nuns, he remembered. It would not be too difficult to find a form that included them. "Very well then," he said, "there is one more point I have in mind. The men you are—how shall I say?—training. . . ."

"Yes," said Dominic.

"No," said Francis.

"The men you are shaping, then," the cardinal corrected himself, "and I think that will be an expression you can both agree to—you can? Excellent . . . these men, then, should be hardy and ascetic, strong in faith and ready to shoulder responsibility. I think such men should be the best material for the kind of bishops the Church needs and wants. You do not seem to like my idea—either of you."

"A bishop must deal with property," Francis said. "My sons are learning to forget about property entirely."

"If some of us were to belong to the hierarchy, they would find themselves respected for their rank." Dominic said. "But we should be respected for only two things: for our way of life and the strength of our arguments."

The cardinal sighed. "I was afraid I'd get those answers. I cannot order you to change your minds. If I did, those minds would become useless. Still, it's a great pity. I must go back to my other guests."

"I must go back to the Portiuncula," Francis said.

"What? Even before the Council has come to an end? You had better stay a few more days. You've got nothing in writing! Surely you ought to have a document, signed and sealed in an orderly fashion. All you have is the verbal assent of the Holy Father."

"And that is quite good enough for me," Francis said, his eyes dancing. "There is no need for any document. The Blessed Virgin shall be the charter, Christ the notary and the angels the witnesses."

CHAPTER TWENTY-FOUR
A.D. 1216

The Brothers at the Portiuncula were not particularly surprised when, in July, Francis told them rather curtly that he must go to Perugia at once and then left without any further explanation. About certain matters one could be quite sure what he would say or do, but in others one could never guess, however hard one tried. Besides, since the brotherhood had increased to over six hundred in the North of Italy alone he seemed to withdraw more and more into himself.

"He wants to climb down into his own heart to find out what to do with us all," was Brother Juniper's explanation and it was as good as any. Brother Juniper was simple—though not quite as simple as Brother Giovanni *the* Simple who was so intent on doing everything in his Father's way that he coughed when Francis coughed and was unhappy when he could not sneeze each time Father Francis did. Nevertheless even Brother Juniper's simplicity could become a nuisance. Last month he had given the only altar cloth to a poor woman and he would have given her the chalice as well if someone had not stopped him in time. Sister Clare there in San Damiano had given him a nickname: the Plaything of God. Not at all a good thing to do, as it were, for at the next opportunity Brother Juniper was seen sitting on a seesaw, with four children occupying the other side of that favorite teeter-totter playing device. He was grinning like a fool and apparently enjoying himself hugely. Yet Father Francis had a special love for him and had said once to Brother Masseo: "I wish I had many such junipers!" And Brother Elias put it: "If he had said, 'I wish I had many more Pietro Cattaneos or Giuseppe Calvis,' I could have understood it." For they were both learned men and so, indeed, was Brother Elias, although he had been a saddle-maker before he joined the brotherhood.

Brother Juniper had an explanation for Francis' journey to Perugia too. "I think he's going there because he had a dream. But when the brothers asked him whether Father Francis had told him that and perhaps also what it was that he had dreamed Brother Juniper said only: "He didn't tell me anything, but I can always see it in his face when he has had a dream," which was just the kind of explanation he would give.

Francis arrived in Perugia in the afternoon. The day was very hot and sultry, with a leaden sky, cloudless and yet threatening. The streets were almost empty and there was something furtive and fearful about the few people scurrying by, as if they did not feel safe.

The palace, the papal summer residence, seemed to be asleep. Francis entered it with the same quick, purposeful stride with which he had entered the Lateran Palace four years ago. But this time there was no dignitary to ask him what he wanted and where he was going, no magnificent officer to stare at him. There were no guards, or if there were any, they did not see him, nor he them. The huge building seemed to be entirely empty. It could not have been empty for very long, however, for there was a plate with some fruit in one room and a chessboard with the figures in the natural disarray of a game half-finished in another.

Francis did not appear surprised. He just walked on. He had never been in the building before and knew nothing of its plan. The ceremonial rooms through which he passed were hot and stuffy. All the windows were closed. He climbed up a broad staircase, and as he did, he caught a whiff of something sharp and sour . . . vinegar. The smell became much stronger in the upstairs corridor. The door to one of the rooms was open and he could see the purple of a bishop's robe.

Bishop Nicholas, the Pope's chief secretary, was on his knees, but he seemed to have heard the clump-clump of Francis' sandals, for he looked toward the door.

Francis knew him well. A year or so ago Bishop Nicholas had wanted to join the Friars Minor, but the Pope recalled him almost as soon as he had gone—he could not do without him, he said.

Bishop Nicholas crossed himself, rose and went up to Francis. "He is very ill," he said in a grave voice. "May God give us all strength . . . he may be dying."

Francis nodded. "Where is he?" he asked.

"That's his study, behind the door with the crest on it. And behind the study is his bedroom. But wait! You can't go in. The physicians won't let you. Oh, Brother Francis, what a calamity for Christendom! Now, on the verge of the greatest events! You know why he came here, don't you? We were on our way to Pisa and Genoa, to bring about peace between them. He had it all worked out, he knew every argument, every single point about which they disagreed, every mistake, every crime of their leaders, even their thoughts deep down under the surface. He could point with his finger, see here, this is where you went wrong. And now he's lying there, racked by fever . . . he's been unconscious for hours. This is the third day. Yesterday he received the Viaticum. The physicians have given up hope. They don't say so, but I know. They are afraid, too, as much as anyone else. Almost all the staff has left the place—some are in the other wing. . . ."

"The physicians are afraid?"

"Yes. They think it may be the plague. They're not sure. There are no . . . no spots, you see, and no boils. It may only be a marsh fever. They don't know. But the rumor that it's the plague got around very fast, and people fled. The physicians themselves spend no more time in the sickroom than is absolutely necessary."

"May I go now, my lord Bishop?" Francis asked courteously.

"Go? Oh yes . . . yes, of course, Brother Francis. You are quite right. It may be the plague, and you have the responsibility for so many of your brothers. The lifeblood of the Church . . . by all means, go."

Francis bowed but he did not, as Bishop Nicholas thought, go back the way he had come. He walked on toward the door with the crest.

"What are you doing," the bishop called out, "you can't—"

Francis could no longer hear him, he had entered the study.

Three physicians looked up from behind heavy white towels, drenched with vinegar as a disinfectant. He gave them a grave nod and slipped into the adjacent room.

Innocent III lay in his huge, canopied bed. He was breathing quickly, irregularly. His small hands were clenched. He had torn open his nightrobe, baring his throat and chest, white and frail.

Francis knelt and reverently kissed the ring on the Pope's damp, feverish hand.

And Innocent became conscious. For a while his eyes, sunk deeply into their sockets, gave no sign of recognition. "I must go," he murmured. "They must stop fighting. I must go to Pisa at once. Tell them . . ." And a moment later: "The fleet must assemble . . . I have chosen . . . eight ports. The meeting point . . ." He broke off. Francis was praying quietly.

"He is a traitor," Innocent said firmly. "He . . . is going to . . . betray Christ. The imperial crown . . ." His voice again trailed off into a murmur. Then, quite suddenly, it regained force. "Jerusalem," the Pope said aloud. "The Lord's sepulchre. Jerusalem. How can it be . . . denied us? . . ."

"It will not be denied us," Francis said.

"I fought and fought," Innocent said in a voice full of anguish. "But I must carry them all and . . . I can't. . . ."

"There is only One who can," Francis said. "And He did."

"Jerusalem," the Pope whispered. "I will go . . . on the crusade . . . myself. They . . . they don't know it yet, but . . . I will. And if I die . . ." He gave a long, deep sigh.

"I will go for you," Francis said, closing the dead Pope's eyes.

202

CHAPTER TWENTY-FIVE
A.D. 1219

"I am sorry Otto died last May," Frederick said to Roger. "He made such an excellent pretext for not going on that thrice-accursed crusade. How could I leave Germany and indeed Europe, with the Ox waiting behind his fence, ready to jump it as soon as I turned my back. Now I shall have to look for other excuses. . . ."

"You will find them, Your Majesty," Roger said dryly.

"Thank you for your confidence in me." Frederick leaned forward to warm his hands at the fire, burning lustily in the large fireplace. It was early March—spring had not yet come to Germany. The huge trees around the castle were leafless and looked as forbidding as the puddles of ice on the road to the draw-bridge. "In other respects it's just as well that the Ox is no more," Frederick went on. "It makes the princes cheaper. What a greedy lot they are, to be sure! Concessions here, privileges there . . . above all, money and again money. But I've got most of them where I want them."

"About the election of King Henry of Sicily as the German king?"

"Yes, of course. They'll elect him all right. I won't be present, but my money will be. When I hear of it, I shall be quite shocked, unbelievably shocked. 'But, my dearest Holy Father, what could I do? I feel most uneasy about it, having sworn so solemnly that I would never, never unite Sicily with the German kingdom! But the princes have the power to elect a German king and they're free to make their choice. Also, I do admit, it's difficult for me not to be proud, after all the child's my flesh and blood. But my conscience is clear.' And so he won't be able to throw the ban at me as Innocent did at poor Otto. I'm out of it."

"And your conscience is clear," Roger repeated.

"Certainly. It's as good as new. I've never used it. I'm not like Otto who made such a fuss about repentance and absolution at the end. If there is a beyond, they'll have to take me as I am."

"But Sicily . . ."

"I'm not King of Sicily, my boy is. I've nothing to do with it any more. Or . . . not much. I shall have to pay a visit there, in due course. Can't a father pay a visit to his son? Also, I still have a few debts to pay there. One to you: you must get your Vandria back. Another is the payment for the purple cloak that Emir Ibn Abbad sent to Otto when he thought I was finished. I'll make him eat that cloak until he chokes to death."

Roger nodded. "That election will be a master stroke. Since Innocent died, you are the leading statesman in Europe, Your Majesty."

"Maybe," Frederick said, "but I'm disappointed in the Pope all the same."

"Poor old Pope Honorius? I thought you were rather glad they elected him instead of Cardinal Hugolino of Ostia."

"So I was, at the time. Cardinal Savelli was a gentle old man, although I did have a clash with him once, when he wouldn't give me enough money. He and his Sicilian account! Well, I'll settle *that* debt soon enough. Savelli . . . I beg his pardon, Pope Honorius III is gentle, which is another name for weak. But he knows it. And that has had two bad consequences. He leaves most political matters to Cardinal Hugolino of Ostia which is almost as bad as if they had made *him* Pope. And he's absolutely adamant about his damned crusade. Maybe Innocent made him swear to insist on it if ever he became Pope, or maybe he feels he must stick to it for some other reason. In any case I never get a letter from him that doesn't mention it and ask when I shall be ready to go. . . . I tell you, my good Roger, I begin to believe the papal crown makes them all alike."

Roger looked into the fire. "Perhaps it does. There are certain things a man may have to stand for in that position."

"My good fool, *if* there is such a thing as eternal life and *if* a pope has to appear before the judgment seat of Christ, do you think Christ would care much whether Jerusalem was in Christian hands or not? One would think he'd had enough of the dear place and of those Jews. Yet they all seem to believe they're doing him a great favor by conquering it. The place does have its merits, mind you, for an expansion toward the east."

"There's some rumor that Pope Innocent died with the word 'Jerusalem' on his lips," Roger said. "But speaking of belief . . . and without witnesses . . . I often wonder what you really believe in, Your Majesty."

Frederick laughed. "I'm only twenty-four, and I have other things to think about. But I do believe in kingship—in mine, that is. And I believe in emperorship, with the same little addition. And if religion helps to keep me in authority—and such is its duty—then religion will be quite welcome. I'll make a wonderful show of it, in fact I am doing so now. No one is so good at stamping out heretics. But the Pope seems very reluctant to give me any credit for it."

Roger raised his head. "What is your real objection against the crusade?" he asked.

"Oh well, if you want to be serious: I must get my house in order first. And Sicily is part of my house too, never mind what the Pope says or what I had to swear to when I needed his help. Can *you* forget Sicily? Vandria? Of course not. And then I must have my coronation in Rome. I told old Honorius so very clearly. I won't budge before that."

"They're shouting for help out there in Egypt, before Damietta . . ."

"So they are. Let them shout. Serves them right for going there in insufficient numbers, to say nothing of old Pelagius. Never allow an army to be led by a cardinal. If he's a bad priest, why should he be a good general? And if he's a good priest, he *can't* be a good general. Besides . . ."

Now it's coming, Roger thought. He had known Frederick long enough to be sure he had not been asked here for a mere chat. Everything that the Emperor-elect said had some importance, some relevance to the point he wanted to make.

"I must think ahead," Frederick said. "Further ahead than muddleheads and fanatics. The Orient is a powerful factor and sooner or later I shall have to deal with it. That I know. What I do not know is how I am going to deal with it. Not, most certainly, by launching a frontal attack. First, I want to know as much as I can about the important personalities there. Above all, about Sultan Al Kamil. He may not be as great a man as his late uncle Saladin was, but he interests me. They say he's very erudite, reads a great deal, debates matters of philosophy and mathematics for hours on end. I wonder whether he really believes in his Allah, in his Mohammed and in his Koran. I'd like to find out. I'd like to find out many things. Will you go out there for me, Roger, *Duke* of Vandria?"

So that's what it was.

"Your Majesty wants me to join the crusade under Cardinal Pelagius?"

"That's probably the only possible way—for the beginning of your mission. Later, you will have to see how you can get in touch with the Sultan. You speak Arabic well. And you've done very nicely for me in Umbria, especially in Rieti, it seems, and in Foligno and Spoleto."

I was not too successful in Assisi, Roger thought. But now he had to concentrate on his new mission, in comparison to which his tour through Umbria was mere child's play.

"I have worked out certain ideas," Frederick said. "Yours will be rather a strange mission, I think. I'll tell you what I want."

And he did.

CHAPTER TWENTY-SIX
A.D. 1219

The Friars Minor from many countries were assembling around the Portiuncula for the Chapter to be held there, just as they had two years before. Huts made of branches and rushes sprang up like mushrooms. "More mushrooms than I've ever seen on one heap," as Brother Juniper remarked, "even when I had to prepare mushrooms for our dinner."

"That I well believe," Brother Carlo said wryly. "Last time we had mushrooms I got exactly two."

"Two?" Juniper exclaimed. "But you're only one man!"

"I see," Brother Carlo nodded. "Very well. Next time we have horse meat, I shall content myself with a single horse." They all remembered the first meal Brother Juniper had prepared. He had cooked every scrap of food they had, "to make it easier for the brother who would be in charge after him." He had put everything together, meat, bread, cheese, honey, fish, milk and several chickens which he most carefully plucked but never thought of cleaning. Something had gone wrong with the cooking itself, too, and the result was a hideous, blackish, oily mess and a general fast by all the brothers for three days running.

"The Order has increased in these two years," Brother Tancredi remarked, watching the huts going up. "We were about nine hundred then."

"And now?"

"Brother Elias says we'll be over five thousand."

Brother Juniper clapped his enormous hands together. "It would take me two years to count that far . . . if I could count that far."

"Well, at least no one's going to throw us in jail here, as they did in Portugal," Brother Anselmo growled. He did not growl out of discontent; his voice always sounded like that, and when he sang a hymn of praise one would have thought he was severely reproaching God for all the good things he had received from Him.

There was discontent enough that May, however, in some parts of the ever-growing camp. Many of the new brothers had never seen Francis himself, they had joined the brotherhood in France or Spain and now had come to Italy for the first time in their lives. All of them had suffered hardships; many of them complained; and some quite loudly.

Brother Elias approached Francis: "The brothers from England have arrived," he announced. "What arrangements have you made to feed all these people?"

"None," Francis said. "Our Lord did not make any arrangements when the people gathered around Him. He told them not to be anxious about what they would eat and drink."

"But when five thousand people were assembled to hear Him, He did think of how to feed them," Elias replied firmly, "and I doubt whether you will be able to multiply the bread and the fishes as He did."

"I can't do that," Francis said softly, "but He can, just as He did then."

Elias left him, shaking his head and muttering to himself.

"Hey, take care, Brother," a rough voice shouted behind him and he had to jump aside not to be pushed over by a mule cart, by three, by five, by a dozen mule carts, rumbling along across the soft grass.

Elias' eyes widened. The carts were full of food.

"We're from Armenzano," the mule driver cried. "Can you tell us where we can unload the stuff?"

"You mean . . . this is for us?"

"For who else? Do you think there are no Christians in Armenzano?"

"Over there would be the best place, I think," Brother Elias said in an unsteady voice. "Between those six huts in a row and the woods."

The muleteer shook his head. "No go, Brother. That's where the men from Rieti are unloading, twenty carts full and more. No space left."

"From Rieti . . ."

"Yes, we passed them a minute ago. Never mind, Brother, we'll find a place." And he drove on.

207

Elias, too, walked on, his head awhirl, and promptly ran into a caravan of wagons, horse-drawn and full of bread and cheese and wine from Gubbio.

A man of system, Elias now patroled the entire camp. He saw the oxcarts with food coming from Bastia and the long line of heavily packed donkeys approaching from the direction of Spoleto.

He sat down heavily on the nearest rock. After a while he raised his strong, jutting chin. "It's all very well this time," he said aloud, "but we can't expect it to happen at every Chapter."

To the majority of the brothers the arrival of the food was no great surprise. Among them were the best who in devout simplicity trusted God to look after them who served Him; but others took it for granted that the head of the Order had arranged it all for them.

The atmosphere of the meeting did not change. At the last Chapter Francis had appointed "provincials" to be in charge of a number of provinces. The provincials now reported and after them the missionaries who had been sent to various countries in Europe. Here the waves of discontent broke through. The missions were largely failures.

The brothers sent to France told how they were taken to be Albigenses and found themselves thrown in jail. The missionaries to Portugal had been jailed too, as vagabonds. In Hungary they had been insulted and ill-treated as tumblers and heretics. The unfortunate brothers arriving in Germany knew only one single and simple word of German: "*ja*," which they had used with rather variable success, until a martial squire asked them point-blank whether or not they were heretics, considering they had come from Lombardy where heresies abounded. Their cheerful *ja* earned them the thrashing of their lives and they fled, completely bewildered and fully convinced that Germany was a heathen country.

"We must know the languages of the countries to which we are sent," the brothers declared. "And we must have documents issued to us, to prove that the Church has granted us the right to preach."

Now Francis spoke for the first time. "Our Lord did not learn the Phoenician language when He went to Tyre; nor did He have letters commending Him as a true authority. He suffered Himself to be beaten and spat upon, to be whipped and tortured. Shall the servant be treated better than his Master? Other Orders have other ways. God does not lead all men in the same fashion. But my sons must imitate the life and work of our Lord, using only the way of the spirit, unshielded by the influence and power of those of high authority in the Church. Not for us the prudence of the world. Instead, a life of obedience and love, of prayer and chastity and humility without learning. Thus it has been with my first sons and thus it must be with you all."

But for the first time his words evoked little echo and the muttering would not cease.

Pale and unhappy, Francis stood in their midst. Bernard of Quintavalle, the leader of the missionaries to Spain, and the only one who could report some measure of success, looked at him sadly. Pietro Cattaneo looked down. He knew only too well how justified the demands of the brothers were on the basis of common sense. But he knew also that it meant watering down the very essence of the brotherhood if one gave in to them. He was shaken to the core. This was tragedy. For was not the root of all tragedy an impasse between two duties, two ideals, two people who must agree and yet for some *good* reason could not?

"The cardinal," somebody shouted. "The cardinal is coming . . ."

Far away a large group of riders on mules came up the road. The flaming red of the cardinal's robe was unmistakable.

At once Francis moved toward him and the brothers followed by the hundreds. A procession formed itself spontaneously.

Cardinal Hugolino of Ostia came from Perugia, where he was residing for the time being. The sight of the multitudes sworn to an evangelical life moved him profoundly. Long ago, Innocent III had told him the story of his dream—the Lateran falling and held up and kept in place by one little friar. Here was the little friar's army, grown to unbelievable proportions in the course of a few years. With men like that one could hope for the fulfilment of that dream, for a new life within the Church.

He dismounted, took off his magnificent mantle and his shoes. Two years ago he had asked Francis quite seriously whether he, too, could become a friar. Francis would give no answer. But for today he was going to be a friar.

When Francis wanted to kneel and kiss his ring, he raised him up at once and embraced him. Side by side they approached the huge camp.

Half an hour later the cardinal sang High Mass in the Portiuncula, with Francis serving as the deacon. He shared the meal of the brothers and then withdrew with the head of the Order for a while, before taking the seat of honor in the Chapter. He had studied spiritual men for a lifetime. Before Francis had said a word he knew that there was trouble ahead.

"Lord Cardinal," Francis said almost brusquely, "two years ago, when I wanted to go on a mission, just like my men, you told me to stay in Italy and to defend my cause against those who might wish to harm it."

"I did."

"My sons have met with rebuffs and not all of them are taking it as they should. I can no longer ask them to do what I am not doing myself. Therefore I ask for your permission to leave Italy."

"You need not ask," the cardinal said gently. "I did not forbid it then, I only advised you against it."

"You are the Protector of the Order. I will not go against your wishes. But I entreat you to let me go."

The cardinal looked at him. "I will give you the answer later in the day," he said slowly. "Let us hear your brothers first— and then take council."

"I gave the promise to go to one whose memory I hold in the highest esteem," Francis said.

"Then you must fulfil your promise. But let us see whether or not this is the right moment to do so."

Francis bowed his head. He said nothing.

The Chapter was stormy. The brothers sensed that they were more likely to find support from the cardinal than from their own ascetical leader and they repeated their clamor for documents. There were many voices asking for a more ordered life with provision taken for the morrow.

Francis jumped up. "My brothers! My brothers! The Lord has called me to the way of simplicity and humility; such is the way He wants of me and of those who believe in me and follow me. Therefore, I will not have another Rule, be it St. Benedict's or St. Augustine's or St. Bernard's, nor any other manner of living but what the Lord has shown and given me. He wants me to be poor and foolish in this world. But with that learning and wisdom of yours may the Lord confound you and through His stewards punish you, so that you will return to your vocation for all your faultfinding, whether you want to or not."

The silence that followed this outburst was terrifying.

The cardinal rose and proclaimed the session closed; it would be reopened in two hours' time.

The friars dispersed in glum silence, but in the most orderly manner. It was as if they wished to indicate that they were all for discipline and obedience and demanded only what was reasonable, and the cardinal remarked on it when he was alone with Francis in his tiny hut.

"I care little about discipline," Francis said. "Obedience, yes, but not discipline; that is a thing for the schools and for soldiers. Every man who comes to me does so of his own free will. He is a volunteer of God. And when he has become a friar, he must still offer up his life voluntarily. There is no other way for me."

"Yet you wish them to come back to your vocation whether they want to or not," the cardinal said evenly.

There was a long pause. Francis dropped on his knees. "I have sinned," he said.

"And I absolve you," the cardinal said very gently. After a while Francis rose. "What am I to do?" he murmured.

"Think," the cardinal said. "In your life you are attempting the imitation of the greatest life ever lived. That is really what every Christian ought to do to the best of his ability. There were a few men who became your early followers. Some excellent, some less than excellent. But you cannot expect to find five thousand men like yourself."

"But I am nothing!" Francis cried. "All I do is to try and live . . ."

". . . as near to our Lord as you can. But do not expect every one of your sons to be able to do so to the same degree. A robe cannot consist of jewels only. You will be the first to acknowledge that your Master's life was greater than yours and that He surpassed you in all things. . . ."

"He is the sun. . . . I am a glowworm."

"But do you think our Lord expects you to be as great and good as He is? And that He will threaten you with punishment unless you are? As He has compassion for you—have it for those who are less ardent, less humble, less self-denying. Oh, I know you have shown it many a time in the past. You allow those who need more food than others to eat more. You look after them like a father and a mother in one. But the Rule that is good and practical, however severe, for twelve men, may no longer be so good and so practical for five thousand. And next year there may be eight or ten thousand!"

"The Rule—" Francis said vehemently, and then broke off.

"In a mystical sense you *are* the Order of the Friars Minor," the cardinal said. "Your body has grown, as the Church, the Mystical Body of Christ, has grown. The Church is a living entity. So is your Order, built into the Church. That means development and through development, of necessity, changes. No truth can be ever abandoned. But new ways must constantly be found to spread what St. Paul used to call the Way."

"He lived in poverty."

"But he did not beg and was yet pleasing to God."

"I have never said my way was the only one, my lord Cardinal."

"I know that. But you now have only the choice of withdrawing from your own Order with a few elite men, leaving the others to find their own level—or of being more sympathetic to their claims, even if you and all those who are strong enough continue to adhere to the Rule as you have to this day. Remember the words of the great Innocent, when you stood before him in Rome and he told you that your Rule was too severe and that he must think ahead? He saw what was going to happen, inevitably, when your sons multiplied. Now you, too, can see it. In fact, you started paying heed to it two years ago when you instituted the rank of Provincial."

Francis said nothing. After a pause the cardinal went on: "A king cannot administer a country as if it were a mere village. The commander of a great army cannot lead it as if it were a mere patrol. The Pope cannot lead the Church today as Linus, Anacletus and Clement led it after the death of St. Peter. I know exactly how you feel, Francis. But much depends upon you and your army and I can think of few things so sad and so dangerous as permanent discord between your brothers and yourself. When one of your brothers needed more food than you did and yet was ashamed to eat, you yourself ate more than you needed to help him overcome his shyness."

Francis looked straight ahead, from tortured eyes.

"Brother Francis," the cardinal said, "dear Brother Francis— I am your deeply devoted friend."

"I am your very humble son and servant," Francis said. "The matter of new missions will be debated in the Chapter. May I ask once more for your permission to go on such a mission myself?"

There was a long pause. The cardinal sighed deeply. "You have my permission, my son . . . and my blessing."

At the Chapter of Pentecost, 1219, a number of new provinces were instituted. The matter of commendatory letters to the brothers to be issued by the Holy See was shelved. A great number of brothers came forward to volunteer for missions to the infidels. Brother Vitale was put in charge of those who were going to Morocco. Brother Giles was to lead those destined for Tunis. And Brother Francis was to head the mission to Egypt.

During his absence two vicars-general were nominated: Brother Matthew of Narni and Brother Gregory of Naples.

CHAPTER TWENTY-SEVEN
A.D. 1219

The harsh, guttural voice came wailing across the sand: *"Amân . . . ia Allah . . . amân . . . moje . . ."*

Hurrying toward the man Francis could see that he was lying on his stomach; his turban, split on top, was caked with blood; his hands moved feebly.

From behind came the muffled sound of hooves and before Francis could turn his head, an armored squire on a heavy charger rode by, without giving him a glance. Francis caught a glimpse of a narrow face, a hooked nose and a flowing moustache. The squire reached the wounded Saracen, reined in his horse and thrust his lance through the man's back. The Saracen gave a shriek, his legs twitched convulsively. He was dead when Francis arrived, gasping with the effort of running in the glaring heat.

"You shouldn't go about here without an escort," the squire said amiably in French.

"He said, *'Amân,'*" Francis said in a trembling voice. "What does that mean?"

"Mercy."

"And *moje?*"

"Water."

"That is what he asked for in the name of God," Francis said. "And you gave him death instead."

"So I did. You are new here in the desert, aren't you? I thought so. That brute still had enough life in him to kill you with this," and he touched the Saracen's curved bow with the reddened tip of his lance. "See, he had the arrow ready? Perhaps he wouldn't have had the strength to draw his bow and perhaps he would have. But in any case: What did you expect me to do . . . is it Father or Brother? Brother, then. Should I have given the dog water? Should I have nursed him back to health so that he could do to me what they did to my two cousins? The Saracens caught them on patrol, six months ago. We found what was left—by them and by the vultures and jackals. It wasn't pretty. When you've been out here long enough, you know the difference between a wound caused by the fangs of an animal or the claws of a bird—and wounds made by man. What the Saracens do is much worse. They are fiends. Come along, Brother, you shouldn't be here at all."

"But . . . the body?"

The squire laughed. "They'll send out men to bury him according to their rites, never fear."

They turned back to the camp. Francis felt like weeping, but the tears would not come, not in the terrible, treeless, flowerless, grassless, sun-parched bleakness that was Egypt. It was said there were lovely oases here, gardens full of slim palm trees, heavy with their fruit, but he had not seen them; only the desert and the stretch of the sea, gray and leaden under the searing sun, as if the Mediterranean had lost color at the sight of this land.

"The Holy Land," the squire grumbled. "What's holy about it? Infidels, locusts, scorpions, sand vipers and sand fleas . . . never go barefoot here, Brother, and keep a rag tied over your feet at night, or you'll wake up with a couple of hundred sand-flea eggs embedded under your toes. They love toes, the devil may know why, and you'll get swellings and ulcers. A thousand good men became invalids for weeks and months, before we found out what the trouble was. Holy Land! Look at that sun, or rather don't, or you'll get a stroke."

"The sun," Francis said, "is strong and beautiful. It is we who are weak."

"The sun is a plague in Egypt, Brother. Even St. Lawrence was only roasted once . . . to us it happens day after day."

"The Lord would not have been incarnated in the loveliest part of the world," Francis said, "or what would people say who have to live in less lovely parts?"

"Eh? Maybe so, maybe so. But when He's given us better parts, why should we come here, instead of being content with our lot? It's warm at home too, now, but it's beautiful. I'd give an arm to be there this minute—God knows no one's ever going to persuade me again to go on a crusade."

"Will you leave the places sacred to every Christian in the hands of people whom you called brutes and fiends? To desecrate them, to destroy them? If robbers played dice on your parents' graves would you not feel indignant?"

"Probably," the squire said. He wanted to scratch his head but was hindered by hauberk and helmet. "But fortunately my

214

parents are very much alive. At least they were when I left," he added glumly. "But God knows whether . . ."

"God knows," Francis interposed not unkindly. "Let that be sufficient for now."

"Why did you come out here, holy Brother?" the squire asked. "I don't mean why you are with the army, though that, too, is more than I can fathom. But this is part of yesterday's battlefield."

"I know, and that's why I came. There might have been a wounded man left who needed help and solace. And there was, but . . ."

"I gave that fellow all the help and solace he needed," the squire said grimly. "You don't speak Arabic, Brother, do you? No, of course not, you asked me about *amân* and *moje*. What do you want in this part of the world? Convert the heathen? How can you, without speaking their language? Mind you, even if you could . . ."

"I picked up some of the lingua franca."

"That does help a little. Though how you're going to explain Christian dogma to an Arab in the lingua franca is beyond me. It would be difficult enough in good, simple French. Believe me, Brother, you're wasting your time on these people. You'll never get anywhere with them."

"Don't you think, Brother Frenchman, that that is what the Devil might have said to our Lord, if he had known that He was going to be incarnated on earth?"

The squire began to laugh. "So I'm the devil, am I? Well, if I am, I'm a poor devil. And so are we all in this god-forsaken army."

They were approaching the camp now. A thin chain of sentinels was drawn entirely around it, to guard against one of those lightning-swift attacks of Arab cavalry. Even from a distance they could hear the shrill voices of women and drunken laughter.

"This God-forsaking army, you mean," Francis said sadly.

"Eh? Oh, that. That's army life, Brother, always has been, always will be. You can't stop them from having their fling when they know it may well be their last."

Francis stopped in his tracks. "How can they fight and win for the cross, if they behave like that?"

"They'll fight all right, Brother, but they won't win. Look at what happened yesterday."

Francis nodded. It had been a grave setback, to say the least. The men were talking about it in whispers. All through the night bodies had been buried hurriedly in mass graves, a single cross for fifty, a hundred men and more. No one seemed to know how great the losses really were. The tents were filled with wounded whose shrieks rent the night so that no one slept. Francis had gone from one bed to another, comforting, carrying water, bandaging wounds, holding the torch as the physician tried to save a man's life by making him a cripple. Few men survived amputations here. Almost invariably mortification set in, as they called it, the wound became black and putrid and the man died in torments. There were many who would die tonight.

But they said that Cardinal Pelagius had not lost confidence for a moment, not even when the Saracen cavalry broke through in the rear of the Christian army and for two long hours they had had to fight on all sides at once.

The sentinels let Francis and the squire pass without question.

"I feel sorry for you, Brother," the Frenchman said. "This is no place for you. Go home—that's the best advice I can give you and if you say the Devil would say the same, at least you can be sure that he wouldn't say it out of compassion as I do."

Half an hour ago the man had stabbed a wounded Saracen to death. Francis stared at him. "I will not go," he said, "not as long as there is a glimmer of hope for our cause and how could there not be? But you mean well, I know. If I was harsh with you, remember that our Lord was harsh with St. Peter when *he* tried to prevent Him from doing what He had to do. But never again kill a man who lies helpless and wounded. If the heathen do so, we must not imitate them. How else can we say that our belief is better than theirs, and be believed?"

"You are a child, Brother," the Frenchman said. "But I wish you'd say a prayer for me some time. I'd like to go home to my parents alive."

"That will be as God wills it," Francis said. "But I will pray."

Cardinal Pelagius had the snow-white hair and beard of a venerable patriarch, the features of an eagle and the carriage of a military man. The most orthodox of Catholics, he bore the name of the famous fifth century heretic. When one of his commanders, a witty Portuguese, remarked on it, the cardinal answered dryly: "If my namesake had had the pleasure of leading this army, he would have never denied the dogma of Original Sin."

Sitting at his field desk, a wooden crate covered by a woolen rug, he listened, stony-faced, to the report of Count Guy de

Choisy, whom he trusted although he was not a Spaniard. In fact, Choisy was the only commander whom he had dispatched to collect the lists of losses of the black day that was yesterday.

The cardinal's eyes were fixed on the large crucifix on the side of the tent; his hands encircled the hilt of his large sword.

"The Italian contingent lost one hundred and fifty-three knights," the Count de Choisy said, "and four hundred and eleven wounded. The dead include the Duke of San Telmo and the Count of San Mauricio."

"Go on, come to an end," the cardinal said somberly.

"The Sicilian contingent: fifty-seven knights dead, one hundred and thirteen wounded. And the Count of Vandria is missing."

"The Count of Vandria?" The cardinal looked at Choisy from under his thick white eyebrows. His eyes were fiercely alive, despite the rings of sleeplessness.

"Yes, Your Eminence. He was not really a member of the Sicilian contingent. He only arrived ten days ago."

"Nine," the cardinal said.

"There are many such single volunteers, some with a small retinue, some without any."

"I know that. But . . . missing, you say?"

"He was taking part in the defense of the Nile bank, at the end of the battle, when it was growing dark. The Sicilian commander does not know what happened to him. He does not seem to have liked him, because the count always kept to himself and would not be drawn into talk."

The cardinal nodded, as if the report fitted in with his own thoughts. "He may have been a spy," he said brusquely. "There are renegades enough in the Sultan's camp. But if he was, he cannot tell the Sultan much he doesn't know. Al Kamil knows how many we are—or rather how few. And neither he nor the Count of Vandria can know that we have lost over five thousand men."

"If only the Emperor would arrive," de Choisy said between his teeth, "or at least the reinforcements we were promised so long ago."

"They'll arrive, I think," the cardinal said. "I'm not so sure about the Emperor himself."

"He has sworn to take part in the crusade."

"In my lifetime every emperor has proved to be a perjurer," Pelagius said coldly. "Why should this one be an exception? Besides—" He broke off.

Besides he would insist on taking over the command of the entire army, de Choisy thought.

"Reinforcements," the cardinal said, "that's what we must have. I cannot attack Damietta with any hope of success with the army as it is now. When we conquered the Tower of Chains I thought it would be a matter of days, of two weeks at the utmost. But they seem to have inexhaustible reserves. Now we must wait." He sighed deeply.

It is difficult to wait when one is Pelagius, de Choisy thought.

"The fortifications of the camp must be improved," the cardinal went on. "And the camp itself is to be enlarged toward the southwest."

Choisy looked at him in surprise. "It has proved quite big enough so far, Your Eminence."

"There is no harm in letting the infidels believe that it isn't," the cardinal replied, with a wintry smile. "At least it will *look* as if we were certain of reinforcements arriving shortly. And, Choisy! Not a word about the figures of our losses to anybody! Not even to Count Jean of Brienne. You just don't know them, not the sum total. The spirit of depression is worse than ten thousand Saracens."

"Yes, Your Eminence."

"Go, then. And if there's anybody out there to see me, you may send him in."

"I will, Your Eminence." Choisy clanked out and the cardinal sank into deep brooding. The infidels, too, had had losses, heavy losses, as usual when there was hand-to-hand fighting. Their best results were always obtained when they would employ their usual cavalry tactics, of rushing up, shooting a volley of arrows and fleeing, with their shields thrown on their backs, the same tactics that their Parthian ancestors used against the Roman legions twelve centuries ago. War never changed very much. What if the Sultan, too, felt that he could not afford another large-scale attack? A stalemate . . . for the time being at least?

Someone was in the room. Instinctively, the cardinal's hand flew to the dagger in his belt, a better weapon than a long sword in the limited space of a tent. Then he saw that the man was unarmed; that he was small; that he was a friar, one of those brown mendicants Cardinal Hugolino of Ostia had recommended to him by letter. "But do not, I entreat you, mention to them that I have written you on their behalf, for they wish to undertake their mission without commendation on the part of the Church, and to travel as the apostles used to do." Strange people. They all looked very much alike in their brown rags, but this one was their leader.

"Brother . . . Francis, I believe?"

"Your servant, lord Cardinal." Francis knelt, but there was no way of kissing the ring on a hand covered by a plated glove.

"What is it you want, my son?"

"Lord Cardinal, it has come to me that our Lord may want to use persuasion rather than force. I beg your permission to go to the Sultan's camp."

Pelagius frowned. "That's asking for certain death," he said curtly. "The Sultan has issued an order to have a gold piece paid for every Christian head delivered to him. You have been long enough with us to know that. What happened to your three companions?"

"We were thirteen when we set out, my lord Cardinal, but nine fell ill in Acre where we landed and the others here in this camp."

"It would probably be better for you if you had fallen ill as well," Pelagius said with bitter humor. "From illness one may recover, not from death. This idea of yours is madness."

"It is not my idea, lord Cardinal."

"You mean you were inspired by God? But can you be quite certain that it is not really a temptation on the part of the Devil?"

Francis smiled cheerfully. "I have no dealings with him, lord Cardinal."

Not the ordinary fanatic. They could smile only in some superior way, as if to suggest that they alone knew what God wanted and that they did not expect lesser people to understand them. Still, it *was* madness.

"What do you want to do when . . . if you get through the enemy lines?"

"I will speak to the Sultan, lord Cardinal."

"You'll never get anywhere near him."

"That will be as God wills it, lord Cardinal."

"Of course," Pelaguis said dryly. But his mind was working. They might take the little man for a spy and kill him at once. Torture him, perhaps. On the other hand, they might think he was a kind of unofficial emissary sent to start negotiations—the kind of emissary one could always disavow without danger to dignity. They might . . . it was quite incalculable. "I can take no responsibility for such an undertaking," he said briskly. "I will neither permit it nor forbid it. But there is one thing I must

219

be sure about: you must do nothing that will bring shame upon the Christian name."

Francis smiled. "Thank you, lord Cardinal," he said, knelt once more and departed.

Friendly little fellow, the cardinal thought. One might at least have given him a blessing.

Ibrahim ben Masud, patrol leader of the camel riders of Bishar, saw him first, a ragged little man walking all alone across the sand as if the desert belonged to him. He did not seem to be armed.

"Wait here," he told his men. "No . . . don't shoot the *giaour* yet."

He drove his magnificent camel out of the hollow and up the dune, the short jereed ready for a throw.

The little man went on as if he had not seen the almost ghostlike appearance of rider and mount. Perhaps he was blinded by the sun—he was walking straight into it.

"*Wakkif* . . . Stop!" Ibrahim ben Masud said sharply.

The little man stopped, turned his head a little, saw him and . . . smiled. Smiled! Ibrahim ben Masud looked around quickly to see whether there was any reason for a smile. But there was no one in sight, not for seventy or eighty paces anyway, and the Franki were not good enough marksmen for a distance greater than that.

What in the name of all the holy caliphs did the *giaour* have to smile about, unarmed and alone at twelve paces from a sharp jereed?

Ibrahim ben Masud approached and as he did the Frank said: "Sultan!" and pointed to himself. Ibrahim threw back his head and laughed. "You a sultan," he said. "They choose them strangely in Frankistan." But then it occurred to him—and he was far from being the first to think so—that the ragged little man was *deli*, crazy, a madman, and was it not said that such men enjoyed the favor of the Most High? "Who are you?" he asked warily.

"Sultan," said the little man again, but this time he pointed to some distance behind his interrogator. Then he said in the lingua franca: "Take me to the Sultan, O commander."

Ibrahim laughed again. "The Malik al Kamil, Ruler of the Faithful, Unconquered, Lion of the Desert . . . what has he to do with the scum of Frankistan?" he replied in the same language. "You are my prisoner." He uttered a sharp, guttural noise and at once six more camel riders appeared on the crest

220

of the dune and rode down. The little man was surrounded. Still smiling, he walked up to Ibrahim's mount and patted its beautifully curved neck.

Ibrahim grinned. No stranger could dare to do that unpunished to a camel reared by the tribe of Bishar. It would snap at the madman and he would find himself with an ear less or with a very painful wound in the arm. There . . . it was bending down its head. But instead of biting, it began to rub its head on the little man's shoulder, uttering the rough, bleating noise it usually made when it was given a handful of dates.

The seven Arabs looked at each other, bewildered.

"Are you a *sachhar*, a magician?" Ibrahim asked in an uneasy tone.

"I am a messenger," the little man said amiably. "May it please you to lead me to the Sultan."

Once more the Arabs stared at each other blankly. It was scarcely conceivable that the Franki, infidels though they were, would send such an ambassador to the Sultan.

"Who sent you?" Ibrahim asked point-blank.

"The highest authority there is," the little man replied, "and I have a great and joyful message for the Sultan."

Ibrahim clicked his tongue. "This is too much for us," he said in Arabic. "Lift him on your camel, oh Amed. We'll take this wizard to Emir Mottaleb ben Tarik. Let him be the judge of what is to be done with him."

Amed made his mount kneel. Then the little man found himself seized and lifted up bodily by sinewy brown arms and placed ungently on the high saddle in front of the rider. Immediately the camel rose with three sharp jerks and the cavalcade sped away, riding so fast that no armored knight on horseback could have kept up with them.

Half an hour later they reached a large camp, outside the south walls of Damietta, and Emir Mottaleb ben Tarik's tent.

The emir was a man feared for his temper. He was known to use his whip of hippopotamus hide freely on those who incurred his disfavor and it was said that he had to renew his harem frequently because so many of his wives suddenly died. But he was great in battle and his family one of the leading in Kurdistan. Salah-ed-Din himself had hailed from Kurdistan and so of course did the Malik al Kamil, his nephew and successor. The emir was a tall man with a short black beard, sprinkled with silver, and his face was the color of a walnut. He listened to Ibrahim ben Masud's report with some indifference. "Where is the *giaour?*"

"There, O Emir. Amed is holding his arm."

"That little dog? You've been wasting my time and yours. He's either mad or a spy. Here's your gold-piece. Tell Ali to have him killed."

CHAPTER TWENTY-EIGHT

Francis heard nothing of the talk between the emir and Ibrahim ben Masud. He was standing at no great distance, but he was feeling rather dizzy. He had never been on a camel before —from Acre to the Christian camp he and his brothers had used donkeys—and he felt as if he had been on a small ship in a heavy storm, lurching back and forth and moving up and down at the same time. Half a dozen times he would have fallen off, if the man behind him had not held him in the saddle.

Now he could hear a strange noise, rhythmic and thumping, as of distant drums but he thought at first that it was only in his head.

The leader of those who had captured him came back and said something, but it was in Arabic and Francis stared at him, trying to find the meaning of his words. The thumping, drumming noise became louder.

Then, to Francis' utter surprise, the man suddenly turned away, dropped on his knees and stretched out his arms in a gesture of prayer. And he was not the only one—all around turbaned and burnoosed figures prostrated themselves. The sentries at the emir's tent, the groups of Saracen soldiers to right and left, the traders, inevitable here as they were in the Christian camp—they all fell flat as if they had been mowed down by a gigantic scythe. What had come over them all?

But the rhythmic, thumping noise grew louder; it hurt one's ears, and then between the rows of tents appeared a large group of men in emerald-green jelabs and white turbans, all pounding away on large copper kettledrums. Behind them came a procession of dignitaries, so richly clad that their clothes were almost invisible under golden ornaments and tassels; following the dignitaries a solitary rider rode on the most beautiful horse Francis had ever seen. It was milk white, with rose-red nostrils and its mane and tail were cascades of spun silver. The rider was wearing a black-and-red turban and a burnoose of some shimmery material, which so blended with the color of his horse that rider and mount seemed to be one silvery creature. His face, the color of ivory, showed fine, regular features, and his beautifully groomed beard was studded with pearls. He was the Sultan. There could be no doubt about it.

Francis' dizziness vanished, and as he looked at the magnificent apparition he gave thanks to God who had brought him eye to eye with the man he had come to see, all the way from Assisi.

The Malik al Kamil, Ruler of the Faithful, Unconquered, Lion of the Desert, was mildly amused to see among the thousands of prostrate backs one ragged little man standing upright and looking at him, neither in adulation nor in anger, but with what seemed to be the most lively interest; and, on the spur of the moment, he stopped his horse.

At once Francis called out in the lingua franca: "I have come to talk to you, O King of the East." The title appeared natural enough to him, but to the Sultan it was not only refreshingly new but also intensely flattering. It was tantamount to calling him the ruler of all countries east of Europe, and there were many of them—indeed many more than Francis could have enumerated.

So the little man had come to talk to him. He was obviously not a Moslem. How had he got here?

"Emir Mottaleb ben Tarik," said the Sultan.

The emir jumped up, approached and knelt in front of the shimmering man, who said a few words in a low voice. The emir murmured the obligatory "To hear is to obey," and the Sultan rode on.

Behind him the prostrate forms came to life. Everybody had risen when the emir said to Ibrahim ben Masud: "By order of the Ruler this prisoner will be sent to the green tent at once."

The patrol leader touched his forehead with his right hand, turned and seized Francis' thin arm. A quarter of an hour later he delivered him at the green tent to the officer on duty. "A Franki prisoner sent by Emir Mottaleb ben Tarik at the special order of the Sultan, may Allah give *him* a thousand years."

The officer looked at Francis with some astonishment. Then he shrugged his shoulders. "It is well," he said with great equanimity, and Ibrahim ben Masud withdrew. For the rest of the day he carefully avoided being seen by the emir. The Christian magician still had his head on his shoulders—the best possible proof that he was a magician—and the emir was quite capable of demanding his gold-piece back.

Francis was given a small tent for himself, fresh clothes and food enough for ten friars. He refused to shed his tattered robe for the silk and muslin garments, ate only what was necessary for the sustenance of Brother Ass, as he had come to call his body, and asked several times to be allowed to speak to the Sultan.

The large Negro who served as his waiter, cook, general servant and jailer grinned. "When the great Malik want to see you, he say so."

"When will he say so, do you think?"

"Me no think. The great Malik say so today, tomorrow, next year, . . . when it is written in Book of Life. Meantime good eat, drink, sleep. You want singing girl perhaps? Dancing girl? White Circassian? Brown girl?" He was surprised and looked mildly reproachful when his kindly offer was declined rather coldly.

The Sultan looked at Roger of Vandria and smiled. "Our clothes suit you well," he said. "One would have to look very closely to discover that you are not a Moslem, a noble of the Hauran, perhaps, or even of Kurdistan."

"This is great courtesy on Your Majesty's part," Roger said, looking down at his burnoose and slippers. "And, aside from concealing the presence of a Frankish envoy in your camp, I must admit it is a much cooler way of dressing than ours. The Christian army would do well to adopt the fashion."

"They never will," Al Kamil said. "The Arab traveling through the mountains of Kurdistan will not shed his garments, made for the sun of the desert, and I had great trouble before I could get my Kurds to dress like Arabs here. Man is a basically stupid animal, clinging to what he is accustomed to. He will not learn from his fellow man and is convinced in some obstinate and vainglorious way that he and his tribe or people or religion alone are right in everything. There are very few exceptions."

"That is exactly what my imperial master says," Roger exclaimed.

"I said there are a few exceptions," the Sultan replied, "and from what you have told me, I gather that *Imberadour* Frederick is one of them. Perhaps one must stand on the summit of the mountain to see how small the difference is between two towns in the valley. Yet when we descend again we lose our feeling of distance and once more embrace a cause we have learned to disdain. Your master has spoken beautiful and wise words through your lips. Yet I have heard that he, too, has sworn to join this mad and senseless enterprise."

"He had to," Roger explained. "He could not, at that stage,

risk incurring the enmity of the Pope—not before he was safely in the saddle. But he has been playing a vacillating game from the first."

The Sultan nodded. "I know that the High Priest of the infidels is powerful in your lands. We also have similar little troubles occasionally. How can your master hope to escape from the oath he has sworn? There will have to be an end to his vacillation at some time."

"The Pope is old and may well die before that happens," Roger replied. "But there is a better answer, thanks to the fact that I have the honor to be a living bridge between the two greatest men and greatest minds of our time."

Al Kamil did not bat an eye at the outrageous flattery. He was accustomed to it. "What is the 'better answer'?" he asked directly.

Roger smiled. "There is always the possibility of an understanding between two such men—an understanding known only to very few. We Sicilians have a proverb: If a man is too strong as an enemy, you will fare better as his ally."

Al Kamil closed his eyes. "You have alluded to such a possibility before," he said, "but an alliance is made against a common enemy. Who is he?"

Roger could still hear the inflection in Frederick's voice, back in the castle in Germany: *He will then say: an alliance against whom?* He gave the answer as instructed: "Our common enemies are very powerful. Stupidity, backwardness, misunderstandings, narrow mindedness and fear. The greatest of them all is fear."

"Fear of what?" the Sultan murmured.

"The fear of both East and West is that each will be overrun by the other and forced to adopt the other's religion as well as endure his tyranny. An alliance would end such a fear and would lead to exchange of knowledge as well as goods."

Al Kamil sat motionless. He said nothing.

"Beyond that," Roger continued, "there could be a military alliance as well. My imperial master is not blind to a new danger that has arisen in the East—your East as well as ours—in the form of a conqueror of great ruthlessness: the Great Khan of the Mongols."

A week ago news had reached Al Kamil that Jenghiz Khan had conquered both Samarkand and Bokhara. It was most unlikely that this emissary knew that and entirely impossible that the *Imberadour* had heard of it. He said: "The Mongols are far away," and he shrugged.

"There are other enemies nearer at hand," Roger said. "As long as man has lived on earth there has been the danger that can come to the father from the son and from the brother to the brother."

(*"I'm told his cousin Al Muazzan, the King of Damascus, is a thorn in his flesh. Each of them regards himself as the true heir of Saladin. Allude to Al Muazzan, but never mention his name."*)

The Sultan said in a flat voice: "We shall be pleased to hear you again on another occasion." It sounded like a rather abrupt end to the audience and Roger feared that even his vague allusion to Al Muazzan had angered the Sultan. But suddenly Al Kamil added: "You spoke of fear. I can well believe that an army has been sent to attack us because the Franks are afraid we might attack them. Yet all the talk is about certain places which must be regained in the name of your religion. . . ."

(*"When he asks you about the Emperor's point of view in regard to the crusade, and whether the Emperor himself will partake in such an enterprise—that is the moment when you will have to speak the truth. He will believe it only if he is a great man. If he is not and therefore does not, it will have done no harm: if he is and does, he will then have to show his own innermost thoughts on the subject and that is what I want."*)

"Most gracious Sultan," Roger said, "a wise ruler must always heed the great currents of his age. The religious fervor of the masses can be made use of for better purposes than those the priests desire. But a sop must be given to both priests and masses. Therefore it is possible and in some circumstances even likely that the Emperor may go on a crusade in his own good time, and appear in what we call the Holy Land with a mighty host. But if then the great Sultan were to grant his imperial brother certain small advantages—including the possession of Jerusalem and a few much smaller places, like Nazareth and Bethlehem—he would have satisfied those powers and there would be no need for a war to weaken us all. It goes without saying that concessions would be made on his part as well. Thus for instance, the Emperor has many thousands of Moslem subjects in Sicily; not only would he treat them in every way as equals with his Christian subjects, but he would also give them full liberty to live according to the rules and rites of their own religion. Also he would introduce Eastern teachings in the West, in schools and universities."

(*"If he is a great man he will then understand that this may* mean the possibility of spreading Islam without a war. Whether it would actually be so or not, I do not know, nor do I care much one way or the other, except that it would weaken the political power of the Pope and to me that is very desirable. In any case, we may see from his answer how much he himself cares about his own religion.")

The Sultan's silence was more enigmatic than ever. From afar came a long-drawn cry, echoed almost at once by a second and a third.

Roger had heard it hundreds of times before, both in Egypt and in Sicily. It was the cry of the muezzin, standing on the tiny platform of his minaret and calling the faithful to prayer.

The flap of the tent was drawn back, two slaves, black as ebony, came in, prostrated themselves, rose and unfolded a small carpet, a priceless piece from Tabriz. After another prostration they withdrew.

The Sultan rose, and now Roger knew certainly that his audience had come to an end. For one more moment he looked into the ruler's face to meet only an expression of studied indifference; and as he withdrew, bowing deeply, he saw the Sultan turn away and kneel down on the carpet to prostrate himself before his Allah, just as his slaves prostrated themselves before him.

Back at the large tent put at his disposal, Roger tried to recapitulate the whole discussion and to come to some conclusions about the ruler's reactions. Al Kamil was interested, that much at least he believed was certain. But there was little if any indication of what he would do. Was he really interested in the spreading of Islam? And did he really believe in it? The fact that he prayed meant little or nothing. He was watched by countless unseen eyes. He must pray and visit the mosque regularly, just as Frederick must go to Mass.

And was he a great man? Impossible to say, at present. Even a second-class diplomat knew how to hide his emotions, and the Sultan's words did not sparkle like fireworks as did Frederick's, but came slowly and quietly, constantly probing. He was not a fanatic, but whether or not—or, better perhaps, how much—he believed was an open question.

So, for all the fireworks, what Frederick really believed was hidden. . . . He jeered and jibed at most things held holy by his subjects, when he could do so without compromising his position. But was that his real self? If it was, why should he be so interested in what Al Kamil believed? Thus both the Western and the Eastern ruler were enigmas

It was too early to come to any conclusion; but, on the other hand, one had, so far, no reason to be dissatisfied. One had managed to get here. That alone was no mean achievement. There had been a few moments of very real danger. Now he was an honored guest, provided with all the luxuries and comfort the Sultan's camp had to offer and shielded against fanatics and spies alike by wearing Oriental garments. Moreover, he had been able to pass on a good deal of what Frederick wanted Al Kamil to know about him and his intentions—if they were his intentions. And all that in less than a week. Another week, or two or three, and he could take back at least a "maybe," and perhaps more. And if it was more, it would be a triumph.

A triumph. Or a betrayal? Well, both, of course. He would be Duke of Vandria at long last. And he would have served his master well—whatever Frederick's real intentions were. But at the same time it was a betrayal. At least, many would regard it as a betrayal of the Christian army or cause or even of the Christian faith . . if they knew about it. He would have opened the way to Europe for Frederick's favorite saint, St. Mohammed, and for the Islam.

Beyond triumph and betrayal lay a third thing: vengeance.

Vengeance against the power that had robbed him of the only woman who could have given him happiness.

They had sent him three lovely young women slaves to look after his needs. They were graceful and submissive. Looking into their beautiful, empty faces he felt that they were wraiths, dreams, charming spectres. They had no meaning.

As for the Christian cause: his ten days with the Christian army had shown him what these men were really out for. Military glory at best, adventure, loot, and often enough merely escape from some tiresome situation in their homeland, a nagging wife, an unpaid debt, the enmity of some petty ruler. Crusaders!

Perhaps Frederick was right. If only one knew what he really believed in, he, who was so keen on knowing what Sultan Al Kamil believed. However much one hated the idea, apparently a man had to believe in *some*thing. . .

Bah. He had been able to pass on Frederick's words to the Sultan. Not many people would have dared undertake such a mission in the midst of a war. It was a feat of courage and it might well turn out to be a diplomatic victory. Why, by the hooves of Satan, could he not feel happy about it?

CHAPTER TWENTY-NINE

Roger was again called to the Sultan two days later, but this time he was led into the largest section of the enormous tent, where councils were held or deputations received in state. To his surprise he found the Sultan surrounded by a number of grave and somewhat sullen-looking men whom he recognized as mullahs and imams, priests of the Moslem faith.

Al Kamil was all smiles. "This should be a diverting experience," he said. "Another emissary has come to see us—some kind of dervish, I think—though he says he has come on his own, or rather, backed only by his God. In the circumstances, it is perhaps not too surprising that he is not in the position to submit an introductory letter. My men would probably have made him a head shorter, if I had not passed by, purely accidentally, if indeed there is such a thing as pure accident except in the theories of certain philosophical schools. I would like to know what he has to say and I want to give these pious and learned servants of Allah the opportunity to hear him. As for you, I want you to be present to tell me afterward what you know of the likes of him. Like you, he has come over from the Christian lines, so there is just the possibility that you may have met before. Therefore you had better take your place over there, in the back."

"To hear is to obey," Roger said, smiling. The place the Sultan pointed out to him was in the shadow and he was dressed in the Eastern fashion. Even if the man had seen him before in the Christian camp, it was not likely that he would be recognized. But who was he? An emissary "backed only by his God"? Perhaps Cardinal Pelagius wanted to open negotiations unofficially and had instructed the man to say that he had come on his own, so that no one could accuse the leader of the Christian army of having tried to make peace with the infidels? Perhaps the wily old cardinal had had an idea similar to Frederick's, but from the military point of view?

Roger's eyes narrowed. Perhaps the Sultan had called him in to show him that he was getting another offer; that he did not have to rely on Frederick alone, and this was his answer, a typical Oriental answer, to his last audience? Anything was possible.

Here was the man, a bearded little fellow in a ragged, brownish robe, not exactly a dignified ambassador. He looked familiar in a way, although Roger could not remember having seen him in the Christian camp. Not an old man; his beard made him look older than his years, no doubt. He might be in his late thirties and he looked ill. While he seemed to hesitate whether or not to approach, Roger saw that three oblong carpets were spread out on the ground parallel to each other and on each was embroidered a large cross.

Suddenly the man walked on, stopping about three yards from the Sultan. There he bowed rather gracefully and courteously. "My Lord offers you peace and happiness, O King of the East," he said in lingua franca.

Roger started. Peace negotiations after all, he thought, and at the same time: Where have I heard that voice before?

The Sultan asked: "Who is your Lord, little dervish?"

"Who else but Jesus Christ, the King of Heaven and Earth, from whom all earthly beings and things receive their bounty."

There was some stirring among the Mohammedan clergy, but Al Kamil said with a twinkle: "Do you realize, little dervish, that you have trodden on the cross?"

The imams and mullahs broke into laughter.

The little friar did not laugh, but he smiled. When the laughter subsided, he said: "Great King of the East, the world knows you as a man of much knowledge. Doubtless you know what every Christian child knows, that our Lord was crucified between two thieves, one repentant and one not. I walked only on the cross on the left side, that of the unrepentant thief."

Al Kamil, too, broke into a smile. "You are a man of quick wit, little dervish from Frankistan. It is a pity that you should belong to those who say that they worship one God and yet worship three; that their supreme leader is the Prince of Peace, and yet wage war against us: that they should love their enemies, and yet come into our lands with sword and lance. But we, too, give honor to Isa ben Marryam, whom we regard as a prophet, though of smaller stature than Mohammed. Why do you not join the true faith?"

"Because I did so when I was still a babe," the little friar said very cheerfully. "It is true that we believe in God the Father, God the Son, and God the Holy Spirit. Yet these three Persons are but one God. Do not seek to understand this mystery, O King of the East, for even the wisest of men is but a little child before God and how could you teach a little child the laws of the stars or of the human body, which it will be able to grasp only when it has grown up? Our Lord is indeed the Prince of Peace, but those who love him wish to see the places where He

230

walked on earth held in reverence by those who believe in Him. And for this they are ready to lay down their lives in combat, if need be. Yet my very mission to you is proof that the Christian prefers peace to war and is ready to call on you to make peace."

That voice, Roger thought, I know that voice. But where have I heard it, and when? The man was some kind of monk, but of what Order? Not the Benedictines, not the Augustinians, nor the Cistercians either. Besides, one did not have so many friends or acquaintances who were monks . . . one did not have any, really, and as for the followers of Brother Francis . . . Brother . . . Francis . . . Roger leaned forward, staring hard. Off with that beard—a little filling out of those hollow cheeks—could it be?

"Does the high imam who is in command of the Christian army know that you are here on this mission?" the Sultan asked innocently.

"He doesn't know it for certain, King of the East," the friar replied, "but I think he guesses it by now. I told him I wanted to go and he would say neither yes nor no. If I tried, he said, I must do nothing to bring shame upon the Christian name."

The Sultan's eyes were slits. Was this supreme adroitness or supreme simplicity? In any case: the Christian leader knew— which was tantamount to at least half agreeing. "Your leader does not seem to hold you in high esteem, little dervish," he said slowly, "if he thinks you capable of bringing shame upon your cause."

"There is no reason at all why he should hold me in esteem," the friar said. "I am neither a priest nor a learned man. But what does it matter? I am concerned only with the honor and glory of my Master and I have come to you to tell you about Him. If you accept Him as what He is—the Son of God and therefore your Master as well as mine—all the rest will be easy. For if you were to become a Christian, O King of the East, and your people with you, then the Holy Places would be in Christian hands and there would be no reason for any Christian to come to you sword in hand. Accept my Lord and all is well. He said so Himself: 'Seek ye first for the kingdom of God, and all these things shall be added unto you.' "

An admirable short cut, no doubt, Roger thought grimly. It was Brother Francis, Francis Bernardone, the gaily plumed little bird from Assisi turned friar, the little coward from Spoleto bent on becoming a Christian martyr. Where did he find the courage to walk into the Sultan's camp, entirely on his own, without any written introduction to back him up? It was dangerous enough with a letter signed by the Emperor himself. And the Sultan seemed to be quite amused, which was more than could be said of the Mohammedan clergy. The pious and learned dignitaries were ablaze with anger.

Al Kamil saw it, of course. "You see around you some of our most devout and high-ranking priests, as you would call them, little dervish. They know a great deal about the prophet whom you believe to be the Son of God. Be careful, then, what you say in their presence."

"What good can it be to them to know anything about our Lord, if they do not believe what matters most?" Francis said. "Namely that He was the Son of God, co-eternal with the Father, who was incarnate by the Holy Spirit of the Blessed Virgin Mary to die for our sins on the cross—your sins, O King of the East, those of your learned priests, and my own—and that on the third day after His crucifixion He rose again from the dead and that He ascended into heaven whence He shall come to judge the living and the dead."

"Ruler of the Faithful," a gray-bearded imam said in Arabic, "will you really go on listening to this dog of an infidel? Will you not rather have him killed and by that very order come nearer by a step to paradise yourself?"

There was a general murmur of assent and Roger felt that the end was very near. Al Kamil was a broad-minded man and very powerful, but even he had to take heed of the clergy. Strange that Roger of Vandria should be avenged for the loss of his love by a bevy of mullahs.

"My priests," the Sultan said in the lingua franca, "do not wish me to listen to you, but rather to have you killed."

"Yes, I thought the learned sirs were not eager to bear with me," Francis said amiably.

"I don't think I shall order your death—at least not at present," Al Kamil said, observing him sharply. "You are, no doubt, misguided, but you seem to be a man Allah Himself would find it difficult to be angry with. Stay with us and see how you like life at my court."

"I will do so with much joy, O King of the East," Francis replied without a moment's hesitation, "if you and your people will accept Christ as your Lord."

"You are asking for too much, I fear," Al Kamil told him indulgently. "And, believe me, there is a great deal to be said for our great prophet, Mohammed, and his holy book, the Koran."

"In that case, why not make a test?" Francis suggested. "Let a great fire be lighted before your tent and these learned priests of yours and I will enter it. Then God may show which is the true faith."

Roger gasped. If that was supposed to be a bluff, it was a very dangerous one. There were fanatics enough among Moslem priests and at least some of them might accept the challenge.

The Sultan glanced at his imams and mullahs. They looked a little vague, as if they had not understood the little dervish's words, and one of them, standing at the back, began to move with great dignity toward the exit of the tent.

"I don't think my priests are very likely to consent to this test of yours, little dervish," Al Kamil said, smiling.

He's got out of it, Roger thought, half relieved, half angry.

"Then I will enter the fire alone," Francis said quietly, "if you promise for yourself and for your people that you will worship Christ if I come out of the fire unhurt." After a little pause he added: "If I should be burned to death, it will be due only to my sins. But if God protects me, it is a clear sign of His holy will and you must all accept Christ."

Now he has killed himself, Roger thought. This is too good a spectacle for the Sultan to miss. The man is mad. He is a fanatic. He is magnificent. By all the angels and devils, he is the only crusader in the army. What a pity he is done for. Those priests will take him at his word, even if the Sultan doesn't.

But just then the gray-bearded mullah said angrily: "This man is probably a magician. He will use tricks known only to the *afreets* and jinni or to the Shaitan himself, to lure the faithful away from the true teaching. Do not listen to him."

"Can you work magical feats, little dervish?" the Sultan asked with some curiosity.

Francis shook his head. "A man cannot expect help from Satan when he is trying to win souls for God."

"I shall never be able to convince my priests that you are not a magician," Al Kamil said, with a wry smile. "But I am pleased with your courage. Ask me for any reasonable favor and I will grant it to you."

"Lord Sultan," Francis said softly, "the arms of Christ are wide open to you."

"We seem to differ about what is reasonable," Al Kamil said. "Tell me, are you the member of some Order?"

"Yes, lord Sultan."

"And they believe as you do?"

"Yes, lord Sultan."

"I shall allow *you* to go to Jerusalem," the Sultan said, "and to the other places so dear to your heart. I shall allow some of your brothers to come and stay there and watch over them. No, do not speak! If you were about to thank me, there is no reason for it, for you gave me a pleasant hour and this permission of mine is my thanks to you. And if you were going to ask for more, I will not listen. Stay in our camp, as long as you wish, but if you prefer it, go visit your shrines. Go in peace, little dervish." The Sultan clapped his hands and Mustapha appeared, the head of the bodyguard, a man of herculean build, splendidly dressed and armed to the teeth. "Mustapha," Al Kamil said, "this little man is my guest as long as he wishes to stay. Watch over him carefully, so that no harm comes to him. Should he wish to depart, see him off safely, wherever he may wish to go and arrange his journey for him in a manner suitable to one who enjoys my favor."

"To hear is to obey, Ruler of the Faithful."

When Francis and Mustapha had left, the Sultan turned to his priests. "You came here, armed with arguments and contempt," he said, "and you let a little Frankish dervish surpass you in courage. He was ready to die for Isa ben Marryam. There was little readiness on your part to die for Mohammed. By the black stone of the Kaaba, our prophet was not well served today. You may go."

They filed out in silence.

Al Kamil began to chuckle. "Come forward now, O Emir of Frankistan. Why, you look almost as perturbed as my poor mullahs! Why is that? You can scarcely be afraid that the little dervish will make a Christian out of you . . . you already are one. Oh well, I will probe no further into your mind. But you can see now that your imperial master is not the only one to offer terms. However, his conditions, difficult as they are to fulfill, are still lighter than those of that ragged little dervish. Let us hope, though, that they are equally sincere. So far our contact with the Occident has been made only by sword and lance, and although there is, at present, a lull in the fighting, it may be resumed very shortly. But in the meantime we are glad to have made two more contacts of an entirely different kind: through you, O Emir of Frankistan, we have made the acquaintance of your master's mind, the mind of the Occident; through that little dervish we have met the heart of the Occident. Allah alone knows which of the two will prevail."

CHAPTER THIRTY
A.D. 1220

The little band of friars was crowded together in the garden of the tiny monastery at Acre.

"We look like so many prisoners after a long period of hardship and privation," Brother Elias said.

"Like so many moulting sparrows," Francis suggested, and his smile lit up most of the faces around him. None of the brothers had escaped the ravages of an alien and dangerous climate. Francis had resisted its earlier attacks, but now his eyes were red rimmed, swollen and painful to the touch and he had sudden bouts of sharp pains in the abdomen. "Brother Ass likes to be rebellious," he said, when the others looked at him with anxiety. "But in the end he always does what he is told."

"I often wonder whether you should not have stayed longer with that sultan," Brother Elias said. "From all you have told us he must be a remarkable man."

"I stayed for several days, after my audience," Francis replied, "and I talked to many of his men, but there was no response. As for the Sultan himself, I fear that his learning has done to him what it so often does to men. Remembering what Brother Giles used to say: 'Who is richer—he who has only a little garden and cultivates it, or he to whom the whole world was given and who does nothing with it? So much wisdom does not help salvation, but he who really wishes to know much, must work much and keep his head low.' And the call of the master of the vineyard at Monte Ripido to his laborers: 'Work, work, and don't talk.' A learned man loves to talk about what he knows, and as he knows much, he talks much. But God wants him to *listen*. A learned man often makes a storage room of his mind, where so much is stored that there is no room left for God to enter and dwell in it. St. Paul himself battled in vain against such men, in Athens."

"Well, it depends," Brother Elias said slowly. "It depends on who has the better argument."

"Can an argument cause love to grow?" Francis asked. "Besides, the learned man likes to argue for the sake of arguing. It becomes a game with him, and in the end he loves his argument instead of loving God."

Peter Cattaneo nodded. "It was my learning that kept me for a long time from joining you."

"But you overcame yourself. Why do you think our Lord asked us to be like little children if we wanted to enter the kingdom of heaven? It is difficult for a rich man to enter it. Knowledge, too, is wealth."

"But the Sultan did give you a final message." Elias had a knack of always coming back to what was on his mind.

"Yes, he passed by on the day before I left his camp and stopped for a moment to ask me to pray for him that God might reveal to him which faith was most pleasing to Him. He said it in a whisper, lest one of his servants hear it."

"Who knows," Elias said, "perhaps if you had stayed on, you would have triumphed in the end."

"Much has happened since, Brother Elias."

"The great victory in battle, you mean?"

Francis gave no answer. His experiences during the last few months were such that he could not talk much about them, even to his brothers. He had gone back to the Christian camp first, and Cardinal Pelagius gave him an audience. It lasted only a few minutes and consisted of a number of sharp, precise questions about what Francis had seen in the Sultan's camp, fortifications, distribution and number of troops and whether the Sultan was expecting reinforcements in the near future, questions to which Francis had no useful reply. On the other hand, the cardinal's interest in the Sultan's theological views was extremely limited. In the end he gave him his permission to visit the Holy Places, if he could, and Francis set out at once.

Thus began the journey through country where every stone was holy and every tuft of grass. But tradesmen were haggling in the street through which the Lord had carried the cross, Mohammedan soldiers were training on Mount Olivet and in the Garden of Gethsemani and—it was too painful to think of the thousand and one humiliations that were being inflicted on the Lord today even as they were twelve centuries ago. And yet, being there, having been there, caused a new kind of union with Him: Look, here is where I was born. Look, there it was that I went with Peter and James and John to pray and My Father acknowledged Me in front of them. Here it was that I raised Lazarus from the tomb and here they buried Me. This is the spot where I overcame death for all time. It was too much honor, it was overwhelming to be taken like this into the one life that really mattered.

Francis came back to the Christian camp just before the

Feast of the Purification and on that very day the cardinal ordered the great assault on Damietta, the assault that succeeded. The slaughter was frightful, but what followed was worse. There was no crime, no horror, no mortal sin that the crusaders did not commit in the fallen city. He remembered the day and those that followed it as one remembers a nightmare, incoherent, mad and horrible. He wandered through strange streets full of corpses, giving water to the wounded, leading priests to the dying, rescuing a girl from a troop of drunken soldiers, knowing all the time that for one to whom he could give water there were hundreds dying of thirst, that for each one to whom he was able to lead a priest, a thousand died unshriven and that even the very girl he saved was almost certain to fall into the hands of other attackers a few hours later. If this was victory—blessed be defeat! He threw himself between soldiers fighting for some piece of loot, he covered a blind old man with his body, whom the soldiers had been about to run through with pikes. . . .

On the third day after the conquest of Damietta he left the army and returned to Acre. But he would not talk of the Holy Places and he would not talk of what he had seen in the conquered city, except to God, to pray for forgiveness for what Christians had done, and done in God's name.

In the early afternoon a lay brother of the Order arrived. When he saw Francis he fell on his knees, sobbing. "You are alive!" he cried. "Oh, thank God, thank God, you are alive!"

"Brother Stephen," Francis exclaimed, startled. "What are you doing here? Who sent you?"

"No one, Father Francis," the brother said, rising and trying hard to control himself. He was a man in his early thirties and of sturdy build. "I have come without the authorization or knowledge of my superiors."

Francis looked at him. "I know you as a conscientious man," he said. "There must be a very grave reason."

"There is, Father Francis. The five brothers sent on mission to Morocco have died for the faith."

Francis rose. His face was as white as a sheet, his poor, red-rimmed eyes burned like live coals. "Now I truly have five brothers," he said in a steady voice. "Five—but we sent six brothers to Morocco . . ."

"Brother Vitale fell ill during the journey and had to remain in Spain, to his great sorrow. Brother Bernardo became the leader in his stead."

"Bernardo," Francis said, "Otho, Pietro, Accurso, Adjuto—

237

pray for us!" He crossed himself. "*This* is victory," he said. "For it will bear good fruit."

"It has already done so, Father Francis," Stephen said soberly. "The infidels beheaded our brothers after many tortures and threw their bodies to the dogs. But Dom Pedro of Portugal, who is resident at the Sultan of Morocco's court, rescued the bodies and sent them by night in a felucca to the Christian coast. They were taken to Coimbra, where they were laid in the church of the Canons Regular. One of them, a nobleman, Dom Ferdinand de Bullones, was so moved that he asked for permission to enter our Order. He was received by our brothers at the Church of San Antonio dos Olivares and for that reason assumed the name of Anthony."

Francis nodded absent-mindedly. For some inexplicable reason he was thinking not of Dom Ferdinand de Bullones or the church of the Canons Regular in Coimbra with the poor remnants of his five martyred brothers lying in state, but of another church, a cathedral in Italy. He noted mechanically and with mild surprise that it was the Cathedral of Padua and at once he recollected himself, frowning at the strange vagary of his mind. He promptly punished himself for it by banishing all thoughts of his lost companions and concentrating on the matter at hand, Brother Stephen's unauthorized voyage.

"You have given me grave and glorious news, Brother Stephen," he said, "but why could this not be done with the knowledge, and indeed at the command of your superior?"

"They would have forbidden me to leave." Brother Stephen's lips were twitching and Francis' first idea was that the friar felt himself wronged by his superiors in some way and had therefore come running to him to complain. That kind of thing had happened before. But a voyage all the way from the Portiuncula to Acre was not easy for a simple man without any money; and somehow Brother Stephen's character did not fit in with the idea either.

"Why should they do such a thing, Brother Stephen?"

"They have done so to other brothers," Stephen said. "They don't want you to know what is going on, not they."

Francis looked grave. "That is no way to speak of those in authority, Brother."

"I know it isn't, Father Francis, but when you have heard me, you shall decide whether or not I must do penance, and whatever your decision is I will abide by it without so much as a murmur. I love the Order, Father Francis, and it's for the Order's sake that I have come—and for yours, whom I loved even

238

before I came to love the Order. The news about the brothers in Morocco I received only on the day of my departure—or rather, of my flight. The brothers you left in charge have betrayed you, Father Francis. They have changed the constitution. . . ."

"No," Francis said tonelessly.

"I know it's difficult to believe—that's why I brought copies of the new constitution with me to show you. Here is one. And that is not all. The Order is in a turmoil. Everyone is going in different directions. Factions and parties keep quarreling with each other and we don't know what to do. Some say we must have schools and live in larger houses. Those who try to oppose such counsel are given severe penances and many have even been cast out of the community altogether. . . ."

"Thank you, Brother Stephen," Francis said in a gray voice. "You may go and join the other brothers here. You can tell them everything you have told me. I must be alone now."

After three hours of solitude Francis had mastered himself, and when the bell of the refectory sounded he took his seat as usual next to Brother Peter Cattaneo. He found him reading a copy of the new constitution. It contained among other things new rules about fasting and abstinence. A lay brother put a steaming dish of meat and vegetables in front of each friar.

"Today is Monday," Francis said. "What shall we do, Lord Peter?" He liked to call Peter Cattaneo that and the former canon reciprocated the merry courtesy. He now looked at Francis from the corner of his eye. Monday according to the new constitution, was a day of abstinence. But that was quite obviously only part of the meaning of the question.

"Ah well," Peter Cattaneo said with a shrug, "it's for you to decide, Father Francis. *Yours* is the authority."

"In that case," Francis said, "we shall follow the Gospel and eat what is set before us. And when we have eaten, we shall inquire about the next ship that will take us back to Italy."

CHAPTER THIRTY-ONE
A.D. 1224

There was no country where the caravan would not have created an uproar. Even in India or in faraway Cathay people would have flocked together to see what surely was a royal progress, and even there they would have stared, open-mouthed, at least at some of its features. But this was Italy, the road from Ancona toward the south, along the Adriatic coast, and here the thing was entirely unheard of, a wild dream brimming over into unbelievable reality.

The first animals, some laden with huge packs, others ridden by brown men in flowing white robes, were strange enough. The inhabitants of Pescara stared round-eyed, and a shrill voice said: "Who has ever seen such ugly horses! Look at the big boils on their backs—some have one and some have two." The oldest inhabitant knew the solution of the riddle: "That's what happens to horses when they are ridden by devils. You, too, would get boils if a devil were riding you." After which the people dispersed rapidly in all directions to watch the progress of the caravan from what they hoped was a safe distance.

There was no stench of sulphur and pitch and brimstone, but there was a strange odor nevertheless, wild and suspicious.

The thing following the devil-ridden horses was without any doubt a devil, and one of the largest imaginable, an enormous, gray mass with tiny, reddish eyes, huge, flapping ears and a nose longer than a man, which kept moving up, down and sideways. The creatures that came after him were like overgrown cats, with tawny fur, full of black spots; six of them, each led by a black man. And then appeared something that from a distance looked rather like a flagpole, or the mast of a ship, but they saw that the flagpole or mast was alive, the upper structure of a beast higher than a house, due to a neck of perfectly absurd dimensions.

A caravan of demons. There was no doubt about it, hell had broken loose, and no wonder, what with all the goings on.

A number of carts following the demons were full of young women, scantily dressed in filmy garments.

The Pescarese exchanged knowing glances. Where the Devil was, women would never be far away. The knight who rode at the end of the procession was of a certainty one of the many who had sworn fealty to Lucifer. The four brown demons with him, posing as his varlets, were keeping an eye on him all the time so that he could not escape.

There had never been anything like it and never would be again. This was the end and Abbot Joachim of Floris, down in Calabria, was right: the last day was coming, the signs and wonders had started and the next thing would be a darkening of the sun and moon.

The caravan made its way past Ortona, Paglieta and Vasto. The knight and his men were by now quite accustomed to seeing people flee and hide at their approach. But when they turned inland, near Termoli, they were due for a surprise themselves.

A cloud of dust came rolling along the sun-baked road toward them and a minute or two later they saw a troop of riders.

"Saints in heaven," the knight ejaculated, "what magic is this? Are we back in Egypt?"

The riders were Saracens. Saracens . . . in Italy. Before one could even think of any defensive measure, their leader, a black-bearded man with golden tassels around his kaffiyah, stopped his horse before the knight. "I am Nureddin Mahir," he said. "Are you the Emir of Vandria?" The sight of the animals did not seem to impress him unduly.

"I am Count Roger of Vandria, yes," the knight replied, bewildered. "But how . . ."

"The *Imberadour kebir*—may Allah give him a thousand years—has heard of your arrival and sent me to lead you to his palace. He is staying in Fojah."

"In Foggia, yes, I was told so in Ancona, when we landed. But . . ."

"I shall ride before you with half my men. The others will ride behind your caravan, to prevent any of your men from running away, if they should try."

"They won't try. But I wish you would explain . . ."

But Nureddin Mahir, after touching his forehead, was riding toward the vanguard, leaving Roger with a dozen questions unasked. The *Imberadour kebir*—the great Emperor. It could only be Frederick. But why Saracens?

Roger's surprise increased when, sometime later, they passed a large, quadrangular watchtower, manned by Saracens. A long-drawn cry came from its high platform and Nureddin Mahir answered with a similar cry. A password, obviously.

But the real shock came when Roger saw, a little on the right, the minarets of at least a dozen mosques stabbing the sky. It was too much. He spurred his horse and rode in a canter past the women, the giraffe, the leopards, the elephant and the camels to the van.

"Nureddin Mahir, what is this place on the right?"

The brown leader grinned. "Lucera, O Emir. That's where we live, twelve thousand of us, and more coming every month."

"But where did you come from?"

"From Sicily, O Emir. The great *Imberadour*—may Allah

give him a thousand years—wishes us to live here and we are doing his bidding."

Roger's head whirled. A Saracen colony in the very heart of Italy, in Lucera. What had happened to its original inhabitants?

The way to Foggia led past the place, not through it and they were never less than two miles away, but he could see the venerable old Basilica, dwarfed by the minarets of the mosques all around it. The frontiers of the Papal States could be reached in two days. This was an open challenge to the Pope.

The reception of the caravan in Foggia was at first the same as in Pescara and all the other places along the way. The inhabitants fled and then observed the fantastic show from a distance.

But the Saracen guards at the palace gate grinned hugely and the courtyard was full of a checkered assembly of noblemen and women, court officials of all ranks and degrees, and varlets, all shouting and laughing and treating the matter as an enormous joke got up for their benefit.

The men leading the animals were worried, especially those who had to look after the leopards, and so was the commander of the guard, an elderly Saracen of great dignity. Much to his and Roger's relief, the noble mob withdrew a little, when the elephant, made nervous by so much noise, decided to add to it and gave off a series of trumpetings.

Then Frederick appeared in the main portal and Roger bowed. "Back from the East, Your Majesty," he announced, "with presents from Your Majesty's respectful admirer, Sultan Al Kamil of Egypt."

"By the Kaaba of Mecca," Frederick said, "what have we here? You I remember, though dimly; camels I know and leopards, and I once saw a drawing of the animal *elephas*—but what is this thing with the neck?"

"A giraffe, Your Majesty. It hails from deep Africa, lives on herbs and leaves and is voiceless."

"What a mount," Frederick said. "One could invent a new type of cavalry. And I see the Sultan has sent us also some of his beauties. The animals I shall keep for myself; the girls I may use as presents to friends of real merit."

"Consider my merits, then, I beg of you, Your Majesty," said a richly dressed young noble at his side.

"You, Eccelino? And what might they be, except for a great capacity to deplate the best vintages in my wine cellar?"

"If you'd give me one of those girls, I'd have no thought for

242

anything else for at least three weeks," Eccelino of Romano replied, "and that would save a lot of your best wine. By the knees of Venus, they're lovely things."

"Slave girls for Your Majesty's service," Roger said, "picked not only for their beauty, but also for their prowess with the needle. They do silk embroideries and weave carpets worth a king's ransom."

"There you are, Eccelino," Frederick said. "I know you are not interested in carpets. Caserta—where is Caserta?"

The Master of the Emperor's Stables stepped forward.

"Here's work for you," Frederick said, smiling. "You had better see about finding a stable high enough for this yellow-brown monster, to say nothing of *elephas* and the rest."

"I shall need a little talk with this knight," Count Caserta said. "Leopards eat meat, I know, and camels hay or maize . . ."

"Muley here knows all about it," Roger told him, pointing out one of the brown varlets, "and what's more he speaks Ialian as well as Arabic and the lingua franca."

"Dobbio," Frederick called out.

The Count of Dobbio, white-haired and dignified, came forward. "Your Majesty?"

"How old are you, Dobbio?"

"Seventy-four, Your Majesty."

"In that case you're the one to see that these . . . ladies are well looked after."

Eccelino and a dozen other courtiers broke into loud laughter. The Count of Dobbio bowed, his face without expression.

"As for you, Roger, I want a word with you at once. Come with me."

When they had left, Eccelino said: "I never saw a knight with a stranger retinue. Who is he?"

"The Count of Vandria," an elderly nobleman said.

"Vandria?" Eccelino asked sharply. "Did you say Vandria, Lord Beraldo? Vandria in Sicily?"

"Yes."

Eccelino laughed. "That's good. That's excellent. Well . . . he surprised us all with his animals. It's only fair that he should have a surprise as well."

"By all the caliphs and saints," Frederick said, "I was very pleased to get the report of your landing in Ancona." He had changed considerably in the last four years. The broad forehead seemed to bulge a little; the furrow between his eyes was much deeper; cold mockery lay in ambush in the corners of the thin mouth. He was twenty-nine years of age. He looked nearer forty.

"Your Majesty is remarkably well and quickly informed," Roger said.

The Emperor laughed. "When the Holy Father sneezes, I know about it within the day; and you may imagine that your arrival with all those beasts could not remain unobserved. So I sent my faithful Nureddin Mahir to guide you here safely."

Roger said: "When I saw Lucera I thought for a moment I was back in the East."

"Ah yes," Frederick said, chuckling. "I had to settle them somewhere, poor things. I also went on a crusade, you know. Not in Egypt—in Sicily. Settled my old account with Emir Ibn Abbad, remember him? He once sent Otto the Ox a purple cloak. I smoked him out of his mountain stronghold. When he was brought into my tent with his three sons, they all fell at my feet. I wasn't in a good mood, so I gave the old rascal a kick in the face, and would you believe it, it killed him outright, so I couldn't make him eat that cloak as I said I would. I had him hanged instead dead as he was and his brood with him. That was the end of my crusade, because most of the other tribes and bands gave up after that. There were about sixty thousand, so something had to be done about them."

"But, if I may be permitted to ask . . ."

"Why Lucera? Oh well, I'm the Holy Father's most humble and devout son, but it's always wise to remind him that such qualities are worthy of his appreciation—which isn't always forthcoming, you know. I had to think of some way to make him see the light. So, having shown severity to Ibn Abbad and family, I began to treat my Saracens well and now they eat out of my hand. You've seen my guards? They're absolutely reliable, because they know that only I will give them what they want: a place of their own and the right to live according to their own specific brand of superstition or faith, whatever you wish to call it. I am not particular. I shall have thirty thousand or more here in the end. We're beginning to have a bit of trouble, though; there's a shortage of women. I can't blame them if they make an occasional raid to get in a few more pretty girls, can I? They're very useful to me. If the Holy Father should ever think of trying on me what Innocent tried on Otto the Ox— my Saracens will care precious little about his ban. He knows it, too, so he probably won't try."

"But why should there be any danger of that, Your Majesty?"

Frederick laughed. "You ought to remember that my relations with the Holy See were often far from cordial. Old Honorius still insists that I go on a crusade for *his* specific superstition which unfortunately I must still pretend to share." Suddenly he turned serious. "I wonder how much you know about what has happened here. The queen died during my Sicilian campaign. . . ."

"I know that, Your Majesty," Roger said. "I heard it in Cairo, last year, and felt very sorry. God rest Her Majesty."

"She was quite a good woman," Frederick said, "except that she exasperated me with her Spanish views and her submissiveness to the old man in Rome. But the boy . . . there are times when I worry about the boy. I shall have to marry again, of course, but there is no hurry. I'm glad the queen lived long enough for the coronation in Rome, anyway."

"Of that, too, I heard at the Sultan's court," Roger said. "I often wondered how he gets his information so quickly."

"His intelligence service is not bad." Frederick nodded. "But now tell me why you delayed your return for so long! Frankly, I thought you were dead."

"I was afraid Your Majesty would think that, but there was nothing I could do about it," Roger replied. "I sent you letters by various means, but I doubted very much whether they would arrive."

"They didn't."

Roger nodded. "The Sultan had them intercepted, of course."

"But why? From the presents he sent me I must assume that he received you well."

"He did indeed," Roger said dryly. "He told me he wanted me to see as much as possible of his realm so that I could tell you all about it; which meant that I had to travel with him from one place to another. On at least two occasions he dropped a hint that he would prefer you to have a thorough and complete picture rather than merely casual impressions."

"And what was the real reason?" Frederick asked.

"The loss of Damietta," Roger said. "He wasn't going to send me back when he had just lost a battle. He bided his time and built up his army: Arabs, Kurds, Nubians, Negroes, tribes of all colors from near-white to pitch-black. Also he thought your own arrival in Egypt was imminent."

"He wasn't the only one to think so," the Emperor said scornfully.

"A number of German troops arrived to reinforce the crusaders . . ."

"Under Hermann von Salza and Duke Ludwig of Bavaria."

". . . yes, and there was the rumor that Your Majesty would yourself follow."

"Of course."

"So Al Kamil decided to act before you did. He attacked at Mansura and at the same time gave orders to pierce the dikes of the Nile. The Christian camp was flooded and the situation became desperate."

"I know all about that." Frederick politely stifled a yawn. "So they had to negotiate and the Sultan insisted on complete evacuation of Egypt and a guarantee of peace for at least eight years. I was terribly upset about such a blow to the Christian cause. You should have seen the letter I wrote to the Holy Father. Even so, there were many who said it was all my fault and that I had brought it about by my vacillation. I was quite shocked. People will say *anything*."

Roger said nothing.

"But Al Kamil? Why didn't he release you after that?" Frederick went on.

"He forgot all about me for a while, after his victory."

"Forgot about my envoy?" Frederick's tone was suddenly sharp.

"Well, I wasn't anywhere near the battlefield, Your Majesty. He left me in Cairo as his much esteemed guest, of course. I was living in the palace. But that was extremely well guarded. However, when he came back, and after sumptuous victory celebrations, I was commanded to see him and he told me quite graciously that I would have to take back his presents to you, but that I could travel only during the summer. He did not wish to risk the lives of the rare animals he was sending you. What would the *Imberadour* say if the Sultan of Egypt were to send him the corpses of a few beasts as his present, he said. Later I heard that he had sent a hunting expedition into Africa to get hold of a giraffe and it took the better part of six months to get it. The elephant, too, had to be acquired. He comes from India. There are many in Africa but they are too wild and usually do not survive captivity even if one manages to catch them. Time means little in the East."

"If I were an elephant," Frederick said, "I'd be an African one. You told the Sultan my thoughts?"

"Most certainly, Your Majesty. He was very much interested, but I could not get a clear response from him. It was neither yes nor no."

"Which means yes, I think," Frederick said. His eyes narrowed a little. "Otherwise he would have been shocked."

246

"Nor can I tell you with any certainty what he believes in," Roger said. "In that respect he rather resembles my emperor."

"I told you years ago, I believe in kingship," Frederick said, smiling frostily. "And do you think Al Kamil is a great man?"

"As a soldier he still has to prove that," Roger said. "At Mansura his army was at least four to one against the crusaders. In other respects—I don't know. He has difficulties with his clergy and pays lip-service to them. . . ."

Frederick laughed outright. "You seem to have found some striking resemblances between East and West."

"His philosophical talk is witty," Roger continued, "and often full of half-hidden irony. He carefully avoids identifying himself with anything and prefers the role of the observer. I doubt whether there is anything he would be ready to die for."

"An interesting yardstick," Frederick said.

"The Sultan would have said exactly that, I think," Roger said.

"But men have died for the most questionable ideas." Frederick shrugged. "From what you tell me I gather that my efforts to keep my Islamitic subjects happy will please the Sultan only because he will be able to point out the fact to his priests as a sop for giving me Jerusalem . . . if he does give me Jerusalem. Mansura diminished my chances for that."

"In the meantime," Roger said, "I wonder what the Pope has to say about Lucera."

"I'm told he intoned one of the old psalms. How does it go? 'O God, the heathens are come into thy inheritance'—something like that. He'll quote some more psalms, when he finds out that I need the stones of the Basilica for a couple of new mosques. I do, you know. My Saracens are very devout people, they haven't got enough houses of prayer and good building material is scarce, at least in the vicinity. What's more there are practically no more Christians left in the town, except the pious bishop. He would like to leave, but he can't. I need him there. As long as he still resides there, Lucera has its episcopal see, even if the Christian congregation consists of only a dozen people."

Roger shook his head. "I no longer understand, Your Majesty."

"Why, it's easy. The Saracens had to go somewhere. Should I have sent them back to Moslem countries and have them fight against me, when I go on my crusade? I'd rather keep them safely under my control. Why should their presence here disturb the Bishop of Rome any more than it used to when they were in Sicily? Quite apart from their value to me in certain

247

circumstances. But I must keep up appearances. As long as there is a bishop in Lucera, no one can call it a Moslem town. One has to take precautions, you know. Times aren't what they used to be, thanks mainly to that repulsive new institution of the Pope's . . . the mendicant friars."

"Mendicant friars?"

"Beggars," Frederick exploded. "Dirty, unkempt, stinking scum in brown rags. You can see them everywhere, all over the country, there must be thousands and thousands of them. It's a disease, an epidemic. They're cropping up in other countries as well. Tramping through the countryside and aping the life of Christ. They aren't good for anything. You can't make soldiers out of them because they have the status of religious. They don't pay taxes, because they have no money. They go about preaching and people listen to them because they are 'selfless' —as if there could be such a thing. It's the greatest trick ever played. Some call them the Friars Minor, others the Franciscan Brothers after their leader. Perhaps he's a Frenchman. The Pope should have condemned them as heretics, but oh no, he takes them under his protection and encourages their machinations. Diabolical, that's what it is. These holy good-for-nothings go about preaching the return to Christian simplicity, only the kingdom of heaven is important, that's all that people should think about—and so on and so forth, all sweet twaddle, but the people lap it up. And now they have created what they call the Third Order which can be joined by anybody—they join by the thousands. Members do not have to beggar themselves as do those in the other two—the first for men, the second for women-religious which is under some crazy witch in Assisi—but they have to live simply, avoiding all luxury and the men are forbidden to fight in an unjust or aggressive war. Can you see it? Can you see the damnable trap? Who's going to judge whether a war is just or unjust, aggressive or defensive? The Pope, of course, through Cardinal Hugolino of Ostia who has been made the Protector of the three Orders."

After a pause Roger said slowly: "I know the leader of the movement, Your Majesty. I knew him even before I first met you. And the last time I saw him was in the tent of Sultan Al Kamil."

Frederick jumped up. "And what mischief has he been up to there?"

"He tried to persuade the Sultan to embrace Christianity."

"Excellent news," Frederick said. "For in that case he must be dead."

"No, Your Majesty. The Sultan did not become a Christian; but he was impressed enough to call Francis the Heart of the Occident and to let him go unharmed—very much against the wishes of his clergy, whom Francis challenged to enter a big fire with him to see whose faith was more pleasing in the eyes of God."

"A mad fanatic, just as I thought."

"There was a time," Roger said, "when I might have come to the same conclusion. But now it seems to me that it would hardly be just to call a man a fanatic simply because he is ready to die for his faith."

"You mentioned that before," Frederick said quickly. "Have you by any chance joined the man's famous Third Order?"

"I knew nothing of its very existence until Your Majesty told me about it," Roger replied evenly. "You said men have died for the most questionable ideas. No doubt that is very true. They have died often enough for the most questionable personalities, too, so long as these men were alive to reward or punish them. But who will die for a man who is no longer alive? Will men die for Jenghiz Khan when he is dead? Of course not. Yet here is a man who is willing to die for Christ whose death took place twelve centuries ago."

"So?" Frederick asked contemptuously.

"So it seems to me that this must be more than a mere superstition," Roger said. "And that is what I learned from observing the man Francis. Then you have mentioned the foundress of the Second Order and called her a crazy woman or witch in Assisi. I know her too. She is a great lady and her beauty is second to none. There was a time when I thought she was the only woman in the world, and I hated Francis when he made a nun of her. But now I begin to think that he was right."

"Why?" Frederick asked sharply.

"Because she may well be a saint—as he probably is, too."

"Just as I thought." Frederick nodded. "As soon as a man acknowledges that Christ was more than human, all the other superstitions come rushing into his mind. I sent you to the East, where people really know something, and you come back to preach at me like a village priest."

"You sent me to the cradle of Christianity," Roger said. "I was in Jerusalem with the Sultan, too."

Frederick nodded. "You have changed a great deal, I can see that. It is a pity. But it makes it easier for me to tell you what I have to tell you. As you know, I thought you were no longer alive. Normally, you should have been back within a year, at the utmost. I knew from your own lips that you were the only one of your name. So I had to regard the family of Vandria as no longer existing and I gave castle and land to Eccelino of Romano for his winter residence."

"I see," Roger said. The world was going to pieces. All hope was extinct. Yet he was still there, wondering why he did not care, not really, why he could stand here, smiling at the crowned hawk before him who was trying to claw his heart out because he could no longer bear to have a man disagree with him, because he was his own god and would tolerate no other gods beside him and, therefore, hated anyone who would say Faith and not mean Frederick.

In a flash Roger saw him, carried on the crest of a wave bound to smash itself against the rocks; carried in blind, malignant triumph as so many others had been before him. The rocks were waiting, rigidly, patiently, for the inevitable smash.

"Your Majesty," he said in a steady voice, "I have tried to serve you faithfully and well. Now you have no more need for my services and I beg your permission to go."

The unblinking eyes stared at him.

"As you wish," the Emperor said icily. "Go."

CHAPTER THIRTY-TWO
A.D. 1224

The nun behind the gate of San Damiano could not be seen from outside. Even when she opened the wooden shutters in front of the iron grille she was no more than a blur. "Praised be Jesus Christ," she said.

"Forever and ever. Amen," the knight at the gate replied. "May I come in and have a word with the Reverend Mother Clare?"

"Do you have the written permission of the Holy Father?"

"N-no, I don't. . . ."

"Or from the Cardinal-Protector of our Order?"

"No, but . . ."

"You cannot come in."

"I have come a long way, Sister Doorkeeper. Won't you tell the Reverend Mother that Roger of Vandria is here and in great need?"

"If your need is material, all we can give you is a plate of soup and a piece of bread. We have no more ourselves. If it's spiritual need, speak to the chaplain. He lives on the other side of the church."

"You misunderstand me, Sister Doorkeeper. It's about Father Francis whom I have known many years, and . . ."

"Wait," said the nun and she closed the shutters. For some strange reason Roger felt that it was he who was exiled, not the Poor Ladies behind the wall.

Nothing happened. The road looking toward Assisi was bright in the September sun and the sky cloudless. The world was at peace.

Then the shutters opened again and a voice came through the iron grille. "Blessed be Jesus Christ."

"Forever and ever. Amen," Roger said, trembling. It was her voice.

"You wished to speak to me about Father Francis," said the grille.

"Yes . . . Reverend Mother Abbess. I am trying to find him and can't."

The grille was silent.

"I have been at the Portiuncula," Roger went on, "but they didn't know where he was either. So I thought perhaps you did. He is your spiritual father."

"We also do not know where he is," the grille said.

Roger nodded. "I was afraid of that. There seems to be no help for me. I am a fool and a failure. Forgive me for having bothered you, Reverend Mother Abbess; and if you think of me at all, do so in kindness and compassion."

"My Lord of Vandria . . ."

"I am that no longer," Roger interposed. "At least . . . the Emperor has given my castle and land to one of his courtiers. But why should I plague you with my misfortunes and sufferings?"

"We are here for the sake of all suffering," the grille said. "Go on, speak."

"I suppose it was bound to happen," Roger said. "But here's a strange thing, Reverend Mother. For a long time Vandria meant everything to me. My family was exiled from Sicily when I was a child and the one dream of my childhood was to return. My father failed to get Vandria back. I was determined not to fail. I joined the expedition of Assisi against Perugia to acquire booty enough for the journey to Sicily. I joined Walter of Brienne for the same reason and after him Count Diepold and in the end King Frederick who promised to give

251

Vandria back to me as soon as he had the power. Yet when I came back from the East and he told me he had given Vandria away it was as if something had happened which I had always known would happen. It was no more than a confirmation of what I had known in my heart."

"Vandria was your idol," said the iron grille. "You are well rid of it."

"It means that all I ever did was to chase a phantom," Roger said bitterly. "That is what I want to tell Father Francis. I want to ask him what a man can do when he finds out he has wasted his whole life. A man who isn't cut out to be a friar."

"Chasing a phantom is not all you have done," the grille said. "You once saved another man's life. You told me so yourself."

"In the battle of Ponte San Giovanni, you mean? True enough. But that was long ago. Also, I merely acted on impulse. I shouldn't have told you. I hope you never told Francis."

"No. But God knows it. You obeyed God."

"Perhaps for once I did. I regretted it many times—when I had to spend months in the dungeon of Perugia; and later, when Francis robbed me of . . . of the lady I loved. At least that was how I saw it at the time. Forgive me . . . Reverend Mother."

"When did you learn that it was not so?"

"I began to learn it when I saw the lady . . . as a nun. But it became really clear to me when I saw Francis in the tent of the Sultan of Egypt and heard him speak as the advocate of Christ. There was a time when I took him for a coward. Now I had to learn it was I who was the coward—and a traitor to boot. I didn't learn right away. But I did know that Francis was the most courageous man I had ever met, and a crusader greater than Godefroy and Richard Coeur-de-lion."

"So he is," the grille said. "And then you began to think of his Master, who is also your Master and mine."

"Yes. But when I stood before Emperor Frederick I was not half as courageous as Francis was before the Sultan. I did not deny Christ, but I still hoped for Vandria until he told me that he had given it away to someone else. And only then did I ask for permission to leave his service. Not before! Ever since, I have been trying to find Francis to ask him for his counsel. But I cannot find him. I wish I knew what he would say. . . . Perhaps he would tell me to become a friar; but I know I couldn't be a good one."

"There are other ways to serve God."

"Nevertheless I may soon have to beg like a friar," Roger said. "Almost everything I possess are the clothes I stand in, my horse, and my armor. Francis gave me that armor, many years ago. I never even thanked him for it. Yet it has saved my life on more than one occasion."

"I cannot say what Father Francis would tell you," said the grille. "It would be utterly presumptuous if I thought I could. But I will pray for you."

"You told me that once before," Roger said. "Perhaps that is what has kept me alive all these years. I only wish my life were not such a failure."

"He who says that without despair is just beginning to live. God has permitted you to save Father Francis' life—He will not let you remain a failure. Perhaps He will test you again. Be brave, then. Blessed be Jesus Christ."

"Forever and ever. Amen." On a sudden impulse Roger went down on one knee as soldiers do before battle, rose again and went back to his horse. A minute later he rode off on the road to Assisi.

The abbess closed the shutters with a firm hand, turned round, staggered and fell into the arms of two other nuns who had been standing behind her all the time. They half carried her back to her cell and put her down in the corner she used for sleeping. There was no bed or cot or straw mattress, nothing but a wooden wedge serving as a pillow for her head. One of the two nuns gave the sign asking for permission to speak.

The abbess said in a voice drained of vitality: "What is it, Sister Verena?"

"Permission to treat this cell as the infirmary, Reverend Mother."

Only in the infirmary were the nuns allowed to converse with each other, if it was good for the health or the treatment of the patient. In the cell only the absolutely necessary words were permissible. But the abbess refused to go into the infirmary.

"What is it then, Sister? Speak up."

"I implore you, Reverend Mother, to abstain from the complete fast you impose upon yourself on Mondays, Wednesdays and Fridays while you are ill. Also it was most hazardous in your present state to get up and go to the gate."

"It was necessary. There might have been news from Father Francis. And perhaps I could give a little help to that poor knight. As for my fast, there is no need to worry. There is no need to worry about *me*. . . ."

The two nuns sighed. Sister Verena was a strong-boned, gaunt woman of fifty. In the world she had been the Duchess of Soriano. Sister Martina was in her twenties, a sturdy, kindly creature with a face like a well-polished apple. She was the eldest daughter of a peasant from a village near Rieti.

They knew what the abbess meant and they shared her anxiety for their spiritual father. They had not seen him for so long. He used to come and preach in the little church and it was like immeasurable wealth being poured over them, riches to fill their hearts for months. But then he stopped coming and for a long time they did not dare send word to him and tell him how much they missed him.

In the end the abbess did send him a message through some of his brothers and it was very short and to the point. "You have given us a fine promise to look after our needs, yet in so short a time you forsake us and let us starve."

Then he came—but only to intone the Fiftieth Psalm: *Miserere mei, Deus, secundam magnam misericordiam tuam . . .* "Have mercy on me, O God, according to thy great mercy" —and for a month they all fasted on Mondays, Wednesdays and Fridays, like the abbess, to respond to his call for repentance.

It's because the brothers are not enough like him, Sister Martina thought.

If only he had not abdicated the leadership of the Order, Sister Verena thought. Surely, no one can replace him. The Lord showed His displeasure when Peter of Cattaneo died, only a few months after Father Francis appointed him his successor; and Brother Elias won't be able to replace him either. No one can.

It's because of the new Rule, the abbess thought. They did ask him to write it, but they did not know what they were asking of him. Our Lord Himself dictated the old Rule, so how could he change anything, anything at all? But they pled with him day after day, the brothers, the Cardinal-Protector, the Holy Father himself—change the Rule, soften the Rule, only a few can live by it as it stands and we want the Order to be big and strong. And he cried in anguish, "Would that there be fewer Friars Minor." They were sensible, of course, they were quite right in their way, but Francis' way was not their way. Obediently he had done what they asked, he had rewritten the Rule even though it almost broke his heart. It was his Gethsemani. His life was the greatest imitation of the life of the Saviour the world had ever seen. He had had his Gethsemani. But after Gethsemani came . . . Calvary.

The two nuns saw a terrible pallor come over the abbess' face. Her eyes were closed, both her hands twitched with pain as if they had been stabbed; then one of them, the left, worked its way to her heart and pressed against it and she groaned aloud.

The two nuns stood still, trembling. But before they could think of what to do, the abbess' body relaxed, her pallor softened, her hands unclenched. Two large tears rolled down her thin cheeks.

The two nuns tiptoed out of the room and ran to see old Sister Antonia in the infirmary. Sister Antonia had been a Benedictine nun for over thirty years before she asked for and, in due course, received permission to join the Poor Nuns of San Damiano. She listened and nodded.

"Mother Abbess has often taken on herself the sufferings of others," she said, "but this time she couldn't. And that also is suffering and perhaps the worst suffering of all."

The two nuns looked at each other. They said nothing. Sister Antonia, after all, was very, very old.

CHAPTER THIRTY-THREE

It was a strange, dreamlike experience to ride once more through the streets of Assisi. Over there was the house of that rich man, what was his name? Quintavalle, that's right, Bernard of Quintavalle, whom a penniless adventurer had asked in vain for a loan to enable him to go south and regain Vandria. Here was the Cathedral square where that troubadour had spoken so eloquently about the Sicilian campaign and where a gaily dressed and plumed young Francis had swapped armor with him—the very armor he was still wearing and it fitted as well and better. Here was the entrance to the great house of the Scifis and . . .

"Lady Clare!" Roger shouted. He reined his horse so sharply that it reared, and now the two ladies stopped and gazed at him, incredulously.

He managed to quiet the horse, but as he dismounted his legs were leaden under him as in a dream. "Lady Clare," he said again, as if he were afraid that the appearance before him might dissolve and vanish at any moment.

"I am still Beatrice," said the lady. "My, but you've grown old."

The other lady began to giggle, the inevitable aunt, ample and button-nosed as ever, but gray of hair, it seemed, and he remem-

255

bered his manners and bowed. "I am sorry," he said, rubbing his forehead, "my stupidity is quite unforgivable—especially as I have just talked to Lady Clare—to the Reverend Mother Abbess, I mean."

"I don't believe you," Lady Beatrice said, frowning. "It's more than five months since *I* talked to her. She sees no one."

"I didn't see her either, of course," Roger said, smiling. "She was behind the grille at the gate, yet talk we did, and thank God for it. But it's uncanny, Lady Beatrice—twelve years ago you looked exactly as Lady Clare did when she was eight—and now you look as she did twelve years ago."

"I don't think that is so surprising," she said, raising the eyebrows that might have been Clare's. "I think it's logical, as Father Vincente would say. After all, we are sisters. It is much more surprising that you should commit the same error twice."

"And you do remember me," he stated, absurdly pleased.

"Even I do," Bona Guelfuccio said, "but I don't think it's at all seemly that we should stand here in the street, conversing . . . if you would honor us by a visit, Count. . . ."

"You are most gracious, noble lady," Roger stammered, "but I am not sure whether the count and countess, and especially Count Monaldo would . . ."

"Count Monaldo died ten years ago," Bona Guelfuccio said with well-mannered regret, "and Count Favorino three years after him."

"Mother has gone into a convent," Lady Beatrice added, "and so has Agnes. You will have to be content with Aunt Bona and myself."

The house was just the same as it had been, except that the staff seemed greatly diminished. "We are no longer as rich as we used to be," Lady Beatrice said and her aunt gave her a reproachful look. "Young ladies do not speak of such matters," she murmured, rather resignedly.

"I have lost practically everything," Roger said, and to his own surprise it sounded almost gay.

However, a varlet took charge of Roger's horse and when Bona Guelfuccio tugged at a bell-pull, another appeared and was ordered to get the noon meal ready.

"We live in only part of the house," Lady Beatrice said, "the west wing is full of very nice little people Clare sent us because they don't know where to go. There have been such a lot of burnings lately."

"Burnings?"

"Yes, didn't you know? The infidels down there in Lucera

256

keep raiding the countryside. There have been many complaints and the bishop has written tô the Holy Father and even sent a special courier. The last we heard was that the Holy Father is sending envoys to the Emperor about it. I suppose he'll just laugh. They say he believes in nothing at all. It's difficult to believe because everybody says he is quite intelligent."

Roger tried to answer and found he could not. He smiled rather ruefully.

"You shouldn't have said that, Beatrice," Bona Guelfuccio said, embarrassed. "The count is at the Emperor's court."

"If that is so I'm very glad I said it," the young lady declared emphatically.

"You are quite right, Lady Beatrice," Roger said, "and I am glad to say I am no longer the Emperor's man. I broke with him —and the Saracens of Lucera had something to do with it. So, incidentally, had Father Francis."

Lady Beatrice clapped her hands. "I'm so glad," she declared. "You are much too nice for him."

Bona Guelfuccio rubbed her button nose. "I don't know what you must think of us," she said, flustered. "Really, Beatrice! Since her mother left us, there's no one to be severe with her. The girls of this house were always terribly headstrong and out-spoken, Count. Sometimes I almost think they ought to have been boys."

"Even the Reverend Mother Abbess?" Roger asked, amused.

Beatrice laughed. "Clare is a great commander. She's a gen-eral. Have you forgotten how she became a nun in the teeth of the whole family, including poor Uncle Monaldo? She outgen-eraled them all. I may look a little like her, but I am nothing in comparison. And that's only part of her. She . . . I could never be half as good as she is. She is a saint—no, don't deny it, Aunt Bona, you've said so many a time yourself and, anyhow, every-body knows it."

"I know it, too," Roger said.

"There, then. But I am a very ordinary girl and I couldn't even be an ordinary nun, if there is such a thing, which I doubt, because a nun is always something special, isn't she, Aunt Bona? Mother, for instance, and Agnes."

"We cannot all be nuns and friars," Roger said quickly, and just then the varlet announced that the meal was ready.

He had to tell them about the Emperor, about Sicily, above all about the crusade and what he had seen in the Sultan's camp. And still he felt he was dreaming. The ghost of Count Mo-

naldo was sitting in the high chair, stroking his beard and babbling about politics; there was the spectre of Count Favorino,
always ready to echo his domineering brother; the mild countess
—he could very easily see her in a convent, and Agnes too, all
eagerness and devotion. But Clare was there no longer. She was
too powerful, too great a being. She was standing at the altar,
her head shaven, her arms extended, raised to a fate beyond
that of a mortal woman—or almost. It was right and meet that
one should not stand face to face with such a one, but be sepa-
rated from her by the iron grille. The world ended in front of
that grille, as the pagan world ended at the banks of the
Oceanus, the great stream, circling the earth. Yet there was
salvation this side of the grille too . . . though it might be due,
at least in part, to the incessant work of those on the other side
of it.

Yes, the Sultan was a man of goodly appearance, a wise man
they called him, too, though those who did so were not themselves wise and therefore, perhaps, were bad judges of wisdom.
The Sultan was always asking questions and never seemed to be
satisfied with the answers. If you told him that two and two
made four, he would say: This is indeed most interesting and it
does seem to fit in with certain practical experiences, but one
must be so careful: there may be a country, hitherto unknown,
where these two figures do not add up to four and may not even
add up at all, to say nothing of the possibility of a country where
figures did not exist.

"Then he must be a fool," Lady Beatrice said, and she bit
with gusto into a ripe apple.

"I have come to believe that very intelligent people often
suffer from a special brand of foolishness," Roger said. "Sometimes it serves as a kind of armor for them. As long as they can
doubt something, they do not have to believe it. And as long as
they do not believe it, why should they acknowledge the obliga-
tions it entails?"

"So the Sultan doesn't know that two and two are four," Aunt
Bona said. "I must tell that to the Countess of San Severino.
She'll be delighted. She always says . . ."

"Count Roger did not mean that, Aunt Bona," Beatrice interposed. "What he means is that intelligent people often fall
over their own feet."

"I'd love to see the Sultan fall over his own feet," Bona Guelfuccio declared. "Not that I wish him any harm," she added
quickly.

Beatrice leaned over and kissed her aunt's cheek. "You'd better be careful or you'll become a saint too," she said tenderly.

"What nonsense!" Bona Guelfuccio protested.

From outside came a diffuse noise as of many people running. Then a woman screamed and screamed again.

"What is going on now?" Bona ejaculated.

Beatrice jumped up. "I'll go and see."

"No, don't," her aunt cried. "I'll send Giacomo. . . ."

But the girl was already crossing the hall.

There was another scream. Frowning, Roger rose and followed Beatrice to the door. Aunt Bona brought up the rear.

"What *is* going on?" Beatrice asked, startled. Over her shoulder Roger saw a swarm of people running across the square in all directions as if the devil were at their heels.

There was a clattering of hooves and a troop of riders appeared, on small, long-maned horses.

"Power of God," Roger swore. The men were Saracens. One of them, riding fast, picked up a young woman and swung her across his saddle. She screamed and screamed again.

"Close the door at once," Roger ordered.

Beatrice obeyed, but at least two of the riders were looking in her direction.

"Call the servants," Roger continued to order. "How many are there?"

"Three—and old Maddalena, of course. But why . . ."

"We must barricade the door. Is there another entrance?"

"Yes, there is," Bona Guelfuccio said, trembling. "That's how Clare and I got out, when . . ."

"They must barricade that, too." Roger began to put on his armor which he had left in the hall.

"Why did that awful man lift the woman onto his saddle?" Beatrice asked, wide-eyed.

"Here, fix that leather strap for me," Roger said. "Tighter . . . that's it."

The servants appeared and Roger saw at a glance that not much help could be expected from them. They were all elderly men and looked thoroughly frightened. "Go to the back door and barricade it as best you can," he said. "These fellows are not likely to break in, if it's made difficult for them. They haven't the time. In an hour or so there should be far too many armed citizens about. When you've finished, two of you will join us here. The third must stay and keep watch. If there should be an attempt to get in, he must come and tell me at once. Understand?"

They nodded and vanished.

"Nothing at all may happen," Roger told the two women, "but it's better to take all the precautions we can."

"I'm not frightened," Bona Guelfuccio said and then gave a shriek as a fist thundered at the door.

"Who is out there?" Roger shouted in Arabic.

There was a pause. Then a baffled voice said in the same language: "You speak Arabic. Are you a Moslem?"

Roger bit his lip.

"If you are," the voice came again, "we'll pass by this house."

To tell the truth was madness. To tell a lie was high treason. But they were out for women. There was a shortage of women in Lucera. And they had seen Beatrice.

"What does he say?" Beatrice asked in a whisper.

"He's asking whether we are Moslems, Mussulmen," Roger said. "If we are, they will spare this house."

"Santa Madonna!" Bona Guelfuccio exclaimed. "Mussulmen! Whatever next!"

Beatrice stared at him with bright expectancy. She said nothing.

Roger took a deep breath. "You two go and join the old fellows at the back door," he said. "I shall have work to do here." He loosened his sword in the scabbard.

"No," Beatrice said. She drew the dagger from Roger's belt. "Get yourself a knife from the kitchen, Aunt Bona," she said. "A nice, long one. There is no Mussulman in this house."

In a wild, jubilant intoxication Roger shouted in Arabic: "We are all Christians here. Slink back to Lucera, you dog and son of a dog. If you try to enter here, you'll die."

The answer from outside was a heavy kick against the door and a hubbub of at least a dozen voices. Another kick shook the door and a high-pitched voice shouted something.

"They'll try to break in," Roger said, drawing his sword. "Stand back. . . ."

There was a much louder crash, and Roger guessed that four or five of them were throwing themselves against the door simultaneously. The door began to give.

Another crash, and it burst open. Turbaned heads appeared and Roger struck and struck and struck again, they were caught off balance and one of them was dead and two were badly wounded before they knew what had happened. But there were many more outside, eight, ten, or more and still more of them holding the horses in the square. They were not armored, light cavalry, what an insane thing that they should be here and not at Damietta or Mansura. They rushed forward and he struck again, twice—the body of the first man impeded their progress, but then they were over him like a pack of hounds and a curved yataghan was feeling its way through his armor and promptly broke. He stamped on a naked foot, brought up his knee into a groin, but the weight of four of them was too much and he was going down—and couldn't because the wall was holding him upright. Another dagger broke, but a third one bit deep into his cheek, a brown face grinned at him, but then coughed and dropped out of sight and here were the varlets, all three of them, armed with axes and knives and the brown devils shouted for those who were holding the horses, but trumpets had begun blaring and suddenly the attackers ran back to their horses, up and off like an evil cloud, as the town guards came clattering up the square, forty, fifty and more.

The square was spinning and Roger shook his head to clear it, but it hurt abominably and he heard Beatrice say: "You can put that knife down now, Aunt Bona," and he laughed and that hurt too.

An officer of the town guard came up. "By San Giorgio," he said, "we seem to have come in time."

"I wouldn't have minded if you'd come a little earlier," Roger said, panting.

"Five here," the officer said with great satisfaction, "and we got eleven, and Bruccio says he got eight at the south gate. But what effrontery to come here in broad daylight. There can't have been more than a hundred of them. They crept up on the guards at the gate and killed them."

There was a clatter of hooves and both men instinctively gripped their swords, but it was another troop of Assisans. Their leader, a grave-faced, thickset man dismounted. "All gone," he reported. "But I'm told that they tried to break into the convent at San Damiano."

"What?" Roger ejaculated.

"One of the lay brothers, living outside the convent wall, told me. When they stopped at the convent wall the abbess who was ill in her cell, gave orders to carry her to the door and there she lay, praying for her nuns and for Assisi and behind her stood the chaplain with the Blessed Sacrament in the ciborium. Six of the infidels climbed the wall, but they shrieked with fear when they saw her and jumped back and the troop left as if the Archangel Michael were after them with his flaming sword. 'She has beaten them off,' the lay brother said, 'she and the Blessed Lord.' He may be a liar, of course. It's hard to believe."

"I believe every word of it," Roger said. Then the square began to whirl again and he could not hear a word of what the officer was saying. Two of the varlets, smiling at him and praising him from toothless mouths, helped him back to the hall, and there was Beatrice and . . . he knew that this time he had not failed.

CHAPTER THIRTY-FOUR
A.D. 1226

The saint was back in Assisi. He was dying, but he was back where he belonged on earth. They all knew him, from bishop and consul to the last street urchin, he was their very own, however much the rest of Christendom might claim him, he was one of them and they were one with him and no one could take that away from them.

"Francis will live longer than Assisi or any town built by human hands," the consul said, "but as long as Assisi stands it will be inseparable from the name of Francis."

Some reported the bishop as having said this and not the consul, but others contradicted this sharply: in the end it was agreed upon that they had both said it and that it did not matter which of them said it first, considering that each one certainly meant it and that it was true.

The saint would not stay long in the bishop's palace because he longed for his Portiuncula. He had told the brothers never to relinquish it. "If they throw you out by one door, enter again by the other, for this place is holy and the habitation of Christ and His Virgin Mother."

For a while they dared not transport him there because he was so weak, as who would not be, after what he had been through during his life and especially during these last years, ever since he had come back from Egypt; and most of all, since he had gone to Mount Alverno. However much the brothers, on the saint's command, tried to hush it up, they could not and, in the end, the brothers did talk, to prevent people from making up stories about it. Yet the truth was more astonishing, more terrible and glorious than anything that could be invented.

That mountain! Duke Rolando of Chiusi had given it to the saint as a present. Whoever heard of such a thing? A man might get a castle as a present, a piece of land, a garden, a house, a palace. But who had ever been given a mountain? A great big one it was, with long slopes and steep cliffs, the fishers of the Arno and Tiger rivers knew it well and somewhere halfway up was a chasm of which it was said that it had opened when the earth quaked at the moment of Christ's death. A little bridge led over it—the bishop preached about it at San Giorgio's: the bridge was like the Church, he said, leading across to life eternal —and not for nothing was a bishop named in Latin a *pontifex,* a builder of bridges.

The saint had crossed the bridge and gone up the mountain for a fast of forty days, ending with the Feast of St. Michael on September the twenty-ninth. With him were six brothers, but only one of them, Brother Leo, was allowed to remain near by. The other five were Angelo, Tancred, Ruffino, Sylvester and Illuminatus.

The birds came to greet the saint when he came to the bridge, a whole flock of them, chirping and twittering away all around him and alighting on his shoulders and arms as if they had a share in him, and maybe they had, saints being what they are; but they would not go with him to the other side, except one and that a falcon.

And the bishop said that was just right, as Brother Francis had always been a knight of God, and knight and falcon were good company for each other.

During the period of fasting the saint was sorely tried by the Devil and that again was not surprising as the same thing happened to the Blessed Lord Himself when *He* was on a high mountain and just as He knew what to do, His saint would know, too and he had.

But then *it* came to pass and though that had been two years ago, people still spoke about it only in a whisper.

"It was perhaps inevitable," the bishop said, "for a man whose life was the most perfect imitation of the life of our Saviour."

There were some who said that it was the Reverend Mother Clare of San Damiano who had said that and not the bishop, but here again it did not matter who said it first, though it was more likely that it was the Reverend Mother Clare who was wiser than anybody else in Assisi unless the saint was there, and whose prayers had shielded the town against the Saracens, as everybody knew.

Inevitable or not, the Lord had deigned to let Brother Francis participate in His own suffering in the most direct way and thus once more linked up all human suffering with His own, and Brother Francis' hands and feet were pierced as by nails and there was a deep wound gashed in his side. The crusaders' cross was fivefold and the knights fighting for the holy sepulchre wore it on flag and shield and mantle and breast, but Francis alone had the fivefold cross carved into his own body by the Lord.

"Not Godefroy of Bouillon, nor Richard Lion Heart nor any other of the great kings and dukes, but Brother Francis of Assisi is the greatest of all crusaders," the bishop said, "for our Lord has so designated him by a signal honor. And what other honors it entails for him, the Lord alone knows."

And there were many who shook their heads, wondering what the humble brother would say in heaven if he had to wear a cloak of purple and gold as long as a comet's tail and whether he would not insist on putting on his battered and patched-up old robe instead, having become accustomed to it in the course of so many years.

There were some who would not believe in the wounds, but they soon came to know better when Brother Francis returned to Assisi in November that year—1224—so ill that he seemed very near death and yet eager to set out on a missionary journey at once. The doubters went out to the Portiuncula and came back, beating their breasts.

But the saint said gaily: "Let us begin to serve the Lord," as if all he had done so far were nothing, when the Order to which he gave life was in full bloom in all Christian countries and those who joined the Third Order could no longer be counted there were so many, and when popes and cardinals said where would they be without Brother Francis!

To many the most remarkable thing was that he had shed completely all dejection and worry and in a way was his old self again, jubilant and cheerful.

On the missionary journey he had to ride on a donkey's back, being no longer able to walk on his pierced feet, although the Reverend Mother Clare had made him a pair of sandals with her own hands. But even so he soon broke down and had to be carried back. He could scarcely eat anything and he saw people only as a blur.

His answer to that was to compose the "Canticle of the Sun," an ecstatic poem on God's glorious works, praising Brother Sun, and Sister Moon, Brother Fire and Sister Water, Brother Wind and Sister Earth and all men of good will.

Then Cardinal Hugolino of Ostia who was at Rieti with the papal court, insisted that he be looked after by the Pope's own physician and Francis set out again, this time on a stretcher.

The road was lined with people, healthy people who wanted to be blessed and ill people who asked to be cured, and he blessed them and cured them and for good measure he blessed the cattle and the vineyards as well.

In Rieti the learned physician tried everything he knew and worried a great deal while his patient, growing weaker steadily, stayed joyful and sang whenever he had the strength.

In the end the physician tried a cure that was supposed to be very helpful in certain desperate cases. A red hot iron was to be drawn from the patient's ears to his temples. Before he submitted to the torture Francis said: "Brother Fire, amongst all creatures most noble and useful, be courteous to me in this hour, for I have ever loved you and ever will love you for love of Him who created you."

When it was over, he smiled to his brothers: "I felt no pain."

And the bishop said thus he was given his crown of thorns as well.

But the cure did not help and when Francis asked to be told the truth he was told that he would die very soon.

"Welcome, Sister Death," he said joyfully, and promptly added one more stanza to his "Canticle of the Sun": "Praised be my Lord for our sister, the bodily Death, from which no living man can flee. Woe to them who die in mortal sin. Blessed be those who shall find themselves in Thy most holy will, for the second death shall do them no ill."

Then he asked and even implored the brothers to take him back to Assisi and the Portiuncula.

They were standing around the little hut, incapable of movement, like brown trees implanted in the soil.

He had signed his will, dealing with his wishes for his brothers, for these wishes were his only earthly possessions, except for the body he was about to leave.

It is said that he began to sing cheerfully. When Brother Elias, with gentle severity, suggested that he should rather evoke repentance for the sins of his past, he answered: "I did so this morning. Now I want to praise God's goodness."

Toward evening he sang again:

> " 'I cry out to you, O Lord
> I say, You are my refuge
> my portion in the land of living.
> Attend to my cry,
> for I am brought low indeed.
> Rescue me from my persecutors,
> for they are too strong for me.

Lead me forth from prison,
that I may give thanks to your name.
The just shall gather around me
when you have been good to me.' "

Then he fell silent.

And as he did, there rose the call of a lark, answered at once by a second and a third.

A chorus of chirping, trilling and warbling came from all sides and the rushing of countless little wings, all mounting and mounting, until the air was filled with a song of jubilation and triumph.

EPILOGUE

For the first and only time since its foundation the town of Assisi was empty. All Assisans had left it to take part in the procession.

The body of the little saint was carried by six sturdy brothers. Behind them came Brother Elias, the head of the Order, then Brother Bernard of Quintavalle, the saint's first disciple, then the other brothers in ranks of three and behind them the bishop with his canons and the priests of the Cathedral. But all the others who followed did so without taking heed of class and dignity, and thus the elder consul found himself rubbing shoulders with a tailor and a stonemason, the Count of Vandria and his young countess were walking between a shoemaker and the wife of an innkeeper, and a notorious thief was marching with two town guards who took no notice of him. Notables and street urchins, nobles and beggars, sellers of fish, saddlemakers, monks of San Subasio and vineyard workers, mothers with their children, old people and young, they were all one with no difference between them, as people are after a great victory or in great mourning, and thus also they were on a day that was both.

They did not take the short way from the Portiuncula to the main gate, but went by the road passing San Damiano. For Francis had promised the Reverend Mother Clare and her nuns that he would visit them before their death and his promise was sacred.

So the brothers stopped there, lifted the body of Francis from its coffin and carried it into the little church, the first he had rebuilt, and to the large grille through which the nuns received Holy Communion.

All the nuns were assembled and into the deep silence broke the sobs of the holy women. But the Reverend Mother Clare did not cry. For no one understood Francis as she did and she knew that he had reached the summit and though the earth was poorer, the heavens were richer for it. She knew that she still had to struggle on for a while, and there was no fear in her heart, but a great hope. And she knew Francis could hear her silent promise to persevere in the way he had shown her and that she would defend and uphold that way against one and all as long as she lived.

Then the brothers took up Francis' body again and left the church, and the procession went on. And though they buried the saint, first in San Giorgio's and later in the great church that Brother Elias built, the procession of the people never stopped and is still going on.

PRODIGAL SHEPHERD

FATHER RALPH PFAU
and AL HIRSHBERG

In this frank and intimate story, Father Pfau spares neither himself nor his readers as he tells of his doubts when he received his Sacred Orders, his addiction to drink and his emotional collapse, the parish he lost and the courage he ultimately found to help himself and countless others.

"This is an honest story, told by a man of religion who believes that, by exposing his own problems and suffering, he can bring hope and help to others."
—LOOK MAGAZINE

A Popular Library Giant—35c
Available wherever pocket-sized books are sold

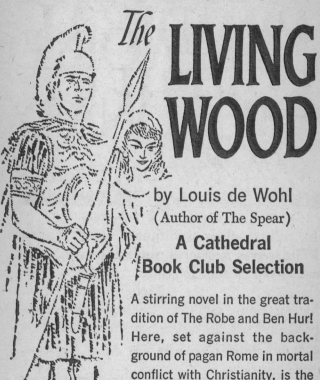